For Josie

Happy Christmas

Helen Matthews

Façade

Helen Matthews

www.darkstroke.com

Discover us online:
www.darkstroke.com

Join us on instagram:
www.instagram.com/darkstrokebooks/

Include **#darkstroke** in a photo of yourself
holding this book on Instagram and
something nice will happen.

For Mum and Dad
Wish you were still here

About the Author

Helen Matthews writes page-turning psychological suspense novels and is fascinated by the darker side of human nature and how a life can change in an instant. Her first novel, suspense thriller *After Leaving the Village*, won first prize in the opening pages category at Winchester Writers' Festival, and was followed by *Lies Behind the Ruin*, domestic noir set in France, published by Hashtag Press.

Born in Cardiff, Helen read English at the University of Liverpool and worked in international development, consultancy, human resources and pensions management. She fled corporate life to work freelance while studying for a Creative Writing MA at Oxford Brookes University. Her stories and flash fiction have been shortlisted and published by Flash 500, 1000K Story, Reflex Press, Artificium and Love Sunday magazine.

She is a keen cyclist, covering long distances if there aren't any hills, sings in a choir and once appeared on stage at Carnegie Hall, New York in a multi-choir performance. She loves spending time in France. Helen is an Ambassador for the charity, Unseen, which works towards a world without slavery and donates her author talk fees, and a percentage of royalties, to the charity.

Acknowledgements

This novel has been some years in the making. An early draft languished in the gloom of my 'drawer of forgotten manuscripts' while two subsequent novels were written and published. Finally I figured out how to replot and polish it so I could bring it back out into the light.

Many people have supported me and helped to shape Façade. Grateful thanks to my publishers, Laurence and Stephanie Patterson at darkstroke/Crooked Cat for believing in my book, for meticulous editing and for the stunning cover design. I'm delighted to be part of the darkstroke/Crooked Cat author community and grateful for the knowledge-sharing in this supportive environment.

Thank you to novelist and editor, Joanna Barnard for your in-depth critique and encouragement, and to Benedicta Norell, writer and editor, for an insightful appraisal.

I'm hugely grateful to my beta readers Gill Swales, Heather Wallace and Linda Firth for your enthusiastic responses to the draft.

As in all my novels, I've blended experiences, places and things I already know with themes and topics I've had to research in more depth. I'm grateful to the team at the Little Venice office of the Canal and River Trust, who gave me their expert insights into the rules, and the joys, of life on the London canals. Also to several houseboat dwellers on the Regent Canal, who chatted to me and answered my novice questions about houseboat living. Patrick Morgan explained the technicalities of DJ equipment and Lindsey Ashton shared advice from her time as a holiday rep in Spain. Many years ago I spent time in Tunisia, visiting a diplomat friend, and exploring local life beyond the tourist trail in that fantastic country. I've drawn on those experiences for the chapters set in Tunisia. I'm lucky to have a family member, who is qualified to check details of police procedure.

Any remaining errors are mine.

Writers' groups are my personal Hotel California – you can go there but you can never leave. I now belong to four and each is brilliant in a different way. The writer friends I met through the MA Creative Writing course at Oxford Brookes University are forensic in their critiquing. Thank you Annie, Benedicta, Helen, Yvonne, Rachel, Rose, Claire and Patrick.

Members of Rushmoor Writers (too numerous to mention) have always given encouragement and sound advice, and I've had brilliant input from my friends in Ark Writers – Katrina, Sue, Jenny, Di, Jenni and Mark.

I'm also delighted to work in a critique partnership (or should it be a trio?) with talented authors, Katharine Johnson and Sherron Mayes.

Author friends, Katharine Johnson, G D Harper and I have recently formed the Noir Collective and had several bookings to appear at literary festivals this year. Sadly, the pandemic and subsequent lockdown brought an end to that but one of the festivals has gone online and other organisers have already rebooked us for next year. We hope to be coming soon to an event near you.

Special thanks are due to many bookshops that have supported my previous books (Peter Snell, take a bow) and to readers who have enjoyed them. I'm especially encouraged by everyone who tells me to 'hurry up and write the next book.' You know who you are.

As some people may know, I'm an Ambassador for the charity, Unseen which works towards a world without slavery. This novel doesn't have a human trafficking or modern slavery theme but, if you're eagle-eyed, you might pick up a tiny reference at the very end. It's a topic I'll be returning to in a future book. In the meantime, I'll continue to donate a percentage of royalties from all my books to Unseen so be assured your purchase is helping to support a worthwhile cause.

A final word of thanks to my family – my husband Alan, my son Alex, daughter Bronwen and their partners, and to my sister Fran, all of whom support my books without showing the slightest hint of embarrassment.

Façade

Chapter One

Rachel
May 1999

When Rachel tried to recall that day, a fog descended. It was as if someone had interfered with her memory, superimposing their own view and erasing hers. Sometimes fragments came back to her: the heat and the clamour; screeching magpies; a pneumatic drill ripping up the main road into the village making it impossible to concentrate on her revision.

She had a hazy memory of tramping across the lawn, away from the house, towards a secluded copse near the boundary wall. The dappled shade of the trees beckoned her in. She sank down on a wooden bench and began memorising the King Lear quotes she'd scribbled on index cards as revision for her A level exam.

What happened next? Did someone call out to her?

More noise. She froze. The voice was barking orders and instructions. Why couldn't they leave her alone? What did they want now?

With an effort, she heaved herself to her feet, preparing to leave the sanctuary of the wood and return to the house, but then stopped. Surely, whatever it was could wait? She'd do it later.

The last thing she remembered was snatching up her earphones and jamming them on; the foam covering was peeling off and black plastic scratched her ears, but she turned the music on her Walkman up louder. The jerky beat of *My Name Is* drowned the clamour and Eminem's lyrics took on a trancelike effect. Sunshine slanted through the leaves, stinging her eyes. She closed them and leaned her head back against the trunk of a silver birch. Just for a few minutes.

A shout woke her, then a scream – awful, curdling – loud enough to penetrate the flimsy earphones. She pulled them off, the wires curled like a tangled necklace. Footsteps pounded on the stone steps that led from the upper terrace of The Old Rectory to the gravel courtyard below. The scream morphed into a wail, followed by more shouting and her mother's voice, shrill and desperate, shrieking, "George, Georgie. Wake up, baby."

Rachel shivered. She crept to the fringe of the copse and peered across the lawn towards the house. Her view of the lower courtyard was blocked by figures bending over something. Above their heads she could see the top tiers of the ornamental fountain: the statue of a nymph, balancing an urn on her head and holding a fish with herringbone-etched scales, under her other arm. The fish's lolling head spouted water into the deep pond beneath.

The air stilled; the birds fell silent. Her mother was cradling a bundle in her arms; her father pulled off his shirt and spread it on the ground. As they both knelt on the grass, Rachel had a clear view of her parents bending over the inert figure of her baby brother, George...

Heart hammering, Rachel shrank back into the shelter of the trees. She shivered, then she ran, her bare feet carrying her rapidly, not towards the scene. But away.

Chapter Two

Rachel
April 2019

Rachel poured herself a gin and tonic, slipped away from the drinks party, and padded halfway up the sweeping staircase to sit, just around the curve, in the place where she used to hide away with her book when she was a child. She'd left home in a rush that morning, so she scrabbled in her bag for a lipstick. She dragged a comb through her shoulder-length hair and a few strands came out, some looking suspiciously grey – odd, because she'd always thought red hair lasted longest and thirty-seven wasn't exactly old. From her vantage point she could see the wood block floor of the hall, with its geometric inlay of light and dark triangles, and watch the front door opening as her father's booming laugh greeted his Sunday lunchtime drinks guests to The Old Rectory.

Today was one of his good days. Now in his early eighties, he'd had decades of practice at hosting and how much memory did you need to host a drinks party? A few well-worn pleasantries and the odd anecdote provided enough circular conversation to last ninety minutes. He could still talk to Rachel about her property business and be perfectly lucid, showing a keen interest and giving sensible advice. It was social niceties he was forgetting, along with the names of friends, acquaintances and, sometimes, family.

Watching her father's struggle was painful. There were days when he was his perceptive self but, at other times, connections between his brain and memory seemed to misfire.

Guests were milling around between the hall and drawing

room, with glasses clasped in arthritic hands. Years ago, her parents had entertained local politicians, academics and business colleagues. Now it was elderly neighbours, but Rachel knew these events were important to her mother, Miriam, as a way of holding on to a lost lifestyle.

Peering through the banisters, Rachel noticed the door between the hall and the kitchen was propped open and she could see straight across to the open French window, rattling in the breeze, and a view of the terrace beyond. On one wall, there were racks of colourful spices, but she knew if she took the lids off the jars, they'd smell as fusty and stale as the house was becoming. She remembered how, when she was a child, her mother had hosted drinks parties effortlessly and prepared Sunday lunch before guests arrived, her manicured fingers deftly rubbing margarine into flour to make apple crumble topping. She would give Rachel a pair of scissors and send her into the garden to clip sprigs of mint for the sauce. But the aroma of roasting lamb was a faded memory. Now there were only ever guests for pre-drinks, but it wasn't pre-anything because, once the neighbours left, the oven stayed cold and lunch was snatched from the fridge.

Rachel glanced down into the hall again and noticed her father standing on his own, shifting from foot to foot. She took a quick sip of her drink, slid her feet back into her shoes and clattered down the stairs to rescue him.

"All right, Dad?" she asked, with a smile.

Max slid his arm through hers and patted her hand. "Imogen... where did you spring from?" His bushy white eyebrows shot up and his brow furrowed into a question he couldn't quite articulate.

"It's Rachel, Dad." She planted a kiss on his cheek. "Come on, we're neglecting your guests. Let's go in and chat."

Max allowed her to lead him a few paces towards the door, then halted. "Where's your mother?"

"I haven't seen her since ..." When was it? Oh yes, it was when the first guests arrived with a bunch of lilies. Her mother had filled a colossal vase and set it down on a console table in the hall, leaving Rachel to fetch drinks for the new arrivals while she arranged the flowers, then repositioned the vase, half an inch to the left. Then the house phone rang, and her mother had wandered away to answer it.

As if on cue, Rachel heard her mother's rare laughter and Miriam appeared in the kitchen doorway, an empty glass in her hand, face flushed. She must have been outside on the terrace. She took a step into the hall, followed by a tall man, with silver hair, who looked around fifty.

"Look who's here!" Her mother's voice sounded unnaturally high and she cleared her throat before continuing. "He's back in England – after all this time."

Her father straightened his spine, so his head came up to the stranger's shoulder as they exchanged a formal handshake. It was obvious to Rachel he was as clueless as she was about the stranger's identity. Miriam drew her husband to one side and whispered something in his ear that seemed to confuse him further.

The man gave Rachel a quizzical look. Despite his grey hair, his face was youthful, and he was clearly some decades her father's junior and probably also younger than her mother, who was sixty-one.

"Didn't you have blonde hair when you were in Tunisia?" asked the stranger.

Rachel recoiled. What sort of man would assume such familiarity and ask such a crass question? Her fingers clenched and she straightened them with an effort, realizing he must have mistaken her for her sister. "No. Mine's always been auburn," she replied. "And I was never in Tunisia. That would have been my sister, Imogen. I don't think we've met. I'm Rachel."

"Howard Dixon," he said, extending his hand. "Apologies. It was a long time ago."

She overheard her mother hiss to Max. "It's Howard, for God's sake. He was your boss when you were working in Tunisia."

The mention of Tunisia seemed to kindle a fresh energy in her father.

"Ah – the gas field in the Gulf of Gabes!" he exclaimed,

slapping the new arrival on the back. "Of course! Those were the days!" He and the man called Howard strolled into the drawing room and Rachel followed, pausing to collect a bottle each of red and white wine from a table inside the door.

The room was elegant but lacked comfort. Sunlight slanted in through the floor-to-ceiling windows and glittered on the gold-lettered spines of books in the shelves opposite. Around the walls, small tables and chairs were arranged in clusters, as if waiting for their Georgian forebears to rematerialize and start a game of canasta, but the spindly-legged antique chairs looked too fragile to sit on, so guests stood around in groups of three or four, holding glasses and not daring to set them down on the polished surfaces.

Despite the Easter sunshine, the air smelled musty to Rachel and she noticed a peeling patch of wallpaper and a malt-vinegar coloured stain creeping down one wall. Her mood dipped. These were only the visible signs of the house decaying. How much more lay beneath the surface in the fabric of the building?

She did a circuit of the room, topping up glasses and taking orders from those who wanted spirits. One of the elderly neighbours, Nadia, asked after her daughter, Hannah.

"How old is she now?"

"Fifteen," replied Rachel.

"Your mother tells me she isn't going to Saint Jude's?" Nadia's tone was accusatory. "I thought you'd want her to go to your old school?"

The memory of the expensive girls' boarding school, where she'd been incarcerated in the mid-1990s when her parents went to work abroad, filled Rachel with gloom. Even after they returned home, her parents had insisted Rachel continue as a day pupil though her elder sister, Imogen, had managed to get herself expelled within a few months. "I'm going back to live at home on my own," she'd taunted Rachel, but their parents had other ideas. To them, The Old Rectory was sacred and remained untenanted, shuttered and closed while Imogen, with a clutch of GCSEs but no A-levels, was flown out to Tunisia to join their parents.

"Hannah's happy at the local academy, thanks Nadia," she replied. "And she's doing well."

"What a shame." Nadia ignored the second part of Rachel's reply. "She won't have the wonderful start in life that your parents gave you."

Rachel turned on her heel and stalked off to the kitchen to fix gin and tonics. She snapped the ice cube tray but missed the glass and ice skittered across the countertop onto the floor. As she bent to pick up the cubes, the kitchen door opened, and someone coughed. With ice melting in her palm, she straightened up. It was that man.

Howard crossed the kitchen towards her and stood a little too close. "Max has been telling me about your property business, Rachel," he said. "Stapleton Kumar isn't it? It sounds as if you've built up quite a portfolio – I'm impressed."

Rachel nodded, without smiling. Why was her father talking about her company to this complete stranger?

"I set up the business and ran it on my own for ten years but now I have a partner, Michael Kumar."

"I'd be interested in hearing more about it." Howard moved even closer and lowered his voice. "Rachel, there's something I wanted to ask you ..." His face was solemn and his eyes a little bit wistful.

Liquifying ice leaked through her fingers. "What?"

"Did you visit Tunisia when your father was there? It would have been around 1997. A year or so after the gas field started production."

She shook her head. "I was at school in England. My mother came home in the school holidays, so I never went." When her mother didn't come home, she was sent to stay with her Aunt Susan in Oxfordshire. She'd been due to go out for a holiday but her mother became pregnant with George and was struggling with the heat, so her visit was cancelled. It had always seemed odd to her. Why didn't her mother come back to England to have the baby?

"I didn't like to ask your parents but ..." Howard's gaze wandered to the window and back, "Your sister, Imogen. How is she?"

"Imogen!" This third mention of her sister in half an hour was too much. Her voice snapped as she replied. "She lives abroad. In Spain, with her husband, Simon. He's a rock musician. I haven't seen her for years."

The scent of the lilies drifting in from the hall was suffocating.

"I see." Howard nodded. "That's good then." He seemed about to follow up with another question when Max appeared in the doorway.

"Ah Howard, there you are." His voice rang out, strong and confident, like his old self, and Rachel looked round in surprise. She dried her hands on a towel. "That business matter we were discussing. I'll have a think and get back to you. Is next week okay?"

Howard looked from Rachel to Max and shuffled his feet.

"Do you know, Max, I need to shoot off," he said. "It's been great seeing you and the family again after so long."

"Well, old chap, if you're sure ..."

Seeing this former colleague must have triggered memories. At eighty-two years old and long retired − what business matters could her father possibly have to discuss? There was something about Howard's over-familiar manner that repelled her. She hoped she'd never have to see him again.

Chapter Three

Rachel
April 2019

Howard's departure set the signal for guests to leave, and Rachel strolled round collecting empties to speed them on their way. Nadia had a reputation for lingering, so when she set down her glass on the windowsill, Rachel sneaked it away. As she closed the door on the last guests, her mother passed her in the hall carrying a plate of cold meat from kitchen to dining room.

Rachel slipped into a seat beside her father, who was spooning dollops of mustard around the rim of his plate.

"That's enough, Max." Miriam took the mustard jar away and served him slices of ham and cold roast beef. She offered him the salad bowl, but he stared at it, so she served that too.

"No potatoes?" Max grumbled, the corners of his mouth drooping in disappointment.

"Sorry. Everyone came early so I ran out of time, but I've made your favourite pudding."

The room's fused aromas of furniture polish and vinaigrette made Rachel feel queasy. She sipped water and listened to her parents' disjointed conversation, hoping they'd talk about their guests, so she could find out about that stranger, Howard Dixon, who had made her feel uncomfortable. She picked at her lunch, pushing most of it to the side of her plate, untasted. When her mother stood up to clear the plates, she followed her out to the kitchen, and stacked the dishwasher while Miriam spooned crème fraiche into a bowl.

"That Dixon man," she asked. "What was he doing here?"

"Oh Howard." Miriam pursed her lips. "We haven't seen him since we left Tunisia in 1998. I think he moved on to work in Nigeria and the US, but he's taken early retirement and come back to England to start some new business venture."

"You seemed to be having a long chat with him out on the terrace." Was it her imagination, or did her mother flinch?

"I had to speak to him first, Rachel, to warn him what to expect, before he met your father."

"Dad was on good form today, wasn't he? Anyway, that man asked me about …"

But her mother wasn't listening. She was staring out of the window. Rachel followed the direction of her gaze, past the raised terrace and manicured lawn towards the rougher grass beyond that merged into woodland. In front of the trees, their old playhouse squatted on its pitch, its rotting door yawning open. It was impossible to look at the garden and not see the view of the ornamental fountain, its deep basin long empty of water, a chunk missing from the scalloped upper tier, where her father had smashed it with a sledgehammer. Clang, clang, clang: the remembered sound of metal striking stone still echoed inside her head.

Miriam turned away from the window, dabbing her eyes with a corner of her apron.

"Mum …" Rachel took a step towards her, arms outstretched to offer a hug, but Miriam side-stepped.

"It must be hay fever." She sniffed, her voice brisk. "It's earlier than ever this year."

Perhaps it was better this way. Leaving things unsaid, skirting away from dangerous memories but, as much as Miriam refused to discuss the past, she was determined to cling on to The Old Rectory and leave it unchanged.

"There's something I need to give you, Rachel," said her mother, tugging at a drawer in the dresser. Paperwork bulged out as she rummaged and took out a chunky manila envelope. She held it out to Rachel, who kept her hand clamped to her side.

"I've only just found this. Your father's had it for weeks but he's such an ostrich." Miriam dangled the envelope by one corner in the no man's land of mid-air until Rachel relented, took it and stuffed it, unopened, into her bag.

"More of the same?" she asked, tight-lipped.

"'Fraid so." Miriam took an apple pie out of the oven and put it down on a cork mat. She laid one hand, encased in a thick oven glove, on Rachel's arm and added. "I'm sorry, darling."

They returned to the dining room, where her father was leaning back in his chair, with eyelids drooping, but the aroma of apple pie revived him.

"Ha! That smells good," he said.

"Wine, Rachel?" asked Miriam, as she topped up her own glass.

"No thanks, Mum. I have to drive home later." She glanced at her watch. Perhaps she could get away before five.

Silence descended as they ate dessert and, when the house phone rang, everyone jumped. Miriam walked across to answer it, but the handset wasn't on its base.

"I'll fetch it," said Rachel, getting to her feet. "I think I saw it in the kitchen." The ringing had stopped but she located it, on a shelf, above the still-open drawer. As she retraced her steps, she clicked the display to check the last number called and saw it was international.

"Here you go." She handed it to her mother. "If it's important they'll call back but it's probably one of those foreign call centres you can't block."

"I'm not sure…" Miriam frowned at the phone. "I know this number…" She tapped redial, her face relaxing into a smile. "I'm sure it's Imogen. I'll put her on speakerphone so you two can listen."

"Imogen. Darling!" said Miriam. "How lovely to hear from you."

Rachel held her breath as she waited to hear her sister's voice for the first time in years. There was a long pause, then Imogen blurted out, "Mum," followed by a spluttering sob.

Max looked up, startled, then carried on spooning pie into his mouth and scattering crumbs on the tablecloth.

Miriam cast an anxious glance at her husband and tapped

13

the phone to mute the speaker. "What's wrong?" she asked, as she got to her feet and hurried out into the hall, letting the panelled door slam behind her.

Minutes ticked by. Rachel fidgeted. Max finished his pudding and swivelled in his seat to look at her with confusion in his eyes. She moved her chair closer to his and slipped her arm around his back. "Don't worry, Dad. It's probably nothing to worry about. Mum will come back and tell us in a moment."

How typical of Imogen, living a carefree, hedonistic life in Ibiza with her husband Simon, rarely giving a thought to Mum and Dad then phoning to upset them when she hits some petty problem. She felt briefly ashamed for harbouring bitterness, because Imogen hadn't lived an entirely charmed life. A few years back she'd suffered an ectopic pregnancy and came home to ask her parents to help with the costs of IVF. As a mother herself, Rachel could understand the pain of being unable to have a child.

Miriam came back into the dining room, head bowed, still clasping the phone in one hand. She slumped into her chair without speaking. Rachel poured her a glass of water, but Miriam ignored it, picked up her wine and drained it in a single gulp. Frown lines, normally kept at bay by Botox, were scored deep on her mother's forehead and her skin looked ashen.

"Tell us what's wrong," said Rachel.

Max patted his wife's arm and echoed, "Yes. What's wrong?"

Miriam set down her glass, a dark red lipstick stain on the rim. Her hand shook as she reached for the tumbler of water. "It's terrible. Simon's had an accident."

"What sort of accident?" asked Rachel.

Miriam rocked back in her chair and covered her eyes with her palms. "Our family is cursed. How much more must I – must we – suffer?"

"Take some deep breaths, Mum," said Rachel, reaching for her mother's hand. "Now exhale, slowly. That's better. You've had a shock. Tell us about Simon's accident. Is he in hospital?"

Miriam shook her head. Her eyes had a haunted look. "He

had a terrible fall. From the balcony of their apartment – Simon's dead."

Rachel gasped and half-rose from her seat. "No!"

"Who is Simon?" asked Max.

Miriam spread her hands and spoke, tripping over her words. "It happened a month ago – no, a fortnight – April? Or was it March? I'm not sure… Imogen's been very ill – too ill to get in touch with us. She's been in hospital and couldn't speak to anyone."

"Oh, Mum. That's horrific. Poor Imogen!" Tragedy wiped the past clean. "I'll fly over and support her," Rachel said, dipping her hand into her bag to grab her phone. "I'll search for flights right now. I could help her with arrangements."

"No, Rachel," said her mother. "It's too late."

"What do you mean?" She laid her phone down on her placemat.

"Simon's funeral has already taken place," said Miriam, her voice breaking with emotion, followed by a rush of tears she didn't attempt to wipe away. "And Imogen's leaving Ibiza this week. She's coming home."

Chapter Four

Rachel
April 2019

Exhausted by the emotion of the day, Rachel parked her car on the road outside, in case Hannah was in bed and crunching gravel on the drive disturbed her. The front windows of Southerndown Cottage glowed like a stage set against the dark backdrop of the sky and she sat in the car for a while longer, gathering her thoughts.

Jack must have heard her fumbling her key into the lock and came out into the hall.

"I was starting to worry." He kissed her cheek. "Let me get you a cup of tea, or something stronger."

"Tea, please." She forced a smile. "Has Hannah gone to bed?"

"She's up in her room but I doubt she's asleep. She's cramming for a test tomorrow."

"Listen …" The urge to unburden to Jack fought with her need to see Hannah. "I'll go up and say good night to her, but then I have something to tell you."

"Sounds intriguing." He smiled. Don't grin, she thought, it's no laughing matter.

She ran upstairs and tapped on Hannah's door. No reply. She eased the door open, called Hannah's name and glimpsed two new posters tacked to the wall next to photos of her favourite singers. The new posters had inspirational quotes by those young YouTubers Hannah admired so much. A sandal with a four-inch heel was hooked over the radiator knob and a red labelled vodka bottle was poking out from under Hannah's bed. A battle for another day.

Hannah looked up from her tablet computer and scowled. "Why are you so late, Mum?"

Rachel took that as an invitation to enter and perched on the edge of Hannah's bed. "Sorry, darling. I couldn't leave earlier. Grandma needed to talk." She stopped – no sense in giving her sad news with a test looming.

"How are you feeling about tomorrow?"

"Cool. It'll be fine." Hannah gathered her blonde hair and secured it with a scrunchie. Now her hair was pulled back from her face, she looked younger, more vulnerable.

"Shall I test you?"

"No thanks. Dad did it earlier."

"Okay." Rachel bit down hard on her lower lip.

Hannah relented and gave her a hug. "How was the party and how was Grandpa?"

"In good form, thanks, darling," she said, though it was untrue. "He enjoyed chatting to his neighbours." The last image imprinted on her memory was of how frail her parents looked, clinging to one another on the front steps, as they waved her off.

"I feel bad about not visiting more. I'll come with you next time," promised Hannah.

"They'd love that." She gave Hannah a quick kiss. "Sleep well. See you in the morning."

Downstairs, Jack was watching Match of the Day Extra with the volume turned down low and leafing through case files for work. His dark hair was damp and tousled and she guessed he'd not long returned from walking their Labrador, Jensen, who was curled up in front of the fireplace, though there was no fire in the grate. Jensen raised his head and thumped his tail on the mat but didn't stir from his cosy spot.

Rachel slumped down beside Jack on the sofa. "Something terrible has happened."

Jack picked up the remote, zapped off the TV and dumped his work files on the floor. Jack never made her compete for his attention, as he and Hannah often had to do for hers. In a crisis he was a rock, and his mind was forensic.

Rachel reached for Jack's hand. "Simon – Imogen's husband – has died in an accident in Ibiza."

Jack's mouth shaped into an O, "That's dreadful. Poor Imogen must be devastated. And your parents! The shock!"

"Dad's poor memory gives him some peace. He seemed to grasp what had happened then forgot about it in minutes but Mum's in a dreadful state. She kept talking about losing George. It brought it all back to her and she's got it into her head that the family's under some kind of curse." It sounded faintly ridiculous yet the Stapletons seemed to be standing in fate's path when it came looking for its next victim.

"Tell me exactly what happened. Was it a car crash?" Jack waited while she gathered her thoughts.

"No. It's all very strange. It seems he fell from the balcony of their apartment."

Jack let out a long low whistle but didn't interrupt.

"Mum was on the phone to Imogen for ages, but we couldn't hear anything with the door shut. She was so upset she didn't make much sense. I tried ringing Immy back, but she didn't pick up."

"What was the gist of it?"

Rachel knitted her fingers together. "It seems that Simon came in drunk in the early hours of the morning, poured himself a Scotch, went out onto the balcony and leaned too far back against the rail. He fell six storeys onto a concrete terrace below." She grimaced. "He broke his neck. But I think he died from internal injuries."

"So where was Imogen while this was going on?"

"In bed. Asleep. The thud of his body hitting the ground woke her." Rachel started shaking. Her voice trembled and Jack put his arms around her and held her close. They sat in silence, clinging to one another, until Rachel stopped shuddering.

"I feel so helpless," said Rachel. "Imogen and I haven't spoken for years. And now this happens, and I feel guilty. How can I support her when she hates me so much? I wish ..."

"You can reach out to her, Rachel," said Jack. "Whatever your childhood issues, you're both adults now. You can put them behind you."

But Jack didn't know the whole truth. She'd only ever shared an edited version with him, and her parents never spoke of it.

"Imogen told Mum that Simon's funeral had already taken place, but Mum was so confused she wasn't even sure if the accident was this month or in March. It seems Imogen had some kind of breakdown and was hospitalised. She had to rely on local friends to arrange the funeral, but they only invited people from the island. They didn't ring us."

"Perhaps Imogen didn't tell them she had family."

"Yes. She probably told them we were estranged." Perhaps Imogen didn't want family support? That would be typical of her. She found it easy to shrug off responsibilities and she'd kept her distance for years, sometimes not even letting their parents know what country she was living in, never mind giving them her address. She never invited their parents to come and stay and visits home were on her terms, usually when she needed something.

"She wasn't exactly close to us. She was always asking for things we couldn't give her."

"Love, you mean?" said Jack. He'd always found Rachel's parents cold and distant, but this wasn't the time to say it. "Sorry," he added, "I didn't mean …"

Rachel shook her head. "No, not love. Money."

"What about Simon's parents?"

"I'm not sure. I think they emigrated to Canada when they retired."

Jack lifted an eyebrow but let it pass. She guessed his lawyer's brain was testing the evidence from a different angle.

"Balcony falls happen often in holiday resorts where young people party all night, take dodgy substances and choose the wrong moment to show off their acrobatics," he said.

Rachel nodded. "But Simon was forty-one."

"Remind me, where did Imogen meet him?"

"He was her boyfriend at school in Blakeswood, but when Dad went abroad to work, they sent us both to that shite boarding school, Saint Jude's. Imogen was furious about being

19

separated from Simon and her friends."

"Didn't she get expelled?"

Rachel nodded. "She'd always wanted to go to drama school but the trouble she got into was serious so Mum and Dad wanted to keep an eye on her. They insisted she went to live with them in Tunisia."

"Where George was born?"

Rachel flinched at the mention of her baby brother's name. She'd told Jack about the family tragedy on a confessional evening when they were sitting up late in her university hall of residence, drinking beer and switching to wine as the night ticked away. It was the first time she'd trusted anyone enough to share her grief and she was soon choked with tears. Jack had listened without judging. She lay in his arms, distraught and miserable – convinced she'd never see him again. Twenty years on he was still at her side. He knew not to open the lid on that tragedy. Over their years together, he'd occasionally strayed into forbidden territory but backed off when she fell silent and withdrawn.

She took a deep breath and forced herself to answer. "They were meant to stay in Tunisia for another year, but Mum found it too difficult caring for a small baby in that heat. So Dad ended his contract early and they all came home – Imogen included."

"What did she do then?"

"I thought she'd try to get into drama school, but she and Simon got back together."

"He waited for her?"

"I don't think so. Simon must have had dozens of girlfriends in the years between, but Imogen only had to whistle, and men came flocking." She paused and hung her head. "Sorry, that sounds really bitchy." She sniffed and wiped away a tear with the back of her hand.

Jack reached under the coffee table and found the box of tissues that doubled as finger wipes when they ate guilty snacks in front of Netflix. "Here you go."

"Thanks." Rachel pulled out handful of tissues and dabbed her eyes. "Simon was quite a catch. His band's first albums sold well, and they were offered a European tour. Imogen fled our messed-up family and went off on tour with them. Perfect timing."

"And she never returned?"

Footsteps slip-slapped across the hall and Rachel turned towards the door as Hannah poked her head into the room.

"Who never returned? What are you guys talking about?"

Rachel summoned a wan smile. "I've been telling Dad about today." The news about Simon had obliterated everything. She forced herself to think of something to say to Hannah. "Their neighbour, Nadia asked about you and gave me a ticking off for not sending you to Saint Jude's."

Hannah made a face. "You wouldn't dare."

"Aren't you tired, Hannah?" asked Rachel.

"I was just getting my phone charger. I'm off to bed now, anyway. Laters."

How lucky Hannah had interrupted. Her head was so full of Imogen, Simon and George she might have given up the secrets she'd been keeping for so long that spread between her and Jack like a stain. Then what?

Waiting for the click of Hannah's closing door, she watched Jack gather up his files and slot them into his work backpack until it bulged so much he couldn't do up the zip. The tea he'd made for her had gone cold.

"Even if Imogen didn't let your family know," said Jack. "There must have been something about Simon's death in the news."

"Of course! I never thought to check. But you're right. How could we have missed it?"

"Quite easily, I should think. It's not like the old days when we both used to read a newspaper from cover to cover. It's just quick online news now."

Rachel reached into her handbag, on the floor beside the sofa, and scrabbled inside for her mobile. She tapped Simon's name into the search engine, followed by 'fatal accident' and 'San Antonio'. Pages of listings confronted her: tragic headlines recounting falls of young men – it was mostly men, mostly young – but no mention of Simon's name.

"I've widened my search and gone back weeks. Nothing."

"That's odd," said Jack. "Have you tried the Spanish papers? There are some English language ones."

"Good thought." She tapped more key words and scrolled through five pages of microscopic text. "This is hopeless, I'm coming up with dates from last summer."

Jack leaned over and squinted at her screen. "What's that – in The Ibizan?"

Rachel clicked on the link. A single small paragraph. She scanned it rapidly and then read it again.

"I think this must be Simon. Listen. It says:

Man dies in Ibiza balcony fall. The accident happened at 01.50 a.m. on Sunday 10th February in an apartment complex at San Antonio. Paramedics worked for over an hour to try to save the man's life. He was taken to hospital where he later died."

She handed the phone to Jack and he read it himself.

"Does anything strike you as odd?" he asked.

"It describes Simon as a San Antonio resident. It doesn't say he was British and it doesn't mention Imogen."

"No, I mean the date. Look at the date."

"It says he died on the tenth of February – that's over two months ago."

Chapter Five

Imogen
May 2019

"Drop me here, outside the gates," Imogen told the taxi driver when they reached The Old Rectory. As she alighted, a breeze ruffled her shoulder-length blonde hair. She patted it back into shape and pushed her sunglasses up on top of her head so the dark circles under her eyes were visible.

While the driver puffed and wheezed to unload her case from the boot, she counted out a pile of coins and tipped them into his hand. He picked out a few one-euro pieces and rejected them, waiting in silence while she searched her bag and found the small bundle of notes she'd slipped into the zipped pocket. He kept his hand held out, waiting for a tip that didn't come. She extended the handle of her suitcase and wheeled it behind her up the driveway. She knew he would be following her with his eyes; men always did.

Whenever Imogen hit a crisis, she followed the familiar trail of breadcrumbs to her parental home, but this crisis was on a different scale. She was in real need. Surely with all the riches they must have accumulated over the years, her parents could dig into their coffers and help her?

There was no sign of her father's ancient BMW in the drive and it couldn't be in the garage because that functioned as storage for excess furniture, so she guessed that her parents must be out. She bumped her case up the uneven stone steps, let herself in with her own key and stepped into the lavender-polish-scented hall.

The empty house beckoned her to make a tour of

inspection. Despite her grief, it was a habit she couldn't break. On every visit home she siphoned off a few small antiques that no one would ever miss – a down-payment on her inheritance and a tiny fraction of the largesse her parents had already bestowed on her sister, Rachel.

Display shelves in the dining room were crammed with ornaments and photographs. There was Rachel's graduation photograph in its walnut frame, pictures of Hannah from babyhood through to a recent one where she seemed to be kick boxing, but no photo of her wedding to Simon. Not that she and Simon had invited her parents, but that was no excuse.

One silver-framed photograph had fallen onto its face. She picked it up. A young child's face stared back at her – her brother, George, his image forever frozen in angelic golden curls. She flinched and slid it to the back of the shelf.

As her breathing steadied, she spotted a silver tea set at the back of a display shelf. Imogen was wary of silver. Max's and Miriam's life and possessions, like their parenting, had all the hallmarks of being silver but fell short of the real thing. Once she'd helped herself to a set of spoons, a ladle and a cruet set that she had found in a drawer but, when she took them to an antique dealer, he had sniffed disrespectfully and announced, "That's not silver; it's EPNS."

"What's EPNS?" she'd asked, her cheeks reddening as other customers listened in on her humiliation.

"Electro-plated nickel silver and, no, we don't buy it. Try eBay."

The cicada-like tick of a carriage clock drew her attention. She picked it up. French, pre-1900 – should be worth a few hundred pounds but, as she was about to slip it into her handbag, she heard the grinding of brakes outside and hurried to the window. Miriam was driving. That was a surprise. Her father rarely let anyone else take the wheel. Her parents got out of the car and picked their way across the gravel; Miriam was wearing stilettos and Max was using a stick. As they mounted the steps to the front door, Miriam held out her arm and Max leaned heavily on her. Had he broken his hip or got a new knee? Still he was twenty years older than her mother so wear and tear was inevitable.

Imogen hurried to the front door and flung it open before her mother could put her key in the lock.

"Mum!" she exclaimed, dissolving into tears.

"Imogen!" Miriam wept with her. Leaving Max to fend for himself, she embraced Imogen and they stumbled to the drawing room, arms around one another.

Between sobs, words spilled from Miriam's lips. "Darling …" and "Simon" and "…terrible tragedy…"

They sat side by side on a sofa while Max hovered awkwardly, patting the arms of each of them in turn, his words of comfort starkly inappropriate. "There, there, don't upset yourself."

He didn't sound his usual self. Where was his regular prescription for tricky moments? A Scotch. She could do with a drink. Any drink. It was hot leaning her head against Miriam's shoulder and she peered at her father through a gap in her mother's embrace and saw a greyish face and watery blue eyes.

Miriam released her, letting her hands fall into her lap. "We've been ever so confused, haven't we, Max? When you didn't ring back and I couldn't reach you, I was frantic."

"Sorry, Mum. It was difficult."

Max's eyes roved the room and lighted on the tray with three crystal decanters. "Ah. We must celebrate," he said, and went to pour out three drinks.

Miriam squeezed Imogen's arm and whispered. "Don't judge him. He gets confused."

Imogen nodded as she accepted the drink from her father's shaky hand. There was no ice and the glass felt warm to her touch, but she swirled it and sipped, feeling the reassuring burn on her tongue.

"Tell me everything," said Miriam. "I can't get it straight in my mind."

What had she told her mother about Simon's accident? Her brain had blanked out so many details, but she'd had to answer questions from the investigators.

"It was too horrible," she said. A tear ran down her cheek.

"I was asleep. Simon came in late. I heard him shout …" She shuddered. "Then a crash and a thud."

"The emergency services had to drag me away from his body. They told me I collapsed. Friends came to take care of me. The next thing I remember was waking in hospital, drugged up. I couldn't accept that Simon was gone. I thought everyone was lying to me."

Fragments came back to her and she shuddered, remembering her friend, Gabriela, telling her it was good that Simon died in hospital because if he'd died at the scene his body might have been left under police cordon until the Court gave approval for forensic teams to remove it.

"But you held a funeral, Imogen. How could you go through that without us by your side?"

"I was totally out of it. The medicines made me numb. Our friends, Gabriela and Rafael made the arrangements. I couldn't do it."

"What about Simon's parents? Did they get missed off the list too?" asked Miriam. "They're not dead, are they?"

"They live in Canada now." They might as well be dead – Simon had cut them out of his life years ago. "Gabriela contacted them, but they couldn't face it."

"Take all the time you need to recover, darling. Stay with us as long as you like." She squeezed Imogen's hand.

As Imogen glanced around the cold, yet stuffy, room, panic gripped her. The Old Rectory had the feel of a mausoleum. If she stayed too long, she'd be buried alive.

"Will you go back to Ibiza?" asked her mother.

"No," Imogen replied. "I'll look for a job in London but, until then, I'm hoping you'll help me out."

Miriam's face tightened and she exchanged a glance with Max. Were they shocked? Did they expect her to channel the weeping widow role for months?

Miriam picked at the tassel of a velvet cushion. "Your father and I are out of touch with the world of work. Why not talk to Rachel about your plans?"

Imogen felt her cheeks grow warmer. "Talk to Rachel! Is that all you can say?" She got to her feet and glared at her mother. "I've been through hell. What would spoilt little Rachel - with her perfect life - know about that?"

Miriam shrank back against the cushions, raising a hand as if to ward off a blow. "Stop it, Imogen. It doesn't help."

"You and Dad always loved her best."

"That's not fair, Imogen," said Max in a firm voice. "And it's not true."

She turned on him. "I haven't forgotten what you did for Rachel – and all those times you turned your back on me."

Miriam began to cry, and Imogen felt briefly ashamed, but she wouldn't apologise. Why should she? She stalked off, heading for the stairs and the bedroom that had always been hers, no doubt dusty and untouched since her last visit.

"Things aren't always as they seem," Miriam called out to her departing back.

Chapter Six

Rachel
May 2019

Hannah had overslept again; her energy drained by late nights and early starts.

"I'll miss the bus," she shouted as she cantered down the stairs and baton-passed her panic to her mother.

"Relax, I'll drive you," said Rachel, picking up her car keys. "Stay there, Jensen. Good boy." She shut the kitchen door. Jensen could move fast if he sniffed the chance of a walk.

"Thanks, Mum. Love you." Hannah planted a light kiss on her mother's forehead and clambered into the passenger seat. Rachel edged her car out of their quiet close to join the procession of school run mums and commuters.

Hannah's head lolled against her headrest and she closed her eyes. Rachel gave her arm a light shake at the school gates.

"Good luck with the test," she said.

"Right. Thanks." Hannah blew her a kiss and strode off, her loose hair streaming behind her.

When Rachel returned, Southerndown Cottage felt like a haven of peace. It would be good to work from home for the morning. She rang her office and left a message for her assistant, Carrie, to say she'd be in later and noticed a missed call from her mother and another voicemail begging her to come over and visit Imogen.

Please come, Rachel. Imogen seems so depressed.

Rachel sighed. She intended to go and, since Imogen's return, she'd phoned several times but only once had Imogen agreed to talk to her. She'd offered condolences but Imogen had snapped *How could you know what I feel?* and ended the call. She didn't need thoughts of her sister in her head just now. She turned her mobile onto silent and dropped it into her bag. She made a fresh pot of coffee and let Jensen out into the garden before turning on her laptop, its magnetic force field drawing her focus onto columns of numbers. Once she had loved poring over figures, teasing them to unlock their secrets, but the property market had changed.

The small buy-to-let company she'd set up alone, working from her kitchen table, was now a complex business. A few years ago she had gone into partnership with Michael Kumar, who was Jack's best friend from university. Michael was a chartered surveyor and, together, they had expanded Rachel's modest portfolio and now sourced land for building. Recently, they had built two small developments, but the housing market had weakened. Michael assured her it would soon pick up, that time would solve everything. She longed to believe him, but anxiety gnawed at her.

Making comparisons with earlier years seemed irrelevant because their business model had changed so radically. A sudden sneeze sent her rummaging in her bag for a tissue and she felt her mobile phone vibrating. She pulled it out and Carrie's name appeared on the screen.

"Hi, Carrie. What's up?"

"Rachel, can you come?"

She curbed the irritation in her voice. "I'll be in this afternoon. Can't it wait?"

"Sorry. No. There's been an incident at one of our new properties at Elmglades. Number 8. I'm there now."

"What sort of incident?" Rachel sighed. Carrie wasn't the best in a crisis and they'd had a few of those in recent months. "Okay. I'll be there in thirty minutes."

When she arrived, Carrie was pacing the paved front garden of number 8. The front door was open and a stench of putrefying meat was coming from inside.

"What the hell's going on?" Rachel asked, striding into the hall. Outside the downstairs cloakroom, brown gunge was trickling out and forming a puddle. She leapt clear but splashed her blue leather shoes. She went inside to lift the toilet lid. It was crammed with disposable nappies. A smell of ammonia swirled in the air.

"Yuck!" Rachel slammed the lid shut and rinsed her hands under the tap.

"Rachel, I'm so sorry." Carrie sniffed, exhaling fumes of blackcurrant lozenge. Carrie had a permanent cold. "When I got in this morning, there was a message on the answerphone from our tenant next door, complaining about sewage leaking into his garden."

Carrie pulled a tissue from her sleeve and blew her nose with a trumpeting sound. "I came straight over to check. The Higgins family have done a runner."

"Wasn't he some sort of international banker moving back from Hong Kong?"

"Exactly," said Carrie. "But they owe us two months' rent."

Rachel stiffened. She surveyed the graffiti frieze crayoned along the hall, and chips in the plaster, where the Higgins children must have scraped their bikes. The rancid meat smell led her to the kitchen.

"What's this?" She ran her forefinger along a six-inch groove scored into the countertop.

"Looks like they took a chisel to the granite." Carrie grimaced but kept a distance.

"Okay," said Rachel. "I've seen enough. I'll call out the emergency plumber. You wait for him here with the key."

She headed back to the office and, fifteen minutes later, was parking her Audi outside the block. The business park was still under construction. Work on it had stalled and unfinished buildings were shrouded in scaffolding and white plastic. With so few interested tenants, Stapleton Kumar had secured a prestige office at an affordable rent.

The fake-marble reception area was like the grandiose foyer of a City bank and echoed to the sound of Rachel's footsteps. The security guard snapped awake and solemnly inspected her pass, even though they were on first name terms. She took the lift to the eighth floor, punched in a security code and entered the compact office suite. There was no sign of Michael and Carrie was still at Elmglades.

Rachel kicked off her stained shoes and sat at her desk, resting her head in her hands. How thrilled Michael had been when he found the plot where they'd built Elmglades Close. It was their first development project – ten houses – and he'd negotiated very favourable terms but, when the homes were built, they couldn't sell them at the eight hundred-thousand-pound price tag. Eventually they sold six at lower prices but were still holding onto four and renting them out while they waited for the market to improve. It was playing havoc with their cash flow. The rental income barely covered the repayments on their bank borrowings. Now they had problem tenants and the hassle of sorting out damage to a brand-new property.

Carrie would handle eviction proceedings and put debt recovery in place – if they could track down Mr Higgins, but the house would be sitting empty while they put the repairs in hand.

From the corridor, she heard the lift ping and seconds later, Michael Kumar breezed in, walking so fast she could almost see the tail wind whipping along behind him. Light from the windows fell on his face, emphasising his prominent cheekbones, aquiline nose and intelligent brown eyes but he wasn't smiling.

"Michael – am I glad to see you!" He had a knack of making problems fade. Michael still wore a tie and often, in meetings, looked like the only grown up in the room.

"Hey, Rachel – good to see you, too. Things are a bit grim over at Woodleaze." He paced the office.

"Tell me about it," Rachel said.

"I got there at eight, but no one was around, so I waited in the car."

He stopped pacing and perched on a corner of Rachel's desk. "Eventually the foreman, Kirkpatrick, ambled up in his van, but there was no sign of any other guys. He gave me a load of bollocks about another job that had overrun."

Michael shifted his seating position, knocking a file to the floor. He bent down to pick it up and shuffled the papers back inside. "I'm afraid my patience snapped. I swore at him."

"I'm not surprised," said Rachel. "The delay on Woodleaze is costing us a fortune. I'll check the penalty clause in their contract."

Carrie filed hard copies of contracts alphabetically on open shelves with the name of the contractor stamped in black capitals on the spine of each file. Rachel strolled across the room and ran her eyes along the row of files, located the right one and pulled it out.

"One thing Kirkpatrick said surprised me," Michael said.

"What was that?"

"It seems his boss told him to slow up the work on Woodleaze. He claimed we hadn't paid their January invoice."

Not paid January's invoice? Could that be possible? Rachel felt as if the room was revolving like a carousel. She put out a hand to hold onto her chair and steady herself. "I'll talk to Carrie when she gets back but I'm sure she must have paid it."

Michael went across to his own desk and began sifting through the morning's mail. She heard someone humming an Ed Sheeran song in the corridor and Carrie appeared swinging an orange carrier bag. Carrie was entitled to a lunch break, but Rachel felt unaccountably annoyed that she'd stopped to do her shopping.

"What is it?" asked Carrie, with a panicky stare. "If it's about the Higgins I'm onto it. I'll start eviction proceedings right away."

"It isn't that," Rachel's throat constricted. "It's Emerald Builders. They're claiming we haven't paid the January invoice."

The colour rinsed out of Carrie's face. She sat down with a flump, switched on her computer and scrolled through payment records. Rachel stood behind her chair, peering at the screen over her shoulder.

"There – see. I authorised payment on the fifteenth of February." Carrie tapped the screen with her forefinger.

"Let me see the bank statement," said Rachel.

Carrie entered the security codes to access online banking

and brought up the February statement. It told Rachel all she needed to know. Stapleton Kumar's payment terms were thirty days from receipt of an invoice. Carrie had processed the payment too early in the month: before their temporary increased overdraft limit was in place. The invoice included quantities of building materials and totalled over two hundred thousand pounds. No wonder the bank had refused it.

Realisation hit Carrie at the same time, a tear slid down her face; she blotted it away with a tissue.

"Haven't you been checking the bank statements, Carrie?" Rachel's voice trembled.

Carrie bit her lip and said nothing.

It was hard to think straight. "Okay, don't bother," said Rachel. "I'll ring the bank and sort it out."

In work, as in the rest of life, everything rested on her shoulders, she reflected. It was as if a suit of clothes had been fashioned before she reached adulthood. She'd shrugged it on, knowing that the life tailored for her didn't fit. But since Imogen's return something inside her had shifted. Her life had become a strait jacket. Why should she continue to carry all the family's burdens while Imogen walked away?

Chapter Seven

Imogen
Ibiza
September 2018

Ibiza was a dream gone sour. Simon hadn't worked for months. The contract on their rented beachside villa ended abruptly when the owner announced he was moving back in. Imogen and Simon were given two weeks to pack up and leave.

"We must find somewhere better," said Imogen. "The swimming pool temperature here is too cold and we need a larger terrace for entertaining."

Simon lit a cigarette and regarded her blankly. "What entertaining?"

It was true. Their social circle had shrivelled. In their early years together, before the band burned itself out, Imogen and Simon were at the centre of everything and others pivoted around them. After they settled in Ibiza, Simon reconstructed the band with new musicians but never recaptured their old magic. Instead he embraced the local scene and segued into the role of celebrity DJ, with initial success buoyed by summer visitors who remembered him as a former boy band heart throb from their teenage years. But his gigs were infrequent, and he never landed a residency. He developed the haggard look of people who drink too much and stay up all night.

Three days after their notice to quit their apartment, Simon returned from one of his benders and informed Imogen he'd found them a place to live in San Antonio.

"I can't live in a villa in San Antonio," she said. "Our

friends are here in Ibiza Town, and in Santa Eulalia."

"You'll get used to it," said Simon. "And by the way, it's not a villa, it's a sixth-floor apartment."

Imogen bristled. "You're joking, right? I can't ride down in a lift every time I want to sunbathe by the pool."

"There's an upside," he offered, grinding out his cigarette under his heel and immediately reaching for another one. "The apartment owner lives in Kent and doesn't use it in the winter. There's only a token rent to pay."

Imogen brightened. Less restriction on their cash flow would be good. "Okay. Let's take a look."

The following day they drove to San Antonio. Simon slowed the car outside an ugly tower block and turned into a barren car park, overlooking a swimming pool with a scummy surface. The windows of all the apartments up to second floor level were fronted with metal security bars. Everything was concrete. Where was the cascading purple bougainvillea and the fine mist of sprinklers keeping parched lawns green? Where was the lawn?

Imogen climbed out of the car and looked up to the top of the building. Above it, the sky was blue, with a white vapour trail from a passing plane, but it was impossible to pinpoint the direction of the coast because other tall buildings huddled together to block the view.

"Well, I can't stay here," she announced.

"Yes you can." Simon's fingers encircled her wrist and squeezed it tight.

"Ouch. Let go of me." She shook off his grip.

"Come up and see the apartment." His lips curled into a snarl and he tugged at her arm as if pulling a dog on a lead. She shook off his grip. It was not yet eleven a.m. but she could smell his whisky breath and the peppermint gum he chewed in a futile attempt at concealment.

It was a sunny late September day, but the block had a forlorn end-of-season look. A hand-scrawled notice on the shuttered door of a mini-market, set into the base of the building, announced it was closed indefinitely and a group of surly teenagers were lounging on concrete benches outside.

35

Shop or no shop, they had bought lager from somewhere and were pouring it down their throats and aiming their empties towards a communal waste bin. When a bottle missed and shattered on the ground, they all cheered and swore in Brummie accents.

"Stop that." Simon nudged shards of glass off the path with his shoe. "Pick it up."

"Who says?"

"I do." Simon marched over to the bench and glared at them. He singled out the skinniest lad, whose skin was raw with acne, yanked him to his feet and marched him across to the pile of broken bottles. "Do it now." He pointed.

Imogen watched, agitated but proud, as the group of lads froze, and she registered how young they were. The tallest boy got to his feet and nodded. Her heart hammered. Was it some signal to attack? But no. The skinny lad bent down and sorted through the glass picking up the largest pieces and dropping them into the bin.

"That's it," said Simon, raising his hand to signal Imogen to follow him. She stepped over a patch of dried vomit on the path and joined him as he opened the heavy main door. It clanged shut behind them.

She shivered in the sunless corridor. "Where's the light switch, for God's sake?"

Simon ran his hand along the wall and clicked it on. They took the lift to the sixth floor and the corridor plunged into darkness as they stepped out, but the light switch didn't work.

"I'm not moving here. No way," she said as Simon groped his way along the corridor and located the right flat. Inside, the lights were working, and the concrete walls were painted white. The kitchen was windowless, the bathroom floor was stained from recent flooding and the shower tray had rust marks.

"This is a hovel!" she exclaimed.

"Take it or leave it. This is where we'll be living."

A week later they were moving in.

"I will never forgive you for this, Simon," Imogen hissed, as she hefted suitcases and boxes up six flights of concrete stairs, because the lift was out of order. Crossing the threshold on her fourth journey, she stumbled and a precious Lalique perfume bottle fell out of the box she was carrying and slid across the tiled floor.

Simon picked it up. "It's not smashed," he said with a shrug, and stalked off to one of the two identical bedrooms, locked the door and strummed a few chords on his guitar.

In the weeks that followed, Imogen and Simon rarely spoke. The management company that ran the block offered to pay Simon from communal funds to look after the swimming pool and keep the weeds on the terrace under control, but Simon couldn't be arsed. He went out in the mornings, walked along the beach and installed himself in his favourite bar, rarely returning before midnight. Imogen gave up making dinner. Did Simon ever eat? She no longer cared.

"There's no money in the joint account," she told him one day, standing in front of the door to block his exit.

Simon shrugged. "Better get a job then."

So she did. Sometimes a few bar shifts, often cleaning. Her fortieth birthday came and went, uncelebrated. She had no children, no home of her own and a husband who barely spoke to her. Christ they weren't even a couple anymore. For the first time, she felt glad not to have children as she contemplated the horror of them witnessing their father's meltdown. She vowed this would not be the rest of her life.

***

Simon fell from the balcony of their sixth-floor apartment in the early hours of Sunday the tenth of February. Sirens blared and lights pulsated across the concrete car park as the first ambulance responded to Imogen's panicked phone call. When the first responder jumped out of the vehicle, she was kneeling on the hard concrete, cradling Simon's head in her lap, as his blood seeped into her flimsy, white bathrobe.

"Do something," she sobbed as a medic gently untangled her arms from Simon's body and led her to one side.

She leaned against the wall as tremors ran through her. Every time she turned her eyes away from the horror, they meandered back to fix on Simon. She strained to hear the medic's assessment, but their words turned to babel in her ears.

"How's he doing?" she whispered in a hoarse voice. They ignored her. Why did they keep checking his vital signs, over and over, why weren't they treating him? Or taking him to the hospital?

More cars arrived. A cavalcade of screeching brakes and slamming doors. First the local police, then the Civil Guard. They acknowledged her with a nod, but left the medics to their work, watching from a distance, smoking, waiting. For what?

After a while, an officer approached and spoke in Spanish, asking her to confirm she was Simon's wife. When she replied, he switched into English.

"Someone should be with you. You must call a friend."

"Yes." She nodded, fumbling in the pocket of her bathrobe for her phone but it was empty apart from a crumpled tissue. The phone was inside her apartment where she'd flung it down on the bed, after calling the emergency services and before racing down the unlit staircase to reach Simon.

"Use mine." He held it out to her. But she didn't know anyone's number.

Her courage fled and she wept, salty tears swilling Simon's blood from her hands. Through misted eyes she saw the ambulance crew fetch a stretcher and felt a faint beat of hope.

Her legs folded under her and she collapsed.

When she woke, in her darkened bedroom, her friend Gabriela was sitting in a chair beside her bed.

"She's awake," Gabriela called, and her husband, Rafael, appeared from the sitting room.

Imogen stared at them. She didn't ask how they'd got there but let Gabriela hold her as they both shed more tears. Gabriela made soothing noises but didn't ask any questions. Rafael brought coffee and placed the tray down on the bedside table. He walked across to the window and pushed the shutters a fraction outward.

"Don't!" shouted Imogen as a blade of sunshine pierced the room.

"If not light, perhaps some air?" Rafael suggested.

"No!"

Rafael nodded and pulled the shutters closed while Gabriela helped Imogen to sit up and plumped up pillows to support her back.

"Simon's dead isn't he?" she asked.

Gabriela nodded, and turned her head away.

"I thought you'd never tell me." Imogen slid back down from the supporting pillows, turned her face to the wall and pulled the sheet up over her head.

Grief engulfed her. Her body twitched. She pushed folds of sheet into her mouth and bit down hard on them to stifle her sobs. Simon's many faces circled in her mind's eye: the poster-boy rock musician, her handsome husband, the rugged DJ, the bloated alcoholic – all morphed into a bloodied head, mocking her. That final image became imprinted. When she opened her eyes, a miniature version of it drifted like a floater in her field of vision.

"No, no, no!" were the only words she could summon. Regret diluted horror. If only Simon had attended those clinic appointments she'd made for him. She'd found a twenty-eight-day rehab programme and they went together to the first appointment. The cost was eye-watering and she was planning to ask her parents for help, but they never got that far. After an introductory meeting, Simon skipped the follow-up medical without telling her. He'd never intended to dry out. So why should she shoulder the guilt?

In the greyness of her bedroom, footsteps padded in and out. Gabriela spoke to her softly but there were other people she didn't recognise, speaking in hushed voices. Time passed.

"You must drink something, even if you don't eat," said Gabriela, easing back the sweaty sheet and forcing a glass into Imogen's hand. "It's not very full. Sip it slowly."

The water soothed her parched throat. Imogen levered herself into a seating position.

"What happens now?" she asked, refocusing her eyes and noticing Rafael standing in the doorway.

"You must rest," said Gabriela in a gentle tone. "And then

some people want to come and talk to you."

"What people?"

Rafael advanced into the room and answered. "An inquiry has begun. The judicial police of the Civil Guard are in charge of the investigation. Are you ready to answer their questions?"

Imogen sat bolt upright, her eyes were stinging, and she pushed damp hair out of her face. She stared at her friends and shook her head. "No."

"It's routine," Gabriela assured her. "They need to take your report."

Imogen let her head drop back onto the pillow. She closed her eyes and waited for Gabriela to leave the room. Heart pounding, she levered herself up on one elbow and rummaged in her bedside drawer for her pack of sleeping pills. With the last of the water she swallowed one day's dose, then another, then a third. Choking and coughing as the glass ran dry, she abandoned an attempt to take more and slumped back, leaving the pills on her cabinet.

She listened as her worried friends called the doctor but were unable to answer the question, "How many pills did she take?"

Within hours she was admitted to hospital, unresponsive, but watching from some strange out-of-body place. She prayed they wouldn't pump her stomach and they seemed to decide on a watch and wait approach. In her hospital bed, her brain switched off and the nightmare vision of Simon's face was smothered by a grey fog.

A few days later she went cold turkey, concealing the hospital's medication under her tongue and spitting it out into a tissue when the nurse moved away. Cold sweats and breathing difficulties followed. Her hands and feet tingled. Little electric pulses prickled her skin like fine rain. The doctors were perplexed and kept her under observation waiting for the symptoms to subside. As her strength returned, she agreed to speak to an investigator in a private room at the hospital.

"I am still confused, because of the medication," she told the young officer. "Can you give me more time?"

His eager face clouded. "Of course, Mrs Wilson," he said, then fired off a round of questions.

"Where was Mr Simon Wilson on the night of his death? What time did he return?"

"Wait." She held up her hand, but he didn't stop although she gave no answers.

"Where were you when he returned? What was his state of mind?"

She shook her head. "No hablo mucho espanol," she said, even though she'd understood every word. Acting confused was easy. She made a mental note of the questions so she could write them down after he'd left.

"I've been unwell. I need more time." Her hand shook as she played with the fastenings of a hospital issue dressing gown. Gabriela hadn't brought her enough clothes and she felt exposed, as if facing this interview naked. When she reached for her glass of water a few drops spilled on the table.

The officer nodded and gathered up his paperwork. Imogen agreed to another meeting in a week's time.

"I need a lawyer," she told Gabriela when she arrived to drive her home from hospital. "Do you know anyone?"

"Why do you need one?" said Gabriela, surprised. "I can be with you if you need help for the translation."

But Imogen was insistent, so Gabriela took out her mobile phone. "I think Rafael knows someone who speaks English."

"I speak Spanish," Imogen pointed out, but perhaps her vocabulary wasn't equal to this challenge. An English-speaking lawyer would make sense.

Gabriela carried Imogen's bag along the echoing hospital corridor to her car. "It's so light!" she exclaimed, as she loaded it onto the back seat.

"I didn't need many shoes in the hospital," said Imogen, and they both laughed, easing the tension between them. "Besides it was you who packed my bag and brought it in to me."

"So I did," said Gabriela as she stowed the bag on the back seat of her car. She drove slowly through deserted streets and, as they reached the outskirts, she took the road towards Santa

Eulalia.

"Where are we going?" Imogen asked, turning in her seat to see Ibiza town receding through the rear window.

"Imogen, you cannot go back to that terrible flat. You must come and stay with Rafael and me."

"No," said Imogen, her face a mask of determination. "I'll have to face the apartment sometime. Delay will make it worse."

She thought about the preparation she'd need for the next round of interviews. And there'd be the funeral to organise – when it was allowed.

Everything was so raw and recent. Thinking of Simon no longer conjured up horrific images but triggered an overwhelming loss that tore at her heart. They'd been soulmates. Survived two decades together when some of their friends had barely made five years before divorcing. But Simon couldn't handle failure and he'd turned away from her – not to other women – but to a harsher, more demanding mistress – alcohol.

"Turn the car round," Imogen demanded. "I'm going back to the apartment."

"Well, if you're sure," said Gabriela, doing as Imogen asked.

Imogen felt another friendship slipping away. It wouldn't take much to cut her ties with Ibiza. Most of the friends who'd been with them in the good times, lapping up tickets to sold-out gigs that Simon handed out, had already drifted away.

Back at the apartment block, Gabriela manoeuvred her car between pots of wizened plants that had blown over in a recent gale. The last few weeks had been wet and windy, but sunny, so the weeds on the pool terrace that Simon hadn't bothered to treat were out in force, poking through the cracked flagstones to greet her.

Imogen wound down the car window and lit a cigarette as she braced herself to slide her eyes up six floors to look at the balcony of her flat. Inch by inch, she lowered her gaze to the terrace beneath, where remnants of shredded police tape flapped in the breeze. She couldn't see it from the car but knew the dark stain on the concrete would still be there to show the exact spot where Simon's head struck the ground.

She stubbed out her cigarette, half-smoked, and took a mint from the packet in Gabriela's glove box. Gabriela's face was taut and her eyes damp with unshed tears. How ridiculous. What was Simon to her, after all?

"Imogen, I wanted to ask, did he … did you..?" Gabriela turned to her with a frank gaze.

"Did he what?"

Gabriela gulped. "Was Simon's death an accident?" She sniffed and lowered her eyes.

"What are you saying?" Imogen's voice trembled with anger. "Do you think Simon took his own life? Is that it?"

"Nothing, nothing. I didn't mean … ignore me." Gabriela's phone beeped. She snatched it up and read the message.

"Rafael has replied about the solicitor." She showed Imogen the screen.

"Ping the number over to me, will you?"

"Sure. I'll do it inside, when I've got you settled back in."

"There's no need for you to come in. I'll have it now," said Imogen, squinting at the screen and tapping the number into her phone.

"Thank you," she said, reaching over into the back seat for her bag. She flung open the car door and clambered out.

Gabriela sniffed and took out a paper tissue to blow her nose. "I will call you."

Imogen waved. As she strode towards her flat, she decided not to see Gabriela again. Their relationship had only ever been transactional, after all. Now she had the lawyer's name, she wasn't worried about the findings of the investigation. The toxicology reports and Simon's non-attendance at the clinic would be ample evidence of an accident. She didn't want a finding of suicide. Soon she'd be leaving Ibiza with all memories erased.

Chapter Eight

Imogen
May 2019

Imogen sat in her bedroom, contemplating greasy-looking spots on the paintwork where her teenage posters had curled away from Blu-tack and slid off the walls. The single remaining poster seemed designed to torment her: a smiling baby in a seascape, fading from cerulean blue to azure, swimming towards a dollar bill. It was the cover of Nirvana's *Nevermind*. The poster and album had been a gift from Simon. She tugged at it roughly and it came away with a strip of wallpaper attached.

She sat cross-legged on the floor and eased her right foot into a half lotus yoga position. As her breathing slowed, she braced herself to make the call. Why had she waited so long? She should have phoned from Ibiza as soon as she received the official investigation report with its conclusion of accidental death and a special note of the amount of alcohol in Simon's bloodstream. She dialled the number of the insurance company where they held a joint life policy.

A message told her that her call would be recorded for security and monitoring purposes, so Imogen set her mobile on speaker and waited in a queue while all their advisers were busy helping other customers. A youthful-sounding voice came on the line and asked for her policy number and the purpose of the call.

When she said she was calling to report her husband's recent death, there was a brief silence. Yet he must take calls like this every day.

"I'm sorry for your loss, madam," the adviser began,

stumbling over his call script. Perhaps he was a trainee. "Our computer system is running slow today. I'm waiting for your record to load. When the screen comes up, I'll take you through security."

"Yes, yes," said Imogen, suddenly desperate to talk, even to this human android who was forbidden to go off script. She launched into details of Simon's accident.

"Can you wait a moment, please, madam? I'll need to enter details on our system after we've been through security."

But Imogen couldn't stop.

"A fall from a balcony, you said," repeated the adviser. "We're getting ahead of ourselves. Wait while I log into the right screen."

Imogen shuddered. "You're going to ask if it was suicide, aren't you? Well, I can tell you categorically that was ruled out. It was an accident. I have the death certificate and investigation report here. Where should I send it?"

"Right. I have your record up in front of me now. Sorry for the delay. Let me take you through security."

Imogen reeled off the answers to his questions. Word perfect.

"Thank you, madam. Wait one moment. There's something else here - a flag on your record. I'll need to speak to my supervisor."

A Beethoven sonata assaulted Imogen's ears, reminding her of the piano exams she'd flunked, while Rachel sailed through the grades. She tapped the loudspeaker icon, put the phone down on the bed and closed her eyes. When the adviser's voice boomed out, she jumped.

"Mrs Wilson, I'm sorry to keep you waiting." He cleared his throat. "I have some bad news. I'm sorry. I'm afraid your husband – err – late husband has discontinued the policy."

"Wha-at?" Imogen's chest constricted. She could scarcely breathe. "That's impossible. No way." Taking out that joint lives policy was one of the first things they'd done after they got married. They'd even joked about which of them would survive to claim the pay-out.

The adviser's voice wavered. "The last premium was paid

by direct debit back in, um, November."

"There must be some mistake."

"No. We sent out two reminders, but the policy has lapsed and your account has now been made inactive."

November! That was nothing. Just a few months ago. Sure, she and Simon had been hard up over the winter but not that desperate.

"I'll make up the payments," she promised. "I'll credit outstanding premiums and any interest due. Today."

"I'm afraid that's impossible, madam. The cover ended automatically when you stopped paying the premiums. There's nothing I can do. Sorry for your loss."

Chapter Nine

Imogen
May 2019

Imogen hunkered down under her duvet. Without the insurance pay-out she would be destitute. Could she contest it? She'd expected the insurers to give her a tough time and to reopen the touchy issue of whether suicide was a possibility but never had it crossed her mind that the policy might be invalid. Did Simon really hate her so much to do this to her?

She locked her door and, for twenty-four hours, ignored her mother's faint tapping and offers of coffee or soup. The next day she staggered down to the kitchen in her dressing gown, made coffee and went out onto the terrace to smoke a cigarette.

Her mother joined her. "Did you have a headache?"

Imogen nodded. "Something like that." She put out her cigarette and they went back into the kitchen and sat sipping coffee in silence.

Her fury at Simon was best kept to herself. At least for now. She picked at her nails; she'd bitten them down to the quick. "You understand, Mum, how it feels to lose someone you love?"

"Oh, Imogen." Miriam concealed her own grief under a brittle exterior but sometimes it broke through. "I know you truly loved him."

Imogen nodded as a wave of misery threatened her composure.

"You can stay with us as long as you like. This is your home."

Imogen shuddered. "The thing is, Mum, if I'm going to build any sort of career, I need to be in London."

How could she move the conversation on to buying a home of her own? The insurance money might have made that possible.

"I know I was unreasonable when we last spoke of this as a family," she began, tentatively. "Ten years ago, I think it was. But I've never had Rachel's luck. Never had the chance to own a property. Simon and I always rented. Couldn't you and Dad help me out? Something quite modest – a flat – would be fine. I could manage with two bedrooms if it's in a good area."

Miriam shifted in her chair and seemed to become selectively deaf. Imogen's mind flicked back to that family discussion some ten years earlier when she'd come home to ask her parents for help with a deposit to buy a place to live in Ibiza. The four of them had gathered in this very room and, for the briefest of moments, it felt like a family Christmas back in the old days. Before Tunisia, before Saint Jude's, before George...

***

Max handed round the drinks then raised his glass. "A toast. To Rachel. Finalist in the Thames Valley businesswoman of the year 2009."

Rachel blushed. "That was last summer, Dad. And I didn't win."

"At least one of you girls has inherited my entrepreneurial spirit and business acumen."

Imogen shifted in her chair and swirled the ice in her drink. "What do you mean, Dad?" She shot Rachel a look of veiled hostility.

Max tugged at his sleeve as if a prompt card with his next lines might be hidden there. Though he hadn't played for years, he was wearing his golf club's V-neck pullover in a shade of pondweed green with jaunty tartan trousers. He opened his mouth but didn't speak. Imogen had chosen a chair with a lower seat than the others. She gripped the arms hard, her rouge-noir nail varnish black against the ivory upholstery.

"I've had a few lucky years," said Rachel, blushing. "But these are difficult times for the property business. After last year's financial crash."

"Never mind, lass." Max moved to sit next to her and draped a fond arm around her shoulder. "You stick with it. Who would have thought you'd have a business brain after all that fancy education and a Law degree?"

He uttered the words 'law degree' as others of his generation might have said 'Media Studies'. Max was an engineer and, as far as he was concerned, all other disciplines were in the 'too easy' box.

"I thought you were dabbling in property," Imogen said slowly. "Mum told me you were running your business from your kitchen table."

"That's right. I did at first, while it was starting up."

Imogen glanced round at her assembled family, levered herself up from her chair and strode across to the window. Outside, Rachel's Audi was gleaming in the sunshine. "Are you telling me it's a real property business – worth, like, hundreds of thousands?" She dropped her voice to a whisper. "Or millions?"

Still no one replied and it was Miriam's turn to look away.

"So how did you fund it?" Imogen asked, spinning round to glare at Rachel. "Did the bank lend the money to you? Or was it the bank of Mum and Dad?"

"I suppose I had a lucky start," Rachel confessed. "But since then, everything has been funded by mortgages and bank loans."

"I don't believe this." Imogen's voice was suddenly high pitched. She faced her parents, hands on hips. "You gave her money, didn't you? While I was out of sight, out of mind?"

Max jumped in. "That's enough, Imogen. Things were different then. We still had our engineering consultancy."

Dust motes hovered in a patch of sunlight above the coffee table, the air in the room thickened.

"So what about my request?" asked Imogen. "When I said Simon and I needed your help to get settled in Ibiza, you said *she* had to be here, that we had to have a family conference. I can't say I get why. But, as she is here, here's the deal – Simon and I need a deposit for our villa. Half a million euros should do it."

"Half a million!" exclaimed Rachel, then clapped a hand over her mouth.

"Yes, Miss Moneybags. Or is it Mrs yet? Perhaps you should make an honest man of Jack before someone more deserving comes along and snaps him up."

Max banged his fist on the coffee table so hard the glasses vibrated. His face reddened and he shouted, "Stop this bickering. Stop it at once."

Rachel looked across at her parents, who sat hunched and tight-lipped. When did she become the family spokesperson? "The thing is, Imogen, Mum and Dad can't manage that amount. Funds are tight."

"Oh funds are tight, are they? And I'm meant to accept that as a refusal? But what about you, sucking up all the available cash? I bet they're bank rolling your business, aren't they…"

***

And here she was, ten years on, no closer to getting what was rightly hers.

"I know you and Dad wanted to help me," Imogen said. "I've always sensed it was Rachel who stopped you. Even if you don't have much free cash, you and Dad are rattling around in this house. Wouldn't it make sense to move somewhere easier to manage?"

Miriam shot her a sharp look. "How can you say that, Imogen? The Old Rectory is our home, our family's roots. You of all people must surely understand why we can never leave. And don't talk to me as if I'm ancient. I'm only sixty-one."

"But Dad's going to need more support what with his memory and everything," said Imogen. "Why wait for a crisis to make decisions?"

"I can manage very well, Imogen, without your advice. And don't talk about your father in that way. Who knows what the future holds for any of us? I won't be forced out of my home."

Imogen fixed her mother with a steely gaze. "Funny. I

thought it was just Rachel I was up against, but now I see it's you, too. How many times are you going to destroy my life and steal what's rightfully mine? After what happened in Tunisia ..."

"Get out, Imogen," Miriam shouted. "I refuse to go through this again."

"I'm going. But I won't forget." As she hurried from the kitchen, she cannoned into her bemused father in the hall.

"Is everything all right, Immy?" he asked, waving his folded newspaper.

She shook her head and waited for him to ask again, but he shuffled past her to join her mother. Imogen stopped in the hall to listen. Would her mother mention their discussion?

"What was all that shouting about?" Max asked, but Miriam dropped her voice so Imogen couldn't make out her reply.

"Help me with this crossword clue then," she heard him say.

Imogen gazed around the austere entrance hall at doors leading to rooms nobody used. No one cared about her – a childless, penniless widow. Only her father had ever loved her, and all he could talk about was his blasted crossword. Rachel was behind this, stealing Imogen's inheritance. She'd let her sister get away with it for too long. It was time to make her pay.

"Daughter of Lear," said Max's voice. "Something O, something E, something, something L – Any ideas?"

"Goneril," replied Miriam and quoted, "How sharper than a serpent's tooth it is to have a thankless child."

Chapter Ten

Rachel
May 2019

Rachel woke to a flurry of icy rain battering her bedroom window. She reached out a hand for her mobile and squinted at the screen: six o' clock. She lay very still, so as not to wake Jack, but he must have sensed her turning onto her back. He stroked her arm, then trailed his hand across her stomach and she tensed under the light pressure. He lifted his head, opened one eye and gave a bleary smile.

"Go back to sleep. It's a bank holiday," she said. His head flopped back down onto his pillow.

She waited for him to settle and, when she heard a snore rumbling deep in his throat, she slid out from under the duvet. Jack rolled over and spread his body into the warm space she'd vacated. She blew him a fingertip kiss. Downstairs in the kitchen, she brewed coffee, carried her laptop into the study and closed the door.

Today they'd all been invited to lunch with her parents for the overdue reunion with Imogen, but her mother had cancelled in a panicked phone call the evening before.

"It's best you don't come," Miriam had said. "Imogen's in a bit of a state. She's had bad news from Simon's life assurance company. They won't be paying out and it's hit her hard."

"I'm sorry to hear that but we can still come, can't we? Perhaps I could give her some advice."

"I don't think that would go down well, Rachel. She's so angry – with life, with us, with everything. She might say something to you she'd later regret."

Despite the years of antipathy between them, Imogen's determination to keep her at arm's length was odd. Rachel's own feelings were in turmoil. On the one hand she longed to reach out and console her but another part of her wanted to force a confrontation. For years Imogen had shirked her responsibilities to their parents and left Rachel to pick up the pieces. She'd spent her life walking away from situations and people with no consequences. And now a dead husband ... Something didn't add up.

The downpour blurred Rachel's view of the garden but she'd been gifted back a free day, she might as well get on with some work. With a sigh, she turned to the March accounts that would form the basis of Stapleton Kumar's year end and were needed for her meeting with the bank though they didn't paint the healthiest picture. Her thoughts wandered to a talk she was due to give to a conference. Working on that might distract her from financial worries. She tapped ideas into PowerPoint starting with the title: *Has the buy-to-let bubble burst?*

It was all a matter of timing, she mused, and her timing had been less than perfect. Everyone around her: her business contacts; her parents; Imogen; Jack and all their friends, assumed she must be rich. But it wasn't that simple.

After Hannah was born, Rachel had renovated her student house in London and rented out rooms. A year later, she took out mortgages to buy a couple more properties, holding her breath that they would turn a profit. The first was a maisonette she'd refurbished and sold on; the other, she kept as a buy-to-let so she could compare the returns. She continued investing and working this formula, choosing the worst house on the best street. Sometimes she made a substantial profit on a sale, but often it was less than ten thousand pounds. Her buy-to-let properties had performed better. Since she started her business there had been two cycles of boom and slump in property and she'd bought too many London properties while the market was at its peak. It was these that had now slumped in value due to economic uncertainty, so she was trapped in a vicious circle. If she tried to sell them in the current market, she wouldn't make enough to pay off the loans she'd taken out to buy them.

My business is a bit like a Tardis in reverse, she thought, sleek and shiny on the outside, but poky and cramped – almost Dickensian – on the inside. Still, despite government changes to the tax rules, most of her rental properties were bringing in decent returns that covered the loans and provided some cash flow. As Michael Kumar often reminded her, property was a long-term investment and things would improve.

She tapped out more bullet points. If her audience was still awake at this point, she'd pause and ask them how they thought the buy-to-let business model could work on such slim margins. Her fingers sprinted over the keyboard to keep up with the flow of ideas.

She heard a footstep outside, and Jack appeared, yawning. "Fancy a bacon sarnie?" he asked, bending to kiss her.

"No thanks. I'll have another coffee, though." She waved her empty mug. Within minutes he returned with a fresh one and settled himself on the corner of her desk, ready to chat. Rachel answered in monosyllables, one eye still on her screen until he took the hint and wandered off.

She worked on steadily through the morning. At around two, the rain eased, and Jack returned to suggest a walk.

"Not now," said Rachel. "Maybe this evening. We could stop for a drink on the way to collect Hannah."

She finished a first draft of her presentation and turned back to the accounts. The unfolding picture of the business made her uneasy. She tried different scenarios, pausing only when her back began to ache after seven hours of sitting. She stood up, stretched her arms above her head and wandered out to the kitchen. There was a note from Jack, propped up against the fruit bowl: *Gone to fetch Hannah from Ellie's.*

She felt a spurt of indignation. Hadn't she suggested going together and stopping at the pub en route? But she'd made it clear she didn't want to be distracted. The rain had stopped. She pushed open the back door, breathing in the loamy smell of damp earth. She went outside and strolled around the garden. Droplets of rain fell onto her hair from the apple tree, but the sun had real warmth. The distant hum of traffic from the main Ferngate Road reminded her other people were out and enjoying their day off work.

Spurning the bland gloom of her study, she set up her laptop in the kitchen, which was an archive of happy memories dating from when she'd run her business from the kitchen table with toddler Hannah playing beside her. Once, she'd been featured in a TV programme called *Property Biz* and a television cameraman and interviewer had come to their house and filmed her working on plans and spreadsheets at this very table. They'd panned the camera round onto three-year old Hannah, who was drawing a picture of a house. Rachel had a DVD of the programme and, sometimes, she and Hannah would cuddle up on the sofa and watch it, giggling at their old-fashioned hairstyles and clothes.

The memory of that golden age made her smile. Soon after Hannah started school, her business outgrew the kitchen table and she had moved to an office.

Rachel worked on steadily as the bank holiday ticked away. Jack returned and she heard Hannah clump upstairs in her much-loved biker boots and felt a tiny stab that Hannah hadn't bothered to come in and say 'hi'. It was her own fault that Hannah and Jack were tiptoeing around her.

The swell of cheering told her Jack was watching football in the sitting room. It was nearly eight. Damn, she'd meant to shop so she could cook a proper evening meal for a change, now it was too late. She rummaged in the fridge and found some cold ham and salad. She was getting as bad as her mother.

"Do you want some supper?" she called up to Hannah.

"No, thanks. I ate at Ellie's," came the reply.

Jack smiled as she entered the room, but his expression shaded to disappointment when she handed him his supper tray. It did look a little meagre. She poured two glasses of red wine and offered him one.

"Not for me," he said. "I'm duty solicitor today. I could still get called out."

"Let's hope the rain has scuppered the plans of our local criminals," she said.

Jack demolished his supper in six forkfuls and slid along the sofa, closer to her as she ate. When she set down her tray and turned towards him, his face was just inches from hers and she could smell spring onion on his breath.

"What is it?" she asked.

"There's something I want to ask you," he said, placing his hand lightly on her right arm. Daylight was fading and they hadn't switched the lights on so she couldn't see his expression, but his pupils looked dilated.

She waited. He cleared his throat.

"I was wondering," he began, "if you'd changed your mind about getting married. You can still call yourself Rachel Stapleton." He grinned. "I don't expect you to turn into Rachel Smith. Let's get married this summer. Go away somewhere abroad and not tell anyone till after. Just us. And Hannah."

The years slipped away. He looked eager and hopeful like the twenty-year-old she'd met at university.

Why did he have to spring this on her now? She had so much on her mind but how could he understand, if he didn't know. Keeping secrets was ingrained in her but if she agreed to marry him, she would be honour bound to tell him everything. She wasn't ready, might never be ready.

Jack must have sensed her inner conflict. His smile disappeared.

She took hold of his hand and squeezed it. "I thought you were happy with things the way they are?"

"Well, I am. But I could be happier."

"Most people don't even realise we're not married," said Rachel, letting her hair swing forward to curtain her face.

"It's none of their business," said Jack, inching further along the sofa, away from her.

"Can I think about it?"

"Sure. I didn't realise it would be such a big deal."

"It's not a big deal. I just wasn't expecting it." Rachel felt unexpected tears prick at the back of her eyes. She reached for his hand, but he brushed it away.

"Forget it." He stood up and walked out of the room.

She watched him go, blinked and blew her nose.

Chapter Eleven

Imogen
May 2019

Imogen perched on the edge of her bed and opened the bottle of gin she'd snaffled from Max's drinks cabinet. Damn, she'd forgotten to bring any tonic upstairs and couldn't be bothered to trek back down to the kitchen. She poured a double measure into a mug and sniffed. It smelt faintly botanical – must have been a gift, because her father would never stray from his favourite brand, Gordon's. In one corner of her room was a wash basin so she added a dash of tap water to the mug and sipped it.

She plumped up a pillow. It smelled of dust, but she stuffed it against the headboard and leant back. The Old Rectory had seven bedrooms, but no one ever came to stay. Why were her parents so determined to soldier on here into their twilight years? It made no sense. Their nest was well and truly empty. If George had survived, he'd be twenty-one now. The thought made her shudder. She couldn't blame her father but felt real fury towards her mother. And, as for Rachel, she would have to pay a price. It might take a while to work out a plan, but Imogen was determined.

In the meantime, she needed to reinvent herself. She was sick of being poor. Staying at The Old Rectory was free, but the longer she stayed the harder it would be to keep equilibrium with her parents. What was the point of sealing herself into an early grave? She needed to be in London.

The shut-in grief of the house was stifling like a museum in mourning for a bygone age. She flipped open her tablet computer and tried to think of people she'd met in the years when Simon's band was still riding high. Then she remembered Gavin.

She'd met him one night in a basement bar in San Antonio, where Simon was playing to an audience of fewer than twenty people. She went up to the terrace to sit at the bar and gaze out at the lights shimmering on the surface of the sea. She'd ordered a cocktail and sat on a high stool to sip it. A pungent smell of after shave made her glance at a stranger, with gold jewellery and visible chest hair, who had taken the stool next to her. She'd noticed him watching the band earlier on. He must have noticed her glass was empty.

"Refill?" he offered. A gap between his top front teeth gave his smile an ironic look. If Simon came off stage and found her chatting to this stranger, he'd be jealous.

"Sure," she replied, and soon they were deep in conversation.

"This is Gavin," she said, when Simon appeared to claim his free interval drink. "He likes your music – and he has contacts in the local music scene."

"Music's not my main business," said Gavin, fishing in his jeans pocket for a business card and offering it, first to Simon, who ignored it, and then to Imogen. "I'm more import-export, but I spend a fair bit of time in Ibiza. I'd be happy to act as your promoter to help get your name out."

He mentioned a percentage that sounded minuscule to Imogen. "How can you work for so little?" she asked. Simon scowled at her.

Gavin laughed. "Music promotion is a hobby," he said. "I make my money elsewhere."

With a brusque nod, Simon strolled away and joined the other band members, who were outside, smoking. Imogen watched the four of them form a huddle, nodding or gesticulating towards the bar with San Miguel bottles. Gavin narrowed his eyes and waited.

Simon broke away and strode back towards them. Imogen slipped her hand through his arm and he smiled and ruffled her hair as he delivered the decision.

"You're on," he said, offering Gavin his hand. "We'll make it a trial period. See if the deal works both ways."

"Great," said Gavin, calling the barman across and ordering another round.

"Where do you come from in England?" Imogen asked Gavin. It turned out he'd lived in Ferngate, the same sleepy commuter town on the Hampshire/Surrey border where her sister Rachel now lived. She stopped herself mentioning that to Gavin because his next question would have been "Where?" It would have been embarrassing to confess she didn't know her sister's Ferngate address.

"It's serendipity," she said to Simon later that night as they celebrated the band's survival. "Fate must have thrown Gavin into our path."

For a while, their new partnership flourished and bookings were strong but Imogen had an uneasy feeling that Gavin was more interested in her than in the band. During the long hours they spent together at gigs and in sweat-drenched rehearsal rooms, he would sit just a bit too close to her. She told him to ease off the sickly aftershave. In airless rehearsal rooms it was making her choke, but at least Gavin didn't reek of sweat and cigarettes like Simon when he came off stage.

What had happened to Gavin? she wondered. He was exactly the kind of contact who'd be able to help her find work in the music business. Back then, he'd split his time between Ibiza, mainland Spain and England. How long was it since she'd seen him? It must be five years at least. The last she'd heard, Gavin was in London but there'd been that falling out when he asked Simon to take a parcel to the UK and post it to some contact in Manchester. That had almost ended badly, very badly.

Perhaps Gavin was a bit high risk? On the other hand, she wasn't going to be offering to carry any parcels for him. What was his surname? Winter. That was it.

A few clicks, a scroll through a list of headshots and Gavin's picture was staring right back at her. He wasn't exactly hiding – thank goodness for social media. Gavin wasn't on Instagram, but he was pretty much everywhere else, including LinkedIn. She checked his biography – he was still claiming to be a music promoter, but he had other profiles, too, including import-export agent and his location was shown as Malaga and London. She followed him on all social media platforms then poured another slug of gin, waiting to see if he'd follow her back. But, unlike her, stuck in her parents' house, waiting for something to happen, Gavin was probably in Malaga, partying.

She crept downstairs and made an instant coffee in the mug she'd used for her gin. She took a glass from the cupboard and two cans of tonic from the fridge and stuck them in her pocket. As she headed for the stairs, she heard her father's loud snores echoing from the drawing room and peered in through the part-open door. He was wearing an old felted cardigan. Why did her mother let him go round looking like a tramp? Her mother was flicking through a magazine, but the television wasn't on and there was no music, no radio, no conversation. If I don't get my life on track soon, she thought, that could be me.

Back in her room, she popped a Ferrero Rocher chocolate in her mouth. She'd bought a box at the airport, intending it as a gift for her mother but never mind. As she sipped her coffee and contemplated her next move, her phone pinged. Gavin Winter had followed her back. Good, now she could private message him.

She tapped out a few words:

Hi Gavin – you might not remember me.

No that was wrong. Of course he'd remember her. She tried again:

Hey – it's Imogen. Remember Ibiza? Good times. I've moved back to the UK.

Should she mention Simon? This probably wasn't the right time. Still she needed something more, so she added:

I'm job hunting. Any contacts in the music world? Or media?

***

For two days she heard nothing and spent her time scouring social media for more contacts, fretting. Her mother seemed to have forgiven her latest outburst – probably put it down to grief – and carried on fussing over her.

"I wish you'd go and sign on with Doctor Hastings, darling. In case you need more medication. Or treatment."

"I've got everything I need, Mum. And I've brought a prescription with me in case I need more tablets."

She was weaning herself off the tablets. She needed to stay focused. Twenty years in a relationship with a musician had taught her how slippery the path could be once you began to spiral down. From now on, she would stick to the things that mattered to her – money, success and admiration. She vowed not to make the mistakes Simon had made.

And just when she thought he'd forgotten her, Gavin replied to her messages and, thanks to his contacts, she had an interview.

Chapter Twelve

Rachel
May 2019

Jensen was snoozing at Rachel's feet on the dog-friendly brown study carpet when a tap on the door surprised her and Hannah took a cautious step into the room.

"Mum, can I talk to you?" she asked.

"Sure." Rachel looked up from her screen and moved an overflowing lever arch file off the guest chair, so Hannah could sit down.

"I bumped into Karen yesterday," said Hannah, "...and Luke." She leaned back and stretched her legs out in front of her. She wasn't wearing her biker boots today.

"Oh yes?" When had she last seen Karen? Three days a week, usually in the mornings, Karen occupied their house like a silent ghost and left her mark in the form of gleaming surfaces and neat piles of folded ironing. Every month Rachel paid the agreed amount into Karen's bank account, increasing it automatically each January. If she wanted Karen to spring clean a particular room, she left a note for her on the kitchen table and Karen always carried out these instructions but never scribbled a reply. Nor did she help herself to the tea, coffee and biscuits that Rachel left out for her.

"I wanted to ask you about Gavin," said Hannah, taking an audible in-breath. "What happened to Luke's father?"

"Gavin!" The question took Rachel back to when she first met Karen at the school gates. It was only by chance that they'd become friends. Luke was older than Hannah and Karen lived on a new estate outside Ferngate town. Rachel sometimes drove past her on the way to school, impressed that she had the stamina to walk two miles, twice a day. On the journey home with Luke, Karen would catch the bus. When she drove past her, Rachel offered Karen a lift. Later, she bought a second booster seat and told Karen she'd borrowed it so she could take Luke, too.

"Didn't you and Dad used to be friends with them?" prompted Hannah.

"Karen and I sometimes had a girls' night out – a film or a Thai meal," she replied. "But Gavin never wanted to socialise."

"He used to talk to you outside school, didn't he?" asked Hannah. "Luke told me his dad was chatting you up."

"Whatever gave him that idea?" She remembered how Gavin would saunter across the playground to talk to her when he came to collect Luke. It was more of a beeline than a saunter because Gavin ignored everyone else. She could feel the eyes of the other mums on them and imagine their gossip. There was something vaguely disturbing about Gavin. He was attractive in a way: relentlessly upbeat, energetic and loud. Probably a teller of tales, the magnetic centre of any crowd: the sort of man who carried a wad of folding money and bought endless rounds of drinks for friends and strangers alike. But not in Ferngate. Here he chose to remain an enigma.

"Everyone was shocked when Gavin disappeared," she said. "He didn't just walk out after a row, he seemed to vanish off the face of the planet." She'd done her best to support Karen who was frozen in a state of stasis, but Karen steadfastly refused to be helped. After six months of unpaid mortgage instalments, the bank took charge and Karen's house was repossessed. "Your dad helped her with legal advice," said Rachel. "And sorting out her finances."

"Is that why you gave her a job?"

Rachel nodded. "Remember how I used to work from home and fit my work into school hours? The business grew; there weren't enough hours in the day, and I needed to move to an office. That's when Karen became your childminder and it suited her because she could look after Luke at the same time."

Karen had also looked after the house and kept everything running smoothly. It was hardly surprising that the thread of friendship between her and Karen had snapped.

"But you still haven't said what happened to him, Mum."

"Sorry. I was thinking back, that's all." She noticed the black tights Hannah was wearing under denim shorts had snagged and a circle of whiteish skin was showing through.

"Karen never mentions him, but I assume they're divorced."

"I don't get it. Why would Gavin take off and leave his son?"

Rachel shook her head. "It's a mystery to me too." She leaned forward and hugged Hannah. "Your dad would never leave you."

"Do you think Luke would have been affected by not having his dad around?" asked Hannah, a hint of crimson dotting her cheeks.

"Not having a male role model, do you mean?"

"Not that exactly. I mean, loads of my friends' parents are divorced, but they still see their dads. Abi goes to Edinburgh every school holiday to stay with her dad; and Lily's grandma drives her and Jake to Oxford some weekends because Lily's mum and dad aren't speaking. Lily says all that travelling sucks."

"Karen's done her best for Luke," said Rachel, slowly. "It's been hard for her."

"Luke told me it's better now he's at sixth form college. He's made new friends, who don't know or care anything about his dad."

So Hannah had been seeing Luke. It wasn't just the one occasion that she'd bumped into him.

"Luke was a charmer when you were both little," said Rachel. "And Karen says he's very bright. He'll be fine. But don't interrogate him about his dad, if you see him. He might not like it."

Hannah shot her a disdainful look. "Honestly, Mum. As if…"

"Sorry, darling. I didn't mean ..." She half-rose from her chair intending to give Hannah a hug.

Hannah tossed her hair and headed for the door. The flesh-coloured hole in her black tights seemed to have grown larger. Don't be ridiculous, thought Rachel, no one darns tights anymore. And yet, somehow, the sight of it reproached her.

Chapter Thirteen

Imogen
May 2019

Imogen's job interview, fixed by Gavin, was with a commercial radio station. Nothing fancy and not one she'd ever heard of, but it was a start. She caught a morning train to London and strolled through the streets to the converted warehouse where the station was based. Her interview was with the businessman who had set up Radio Denim FM. He introduced himself as Victor and, as they chatted, she sensed it was a vanity project he intended to hand over to his son, when the son graduated. She wondered how, if she got the job, she would feel about taking orders from a twenty-one-year-old.

"Your CV says you were a DJ in Ibiza," said Victor. He hadn't bothered to print it out but peered at it on a tablet computer lying on the desk in front of him. "What equipment did you use?"

Imogen froze. When talking to Gavin, and in her CV, she'd pitched herself as having DJ experience but that wasn't true. Her only exposure was hovering in the background when Simon was standing up in front of the decks and battling with temperamental tonearms and bouncy vibrating staging. He'd moved on to using a laptop and some sort of controller-cum-CD turntable. What was it called?

"Um – a laptop and CDJ set up," she replied.

"And which clubs did you perform in?"

Her brain went dead. She could only remember the names of the super clubs like Pacha and Privilege.

"Bora Bora," she said finally, remembering a beach bar club

in Playa d'en Bossa. But Simon had never played there.

"And what music did you play at this club? House? Techno?"

"Both, of course."

"Hmm." Victor rubbed his stubbly chin. "I don't think Radio Denim listeners will enjoy that on their morning and evening commute."

Imogen blushed. He'd been winding her up. Damn Gavin – why didn't he warn her? "My tastes are more mainstream. My husband was a rock musician. His band was well-known in the noughties,"

"Name?"

"Simon Wilson."

Victor scratched his head and a few flakes of dandruff fell onto the shoulders of his dark blue shirt. "Never heard of him. As it happens, the job we're looking to fill today isn't a DJ. It's mainly traffic, weather, continuity announcements. Perhaps reading the news headlines. What do you think about that?"

Imogen felt a surge of relief. "I suppose it might be a start."

"I usually give candidates some tests but, for you, I think we'll start with the voice recording," said Victor. He ushered her into a studio and sat her in front of a microphone. "Adjust your seat while I fetch a technician."

A few minutes later a younger man appeared and introduced himself as Josh.

"This will take around fifteen minutes," Josh said, handing her a set of cards to read from.

"Are there any guidelines?" she asked.

He grinned. "My advice would be to mix it up a bit. Do some different voices. Those traffic reports can sound dire if you read them out in a deadpan tone."

Josh gave her a cue and the recording began. She knew she'd be word perfect so took a calm breath and read each piece in a different voice.

"How was it?" she asked.

"Sounded good to me," said Josh. "Go and sit in the waiting area and I'll fetch Victor to have a listen."

She waited, tapping her foot to rid her body of trapped energy and wondering about the next set of tests. As she checked the time on her phone, Victor opened the studio door and strode towards her, hand extended.

"Welcome on board!"

"What about the tests?" she asked, but she already knew it was her voice. She could do sultry, high pitched, smoky, friendly, even clipped business speak.

"You'll be fine, Imogen," said Victor. "How did you develop such a range?"

"I always planned to go to drama school, and I acted when I was younger, but life got in the way." It was the years abroad and the music scene that had given her the voice with its indefinable accent. She could sound exotic, foreign, home counties or hip.

"You'll have to do some station admin along with traffic and weather," said Victor. "But longer term we might trial you as a presenter. You'll need to build your social media following."

"What do you mean?"

"Presenters bring their followers with them, Imogen. That's how the world works now."

Imogen quickened her pace as she left the radio station. It was cramped, just two studios, some hot desks and a common area shared with other companies in the building. There wasn't even a café, just a grim vending machine. She took the underground to Leicester Square. It was her first time in London since returning to Britain and the defeated face of a man slumped in a theatre fire exit, with his rolled up sleeping bag, cast a shadow over her day. She dug in her handbag for coins and deposited them in the man's enamel cup.

She reached Dean Street and located the Georgian townhouse with a discreet brass plaque outside giving the name of the club. She rang the bell. The door was opened by an impossibly tall and elegant young woman in white shirt, waistcoat and bow tie.

"Name?" asked the woman.

"Imogen Wilson."

"No. Member's name."

Imogen blushed. "I'm meeting Mr Gavin Winter."

The woman scanned the member database and checked off a name, turning back to Imogen with a smile. "Did he tell you which floor he'd be on?"

She shook her head.

"Well, he'll likely be on the ground floor or second floor. Put your phone on silent please." The woman stepped aside and beckoned her in.

Imogen wandered from the corridor into a bar, scanning faces. The bar was quiet, but the tearoom was buzzing. Young professionals of all nationalities, in small groups or alone, sat hunched over laptops. Would she recognise Gavin or, more to the point, would he recognise her? She sneaked into a cloakroom to touch up her lipstick and smooth her blonde hair. Not bad for thirty-nine, she thought, squinting in the mirror. Then she remembered she'd turned forty. In a comfortable sitting room with tall windows overlooking the street a man with a neatly trimmed beard glanced up and caught her eye. She strode toward him. "Hi!"

He raised a quizzical eyebrow. "Were you meeting someone?" Of course, he was far too young. Younger than Gavin was when she first knew him. Muttering apologies, Imogen took a step back and an arm reached out from nowhere and encircled her waist. She spun round.

"Gavin!" The years had moved him on, but his face still had its hungry, angry expression.

He kissed her cheek and ushered her through to the bar where he chose a table with two high backed armchairs. Without asking he ordered her a double gin and tonic.

"I wanted a tea," she protested, but he laughed.

"No, you didn't. So how did it go?"

"What?"

"The interview"

She fluttered her hand. "Oh, you know." She paused to let suspense build. "I got the job. Thanks for setting up the introduction." She noticed a dark stain creeping from his hairline but why shouldn't he colour his hair? Lots of men did.

"Congratulations!" He raised his glass in a toast. "When do you start?"

"They want me straight away. So, I'll start next Monday when I've found somewhere to live." She'd looked online but rents had shocked her, and no way was she going to share. She was considering a small hotel in Marylebone that cost sixty pounds a night with a basic kitchenette. It would strain her finances but, a couple of days earlier, she'd had a stroke of luck. Rifling through her father's wardrobe, while her parents were out, she'd come across some bundles of bank notes, neatly secured with elastic bands, in a jacket pocket. There was no way he would remember he had it – the money was already as good as lost. She slipped it into her bag.

Gavin leaned back in his chair and his jacket fell open revealing a well-toned chest, undermined by a paunch belly. "What area were you thinking of looking?"

"I was wondering about Marylebone. Somewhere accessible for the office as I'll be working late and early shifts."

"Maybe I can help you out."

"You know somewhere?" She hesitated. Was he about to invite her to move in with him?

He nodded. "I do. It's in Maida Vale. I'm keeping an eye on it for the owner and it's rent free."

Chapter Fourteen

Rachel
May 2019

Miriam had a habit of phoning just as Rachel was about to leave the office, and her first words always carried a sting.

"What are you doing at work at this time, Rachel? You should be at home with Hannah."

"Uh – huh." Rachel remembered her mother working late into the evening during her childhood. "I'm leaving soon."

With her free hand, Rachel scrolled through her inbox, deleting some messages, unread. A clanking sound from the corridor meant Fatima, the cleaner was lumbering along, trailing her vacuum cleaner behind her. Soon she would appear in the office and want to chat.

"How is Imogen?" she asked, continuing the spring clean of her messages.

There was a brief pause. "She's moved out."

"Really?"

"She's found a job in London and moved out at the weekend."

"That's quick!" Rachel felt a spurt of admiration.

"Exactly. It's too soon – just weeks since Simon died. I begged her to go and see Dr Hastings, but she wouldn't listen. She's grieving for Simon. Sometimes she's in a terrible state but, other times, it's as if she's forgotten she was ever married. Did she ring you?"

"No. I haven't heard a thing."

Rachel remembered the article she and Jack had read in The Ibizan and the mix up about the date of Simon's death. When her mother relayed her garbled version of Imogen's phone call from Ibiza, she said it had happened only two weeks ago but if Simon died on the tenth of February, Imogen would have said two months. Rolling the calendar forward to today would make it three months ago. Still not long to recover from such a tragedy but why did she tell their mother the wrong date?

"Listen, Mum, I'm viewing a property in Theale tomorrow, so I'll call in afterwards and we'll have a proper catch up."

As she bundled papers for the next day's visit into her bag, her eye caught a brown envelope she'd been carrying around. It was the envelope Miriam had given her weeks ago, containing three quotations for a new roof on The Old Rectory. The cost was eye-watering – in many parts of the country you could buy a family home for less. Rachel had asked one of Stapleton Kumar's contractors to quote. She printed off the email and added it to the envelope.

***

Two bay trees in pewter pots stood sentinel on either side of The Old Rectory's front door and Miriam was hovering on the step, secateurs in hand, tidying up uneven shoots that threatened their symmetry. Rachel drove in through the gates, parked and ran up the steps to greet her mother.

"I expect you're pressed for time," said Miriam. "So I've made sandwiches for lunch."

"That's fine." Rachel followed her into the kitchen, which smelled of hard boiled eggs, and waited for her mother to peel back the cling film from a plate of sandwiches.

"Isn't Dad eating with us?" she asked.

"He had his earlier." Miriam poured elderflower cordial from a bottle and over-diluted it with tap water. "I think he's dozing at the moment."

As they finished the egg sandwiches, Max wandered in and greeted Rachel with a smile and a kiss.

"Is it breakfast time already?" he asked.

Miriam sighed. "You've already had breakfast, Max. And lunch."

"Have I?" He seemed genuinely surprised. "What did I

come in here for?"

Rachel noticed a folded newspaper on the windowsill and handed it to him. "Perhaps the crossword, Dad?"

"Right. That must be it." He took the paper and pottered out.

"How is he?" Rachel asked, biting her lower lip.

Her mother sighed. "Most of the time he's fine. In fact, he's been talking about some business meeting he has coming up. I've found it's best to go along with his fantasies."

"Has he seen the doctor?"

"Not recently. I'll make another appointment soon."

"Let's discuss the roof repairs." said Rachel, reaching into her bag and taking out the envelope of quotations. "I've looked at your quotations and I have this extra one from Garman's. Remember? Jon Garman popped round to have a look?"

"Yes. He came a couple of weeks ago."

Rachel laid the Garman's quotation on top of the pile. "Look – it's thirty-thousand cheaper. Those other contractors were ripping you off."

Miriam squinted at it, then fished in her pocket for reading glasses.

"This one's no good, Rachel. We're a listed building. We have to use original materials for the roof. Welsh slate and it will have to be reclaimed from a building of the same age that's being demolished."

"Surely Spanish slate will do just as well."

"Absolutely not." A flush appeared on Miriam's cheeks. "The council's planning department will never permit it. And I couldn't either. The Old Rectory was here for two hundred years before we moved in and will exist long after we've gone. We're only the custodians. It's our job to conserve it, not wreck its beauty for future generations."

Rachel frowned. It was all very well for Miriam to take that view but it wasn't her who'd be finding the money. If a tree had fallen on the roof, the insurers might have paid up, but this was wear and tear so the money would have to be found. "Then there's no way we can do the whole roof," she said.

"We'll have to repair the parts that are leaking."

Miriam's eyes flashed with a mix of shame and anger. "I didn't expect you to be so parsimonious. After everything …"

Rachel raised her hand, palm forward. Recriminations wouldn't help. "Stop it, Mum. Come on, let's take a look at the roof from outside."

Miriam led the way through the French doors onto the terrace where they both leaned against the stone retaining wall while Miriam pointed out missing slates and bulges. "That's the place where the rain seeps in. You must have noticed damp on the drawing room walls."

Rachel nodded. "I've seen the wallpaper peeling off."

"I have to put a bucket on the landing when it rains heavily."

Rachel swept a practised property developer's eye across the back wall and noticed rust coloured stains. "I think those stains are coming from the guttering," she said with a twinge of dismay. The damage was dotted in patches across the whole roof area. "Even if we just do the repairs, the scaffolding alone will cost a fortune."

Miriam's lips compressed as she changed the subject. "Let me show you the garden. I've done some new planting."

Rachel glanced at her phone and the list of messages waiting for her attention. "Just ten minutes," she said. "I must get back to the office."

There had been no rain for a week, but Miriam fetched her green overshoes and slipped her feet into them. She slid her arm through Rachel's, and they took the steps down from the raised terrace to the garden.

In the decade following George's death, the garden had been neglected but, lately, it had become her mother's solace. Miriam had wrestled the two-acre plot back from wilderness and restored the original classical features. Now it was a relaxed fusion of formal and wild elements with herbaceous plants scampering across flowerbeds like film trailers promising a spectacle coming later.

"You were going to tell me about Imogen's job," said Rachel.

"Oh yes. She's working for a radio station. Radio Denim,"

said Miriam.

"That sounds perfect. It's three months since Simon died so perhaps she's ready."

Her mother bent to move a fallen branch from their path. "No. Not three months. The accident was in early April. Definitely."

"I thought it was February."

But her mother wasn't listening. She began pointing out every tree and shrub and naming them, as if introducing a set of personal friends. "That's a forsythia. Over there is a sweet chestnut I planted five years ago. I think the wisteria is going to be disappointing this year."

Perhaps it wasn't a surprise that her mother preferred plants to people. She certainly seemed reluctant to talk about Imogen.

They entered the walled garden, where Miriam grew vegetables. She picked up a scissors and snipped off some herbs for Rachel to take home and hand-tied them with twine. The aroma of mint and rosemary stirred memories from the past when her childhood was happy. Before Tunisia, before boarding school, before George.

A path made from scuffed terracotta bricks ran through the centre of the gardens, past the silent fountain where Miriam had placed pots of spring bulbs inside the empty pond basin and created a shrine.

All of a sudden Rachel had a feeling she was not alone. Her senses on high alert, her ears tuned in to long ago sounds of birdsong, roadworks, blaring rap music and a child's rippling laughter. From the corner of her eye she thought she glimpsed a small figure near the old playhouse and felt something brush against her leg. Her stomach somersaulted but, when she looked down, it was next door's cat, Monty. She gathered him up in her arms, holding him tight against her chest and feeling his rapid heartbeat keep pace with her own. He struggled and mewed before settling into her embrace.

The feeble sunshine painted The Old Rectory's rear windows into reflective mirrors and the house seemed to whisper to her, as if re-establishing its claim: mend me, fix me, love me. She gave Monty a final hug and set him down on the path.

Chapter Fifteen

Imogen
June 2019

Gavin swirled the ice in his tumbler of bourbon, stretched out on the double bed and beckoned to Imogen to join him. His boots were resting on her new white bedspread and she wanted to yell at him to take them off. If he thought she was going to sleep with him, just because he'd found her a job and offered her a place to live...

Imogen hadn't expected it to be a narrowboat but, after ten days on the Lazy Lucy, she was loving a lifestyle that fitted with her reinvented self-image: bohemian. The sun shone and Little Venice buzzed with activity. All around there were coffee shops and bars, organic butchers and grocers. And it was so central. If she didn't feel like walking, she would take an Uber. She'd invested some of the windfall she'd found in her father's jacket pocket in new linen: 500 thread count Egyptian cotton sheets and a white, pure silk quilt cover. And now Gavin had his feet on it.

She stood stiffly, keeping her distance as she sipped her gin and tonic.

"So tell me, sweetheart," he said.

Imogen cringed.

"What happened between you and old Simon? Did he jump?"

Now she was seriously cross. "How do you know about Simon's accident?"

Gavin laughed. "When were you going to tell me? At first, I figured you must have left him, and I wasn't surprised. He was a bit of a loser, as I recall. I remember that trouble he had with the law. He was lucky to walk away from that."

"How dare you!" Imogen fumed, clenching her fingers. "That was your doing. Simon did you a favour and look where it almost landed him!"

Gavin ignored her rant. "So anyway, when you didn't tell me whether you were divorced, I did a bit of googling to check if Simon was still playing the clubs in Ibiza. It took some detective work to track him down. But when I used the Spanish search engines, reports of poor old Simon Wilson's accident popped up. Balcony fall was it?" He laughed uproariously. "Or did he jump? A man with a lovely wife like you. I'd say he had everything to live for."

"Of course he didn't jump," said Imogen, narrowing her eyes as she turned to face him. "It was a terrible accident. Don't make a joke of it, Gavin." Tears welled up in her eyes. One overflowed and traced a path down her cheek. "I haven't come to terms with it. I doubt I ever will. But I have to face the future and make a living." Her voice trailed off and she set down the gin, ran water into a tumbler and gulped that down.

Gavin swung his legs off the bed and levered himself up to standing. Two paces brought him to Imogen's side. He draped an arm around her shoulders and kissed her softly on the cheek.

"I'm sorry, sweetie. I didn't mean to be brutal. It's just that you were so secretive when I mentioned Simon's name. At first I assumed you'd split up long ago and were over him so it was a shock to find out it was so recent, but I don't remember reading about it in the British press."

Imogen's hand moved to the solitaire diamond she wore on a gold chain around her neck, one of the few pieces of jewellery Simon had given her that she hadn't sold. "Simon was furious about how he was treated when he brought that – err – package over for you. He swore he'd never set foot in England again. And he didn't."

Her heart constricted as she thought of Simon and her tears flowed unchecked. She wiped them with the back of her hand and sniffed. How angry Simon was when his early success didn't continue. He didn't seem to get that most boy bands only have a limited lifespan and even then, they were more popular in Germany and Spain than at home. After the Brexit vote in 2016 he'd turned his back on Britain.

"Simon had taken Spanish citizenship," said Imogen. "I don't think his link with the UK was picked up by the media when the accident happened." He wasn't even famous enough to have a proper obituary in the UK music press, she thought grimly. How Simon would have resented that.

"But that's impossible," said Gavin. "I've lived in Spain – off and on – for years and thought about applying. But you need ten years' residence."

"Simon didn't need the residence qualification. His mother was Spanish, so he went to the head of the queue."

"Is he buried in Ibiza?"

She nodded. "He wouldn't have wanted his body repatriated, so no British coroner was involved. I guess that's another reason why it wasn't reported."

"You seem a bit of an expert."

Imogen bristled. Why did he insist on taunting her?

"Of course I'm a bloody expert! I've worked as a holiday rep, stupid – one of many jobs I had over the years, and I dealt with several accidental deaths of young tourists falling from balconies. It was chilling. Not just dealing with the authorities and looking after their grieving friends but often their devastated parents would fly out and want a guided tour of where their child had spent his last hours. I never thought it could happen to Simon."

A wasp flew in through the open door and hovered close to Imogen's glass. She swatted it with the back of her hand. It darted away and she watched it disappear inside a lampshade where she could hear it, but not see it.

"So tell me," said Gavin, changing his frivolous tone and sounding more serious. "Are you grieving?"

Imogen dropped her gaze and shivered. "Honestly, Gavin. You are unkind. I'm devastated but life must go on. I mean, I'm here and he's not."

"And I'm here, too." Gavin pulled her into a hug. His

aftershave was spicy and overpowering – she'd have to stop him using that, but it was comforting to have a man's arms around her. The Lazy Lucy houseboat belonging to his mysterious friend was ace, too, and Gavin had some useful contacts.

"Let me help you, Immy," Gavin murmured, stroking her hair. "You've had a tough time and I'm going to make it up to you."

She faked a sigh. His caresses were soothing. Why bother to fight him off? She wasn't taking contraception but, after the ectopic pregnancy, her chances of getting pregnant were virtually zero. Why not let this man, who was solvent and a passable looker, take care of her? For a while.

Chapter Sixteen

Rachel
June 2019

In the weeks after Imogen moved to London, Miriam stepped up her campaign for a reconciliation between her daughters and Rachel came to dread her mother's phone calls. She could stand up to relentless pressure but not emotional blackmail. She'd tried to talk to Imogen on the phone and steeled herself to visit when Imogen was staying at The Old Rectory, but her mother had cancelled. What was really going on? It was clear her mother was genuinely upset at the rift.

"I'm so worried about your sister," was Miriam's opening salvo in an otherwise routine phone call. "Widowed at such a young age and, after so many years abroad, she's having to make her own way with no friends to support her."

Was her mother also nagging Imogen to contact her? Unlikely. It dawned on Rachel that she would be the first to crack though the prospect of seeing her sister made her shudder. The last time they were together, Imogen had turned on her and said some terrible things. A decade on, Rachel still sometimes woke in a cold sweat with Imogen's false accusations echoing in her ears. How would Imogen react, she wondered, if she started questioning her about Simon's accident?

On her next visit to The Old Rectory, she broached a peace plan with her mother.

"You need to tell Imogen the truth, Mum. About why you transferred the student house in Streatham into my name."

That bloody house! It had caused nothing but problems. It

wasn't as if she'd wanted her parents to buy her a house. For all they knew, she might have preferred to stay in a hall of residence, or at least rented somewhere more central, but they'd gone right ahead without consulting her or even inviting her to view it. With Imogen abroad and George dead, they couldn't help channelling all their energy into their remaining child.

Following George's death, Rachel missed her last two A level exams but Saint Jude's, the school she so despised, had lobbied the university on her behalf and her offer to read law was mysteriously reissued as unconditional. She moved to London in October 1999, still traumatised.

She rarely went home for weekends. It was too painful. In later years, she asked herself if she should have noticed her parents, and their business, unravelling but Max and Miriam were expert at keeping things under wraps. Her father had put his engineering consultancy on hold while he was in Tunisia and his most valuable clients were lost to other consultancies. Her parents were in the early stages of rebuilding the business when George died. It tore them apart.

Projects in progress were neglected, the firm's reputation suffered, and clients drifted away. They brought in day-rate consultants to fulfil obligations Max should have carried out himself and paid the inflated rates they demanded. The final blow came some years later when Miriam, who was company secretary and ran the office, missed the renewal date for the firm's professional indemnity insurance. When one of their sub-contractors made an error on a project that Max hadn't adequately supervised, the client company sued. It cost millions.

By that time, Rachel was running her small property business and looking after eighteen-month-old Hannah. The bombshell was shared with her at a tearful family conference where her father had explained they were on the verge of bankruptcy and wanted to transfer the London house into her name to put this small asset beyond reach of their creditors. Rachel was already a joint owner on the deeds. Legal fees had gobbled up their investments and emptied their pension pots,

The Old Rectory would be the next asset to go but neither of them was ready to leave.

"There must be something we can do," Rachel had urged, appalled at how her parents had rolled over and accepted their fate. Why hadn't they discussed this with her sooner? "Give me time to take advice," she had said, and watched hope flicker in her mother's eyes.

"Do you have an idea?" asked Miriam.

"Maybe. I wish you'd trusted me with this sooner."

Miriam bit her lip. "We were too ashamed. Whatever the outcome, you must promise never to tell anyone. Not Imogen - not even Jack."

With advice from a lawyer at the firm where she'd done a student placement, and a financial adviser, Rachel had raised a massive mortgage on the Old Rectory to settle the final debts and allow her parents to stay in their home. The stain of the negligence claim against them would make it impossible for them to continue in business and, having liquidated their pensions, they had little income. So it fell to Rachel to take responsibility for the repayments. She accepted the transfer of the London house. From that day on, her property company could no longer be a hobby. She was not yet twenty-four years old, but her start-up business would have to support her own family, her parents, plus one very ancient and expensive house. If she hadn't already hated The Old Rectory, she would have grown to loathe it.

"Unless you tell Imogen the truth, Mum," said Rachel, "we'll never be reconciled. She's convinced you've bankrolled my business – and that you have squirrelled away your wealth and won't share it with her. It's not fair."

Miriam's breathing quickened. "Your father and I have talked about it, but…" She hesitated. "He's not ready."

"Mum, are you sure? I don't think Dad's that sensitive anymore. Even if telling Imogen upsets him for a while, he'd soon forget all about it."

"You'd be surprised, Rachel. Your father's social interactions might have deserted him but, when it comes to business, he's as astute as before. He even has former colleagues calling him for advice."

Rachel didn't believe her. Why was her mother playing along with some fantasy that Max was still active in business? The person whose pride couldn't stand the prospect of losing The Old Rectory was her mother.

"Here – take Imogen's number." Miriam pressed a scrap of paper into her hand.

Rachel folded it and dropped it into her bag. "I'll try calling her, but unless you tell her the truth, it'll be a waste of time." Rachel felt her irritation rising. She got to her feet, anxious to be in her car and driving fast along the motorway towards home.

"You haven't told anyone, have you?" Miriam laid a restraining hand on her arm. Rachel glanced down and noticed the nail polish peeling from her mother's fingernails – a tell-tale chink in her mother's immaculate armour.

"No Mum," said Rachel, "I haven't told Jack, if that's what you mean. But it's not been easy." At times, the weight of putting her business responsibilities before her family had come close to breaking them.

She drove away from Blakeswood with Imogen's number in her bag, and the promised phone call, rated as an A-minus on her mental to do list. But she hadn't been fully honest with her mother. She hadn't told Jack, but there was someone else she had confided in: Michael Kumar.

Chapter Seventeen

Imogen
June 2019

Radio Denim's micro-staffing was stretched across a schedule that ran for twenty hours out of twenty-four but Imogen's colleagues were millennials, used to sacrificing their lives on the altar of their careers. If she ventured a negative comment on her fifty-hour shift pattern, they acted bemused and mentioned friends, who worked as baristas in the day and blossomed into their true DJ selves on community radio night shifts – for zero pay. Imogen was left in no doubt that some people would trample over her to steal her job.

The life was immersive and, when her next weekend off rolled around, she had no plans. Gavin was abroad somewhere, working at his dodgy import-export business and she was alone on the Lazy Lucy. A smell of burning made her glance around the tiny galley. The kettle had boiled dry. Ho hum – good thing Gavin wasn't around. He would give her grief for that. The day she'd moved in, he'd laid on a health and safety tour, highlighting the perils of houseboat living.

"What do you think are the main risks?" he'd asked her.

"Err – drowning?"

"No. That's incredibly rare. People get injured in gas canister explosions or die of carbon monoxide poisoning..."

He'd showed her all the safety features and alarms and urged her to double check everything before she went to bed.

"Now you're scaring me, Gavin," she'd said, trying to lighten the atmosphere.

"I'm always serious about things like this, Immy. I want

you to stay safe." He'd laughed and added, "it's not only boats that are dangerous. A few months back, I had a scare in the place I'm renting. I woke up in the night, smelling smoke."

"Oh my God, what was it?"

"I'd had a plumber in to work on the central heating. It seems he'd put down his blow torch while it was still hot. My cottage has old wooden floorboards and dust gets trapped between the joists. A light draught can carry the heat and start a small fire. Luckily, I smelled it in time, but the odd thing was, it was nowhere near the original heat source. Fires can smoulder for a while before going up."

"Like Notre Dame Cathedral in Paris?" On the fifteenth of April, while she was still in Ibiza but planning to leave, Imogen had watched on TV in horrified silence as the historic cathedral burned. She and Simon had visited Paris in happier times. They'd climbed a spiral staircase to a gallery and posed for photographs beside gargoyles, swapping childhood memories of Victor Hugo's hunchback. The burning cathedral felt like a metaphor for her life.

"Exactly. Historic buildings are like tinder boxes because well-seasoned wood has dried out over centuries."

The kettle was ruined so she boiled water in a saucepan for her second cup of coffee and yawned, wondering what to do with her day. When her mobile beeped and an unknown number flashed up on her screen, she snatched it up.

"Imogen?" said a voice, so uncannily familiar, she could have been talking to herself. These days her voice was her living, so she knew instinctively that this was the voice Simon had sometimes mistaken for hers, when she was in her teens. It could only belong to her sister.

"Rachel?" she whispered, cupping her hand around the phone.

"Imogen, I'm so terribly sorry about Simon," said Rachel, her voice cracking with emotion.

She heard a sniff and realised Rachel was crying. It triggered her own tears and soon she was sobbing too.

Rachel recovered first. "What a desperate thing to happen. Poor Simon. Poor you!"

Imogen blubbered some more. It was pathetic really, not how she'd imagined her first talk with Rachel.

"I'm here for you, Immy," said Rachel. "I wish we'd been able to meet sooner but... you know, you had a lot on your mind, and I didn't know if ... Shall I come to see you?"

Imogen found her voice. "You could have come to see me when I was at Mum and Dad's."

"But Mum said you didn't want to see ME! She asked me to come over and called it off a couple of times."

Imogen hesitated. "Well, of course I want to see you! What gave you that daft idea? I live in London now. Do you come here for work?"

"Not often."

"I thought you owned properties here?"

"A few," Rachel admitted. The London properties were the Achilles heel of her portfolio. She'd bought too many when the market was booming and now they'd slumped. "Why not come to visit us in Ferngate? Jack would love to see you. And Hannah. How about next Friday?"

Imogen glanced at her watch. Today was Saturday and it was only ten-thirty in the morning. Under a cloudless sky, joggers were pounding along the towpath forcing dog walkers to step aside. The day stretched aimlessly ahead, and her next shift was on Monday morning.

"I'm working next Friday," she said. "But I'm off this weekend. I'll come tonight and stay over. Ping me over your address. I'll be with you by six-thirty."

Chapter Eighteen

Rachel
June 2019

Rachel made up the guest room with fresh bedlinen. It was hard not to feel manipulated. After going to great lengths to avoid her, why had Imogen calmly invited herself to stay? It was doubly awkward that Mike Kumar and his wife, Alisha, were coming for supper. Introducing Imogen into their tight circle would be a risk but might dilute some of the tension from this first meeting.

What did Imogen eat? She had no idea, but Alisha was a vegetarian, who occasionally ate fish, so there should be something suitable. She thumbed through her recipe book, easily finding favourite pages stuck together with spots of grease or chocolate. She used to enjoy cooking but lately it was on the back burner, along with going to the gym and keeping in touch with her friends. She turned the radio up as she chopped herbs and vegetables and resolved to face the evening with a smile.

Six-thirty came and went. No Imogen. At seven, Mike and Alisha arrived. Twenty minutes later, a car drew up outside and Rachel opened the front door for Imogen, who was getting out of a taxi.

"Darling," said Imogen, wafting into the hall. Her words weren't directed at Rachel, who was holding the door open, but towards Hannah. She clasped her niece in an embrace. "I haven't seen you since forever!"

"Not since I was a baby," agreed Hannah, squirming out of her aunt's grip. "I don't remember you at all."

"Really, darling? Can it be that long?"

"When I was little," said Hannah, "Grandma used to make us all sit and listen while she read your letters out loud. She doesn't do that anymore."

"Letters are so last century," said Imogen, lifting an arm to smooth her hair and setting her bracelets jingling. "We all tweet and Insta now."

"Not Grandma," said Hannah.

"No indeed. But she does email."

Finally Imogen turned to Rachel. "I see you've re-homed the old grandfather clock." She ran a hand over its polished walnut casing. "Must be worth a few bob. I don't know how you can stand the chimes, though. Every quarter of the hour, wasn't it?"

"Its chime was removed," said Rachel with a tight smile. The lump in her throat and the rush of warmth she'd felt when she saw her sister getting out of the taxi had gone. Trust Imogen to spotlight a family heirloom. Perhaps she would examine all her furniture and artefacts to verify their legal ownership. She'd heard of families where people went around sticking labels on antiques before their parents had even ... She nudged the conversation back to small talk.

"We have a couple of friends over tonight. I didn't have chance to tell you on the phone. Come and meet them."

"Let me freshen up first," said Imogen. "Can we take that up to my room?" She nodded towards a holdall, large enough to hold clothes for a fortnight. Rachel picked it up and Imogen followed her upstairs to the guest room.

"It's lovely, thanks," said Imogen, admiring the ivory walls and painted furniture. "I usually go for bolder colours. The Ibizan sun inspired me. But monochrome can be restful."

"I'm glad you like it," said Rachel. If Imogen was expecting every room in Southerndown Cottage to have a neutral palate, the kitchen would surprise her.

"Now, where's my bathroom?"

Rachel pointed along the landing to the family bathroom.

"No en-suite for guests in the property developer's home? Well, well."

"That's right," said Rachel. "We've kept the original layout of the cottage, but we managed to fit a tiny en-suite into the master bedroom."

"Your house seems vast to me," said Imogen. "You should see the shoebox where I'm living." She opened her holdall and sorted through layers of clothes. Something about her hunched shoulders rekindled Rachel's sympathy. This bravado must be for show.

"Immy, I hope it's not difficult for you – us having friends here for dinner and everything. We're all sorry about Simon. If there's anything I can do…"

Imogen straightened up, one hand supporting her back, as if any pain she was suffering was lodged there and not in her heart. "Thanks." She gave a brusque nod. "It was hard at home, Mum wanted me to wallow in grief, but I have to pick myself up and get on with life."

"Well, I'm here if you need me." Rachel turned towards the door. Supper wouldn't cook itself.

"I'll stick with these trousers and change my top," said Imogen. "See you in five."

Twenty minutes later, as Rachel wiped perspiration from her face and fretted that the starter was overcooked, Imogen appeared. She had changed into a turquoise top studded with hundreds of silver beads and pinned her blonde hair up in a loose knot. Her grey eyes glowed in reflected light from the candles on the table.

Jack rose and greeted Imogen with a kiss. "What can I get you to drink?"

"Is that champagne?"

"Yes, there's a glass left. Would you like one?"

"Sure," said Imogen. She turned towards Alisha, who extended her delicate yet powerful hand: a surgeon's hand, in a formal greeting.

"That's a lovely top," said Alisha. "Is it from India?"

"No, I made it myself. In Ibiza I had a craft jewellery business and sometimes I ran up a few samples of clothes to sell on my stall. Everyone loved these beaded smocks."

Michael's long fingers enclosed Imogen's small hand and

held it for a moment. Rachel had explained to them about Simon and suggested they leave it to Imogen if she wanted to talk about it, but the shadow of tragedy hovered, making the atmosphere tense.

Rachel blotted her clammy hands on a tea towel. "If we're going to eat before everything's ruined, I need to serve the starter."

"Isn't Hannah joining us?" asked Alisha.

"No, she ate earlier."

"How long did you live in Ibiza?" asked Michael, pivoting round on his chair to face Imogen. "It must be strange to be back."

Rachel winced; the conversation could wander in any direction.

But Imogen seemed unruffled. "You'll all have heard about my tragic loss but let's not speak of it now. It was time for a change – I was ready to leave Ibiza to younger people."

Rachel handed round plates of scallops. Imogen took one.

Mike was telling Jack about the problems with the builders on Woodleaze. "What's your take on it, Jack?" he asked.

"Well, contract law isn't my bag, but I'd say if they don't perform in line with the agreement, and you've been keeping to your payment terms, you have grounds for terminating them and getting someone else in to finish the work." Jack turned to Rachel with a frown. "You never mentioned this to me?"

She shrugged. "Sorry – I don't like to burden you with my work problems." The scallops tasted rubbery, but she forced herself to finish before returning to the stove to stir the sauce. From her standing position she watched the guests' body language. Every time Imogen spoke, the men leaned forward to listen, while Alisha moved her chair back and stared at her hands.

Imogen was talking about her job at the radio station and how she'd been chosen because of her voice. She and I have basically the same voice, thought Rachel, but Imogen's hung onto that posh Saint Jude's accent that I've worked my whole adult life to shed.

"D'you think listeners will believe I'm twenty-three years

old?" Imogen joked. "My colleagues are so young. I've got a great face for radio, but listeners will be disappointed when they see my ancient mugshot on the website."

Jack and Michael stampeded to assure her she didn't look a day over twenty-three. Rachel winced. At least Imogen could make a joke of it. Her hand shook as she refilled her wine glass – she'd been drinking since four o' clock when she started cooking.

"You need to open more white wine," she hissed into Jack's ear.

He nodded, took a chilled bottle from the fridge, opened it and topped up everyone's glasses.

Alisha held her palm over her glass. "No more for me, thanks."

"I've been thinking, Mike," said Jack, as he eased back into his seat and patted his stomach. "I should start some kind of fitness regime."

"Good idea," said Michael, whose sculpted body was no different from their student days.

"How'd you fancy training together? We could set ourselves a target, say, a half-marathon by the end of the summer?"

"That could be a plan," agreed Michael. "I'm more of a triathlon man myself – I prefer the swimming and cycling – but if it's running you want to do – count me in."

"Great. Let's do both?" They planned to start the following weekend. Jack would drive over to Michael's house to do some circuits on the South Downs and finish up with a pub lunch.

Rachel smiled. "The pub lunch will undo all your efforts." It would be good for Jack to get fit and have more time with Michael. She sensed he was jealous of all the time she spent with his friend.

She made coffee and poured out cups for Alisha and Michael, but Jack and Imogen waved the coffee pot away and refilled their wine glasses. Rachel sank back into her seat and listened to the ebb and flow of banter, noticing how often Imogen dragged the conversation back to herself.

Alisha bit the heel of her hand to stifle a yawn. Michael looked up and they exchanged glances. He got to his feet.

"Sorry to break up the evening, folks. We must be off."

"Yes, thanks so much, Rachel," said Alisha, kissing her lightly on the cheek. "Sorry if I've been a bit dull." She flashed Mike a grateful smile. "I'm shattered. I'm looking forward to being back on days at the hospital."

"See you soon," Rachel promised, fetching Alisha's jacket and escorting them to the front door.

Back in the kitchen, Rachel blew out the last candle and the room filled with the smell of smoke and hot wax. She gathered an armful of empties and counted them: there were five, plus the champagne. Had they really drunk that much? Alisha had hardly had anything! She opened the back door and carried the clinking bottles out to the recycling crate.

"We've got through quite a few," she remarked to Jack.

"Rach, I was watching you." Jack lifted his eyebrows and the crinkles at the corners of his eyes smoothed out. "You don't normally drink that much."

"Me! I didn't see you hold back! Or Imogen. Where's she got to by the way? Gone to bed? We need to ask her about Simon. What really happened? Why did she tell Mum he died in April when that article we found said it was in February."

"Shush, this isn't the time," said Jack, holding up a warning hand as Imogen reappeared in the kitchen. She must have been on one of her freshening-up trips because she was looking dewy-eyed.

"What isn't the time?" asked Imogen. "Am I keeping you up?"

"Nothing." Rachel busied herself wrapping up leftover cheese and stashing it in the fridge. "I'll leave the rest of the clearing up till the morning," she said. "The dishwasher's full and ready to switch on."

No one answered. Without the candlelight, the kitchen was in shadow apart from task lighting under the units. Jack leaned over to light Imogen's cigarette. When did he start carrying a lighter? And who told Imogen she could smoke indoors? Jack took another bottle from the fridge, refilled Imogen's glass and poured a beer for himself.

"I haven't had a chance to offer condolences," he said quietly, moving his chair closer to hers.

Imogen's composure fractured. She leaned her elbows on the table and buried her face in her hands. Her body shook with sobs. Jack put his arm around her shoulders.

Rachel had a sudden image of Simon as a young man, the way she always remembered him, and felt tears welling in her own eyes. She hovered. Should she sit down and join them at the table? But she'd already pushed her own chair back and pulling it out would make an ugly scraping sound.

"You've been strong all evening," Jack said. "It must have been a strain, putting on such a brave face in front of strangers. You don't need to bottle up your grief. We're family."

He glanced up and met Rachel's eyes above Imogen's bowed head, his expression seemed to say: "I'll handle this."

"I'll go on up, then," said Rachel, as Imogen lifted her wine glass and took a shaky sip.

"Sure, you do that," said Jack, without looking at her. "I'll be up soon."

Chapter Nineteen

Imogen
June 2019

Imogen was in no hurry to leave Ferngate. Sunday was a day for a lie-in, so she didn't stir from bed until ten. When she pottered downstairs, looking for coffee, Rachel was already installed in her study.

"Is it always like that?" she asked Hannah, pointing at the closed study door.

"Most weekends, yes. And most evenings too," said Hannah, as she demonstrated how to work the coffee machine. "But she's always available if I need a lift to sports clubs, or to see my friends. We chat in the car."

"Hmm. Interesting. Where's your dad?"

"He's decided to start his fitness kick. He's gone out for a run."

Imogen sipped her coffee, expecting Rachel to appear and whisk her away for the heart to heart that she must surely be planning. Probably, Rachel would be as bad as their mother: going on and on about Simon, asking her a barrage of questions she didn't want to answer. Jensen the Labrador padded in and settled at her feet and Hannah fetched his lead.

"Are you going out?"

Hannah nodded. "I'm taking Jensen for a walk."

Imogen stood up. "I'll come with you."

Hannah glanced at her aunt's feet in thin strappy sandals. "Are you sure?"

"I wore these every day in Spain. Walked miles in them."

"Wait while I tell Mum we're going out."

Imogen watched as Hannah knocked on the study door and briefly disappeared into the room. What sort of mother made her daughter stand in the hallway, knock and wait to be admitted? Even Miriam, the stiffest woman in the world and also a working mother, had let her teenage daughters bounce in on her with last minute homework or to ask for fashion advice.

"Did your mum wonder what my plans were?" Imogen asked as Hannah fastened Jensen's lead.

"No. But I told her we were going out to walk Jensen and she said she'd see you when we get back."

Outside Southerndown Cottage they turned away from the main road and strolled alongside the green until they picked up a footpath leading into woodland, where Hannah let Jensen off the lead. He raced ahead of them, sniffing out rabbit trails in the bracken undergrowth. Every so often, he loped back to Hannah's side to seek permission for his next adventure.

Remembering Gavin had once lived in Ferngate, Imogen said, "One of my London friends lived around here. We met in Ibiza."

"Oh, what's her name? Perhaps Mum knows her."

Imogen hesitated. Should she play the Gavin card, or keep him up her sleeve? She still wasn't sure if he was a trump card or a joker. She'd hold him in reserve. She improvised. "It's a very common name – Jill Sims."

"I think there might be a girl in the year above me called Sims…"

"Jill doesn't have any children," said Imogen hurriedly.

"Aunt Imogen…"

"Just Imogen, please. Aunt sounds so formal."

Hannah blushed. "Sure. What was Mum like when you were both little? When I ask her, she says she was exactly like me but I kind of wonder. I mean, was she sporty? Did she have lots of friends? Or did she work ridiculously hard in school? She works all the time now."

"Does she?" Imogen filed away that nugget of information. "You're right, Rachel was a hard worker. She played the piano and practised hard for her exams. She was a reader – and a dreamer. She had friends, of course, but they were serious girls, a bit like her."

"Sounds boring. I bet you were the adventurous one?"

Imogen laughed. "I had my wild moments. It wasn't easy living in Blakeswood. There weren't many children in the village, we had no buses, apart from the school bus, and the nearest station was six miles away. I was lucky that Simon, my first boyfriend, lived a couple of streets away. So, once I was fifteen, I hung out with him."

"I thought you went to boarding school?"

"We did, but not until our parents made that ridiculous move to Tunisia."

"Was it like Mallory Towers?"

"What?"

"You know those Enid Blyton books. If I read them, you must have done."

Imogen dimly remembered. It wasn't her kind of book. "I don't know. I didn't stay at Saint Jude's long enough to find out."

"You weren't expelled?" Hannah said, sounding secretly thrilled at her aunt's audacity.

"Yep. I went to Tunisia and lazed around. It was boring as hell. Plus it scuppered my chance of going to drama school."

Imogen could almost taste the bitterness of missed opportunities. It was her mother's fault for refusing to let her stay in England. If she drew up two columns and listed the grudges she held against her mother and Rachel, it was possible Miriam's list might outweigh her sister's.

"Couldn't you have gone to drama school when you came back? You can't have been that old?"

Under the spotlight of Hannah's question, she flinched. Her niece's direct challenge was fair because the answer was nothing had stopped her. Desperate to get away from home, she'd chosen her own path by following Simon and barricaded other routes.

"After Tunisia, it took me a while to readjust. And then everything at home changed so drama school didn't seem so important." That was the nub of it.

"Was that because your baby brother died?" asked Hannah.

Imogen briefly bowed her head. She noticed Jensen squatting at the side of the path and alerted Hannah, who took a bag out of her pocket and bent down to pick up the steaming turd. She fastened the bag and swung it in her hand as they walked on.

"George died a cot death, didn't he?" said Hannah.

Imogen stared at her niece. "Is that what they told you?"

"Yes. Sort of. No one will talk to me about it, but I figured it out. When I was little, Grandma sometimes had a little cry when she was looking after me. She used to say how precious I was and how my arrival made up a tiny bit of her loss. I remember her hugging me tight and saying something like "you're a big girl now, Hannah, not a baby, and you're safe. You'll grow up to be the next generation of Stapletons." I must have been about three, but it made a big impression. That's how I figured out George didn't get past being a baby."

"So you're a Stapleton?" asked Imogen.

"Of course. Mum and Dad don't want to get married. They say it's against their principles. But I think Dad would like it, secretly."

"I'm not really a Stapleton, but I use it for my radio name," said Imogen. "It sounds better than Wilson."

They reached a large grassy area, an oasis in the centre of woodland, where traffic noise faded to nothing. Hannah took a ball from her pocket and offered it to Imogen.

"Do you want to throw it for him?" she asked.

"I think I'll have a ciggie first," said Imogen. The spring sunshine warmed her shoulders and painted patches of light on the coarse grass. The countryside was soft and delicate like a watercolour painting, so different from Ibiza's brash brilliance.

"That was fun," said Imogen, as they made their way back home. "It's been great getting to know my lovely niece. I have to head back to London now but in the next school holidays, you must come and stay with me. We'll go to some shows, and shopping. Would you like that?"

"I'd love to."

Chapter Twenty

Rachel
June 2019

Jack had warned Rachel that Imogen was fragile and to not press her about Simon's death. Rebuild your relationship first, he'd said, then she'll want to confide in you. Yet Imogen had sat up half the night confiding in Jack.

There was so much else they needed to discuss. Their father's health for a start. After staying with their parents, Imogen might have an insight into his condition. So, when Imogen and Hannah returned from walking Jensen and her sister announced she was heading back to London, she felt unaccountably annoyed.

"Fair enough," she said, covering up her feelings. "Jack will drive you to the station." She could have done it herself but if Imogen couldn't spare a couple more hours for her sister, why bother?

She stood on the doorstep and waved them off, then headed straight back to her study to fix a videocall with Michael, who was also grafting at home. The rest of the day sped by.

It was after midnight and Rachel was on her way to bed when she heard music coming from Hannah's room. She knocked on the door and edged it open. Hannah was kneeling on her bed, eyes fixed on her tablet computer and talking at the screen. Rachel caught sight of the on-screen image of a boy – no, a young man – slim-faced with a floppy brown fringe. Was Hannah watching one of her YouTube heroes? The fisheye lens angle decided her otherwise.

"Is that Skype?" she asked.

Hannah started. "Mum! You didn't look, did you?" She snatched up her tablet and cradled it against her chest. "And no, it's not Skype. It's Facetime."

"I caught a glimpse. Anyone I know?"

Hannah laid the tablet back down on her bed, raised her hands towards the screen in a gesture of helplessness, and swiped so it went blank.

"Okay," said Hannah. "It was Luke."

Rachel's eyes widened, yet why shouldn't Hannah chat to him?

"Karen's Luke?"

She nodded. "We're friends, that's all."

A seascape screensaver rippled across the tablet. "Anyway, he's gone now."

"I'm sorry. Did I interrupt?"

Hannah shrugged. "It doesn't matter."

"How was your walk with Aunt Imogen this morning?" Everyone in the family – even Jensen – had spent time with Imogen, except her.

Hannah hunkered down over her tablet, not quite meeting Rachel's gaze. "It was fun, I guess. I asked her what you were like when you were young."

Rachel cringed. "What did she say?"

"That you were the brainy, swotty one, who always did your piano practice. I could have guessed that myself."

Rachel winced, but recognised a core of truth. "She and I didn't spend much time together, you know. She's two years older, so we had different friends."

"Yeah. She said living in Blakeswood was well dull. No escape without a lift from your parents. Just like here. I'm moving to a city as soon as … and Aunt Imogen invited me to stay with her in London."

"Did she?" The idea sounded a negative chord with Rachel.

"Yes. I said I'd go in the summer holidays. She said we could hang out at Camden Lock market and she's going to get tickets for the Harry Potter show."

Rachel's heart bumped in her chest, but she forced a smile. "That was kind of her." The plan was bound to come to nothing. By the time the next holidays came around, Imogen would have forgotten. She'd have a new project, or perhaps she'd be bored with London and swan off back abroad.

She was furious with herself for not clearing the air with Imogen. They should have met up on neutral turf, where she could express the sympathy she truly felt and maybe probe a bit more into Simon's accident. It didn't help that circumstances had made Jack the available confidante, so Rachel felt edged out. But why shouldn't Imogen confide in Jack? They'd met so rarely; he was practically a stranger to her.

Hannah's room was suspiciously tidy, and Rachel guessed it was Karen who tended it and dealt with the dirty washing and crockery. A lump formed in her throat as she looked around to imprint memories of her child, who was almost ready to shrug off her mother's protection. Everything was moving too fast. If only she could stop time in its tracks and go back and relive the years of Hannah's childhood. As soon as she and Michael had solved their latest business crisis, she vowed she would banish all the dross from her life and spend more time with Hannah and Jack.

Hannah was watching her with puzzled eyes, twisting a lock of her blonde hair around her index finger. "Mum, are you okay?"

Outside the wind picked up and rattled the open window.

"How d'you mean? I haven't had one of those pesky migraines in a while."

"Oh, I dunno." Hannah slid her feet off the bed and ambled over to close the window, collecting schoolbooks and ramming them into her over-stuffed bag. Keeping her back to Rachel, she murmured. "You're always so, like, distracted. It's hard to talk to you."

Rachel felt tears pricking the back of her eyes and gathered her daughter into a hug. "Don't say that, darling. I've always got time for you."

Hannah masked her vulnerability with an attack. "Dad's noticed, too. He says it will pass but sometimes …" she gulped. "Sometimes it feels like you're not part of our family anymore. As if you've gone away and left us, like Luke's dad."

"I would never do that!"

"What if I was in trouble or danger?" asked Hannah. "What if I needed you? Would you be there?"

A sharp pain kicked Rachel's ribcage. This was a wakeup call. What was the purpose of all her years of striving, building up her business so she could support her needy parents to stay in a home that was, frankly, a mausoleum? Her sister knew nothing of this. She should never have allowed Imogen to shrug off all responsibility. While she'd been fending off guilt by doing everything for her parents, she'd built a wall. And Jack and Hannah, the people she loved most, were on the other side and couldn't reach her.

Chapter Twenty-One

Imogen
June 2019

It turned out that working for a radio station was humdrum, like all the other jobs she'd done in her life. Imogen counted the days until Gavin returned from his business trip. Although he'd stayed over with her twice on the Lazy Lucy, they hadn't established any kind of relationship so, when he said goodbye, he never arranged a date to meet up. He rarely messaged and she had to restrain herself from calling him, but Gavin had a habit of surprising her. He would simply appear, unannounced, perhaps with a bottle of champagne and some snacks, and be waiting when she returned from a shift. Someone at the radio station must be telling him her work pattern. Gavin had his own key to the houseboat. He'd never told her who the boat belonged to and she sometimes rehearsed what she might say if the owner turned up unexpectedly. She'd find a way of talking him round – whoever he, or she, was.

When Gavin finally returned from Spain, she found it ridiculously difficult to disguise her pleasure at seeing him. If ever there was a sign that her life resembled an old dish rag, wrung out and finished, this was it. In the past she would never have bothered with someone like Gavin, but life had taken her on this journey What could she do? Until she could dislodge some funds from her tight-fisted parents, and their even tighter banker-daughter, she had nowhere to go.

Gavin had ditched the vile smelling after shave and gold jewellery in favour of a Patek Philippe watch and a better hairstyle. She was almost happy to be seen with him.

"Where do you live, Gavin?" She asked as she fetched a couple of champagne flutes. "You've never told me."

"A few miles outside Ferngate," he replied, giving a final twist to the cork so it exploded upwards and hit the low ceiling.

"I thought you lived in London?" So he still lived in the same town as Rachel.

"I've been renting a place about three miles outside Ferngate, off the Old London Road."

"But why there?" Imogen persisted. She didn't mention her recent visit to Rachel. The little she'd seen of Ferngate reminded her of crushing boredom and constricted minds.

"My house is secluded but has outbuildings for storage – perfect for my business. Plus, I need to keep an eye on my lad."

"You have a son?" She watched the bubbles float to the top of her glass. How many more secrets would Gavin unpack this evening?

"Yep. His name's Luke – he's seventeen. I haven't been around for him much in the last decade, but I reckon it might not be too late. His mother doesn't know I'm back, but Luke and I have been in contact for a while. Sometimes he stays weekends with me at the cottage."

"Now you have surprised me. What about Luke's mother? Are you still in touch?"

"Nah. We're divorced. I haven't seen her for years. Getting away from that miserable cow was the best move I ever made."

"That sounds harsh," said Imogen, in a prim tone.

"I tell you, Imogen, that woman was smothering me. She was trying to drag me into some upwardly mobile lifestyle, making friends with the yummy mummies at the school gate. I told her I wasn't having any of it."

Imogen reflected. Perhaps if she and Simon had had their longed-for child, that kind of life would have suited her. With a family, even a gossipy, pretentious life might be tolerable – though clearly not to Gavin.

"I've told Luke," he continued, anger glinting in his eyes,

"not to breathe a word to his mother. If she finds out, I'll take off again. For good. And as I'm paying for his driving lessons, I can't see him taking that risk. Can you?"

Imogen shook her head but this glimpse of Gavin's shallowness unsettled her. He had carved out his own life with little thought of the son he'd abandoned. And why the pent-up bitterness towards his ex-wife?

"What school does he go to?"

"He's at the local sixth form college."

"Ah." So Luke wouldn't know Hannah. She was only fifteen and at a different school.

"I'd like to see where you live," Imogen said, moving closer to Gavin and caressing his arm.

He grinned at her. "Sure. I'll take you on Saturday."

"I'm on a morning shift. Can we go late afternoon?"

"Sorry. No can do. I have to be at home for a morning delivery. Catch the train down when you've finished work and take a taxi from the station."

Chapter Twenty-Two

Rachel
June 2019

Rachel sat at her desk, drinking diet coke from a can and eating a tuna sandwich. A shred of lettuce dropped into her lap and left a smear on her black skirt. She rubbed it with a tissue, but the mark resisted and spread like an oil slick. Infuriated, she wrapped up the rest of the sandwich and dropped it in her bin. The door slammed and Michael strode into the office. She felt a headache coming on. Why did everyone make so much noise?

Michael's face shone with perspiration as he crossed to her desk, brandishing an open newspaper.

"Look at that," he said, pointing to a headline halfway down the front page. "I don't normally buy this rag, but I picked up a copy at lunchtime."

Rachel didn't read the *South Eastern Gazette* either, but felt bad as it belonged to that breed of family-owned regional newspapers, facing extinction.

Builders stop work on Stapleton Kumar's Woking development scheme, screeched the headline.

Rachel blinked. The words didn't register. Her brow creased as she scanned the text of the report. Unnamed 'sources' were quoted, implying that Stapleton Kumar might be in trouble.

"For God's sake!" she said, as realisation dawned. "Do you think Emerald builders have stirred this up? But why?" She let the newspaper drop onto her desk. "We've settled all their blasted outstanding invoices!"

"I know," said Michael. "But here's the damning bit. Look."

He ran his finger along a line that read: "A spokesperson for Stapleton Kumar Developments declined to comment."

"Who the hell's the spokesman?" asked Rachel. "I've not taken a call from the Gazette. Have you?"

"No," said Michael. "I haven't heard a word."

They stared at one another in mute incomprehension. The smell of tuna sandwich lingered, and Rachel visualised it decomposing in the bin, curling at the edges, until it became spotted with mildew and teeming with maggots. The air grew thick and muggy.

A cool draught signalled Carrie's return from lunch. She carried two bulging shopping bags across the room and stowed them under her desk.

"Hi," she said, as she straightened up, followed by, "Is something the matter?"

Rachel swallowed hard. "Did you get a call from the South Eastern Gazette recently, Carrie?"

"I might have done." Carrie plumped down on her chair, threaded her fingers together and clenched them tight. "Two or three days ago."

"And what did they ask you?" Rachel glanced at her hands and noticed she was subconsciously mirroring Carrie's body language. "It's really important."

"I don't remember."

Rachel unlocked her fingers and placed her palms flat on the desk. "What did you say to them?" In the compact office, with its insulated walls and double-glazing, her voice reverberated like a shout.

Carrie responded in a whisper. "I followed our media guidelines. You've always told me not to discuss company business with the press." She moved her eyes from Rachel to Michael, who was standing further away with his arms folded.

"So I suppose you did say 'no comment'," said Michael.

"Yes, of course. Isn't that what I'm supposed to say?"

"It depends on the circumstances," said Rachel. "Why didn't you tell me or Michael about the call?" She picked up the Gazette and showed Carrie the headline. Carrie flinched and scraped her chair back six inches.

"You should have told one of us immediately!" said Rachel. "You know we have a contract with Lowlight PR agency. They deal with any press queries."

Outside, the clouds dispersed and the sun threw the weight of its energy against the windows. As the temperature in the room rose, the smell of tuna was overpowering.

"Let me read it," said Carrie, in a dull voice. She took the newspaper and scanned through the article. When she'd finished, she didn't speak but propped her head on her hands and pressed her fists into her cheeks.

"All right, Carrie, we'll talk later," said Rachel, snatching the paper away. She turned to Michael. "I must contact Lowlight PR for advice. We've got a meeting room booked for our monthly update. I'll call them from there."

***

"Do you think this negative press coverage will harm us?" Rachel asked after their PR account manager had made reassuring noises and promised to call back with an action plan.

Michael shook his head. "Not if they move quickly to close the story down."

As they strolled back along the corridor from the meeting room to their office, Michael said, "I can't remember if I thanked you properly for dinner last week. Your sister, Imogen, is – um - interesting."

"Yes, Mike, you did thank me. And Alisha sent a lovely card."

"You and Imogen seem very different."

"How d'you mean?"

Michael tapped in the security code then paused before opening the office door. "It was something Alisha said – Imogen reminded her of an actor, performing for an audience. I'm afraid Alisha wasn't keen on her."

"I thought she was quiet that evening," said Rachel. "I hope she wasn't bored."

"Oh no, she was fine – just tired," said Michael. "Now she's working days again she's a different person."

As they entered the office, Carrie was powering off her computer and preparing to leave. Rachel placed her papers down on her desk and noticed an envelope addressed in Carrie's looped handwriting, propped up against her keyboard.

"What's this?" she asked, picking it up and turning it over in her hands.

"My resignation," said Carrie, with an audible gulp.

"Don't be rash, Carrie!" said Rachel. "It's been a bad day and I'm sorry if I snapped at you earlier. We don't want to lose you!" She dropped the envelope back onto the desk, unopened.

Carrie scowled at her and slid her arms into her jacket.

"Rachel's right," added Michael, straightening his tie. "It's never a good idea to make important decisions in the heat of the moment. Come on, I'm heading home, too. Those bags look heavy, I'll carry them down to the car park."

As the door closed behind them, Rachel leaned back in her chair, pressing her shoulder blades against its firm padding and shut her eyes. She put a hand to her forehead; no sign of a headache, thank goodness. The office phone jangled, and she answered it.

"Rachel?" said a familiar voice. "Is that you?"

"Dad! What a surprise!" Max rarely made phone calls these days and she could hardly ever remember him ringing her at work.

"I'm calling you about a business matter," said Max. "Is everything all right with Stapleton Kumar?"

Rachel inhaled and doubled the length of her out-breath to a count of six, as a yoga teacher had once taught her. "What do you mean, Dad?"

"I've had a rather strange call from Howard," said Max.

For a moment, Rachel couldn't think who he might be referring to and then it came to her. "Howard Dixon? The man who was at your drinks party?"

"Yes," said Max. "He rang to tell me he'd read something in today's *South Eastern Gazette*. He said it sounded as if Stapleton Kumar might be in difficulties. That's not true is it, Rachel?"

Rachel forced a reply from between clenched lips. "Dad,

I've seen that article. It's a gross misrepresentation. A journalist from the Gazette rang Carrie, fishing for comments on unsubstantiated industry gossip, and she answered without thinking. Our PR people are sorting it."

"Phew, that's a relief," said Max. "But Howard asked me to arrange a meeting with you. When's a good time?"

Rachel pressed the back of her hand against her forehead. "Tell him never!" How dare that man pry into her business. She laid the receiver down on her desk but couldn't dislodge a tightness in her chest. From far away, Max's voice rumbled on, but his words didn't register. Discomfort shifted from her chest to her stomach. She eyed her wastepaper bin with its greasy, decomposing sandwich. Any minute now she might need it. She was going to be sick.

Chapter Twenty-Three

Imogen
June 2019

At Radio Denim FM, Imogen's shift ended. She pulled off her headphones and marched towards the door where Damien, the station's youthful deputy head and son of the owner, accosted her. He'd sat his finals and, without even waiting for the results, moved to London to take up the position his father had created for him at the radio station. Everyone else tumbled a step down the seniority rankings.

"That lad's unnatural," one of Imogen's colleagues complained. "Why doesn't he piss off to Oz, or inflict his volunteering skills on some impoverished country?"

Damien's boyish charm was unfortunately packaged: a round pink face and tufts of brown chin-fuzz that were neither a beard nor designer stubble.

"Thank goodness I've caught you, Immy, darling," said Damien, slicking back his quiff. "Krystyna's called in sick. Can you cover her shift? After your break, of course."

"Sorry, darling," replied Imogen. "No can do. I have plans." She shuffled out of range of his octopus embrace, took a lipstick out of her bag and peered at her reflection in a wall mirror.

Damien came and stood behind her, his over-large head creating a halo effect behind hers. "Who's going to cover traffic and weather, then?" he asked. She noticed his glum expression. His bravado was fading. She shrugged.

"Here's the script, sweetie." She turned around and handed him a wodge of stapled sheets. "See." She jabbed the top page with her forefinger. "Couldn't be simpler. It's all on the system. As the traffic updates come in, delete or insert accordingly."

He scowled at her and she beamed back. Damien often boasted that he knew all the roles around the station, but she'd never seen him do anything but stride around acting self-important. Let him get his hands dirty for a change.

"I suppose I can do it," said Damien, peering doubtfully at the script.

"Enjoy. See ya," said Imogen. She picked up her overnight bag, swung it over her shoulder and headed for the door.

Chapter Twenty-Four

Rachel
June 2019

From now on, weekends would be for family, Rachel vowed, but she wasn't thinking of her parents, or of Imogen who had flitted briefly into her world and then, yet again, stopped answering calls and messages. No, she would focus on her own small nuclear family unit. Humming a tune under her breath, she pottered down to the garage and pulled tarpaulins off their old bicycles. Jack's was a mountain bike, with sturdy patterned treads; hers was an upright town bike, with wicker basket mounted on the handlebars. Even before she'd squeezed the tyres between her thumb and third finger, she knew they were flat. She unhooked the pump and blew off some cobwebs. Jack's tyres quickly inflated to rock hard, but her bike seemed to have a rear puncture.

When Jack came looking for her, she was kneeling on a newspaper, bike upended, trying to prise off the tyre with the end of a spanner.

"Here, give me that." Jack smiled and took the spanner from her. Using only his hand, he twisted back the tyre casing to reveal a flaccid inner tube.

She shot him a grateful look. He hadn't asked her what the hell she was doing, or why.

"I thought we could go for a bike ride later," she said. "Do something together as a family like you're always saying you want to."

"Does that include Hannah?" Jack gestured to a pink, child-sized bicycle leaning against the garage wall. "Because I think she might have outgrown that."

"Does what include Hannah?" she asked, joining them on the driveway. Her skin looked pale in contrast with her kohl-rimmed eyes and eyebrows, painted in a thick rectangle but at least, thought Rachel, she hadn't plucked out all her natural brows as some young girls did.

"Your mother thinks we should take a family trip: a bike ride."

Hannah's smile slipped. "You can't be serious! What if somebody saw me?"

Jack grinned as if ready to play the moment for longer, but Rachel shrugged. "Unless we can get hold of some Alice in Wonderland *shrink-me* potion, you're out of luck." She pointed to the pink bike. "You're not going anywhere on that."

Hannah's smile returned. "Dad!" She punched Jack on the arm in a playful gesture.

"Ouch!" he said.

"Weakling!" She laughed. "I have plans. Can you drive me into Ferngate?"

"Where are you going?"

She shrugged. "Meeting friends, you know. Can we leave now?"

"Sorry, sweetheart. I'm out training with Mike tomorrow so must catch up on some work today."

"Honestly, Jack you're as bad as me," said Rachel.

He kissed her. "I thought you wanted me to get back in shape?"

"Fair enough." Rachel nodded. "I'll drive you, Hannah."

"Thanks, Mum. Can we go now?"

"Before breakfast?"

"Please."

When Rachel returned from fetching her car keys, Hannah was leaning against the car tapping a message on her phone. She didn't look up from her phone on the drive into town and Rachel's attempts to tease out Hannah's plans were politely rebuffed.

"Could you advance me some money?" asked Hannah.

"Don't you have your cash card?"

"Yes, but I've walked Jensen four nights this week."

Rachel drew into the car park in the centre of Ferngate and handed over a twenty-pound note. "Is that enough?"

"Yes." Hannah scrabbled with the door handle, ready to leap out.

"Hang on a minute. How are you getting home?" asked Rachel.

"I'll call you. Love you." Hannah blew a kiss and set off through the narrow passage that led onto Ferngate High Street. Rachel watched her go. On an impulse, she pulled into a parking bay and collected a ticket from the pay and display machine. She made her way past the market stall offering two lettuces for a pound, along the lane onto the high street.

At the Old Swan coaching inn opposite, a blackboard on the pavement said coffee was being served. Next door, the plate-glass frontage of a newly opened lounge also chorused 'coffee', as if psychic and detecting Rachel's need for a caffeine fix. It was a synthetically sweet day in early summer, and she shielded her eyes from the sun as she scanned the street. A flock of pigeons landed near the statue of some ancient alderman in the centre of the market square and pecked up scraps from beneath the outdoor tables of the shack café. Then she spotted Hannah.

Hannah was sitting on a bench, between the public toilets and the bike racks, chatting to a lad with floppy brown hair. His long legs were stretched out, staking a claim on the surrounding territory and his right arm was draped along the back of the bench, behind Hannah's shoulders. As Rachel watched, Hannah leaned her head and rested it on the boy's shoulder.

Rachel's stomach knotted. This was Hannah – her baby. And then she recognised the boy. She hadn't seen him for several years, but it was obvious to her now. It was the same lad Hannah had been chatting to online the other night – Luke, Karen's son.

Suddenly she needed coffee. Badly. If she crossed the road, Hannah might look up and spot her. Now she was being ridiculous. Why shouldn't she stop in Ferngate for a coffee?

Still musing, she glanced at Hannah and Luke again and saw that they weren't alone. A muscular middle-aged man, dressed in a track suit, was strolling towards them and Luke was standing up to greet him. The man had a ruddy, sun-tanned complexion, as if he spent his time outdoors. Perhaps he was a sports teacher from Luke's sixth form college, or Ferngate Town football club's youth coach?

Luke gestured towards Hannah, who stood up and shook hands with the older man. He performed an exaggerated, theatrical bow over her hand. The older man took out a pack of cigarettes and offered it to Luke and Hannah. Rachel craned her neck to peer through the bustling crowd of shoppers and saw Hannah take a cigarette.

Rachel froze. The man produced a lighter and lit it for her. This couldn't be happening. She watched the trio huddled together, chatting, while smoke trailed from their lighted cigarettes. All that care she and Jack had lavished on their daughter: the sleepless nights when she was a baby, the healthily concocted meals, the immunisations, fresh air and exercise. And now she was smoking. She should have insisted on that family bike ride.

Hannah finished her cigarette, dropped it on the pavement and ground it under her heel. As Rachel watched, she stooped to pick it up and put it in a litter bin. Something to be grateful for.

The track-suited man jogged away from the teenagers and they sat back down on the bench, but, moments later, a black BMW pulled up next to them. Luke climbed into the front passenger seat, Hannah into the back. The windows were tinted a smoky black, yet Rachel could make out the driver's profile. It was the man in the track suit. As the car drove off, picking up speed and heading towards the dual carriageway out of town she noted the number plate: GAV 1N. All her suspicions were confirmed.

In a daze, she walked over to the shack café, queued at the counter to give her order, and sat down at one of the outdoor tables. Her head was buzzing, her fingers played with her mobile, hovering over Hannah's number. But if she called and asked Hannah where she was going, her daughter would be furious.

The waitress brought her coffee in a chipped white cup and plonked it on the table in front of her. Scummy white froth swirled on the surface. She lifted the cup to her mouth and took a gulp. It scalded her tongue.

Luke was a good lad, she reasoned. He'd take care of Hannah. But seeing Gavin, Luke's father, was a shock. When did he turn up and what did she know about him? Nothing.

Chapter Twenty-Five

Imogen
June 2019

The sign on the gatepost read *Stonehill Court, Residential Home*. Could this be right? Imogen's taxi swung in through the gates and followed a tarmac drive towards a stone mansion.

At a fork in the road, an arrow pointed right to *Gamekeeper's Cottage* and the taxi driver turned onto a gravel track with potholes, bordered by tall trees and a swaying canopy that blocked sunlight. It was spookily remote. A few hundred metres further on was a red brick cottage with land around it cleared to make a garden. She shivered as she took the driver's card and watched the taxi drive off.

The red brick cottage had the date 1910 scored into a stone panel above the door so it was built more recently than the main house. To one side of the cottage was a jumble of outbuildings and, behind them, stretching into the woods, an expanse of netted pens with a neglected air and full of holes. Presumably the poor little pheasants had been raised there before being unleashed to provide sport for the Stonehill Court gentry and their guests. She thought of Lady Chatterley and her bit of rough.

The garden wall was made of the same flint-grey stone as the main house and clashed with the red brick of the cottage. The gate creaked open and she took the stepping stone path across an apron of front lawn. Splashes of sunshine broke through the trees to form a mosaic pattern on a metal table and three garden chairs. Beside the front porch was a neat stack of chopped logs and the window boxes looked well-tended. She

117

took a deep breath and pressed the doorbell with the flat of her hand.

Within seconds, the door was flung open. Gavin was wearing a blue and black striped bathrobe, a gold medallion and probably nothing underneath. Imogen took a step back.

"Go and get dressed, Gavin," said Imogen, wrinkling her forehead crossly. She caught his eye and they both dissolved into laughter.

"Sorry to distress you, madam! I was in the shower. I've been out for a run this morning."

He pulled her into a hug. She felt the clammy pressure of his body and glimpsed matted, dark chest hair where his bathrobe gaped open. She pushed him away and turned to look at two cars, ancient and modern, parked to one side of the cottage.

"Who does that beat up Golf belong to?" she asked. "I'm assuming your name is on the black BMW."

"Right first time," said Gavin. "What would I do with a Golf at my age?"

Her eyes narrowed. "You're so obvious Gavin!"

He roared with laughter. "Come on in. I'll show you round."

He stood aside to let her enter and Imogen's eyes took in the sleek open plan interior that had been crafted inside the utilitarian box-shaped cottage.

"This is pretty smart, Gavin," she exclaimed. "Though unremittingly macho. Who does the Xbox belong to?"

"That's mine, of course, but my lad, Luke, plays on it, when he comes over. The Golf will be his, too, when I've fixed it up and put it through its MOT."

"Is Luke here today?"

"No. I met up with him and his little girlfriend this morning. They wanted me to give them a lift out to the country park."

Gavin strolled to the fridge, poured a glass of white wine and handed it to her. "Have this to keep you company while I sling on some clothes." He clattered up the metal staircase that spiralled from the sitting room to the first floor.

Imogen carried her drink with her as she toured the living

space, opening drawers, peering inside cupboards and flicking switches on the sound system. At her touch, old-fashioned rock music spilled out from concealed speakers. What a relief. She was weary of the bland music played at Radio Denim. She scrolled through Gavin's database of music; his tastes were eclectic, from rock to classics and even opera. She hesitated over Neil Hannon and the Divine Comedy, then opted for Tom Petty and clicked on *I Won't Back Down*. Just like me, she thought. And Gavin.

Gavin returned wearing a denim shirt and darker jeans, went straight to the fridge and grabbed a Budweiser. After years in Ibiza, she liked to see a healthy suntan on a man. Too many of the guys she met in London had skin the colour of uncooked pastry. On the minus side, Gavin's overgrowth of chest hair and that blasted medallion were such clichés. On the plus side, his muscles rippled in all the right places and his backside was taut, though his bloated stomach needed a workout.

Gavin sat next to her on the sofa, dangling his arm around her shoulders. "Fancy you and me both arriving back in the motherland at the same time," he said.

She nodded. "Life delivers some strange twists."

"Are you over old Simon yet?" he asked.

"That subject is closed," she fumed. "Don't mention his name again." She took another sip of her drink. "Have you got anything to eat? I'm starving."

"Sure, what d'you fancy?" Gavin opened the fridge and inspected the contents. "Some Brie? I have ham - Serrano or York? Hummus? Olives?"

"Sounds good to me."

He took a fresh baguette from a bread bin, unwrapped a selection of meats and cheeses and arranged them deftly on an oval platter. He laid plates, knives and real linen napkins on the breakfast bar and beckoned Imogen over to take a stool. She nibbled on a honey-coloured crust of baguette and sliced herself a wafer of Brie, while Gavin heaped his plate with cheese and two types of ham, the sweaty pink kind and the rotting-flesh Serrano.

"You've explained your family reasons for squatting here in the back of beyond, but you said there were business reasons, too? So, I was wondering if you had any of that – you know – decent stuff, like in the old days. The London scene is so hostile after Ibiza."

Gavin had taken a bite of a chunky sandwich of cheese and two types of ham, on hummus-coated bread. He laughed, inhaled and choked, spitting crumbs across the breakfast bar.

He leaned over and ruffled Imogen's blonde hair.

"Same old Immy!" he said. "Just for a moment I thought you might have come down here because you wanted to see me."

She scowled back at him. "Of course I have!"

"So what do you need? Something from your harmless little dealer for your personal use? Or supplies on a grander scale?"

"Don't be an arse, Gavin," she said, jabbing her pointy-toed shoe into his bare foot. "Just a smidgeon for personal use, of course."

"You're in luck," he said. "I'll show you when we've finished eating."

The Tom Petty collection looped around and blared out *American Girl* for a second time. Imogen noticed a framed painting of olden days America hanging on the wall. It looked like a copy of an Edward Hopper, an old guy lounging on his porch in a wicker chair. Its delicacy seemed out of place in this minimalist environment. Gavin finished his sandwich, crossed the room and lifted this painting from the wall. Behind it was a compact safe, set into a space where bricks from the original wall must recently have been removed because reddish dust swirled into the air. Gavin twiddled with a combination dial and flicked the safe door open. Inside was a cash box and a set of keys on a metal ring. He beckoned to Imogen to follow him and opened the back door, crossing the garden to a concrete outbuilding next to the barn. Something in its construction made it look more like a bunker than a shed, with its row of miniature windows positioned two metres above ground level.

"This was built as the old game larder," said Gavin. "It dates from the days when there was a real Mellors-type living in this cottage and the family in the main house used to have their friends down from London for weekend shooting parties, dontchaknow."

"Hence the name Gamekeeper's Cottage," said Imogen. Her heel caught in a crevice between paving slabs, she bent down to free it. Gavin unlocked a mortice first, then two smaller locks. The door swung outwards. Inside was a black wire-mesh screen door, the mesh so fine, it was near-opaque. Gavin selected another key from his clanking set, unlocked it and pushed it inwards.

He pressed a light switch and old-fashioned strip lighting dangling from the roof glowed, pallid at first but warming to a white intensity.

"Come inside," said Gavin, leaving the screen door open but dragging the outer door shut behind them and sliding a bolt across. The air was arid; cooled by white-washed concrete walls. Whatever else went on in here, it was a morgue for flies, the floor was littered with their tiny corpses. She looked around and gave a low gasp. The walls were racked out with the kind of meccano-build shelves, loved by DIY enthusiasts. But, instead of drill bits and potting shed paraphernalia, these were piled with jars, boxes and bags; and bags inside boxes. Some resembled plump packets of sugar, others were like a stamp collector's miniature envelopes. One whole shelf was piled with bags of brown-black resin. Her eyes widened as she took in powder, ready-packed in wraps, and raisin-sized crystals that were unmistakeably crack.

Her head was spinning with visual confusion: old fashioned screw-top jars that should contain pic 'n mix sweets contained pills she recognised as ecstasy tablets. She felt faint. There was nowhere to sit down, no chairs and only a slab of rough wooden worktop on the end wall, balanced between two rows of shelving, holding a weighing scale, a couple of chopping boards and a butcher's block of knives.

"Ugh, is that heroin?" she asked, stabbing a finger towards an open package leaking its brownish-white powder onto the shelf. She snatched her hand quickly away.

"That does indeed look like it to me," said Gavin, his smile displaying gleaming white teeth against his sun-tanned face. "Smack, gear, junk, H – whatever you want to call it."

Imogen shuddered under her sleeveless top.

"Sorry to offend your delicate sensibilities, but there is a call for it, as they say in the retail trade. And the customer is always right."

Imogen cast her eyes up at hooks fixed into the ceiling: mementos of the time when this building functioned as a game larder.

"Ingenious, isn't it?" said Gavin. "Now, what do you fancy? I have some Moroccan. And I saw your nose twitching while you were eyeing up that charlie."

Imogen's eyes wandered the shelves as she waited for her heartbeat to slow. The merchandise was vibrant with promises, from ecstasy to death. "You choose," she said. "Show me something I won't have tried before. Nothing too extreme."

Why couldn't she say not too toxic or addictive? A frisson passed through her body. She was living dangerously now: this was life on the edge.

"Fair enough," said Gavin, nodding. He lifted down a stainless-steel tray and pottered along the narrow central aisle with the intensity of a connoisseur, selecting bags, some with printed computer labels giving a weight and date, and kneading them between his fingers. He opened some and sniffed or tasted the contents. Those that passed his test, he placed onto the tray.

She monitored his progress, smoothing a hand over her hair to calm her jitters.

"Hold this for me," said Gavin, draping a cloth over the tray and passing it to her while he unbolted the door. She gripped it tight though her hands were trembling, while he repeated the locking up ritual.

Back in the kitchen, Gavin poured two gin and tonics and sliced a half-moon of lime to add to each glass while Imogen selected music and settled on the sofa. As Gavin handed her the glass, he gave her an enquiring look. He sat beside her, stretching out his legs and resting them on the glass coffee table. In the centre of the table sat the tray. He must have nudged the cloth with his foot because it slid to one side, displaying their tasting menu contained in neat transparent bags.

"Are you certain your son isn't coming here tonight?" she asked. The sick feeling had vanished, replaced by a rush of energy. Gavin edged closer; his upper arm pressed against her shoulder.

"No," he said. "When I saw Luke this morning, I told him I was entertaining an old friend. He knows I don't want to be disturbed."

Imogen's eyes sparkled and her hair tumbled around her face as Gavin pulled her towards him. She could feel his heart pounding. He was a little rough, but she didn't mind. Life was full of risks. It was time to grab hold of everything it offered.

Chapter Twenty-Six

Rachel
June 2019

Rachel arrived home to find Jack kneeling on the drive with her bike upended, mending her puncture. She felt a rush of gratitude. Jack had work to do, but he'd spent his morning doing this small thing for her.

He smiled at her, wiping oil from his hands on a rag. "All done. You can go out on it later, if you like."

"Thank you." But she couldn't force a smile.

"What's wrong?" he asked. "I thought you'd be pleased."

"About the bike? I am. I'm worried about Hannah."

Usually she dropped Hannah off at a friend's house and it never occurred to her to wonder where her daughter spent the day. At fifteen, she'd been incarcerated in Saint Jude's, with rare chances to break free, and as for sneaking off with a boyfriend – if only!

"Why?" asked Jack.

"She was meeting Luke."

"Karen's Luke?" his mouth twisted in surprise. "Is that so bad? At least she told you."

"She didn't tell me. I dropped her off in the car park and she practically sprinted away from me, along the passage to the high street. So I followed her. She was sitting on a bench with Luke." She didn't mention the snogging.

"Was that wise?"

"I know. It sounds a bit stalkerish, but I had a weird feeling … now I'm glad I did."

"Luke's a nice lad. What's the worry?"

Why wasn't Jack showing a father's protective instinct towards his little girl? He grinned. "She's growing up fast."

"It's not Luke I'm worried about. Someone else was with them. Remember Luke's father, Gavin?"

"Indeed I do, the missing man. I remember giving Karen legal advice."

"Gavin's back."

Jack's expression stayed deadpan, but his eyes narrowed a fraction. "Did Karen tell you that?"

Rachel shook her head. "No, but I'm ninety-nine percent certain it was him, chatting to Luke and Hannah. A few minutes later, they got into a car with him and drove off."

Jack rubbed his oil-streaked hands absent-mindedly across his forehead. "I can see why you're worried. After he ran out on them all those years ago. Do you think he's living with Karen?"

"I'm not sure. But I rarely see her these days. Hannah's the only member of this family who does."

"We'll have to ask Hannah what's going on. Don't spend your whole day fretting." He moved to hug her. She pointed out his oily hands and they both laughed. The clutch of anxiety inside her stomach eased and she went indoors. The dishwasher was full. Emptying it was Hannah's job. Her emotions seesawed between anxiety and irritation. She gave in and messaged Hannah.

How's your day?

No reply.

She was too twitchy to relax or work.

"Can we take the bikes out?" she asked Jack.

He wavered for a second before he answered. "Sure."

That was why she loved him. He'd drop anything to make her happy. What did she do for him?

It was years since she'd cycled. She made a few circuits of their quiet close before approaching the main road, where traffic pounded incessantly from dawn until midnight. The usual gaps between vehicles had fused into a column of unbroken traffic. On one side of the road was a narrow pavement, where few people walked. Flouting the law, Rachel cycled along it while Jack took to the road and flanked her, protecting her from angry motorists who resented sharing the highway with cyclists even more than they hated the processional progress of their journey.

Two miles on, they turned off the main drag and took the winding road up into the Surrey Hills. It was steeper than she remembered – in her car she hardly noticed but the traffic thinned, and it was good to breathe in unpolluted air.

They rode on for two hours, in single file on the approach to bends, Rachel in front, flinging scraps of conversation over her shoulder that Jack probably couldn't hear. On the next downhill stretch, he overtook her and, as the sign of the Horse and Groom came into view, he made a hand signal to slow her down.

"Let's stop for a drink," he suggested. They dismounted and wheeled their bikes into the pub's car park. "Did you bring a bike lock?"

She shook her head. It had been in her saddlebag, but she'd left it behind to reduce the weight.

"Never mind. Let's sit outside. I'll get the drinks. Cider?"

She nodded.

"How about a sandwich, if they're still doing food."

"Sure. You choose."

The pub garden was quiet apart from a few dog walkers and Rachel chose a table with sun for Jack and shade for her. While she waited for him to order the drinks, she thought about the conversation they needed to have about the future. It was time she confided in him. Her property business was taking too great a toll on her – not just the strain of their current financial problems, but the growing feeling that she was living the wrong life and needed to make a change. How could she explain it in a way he could understand? She felt like Sisyphus condemned by the gods to roll a heavy rock uphill for eternity, only to have it crashing down when it reached the top. The problem was she couldn't tell him why she'd shouldered the burden without explaining her parents' situation and breaking her solemn promise.

"I'm glad you suggested this, Rach," said Jack, putting their drinks down on the table. "We should do it more often."

"Definitely. I feel so much better."

Their sandwiches arrived and they ate in companionable silence. Jack finished first and pushed his plate away.

"There's something I want to talk to you about," said Jack.

"Me, too," said Rachel. "But you go first." The sun had shifted round. Now it was shining in Rachel's eyes, so she put on her sunglasses and hoped he wasn't going to bring up the subject of getting married again. "Is it about work?" she asked, trying to steer him. "How was your meeting with John Sallis yesterday?"

He seemed surprised – and pleased she'd remembered. "That's right. It's partly that. My annual review. It was rushed – as usual. Sallis reeled off platitudes about how much they valued me, then down came the usual barrier: the firm's financial position, can't support another partner ... blah, blah." He leaned forward in his seat, balling up his paper napkin inside his fist.

"Oh Jack, that's too bad." She placed her hand over his. He uncurled his fingers and let go of the napkin.

"The partnership is never going to happen, Rach."

"Then you must move on. To another firm."

"Exactly." His face became animated. "To be honest, I've been wondering about changing direction?"

She felt a flutter of alarm. "But what would you do?"

"Perhaps I could join you and Mike in Stapleton Kumar." He uncurled from his slouch and sat upright, fixing her with a frank, hopeful smile.

"What?" Rachel gaped at him as she digested his words. She shrank back into her chair knowing he'd see her response as another rejection. Her throat tightened. It was hard to speak. Why did everyone – her parents and now Jack – assume Stapleton Kumar was some kind of money tree that could endlessly expand to support more and more people? Wasn't it enough that she grafted to bring in income for them all and performed accounting somersaults to keep everything afloat? Her cycling top clung to her. It felt as if it had shrunk a size since she last wore it.

"I need the loo," she said, scrambling to her feet, and avoiding his eyes as he watched her walk inside the pub.

In the sanctuary of the tiled cloakroom, she splashed cold water on her face but her armpits still felt hot and clammy so she dabbed them with a damp paper towel, leaning against the cloakroom door so no one could come in and find her with her top rolled up.

As she weaved her way between tables back towards the garden, her phone beeped, and she glanced at the message.

"It's Hannah," she told Jack, with a surge of relief that their conversation was at an end. "She wants picking up from Ferngate at seven."

They cycled home, more slowly, though the route was now downhill, Rachel's legs ached, and her breathing was constricted by a tightness in her chest brought on by their unresolved conversation. Jack's quest for a partnership at his law firm seemed unlikely to succeed. Being in criminal law, his pay was low but how did he imagine she could make space for him in Stapleton Kumar? Why had she never explained to him that her business was struggling? Or even that she was sick of it and wanted out. The world was slowly spinning from her grasp. Everything was out of control.

***

"Don't say anything to Hannah in the car," Jack warned as Rachel prepared to set off to pick her up. "If she's not straight with us, it's best we tackle her together. With a united front."

Hannah was five minutes late to meet Rachel at the car park and arrived out of breath, as if she'd been running, but her eyes were sparkling when she climbed into the car.

"Good day?" asked Rachel, sneaking a sideways glance at her daughter.

"The best!" said Hannah. "I spent the day with Luke." She glanced at Rachel and drew a long breath. "We've been seeing each other for a few weeks."

"That's great. I'm really happy for you," said Rachel. "He was a lovely lad when he was young."

"And he is now, too," said Hannah. She launched into

Luke's biography: the subjects he was doing at sixth form college, his hope of going to university to do sports science, his ambition to train as a sports teacher. How generous he was, how kind ...

"What did you do today?" asked Rachel.

"We went up to the country park for a walk and a picnic lunch."

"Did you, err, meet up with anyone else?"

Hannah shook her head and Rachel didn't probe.

But later, when they sat down to supper, Jack asked Hannah, "What's the latest on Luke's missing father? Does Luke see him?"

Hannah flushed. She looked down at her supper plate and coughed.

"Hannah, please tell us the truth," said Rachel. "I saw you and Luke getting into Gavin's car."

"What? Were you spying on me?" Hannah gripped the edge of the table and her knuckles turned white.

"Of course not," said Rachel. "I stopped in Ferngate for a coffee. It's only by chance that I spotted you and saw Gavin pick you up in his BMW. I do know him, remember. From when you were young."

Hannah's face reddened. "He's back," she said. "Luke sees his dad, but he doesn't want Karen to know."

"That seems very childish," said Jack. "He's a grown man, for heck's sake."

"Things were – messy between them," said Hannah. "Gavin swore Luke to secrecy."

"That's ridiculous."

"I know. I thought so too, but Luke told me, if his mother found out, his dad would know whose fault it was and would disappear from his life all over again. Luke doesn't want that, Mum, Dad."

"That doesn't sound like the action of a caring and rational father," said Jack. "Whatever his issues with Karen he needs to sort them out. It's not fair to put Luke in that position – or you."

"Please, Dad. If you tell Karen, Luke would kill me. Well,

maybe not kill me, but dump me. And if that happened, I'd die."

Rachel stayed silent but she felt cold disapproval. How different the world looked through the eyes of a teenager. She worried about what young people had to contend with these days.

"I don't like this, Hannah," continued Jack. "Your mother and I have no problem with you seeing Luke. He's welcome at our house any time but I'm not happy with what you've told us about his father, nor am I happy about not telling Karen."

"I'm begging you, Dad." Hannah had been keeping her hands underneath the table. Now she raised them towards Jack, clasped together like a supplicant. Her fingernails were bitten down to the quick.

"On one condition," said Jack. "You're not to go anywhere with that man. Don't go in his car and certainly don't go to his house. Where is it by the way?"

"I don't know," said Hannah. "I didn't go to his house. I think he lives in London."

Rachel stared hard at Hannah while Jack extracted her solemn promise. A mother's instinct nagged at her – Hannah wasn't telling the truth.

Chapter Twenty-Seven

Imogen
June 2019

The weekend at Gavin's was the kind of hedonistic session Imogen had last experienced in the glory days of Simon's band. Sunday passed in a blur, but Monday was her day off and she lingered at Gamekeeper's Cottage with the blinds drawn, not ready to face the world. Gavin's fridge was well-stocked, but she wasn't hungry, and Gavin was grumpy.

"Let's go out and eat at the pub," he suggested, but Imogen shook her head. This was Rachel's home territory. What if they bumped into her? There was no need for anyone to know about Gavin. His time in her trophy cabinet might be limited, if he turned out to be one of those trophies that has to be handed back.

It was late afternoon when Gavin drove her to Ferngate station. He parked his car and walked with her onto the platform. She put on her sunglasses and glanced around shiftily. When the train appeared in the distance, she dodged Gavin's farewell hug.

"What's wrong?" he grumbled. "I've cleaned up my aftershave act."

She shrugged and moved closer to the platform edge.

"See you then," he said, lifting his hand to wave, then turned and marched off to the car park, before the train pulled in. She felt unaccountably annoyed.

The compartment was stuffy and crowded. She raced a young woman to the last available seat, before noticing the other woman was in the final furlong of pregnancy. She gave it up, the woman nodded her thanks and Imogen squeezed into a space near the interconnecting door, which opened unnervingly whenever her bag hit the button. It was ridiculous to be standing on a London bound train at this time of day.

"Why's it so crowded?" she asked the guard, when he shuffled through the press of passengers to check tickets.

"Didn't you read the sign at the station? Delays and cancellations. Trains are being turned around at Woking. All lines out of Waterloo are blocked."

"And into Waterloo?"

"You'll get there. It's the poor commuters trying to leave London who won't make it home tonight."

At the next station, a cyclist hauled his mountain bike onto the train, and she had to shrink back further to avoid its sticking-out pedal. Wrung-out and sweaty, she kicked off her shoes and sat on the floor until a schoolboy glanced up and offered her his seat.

The station concourse at Waterloo resembled a wartime exodus of refugees. Red-faced commuters ranked in their thousands, stared at departure boards, which uniformly showed no trains.

Imogen forced her way through the crush, with gritty determination. A young mother bumped a pushchair against her shin, and she swore. She was standing on one leg, rubbing the bruise when a tall man cannoned into her.

"Watch out!" she shouted, about to add the word 'arsehole', but his eyes were fixed on the blinking signboard above her head. He looked down and they gaped in mutual recognition.

"Imogen!"

"Jack – what are you doing here?"

"Sometimes I work from our London office," he said. "Looks like I chose a bad day. I doubt I'll make it home tonight."

"Oh yeah – the guard told me there are no outbound trains. Haven't they fixed the problem?"

"I don't think so. There was a fatality at Surbiton. They turned the power off and, when they turned it back on, all the signals failed."

"What will you do?"

"I guess I'll hang around here until there's some information," said Jack.

"I tell you what, I'm starving," said Imogen. "Why don't we get something to eat?"

He seemed to be turning it over in his mind, then he replied, "That might not be a bad plan."

They exited the station and strode towards the South Bank, Imogen staying one pace behind, so Jack could beat a path through the crowds. It seemed as if others had the same idea. The pavements were gridlocked. Pedestrians were spilling into the roads; queues had formed outside restaurants.

"Are you okay to walk across Hungerford Bridge?" suggested Jack, glancing doubtfully at her shoes.

She nodded and they left the commuters behind and weaved their way between tourists taking photos of the city with smartphones and blocking their path across the bridge.

Beyond Embankment station, Jack paused outside a sleek-looking bistro. "What about this one?"

"Fine with me," said Imogen. But, once they were inside and seated, she felt uncomfortable. It had the atmosphere of an old-fashioned works canteen, harsh lighting and silver industrial pipework snaking overhead. Sound bounced off the walls and echoed from the hard flooring. Their aperitifs arrived and they sipped them, struggling to converse above the cacophony. Waiters screamed orders through to the open plan kitchen and chefs shouted back, "Table sixteen – food away."

They exchanged a look of mutual dismay.

"D'you know what? I've got food back at my place," said Imogen. "Let's go there."

Jack shuffled his feet under the table. "I'd rather not go too far from the station in case they get trains moving again."

"It's not far. If we jump on a tube, we'll be there in no time."

He seemed to be thinking it over as the waiter appeared to take their food order.

"Just the drinks bill. We've decided not to eat," said Imogen.

Grumbling, the waiter teased the bill out of his hand-held terminal and presented it to Jack.

"Let me." Imogen snatched it from him.

Jack let her pay. The waiter took Imogen's credit card and tapped it, without asking if she was happy with contactless. She glared at him and led the way out of the restaurant towards Charing Cross underground station. She glanced round at Jack who was dawdling a pace or two behind. Why had she pressed him to visit her home? What was she hoping to achieve? But fate had thrown this meeting in her way. Perhaps it would help her to explore the inner workings of her sister's life. Weariness hovered beneath her smile. She and Gavin had had little sleep in the last two days and Jack, too, seemed to lack lustre and kept sneaking glances at his watch.

"Where are we going?" he asked again, stifling a yawn.

"It's near Maida Vale. Wait and see. I think you'll be surprised."

Chapter Twenty-Eight

Rachel
June 2019

Rachel heard a noise and glanced at the clock on her office wall: five p.m. No sound could penetrate the sealed windows, so she opened the door and peered into the corridor. Nothing. The source of the noise was a roar inside her head. She swivelled her neck from side to side. Nothing changed. It was as if the path to her brain was clogged. She couldn't focus so she propped her head on her hands and shut her eyes. When she opened them and peered through the gaps between her fingers, the room was a bright off-white space with no colour. It was as if only part of her visual cortex was functioning. Trying not to panic, she took long slow breaths and waited. Gradually the dots floating in front of her eyes coalesced into a single image and colour returned. Was it a trick of the light, or the angle of the early evening sun shining through the blinds? It had rattled her.

After a day without Carrie's needling presence, she should feel relaxed. Michael had worked his charm and persuaded Carrie to withdraw her resignation, but it might have been better if he hadn't bothered. Carrie had taken her victim act to a new level and now they tiptoed around one another.

In Rachel's desk drawer, a hipflask of Scotch was waiting to comfort her, but she drew her hand away. She must cure this headache before triggering a new one. The headaches had started when business pressure crowded in. Michael was sanguine, convinced the business had turned the corner. Why couldn't she believe him? How long would it be until she made enough profit to rid herself of the mortgage on The Old Rectory? While she waited for that day to come, her sense of living the wrong life was becoming overwhelming.

She picked up the Law Society Gazette from her in tray and began leafing through it. She could have read Jack's copy for free, but she still paid a subscription to have it sent to her at the office. What did she have to show for all her studies? Only her law degree. She'd never achieved her practising certificate to qualify as a solicitor and it rankled. If she went back into law now, she'd have to take her legal practice course and find a firm to sponsor her through a training contract. It would take years. And would a firm take her on at her age?

Don't be so defeatist, she told herself, you're only thirty-seven. Your years of running a property company would help you. She let the magazine slide from her hands onto the desk. Her experience might qualify her for property, contract or commercial law but she wasn't interested in those well-paid disciplines. When she was at university, she'd done work experience in an immigration centre with refugees and asylum seekers and it had always been her dream to work in an area of human rights law, but how was she going to achieve that while so many people depended on her for their livelihood?

Chapter Twenty-Nine

Imogen
June 2019

Imogen and Jack left the train at Warwick Avenue. She set a brisk pace while he dawdled behind, pausing to shift his backpack from his right shoulder to his left. She guessed he was regretting this excursion. How would he explain it to Rachel? Would he say, 'I bumped into your sister at Waterloo and she was so insistent I visited her home, she practically kidnapped me ...'? Perhaps he wouldn't mention it at all.

She strode on, a breeze catching her hair and whipping it across her face. She stopped to push it back behind her ears and Jack caught up with her. They strolled on, past stucco fronted houses, some pristine white, others grubby, to a junction where the road rose up over a humpback canal bridge and turned left into Blomfield Road.

"Do you really live around here?" he asked. "These houses must be worth a couple of million."

"Correction," she replied. "A whole house is up to seven million. One million might buy a one bedroom flat but, for three bedrooms, you're talking two and a half million." She tugged his sleeve. "Come on, we cross the road here."

"But how can you afford...?" he began, hurrying after her and speeding up as a taxi swung around the corner and threatened to hit him. Ahead of them were the black iron railings separating the pavement from the canal below. Jack grasped hold of two spiked finials, peered down at the line of houseboats and exclaimed, "Little Venice."

"That's right." Imogen nodded. "We've arrived. Come on."

She slipped through an opening in the fence and took the steep steps down to the canal bank, where she turned left and headed towards a metal gate arched over with spreading branches and creepers.

Jack watched as she unlocked the gate and dropped the key back into her bag. "How come this gate is allowed to block the towpath?" asked Jack.

Imogen felt a stab of irritation but, after all, only a few weeks ago this hidden way of life so close to central London had been a mystery to her. Now she was part of a community of boat dwellers with a vibrant social mix: journalists and judges, retired craftsmen and civil servants and people like her, who had normal jobs, all co-existing in friendship and mutual support.

"This is the offside, not the towpath," explained Imogen. "When the canal was originally built there was a towpath on only one side and all the activity took place there. It's all changed now but most permanent moorings are on this bank and there's not necessarily a right of way for walkers." The houseboats were lined up, nose to tail, and instant gardens of grasses, potted ferns and geraniums cluttered the bank beside each. The path was little more than a metre wide but crammed with bicycles and barbeques, picnic tables and canoes. No two boats looked the same. Some had rooftop jungle gardens, others used that space for storage with vibrant orange lifebelts and inflatable dinghies. All the boats were plugged in to a power supply.

"People live here for years – decades, even," explained Imogen. "A mooring in central London is like gold dust. The moorings on the other side of the canal are mostly for continuous cruisers."

"What's a continuous cruiser?" asked Jack, his flagging energy seeming revived. He kept pace with her as they circumnavigated a garden table set up for supper.

"Lots of people live on boats all year round but they don't all have a fixed mooring so they buy a continuous cruiser licence and can travel wherever they want on the canal network. But they have to move on every two weeks."

"So it's fine if you have no ties and can embrace the freedom but what if you have a job?"

"Exactly. There aren't enough moorings in London for everyone who wants one and the costs can be eye-watering. The Lazy Lucy may not be grand, but she has a permanent mooring."

"The Lazy Lucy? So you live on a houseboat?"

Had he really not worked it out? He might have an analytical brain but he was slow at making simple everyday connections. "We're nearly there."

Most of the houseboats they passed were moored side by side, with one alongside the path and another abutting it like a conjoined twin and accessed by stepping onto the neighbouring boat.

The clouds lifted revealing a silver-blue evening sky. The waterbus, Gardenia slipped quietly past, with a dozen passengers on board, its route from Camden to Little Venice via London Zoo emblazoned on its side.

A bearded man was kneeling beside his boat and dipping a brush into a paint pot. He looked round as he heard them approach, scrambled to his feet and greeted Imogen with a shy nod.

"Hey Mark," she said. "Did you finish varnishing my rail over the weekend?"

"I did it this morning," he replied, his paint brush dripping onto the path. "Take care. It might still be a little bit tacky.

"Thank you. Come for drinks at mine tomorrow. I'm not free tonight. I have an old friend visiting."

Mark gave Jack a hostile look.

"I'm Imogen's brother-in-law," muttered Jack. Not being married to Rachel there was no formal term to describe his relationship to Imogen.

"Just a few more paces," said Imogen. "Now – stop. Close your eyes and count to twenty, okay?"

Jack obeyed, raising his palms to cover his eyes. How naïve he was, she thought, obeying her commands. This chance encounter had dropped into her hands and she must decide how to use it to her advantage.

"Eighteen, nineteen, twenty," Jack recited. He uncovered his eyes and blinked.

Imogen had flipped a switch to turn on fairy lights and the Lazy Lucy sparkled like a fairground ride. She leaned on the rail, raised her arm and waved. "Tah dah!" But she'd forgotten the fresh varnish and rubbed her hands together briskly to get rid of the stickiness.

Jack grinned and hurried forward. Men and boats. That was bound to be a thing. All that hands-on old school technology. She tried viewing the Lazy Lucy through his eyes, remembering the thrill of her first encounter. The Lucy had sunflower yellow walls and roof, with a blue stern. Imogen had embellished it with touches of Spain, pottery from Granada and scarlet geraniums cascading from sky-blue planters.

A sizzle of frying and a whiff of garlic drifted across from a neighbouring boat. "I'll put the kettle on," said Imogen. But she didn't move. "You see," she said, "I have everything that's best about Ibiza right here in the centre of London. Except the weather, of course."

"What a fantastic place to live!" Jack enthused. "Who does it belong to?"

"The owner's a friend of a friend of mine, who spends most of his time abroad. I'm boat-sitting. Make yourself at home or have a look round."

Jack explored the deck, opening hatches and twisting knobs. "What does this do? Have you been anywhere in it?"

She shook her head. "I don't fancy taking it along the canal on my own. Once I had to go on foot down to the Elsan point." She grimaced. "It was disgusting. A friend does that for me now, when I'm at work. Or I can book the service boat to come along for a pump out. He brings coal, too, but I haven't needed that yet."

Imogen went down the steps into a galley kitchen and opened the fridge. Inside there was milk and cheese, but mainly bottles.

"You mentioned something to eat?" asked Jack.

"Oh yes," she replied, taking out a bottle of gin. "Cheese

and biscuits?"

"Oh."

The kettle she'd burnt out a few days ago stood cold and idle on the hob, but the gin bottle sparkled sapphire blue as Imogen slopped quadruple measures into two tall glasses.

"Whoa! That's too strong for me," said Jack.

"Sorry, I'm used to Spanish gin. It's quite a bit weaker." She sliced a lime into crescents. "I'll put in some extra tonic."

She noticed Jack feeling in his back pocket for something – probably his phone.

"Damn. It's run out of charge," he said and went back up on deck. He took his laptop, in its soft sleeve, out of his backpack. There wasn't much space on deck. She watched him stash his backpack under the chair and balance his laptop on his knee and guessed he was about to tap out a message to Rachel.

She interrupted him. "Could you move that little mosaic table into position? There are some cushions in the wooden chest."

"Sure." He put his laptop down and arranged the Lilliputian-sized deck furniture while she padded up the steps with the drinks.

They sipped in silence, watching sunset brew on the horizon. Soon after, daylight faded and, one by one, the neighbouring houseboats switched on their lights; a few had coloured fairy lights like the Lazy Lucy. On other boats, the windows glowed in shades of blonde and gold.

A gash of moon slit a cloud and Imogen went below to pour two more large gins. She lit a candle and carried it up onto the deck, cupping her fingers around the flame to shield it from the light breeze.

"It's so quiet here," remarked Jack. "An oasis in the centre of London."

"It depends which way the wind's blowing. Sometimes I hear the rumble of trains from Paddington."

"How long will you stay?" he asked.

Imogen shrugged. "That depends. I guess winter could be a bit harsher but that's ages yet." People who hadn't sampled

141

life afloat had a romanticised view. Gavin had warned her that anything on the boat, including the shower, could unexpectedly fail without notice. He'd advised her to join a nearby gym in case of problems with the water supply, but so far it had been fine.

"Is that a log burner?" asked Jack.

"Yes. I'm told it's toasty in winter. Some boats have central heating and I have solar panels so in summer I don't have to worry about restrictions on running the generator."

Jack rocked forward in his seat, gripped by the minutiae of houseboat living.

"Why don't you go down below and take a proper look around?" she suggested. "It's a bit cramped. I'll stay here."

"If you're sure." Jack got to his feet and descended the steps.

Imogen watched as he examined built-in cabinetry and artful kitchen fixtures. He strolled through the galley into the open plan cabin where her double bed nestled in an alcove behind a voile curtain, billowing in the light breeze. Earlier on, she'd lit two Moroccan lamps and their twinkling light picked out a silhouette, clearly identifiable as Jack, standing beside a double bed. Imogen pointed her phone, clicked, and snapped his picture.

Chapter Thirty

Rachel
June 2019

Summer continued to tease, scattering temptation but failing to deliver on its promise. Sunlit mornings turned ugly by lunchtime and Rachel often drove home under threatening skies. On a morning when the skies were blue with new possibilities, Rachel settled at her desk to crunch through a pile of paperwork before her crucial meeting with Stapleton Kumar's bank.

Around mid-morning, the phone rang. Carrie answered it, calling across to her. "There's a visitor for you in reception. I'll go and meet him."

"Who is it?" asked Rachel, furrowing her brow. "I don't have any meetings booked."

"It's your father."

"Oh! That's a surprise."

Carrie stood up, smoothed down her skirt and strolled to the door, letting it slam behind her. Once so obliging, Carrie had developed a knack of winding Rachel up. She shuffled paperwork back into an in-tray and waited. What had prompted her father to visit? Was his memory causing this unusual behaviour? The lift pinged and Carrie gave a high-pitched giggle as she greeted Max. Then a second voice broke in, clipped and gruff. Oh no, it couldn't be! Not him.

Rachel scanned the familiar walls and windows of her office, knowing there was no escape route. Lifts, corridors, cloakrooms were all located in the central core of the building and Stapleton Kumar's office was in a cul-de-sac: the end of the line. Despite sprinklers and alarms, if a fire started in the lobby and blocked the door to their office suite, they'd be toast.

She watched the office door, willing it to jam itself shut. There wasn't even time to reset the passcode to block Carrie's swipe card. With a looming disquiet, she got to her feet and turned to face the opening door.

"Dad!" she exclaimed, as Max barged into the room, bumping into the first desk. She realised his spatial awareness was also beginning to fail. "What brings you here?"

A few paces behind came Howard Dixon, offering his hand for Rachel to shake. She ignored it and turned back to her father.

"What's this about, Dad?"

"You look a bit peaky, love," said Max. He turned to Howard and, with a wave of his arm that implied some kind of ownership, said, "See - what d'you think?"

Blood pounded in Rachel's ears and left her speechless.

Howard fiddled with his shirt cuff. "Rachel," he said. "I apologise for coming here without an appointment." He cleared his throat. "Max insisted you wouldn't mind."

"So what *are* you doing here?" she asked.

Sensing a drama unfolding, Carrie looked up from her screen and shifted in her seat. "Shall I ring down to reception and book you a meeting room?" she suggested.

"Please do," said Rachel and, as Max opened his mouth to speak, she held up her hand to signal silence. "We'll talk in the meeting room, Dad."

While Carrie made the call, Howard studied the grain of the wooden floor and Max tapped his foot.

"You can have room 825," said Carrie, replacing the receiver. "It's that small one opposite the fire exit. Shall I bring you coffee?"

"No thanks," said Rachel. "They won't be staying long." She led the way along the corridor and the two men filed after her, Max limping, Howard padding behind as noiseless as a panther.

At the water cooler, she handed the men paper beakers.

"Help yourself." She filled her own cup to the brim.

The white walls of room 825 were dotted with Blu Tack, where previous users had hung flipchart pages. There was a square table, four black mesh chairs and a flipchart on a stand, propped against the wall. The room smelt stale but what the interior lacked was compensated for by panoramic views over the surrounding townscape to the countryside beyond. Max fumbled with the buttons of his mac – even in summer he wore a coat when he came into town. He folded it over the back of a chair and strolled to the window, admiring the view.

Howard chose the chair with its back to the light, placed his briefcase on the table in front of him and snapped it open.

"So," said Rachel, taking the seat opposite and narrowing her eyes against the sunlight, "What's all this about?"

"Fine views you have from here," Max butted in.

Rachel glanced out at the angular buildings of the business park, but Howard's voice dragged her back.

"Let me explain, Rachel," he said.

She flinched at his over-familiarity.

"I realise this is unorthodox and I should have spoken to you directly, but I've been sounding out Max about your business."

Rachel felt as if an insect was crawling across the back of her neck. "My father knows nothing about my business," she said, sitting up straight and feeling her vertebrae extend.

Howard took a sheaf of papers out of his briefcase. "The fact is," he said, "that early retirement bores me. I'm keen to get back into the world of business."

"And what's that to do with me?" Rachel interlaced her fingers and placed her hands on the table.

"I worked for years in the States and made good money. Now I want to invest in a growing business." His voice took on a new vigour. "I wouldn't need active involvement in day-to-day matters, if you get my drift, but I have a background in finance, and contacts who might be useful to you." He peeled the top page off the pile of documents and slid it across the table towards her. She flicked her eyes over it and shrugged.

Howard nudged the paper closer. She noticed his fingernails

were clean and manicured. As the silence stretched, Max stepped away from the window and lowered himself into the chair that was nominally head of the table.

"You see, Rachel," he said. "I told you it'd be worth having a chat with old Howard. He knows everything about business."

Her father's words stung. A few years ago, he was bursting with pride at her achievements – embarrassingly so – and would never have patronised her in this way. The gradual loss of his short-term memory was transporting him back to an era when he, like so many men of his generation, were unreconstructed chauvinists.

"Dad, let me handle this," said Rachel, focusing back on Howard. "What makes you think Stapleton Kumar might need a cash injection?" she asked. "Or consultancy in finance or anything else? We have our own advisers."

"I was thinking of a non-executive role, actually," he said. "I'd be prepared to see my investment as a long-term loan, interest-free, with certain options for the future."

The irony wasn't lost on Rachel. She was due at the bank that afternoon to bargain for an injection of credit. In other circumstances, she'd have bitten off the hand of anyone who offered an interest-free loan. "Not interested," she said. She pushed away his offer letter, or financial statement, or whatever it was. Howard seemed rattled and she smiled inwardly. She took the last sip of water from her paper cup and crumpled it in her hand.

"Think it over," said Howard, taking a business card from his wallet and sliding it towards her.

She didn't pick it up. Max wheezed, cleared his throat and slurped his water. She waited for him to recover, then opened the door to signal the meeting was over. She didn't say thank you. Why should she? She'd been ambushed.

"Hey, steady on Rachel, old girl," said Max. "There's plenty more to talk about. Howard and I were wondering if you'd like to join us for a spot of lunch."

"Not today, thanks, Dad. I'm too busy."

While Howard stuffed papers into his case, Max went back and collected his raincoat. She ushered them out and escorted them to the lift lobby where a green arrow showed the lift was on its way up. When the doors opened, Michael stepped out into the corridor.

"Hello!" He raised a quizzical eyebrow. "What's this, a welcoming party?"

No one smiled.

"You must be Michael Kumar," said Max, offering his clammy hand. "I'm Max Stapleton – Rachel's father."

"Pleased to meet you, sir," said Michael, automatically straightening his tie before shaking hands. "And you are?"

"Howard Dixon." The words came out as a grunt. "I'm sure Rachel will brief you about my offer. Here." He thrust his business card into Michael's hand.

"Offer? That sounds intriguing." Michael glanced at the card and sideways at Rachel who had dodged between the lift doors to stop them closing. Max was still gabbling as the lift doors closed and the two men were whisked away.

"What was all that about?" asked Michael. "His offer?"

"Trust me Michael, that man is bad news. I'll tell you later but now I have to dash."

"Oh yes – you're off to that meeting with the bank. Good luck."

"Thanks, I'll need it." She forced a smile. She'd need more than luck to get her through this meeting. How would the bank's business manager react when she said how much extra credit Stapleton Kumar was applying for?

Chapter Thirty-One

Imogen
June 2019

Imogen dialled the office number of Stapleton Kumar and selected the appropriate voice from her repertoire. Her newsreader's voice would be perfect. Her role at Radio Denim had expanded to include reading news bulletins and she'd developed a more solemn tone. It wouldn't do to sound bright and chirpy when she announced yet another stabbing on the streets of London.

"May I speak with Rachel Stapleton?" she asked.

"She's in London. Would you like to leave a message?"

"When will she be back?"

"Possibly late afternoon. Around four."

"And Mr Kumar?"

"He's in London with her."

Imogen brightened. "I'm in the area today and I'd like to make an appointment to see Miss Stapleton later on."

"I'm afraid I can't do that without checking with her. She's in meetings all day so I may not be able to get hold of her."

"I'll take a chance and drop by around four, anyway."

"I don't think that's … who shall I say…?"

But Imogen had already ended the call. She rang Radio Denim to say she was too ill to come in for her night shift. Listening to Damien's grumbles brought a smile to her face. Unless he could bully Krystyna into working late, he'd have to cover and step into her news reading slot. When he was nervous, Damien's twenty-one-year-old voice neighed like a startled horse. Denim FM's listeners were already complaining about him.

She checked her messages. Several were from Rachel: WhatsApps and voicemails, enquiring how she was, suggesting times they could get together. Imogen never replied. The most recent one told her Rachel was in London today – exactly as her assistant had said. What's more, Rachel had suggested meeting up at around three-thirty when her meetings finished.

She wasn't yet ready to meet Rachel. She was still doing her research into Rachel's life and work, looking for ammunition. With Rachel and Michael Kumar both away from the office, what better time to pay a surprise visit.

She caught a lunchtime train from Paddington to Reading and was surprised at how the ancient railway station she remembered from her childhood, had been reborn as a shiny space age cube of gleaming glass and swishing escalators. When she was at school locally, before they were packed off to Saint Jude's, Simon's band had played their first few gigs in Reading pubs. The venues hadn't been gentrified then, but she hadn't noticed how dingy the streets were or seen so many homeless people crouched in doorways. The area had become a fine-dining mecca for pigeons and the occasional seagull that surfed inland on a wave of wind to scavenge on takeaway droppings. On the opposite pavement, she noticed a young police officer talking to a fuzzy-haired man, huddled inside a sleeping bag with a dog dozing beside him. She'd been planning to grab a sandwich and dawdle around the shops, but she changed her mind, turned back towards the station and joined a short queue at the taxi rank.

She gave the cabbie the address of Stapleton Kumar's office and settled back for the short ride. The unmade roads of the part-built business park had turned dusty in the recent heat and the place had a somnolent feel, in stark contrast to London, where hammering and clanking on building sites was incessant. At least Stapleton Kumar's block had a rudimentary polish, she thought, as she strolled up to the reception desk and woke the startled security guard.

"Are they expecting you?" he asked, hitching his trousers

over his beer belly and tucking his shirt back inside.

"Yes," she lied. How to explain herself? It would be a waste of time if she was held in the ground floor reception until Rachel or Michael returned. She needed to get inside the office, so she plumped for announcing herself as Rachel's sister. Imogen Wilson.

The guard put through a call and showed her to the lift, which whisked her up to the eighth floor. A mousy woman of indeterminate age was waiting for her.

"I'm Carrie," said the woman. "Why didn't you say you were Rachel's sister when you rang earlier? It was you, wasn't it?"

Imogen nodded. "I thought I did."

"Rachel's not back yet. But you can wait." She ushered Imogen into the office.

"Thank you."

The office suite had four desks, with sleek, modern computers and a whole wall of filing shelves: a fusion of low-tech and state of the art equipment. In one corner was a seating area with cream leather sofas and a glass coffee table, piled with marketing literature. Luxuriant potted ferns completed the look. It was more anonymous than she'd expected.

"You can wait there," said Carrie, glancing doubtfully at her watch. "It could be a while. Shall I fetch you a coffee?"

"Yes, please. A skinny latte."

"I can only do Americano or Cappuccino."

"Fine. Americano."

Imogen picked up a glossy brochure, featuring residential developments by Stapleton Kumar with sylvan names: Woodleaze and Elmglades. She flicked through, her jaw dropping open as she studied the slick marketing copy. The Elmglades properties were priced at up to a million pounds! A low whistle escaped her lips and bitterness welled inside her. Rachel must be super-rich. She let the brochure drop from her hand back onto the coffee table and glanced across at Carrie, who was tapping her computer keys with furious energy.

"Have you worked here long?" she asked, innocently.

Carrie turned her head and nodded. "I've been with Rachel

for five years." Something in her expression told Imogen she could find out more if she pressed harder.

"You must have seen lots of change? Growth in the business?"

Carrie swivelled her chair round to face Imogen. It seemed she was ready for a break. "Yes. It's unrecognisable from the firm I joined. Rachel and I used to work out of an office over in Ferngate but, since Mr Kumar joined the business, he's dragged us forward."

"You don't seem happy about that," prompted Imogen.

Carrie blushed. "No. It's great. I mean, Mr Kumar is great. It's just that the workload has rocketed. Sometimes it's hard to keep on top of everything…"

Imogen narrowed her eyes and looked at Carrie's desk. It was buried under paperwork. Strange – she would have expected a paperless office with invoices, or whatever, in digital format. Perhaps this chaos was the ten per cent visible above the surface and the rest was buried inside Carrie's computer.

"I can see you're busy," she replied. "You must be really stretched."

"Do you know," said Carrie, picking up her own mug of coffee and strolling across to sit on the sofa opposite Imogen, "it's odd, but I'd never met Rachel's family before this week. At least, only Jack and Hannah. But last week your father was here."

"Really?" It was hard to picture her father venturing far from The Old Rectory and he didn't seem to drive any more. "Did he pop in to meet Rachel for lunch?"

"No, it was a business meeting, I think, but it didn't seem to go very well. He brought a colleague with him. Mr Dixon."

Imogen set down her coffee mug on the glass table and stared back at Carrie.

"Did you say Mr Dixon?"

"Yes." Carrie drew back from the intensity of her gaze.

"Howard Dixon?"

"I think that was his name."

Blood drained from Imogen's face. "What was he doing

here?" she asked.

Carrie fiddled with a silver necklace at her throat. Her face had recently caught the sun, the skin on her neck was mottled pink and her cheeks flushed to a similar shade. "I'm sorry," she said, twisting the delicate silver pendant. "I shouldn't have mentioned it. Please forget I told you."

Imogen reached out a hand and laid it on Carrie's arm. "Please, Carrie. Howard, err, Mr Dixon is an old family friend, but we've lost touch. You don't happen to have his number in your, um, filing system." She tightened her grip on Carrie's wrist and Carrie shot her an alarmed look and tugged her arm away.

Carrie stood up and recited in a prim tone. "That's confidential business information. If you want to get in contact with Mr Dixon, ask Rachel."

She marched back to her workstation, adjusted the position of her screen and chair, so her back was to Imogen, and began typing.

Imogen fidgeted and fretted. Why hadn't she been more tactful? Carrie could have told her so much more. She gathered up a selection of Stapleton Kumar brochures, put them in her bag and contemplated the ranks of files, shielding confidential information. Staying here longer would be a waste of time. She checked her phone messages. They were mostly from Damien, wanting to know if she'd be better tomorrow. Let him stew! She had other things on her mind. The clock on the wall showed three-forty-five. She got to her feet. "I don't think I can wait much longer."

Without turning from her computer screen, Carrie tossed a reply back over her shoulder. "I told you Rachel wouldn't be back before four at the earliest." Her chair squeaked as she stood up and escorted Imogen out to the lift, saying goodbye with the curtest of nods.

Imogen scarcely noticed. As she rode down in the lift, one name was spooling inside her head: Howard Dixon. Carrie might have told her to forget that name was mentioned. But she couldn't.

Chapter Thirty-Two

Imogen
Tunisia 1997

Miriam pleaded, Max ranted, but Saint Jude's was adamant. Imogen was being expelled.

"I'll confirm our decision in writing," said the headteacher, signalling to Max that the matter was closed. "Please hold. I'll have someone fetch Imogen to speak to you now. You'll want to make plans to collect her."

Max's slippers shuffled as he paced the tiled floor of their villa, phone gripped in one hand. "I won't have it, Miriam," he fumed.

"Shush, darling," said Miriam, pulling the sitting room door closed. The headteacher's phone call had woken them from an afternoon siesta and Max was wearing only a cotton bathrobe. Miriam, whose pent-up energy couldn't adjust to the slow North African pace of life, had been dozing in a chair. She stood beside him in stunned silence as late afternoon sunshine slanted in through the louvred shutters and listened to the gentle hiss of a water sprinkler on the lawn.

As they waited, Max scratched a mosquito bite on his forearm until it bled. "I don't get it. Why would asking for extra coaching outside school hours be grounds for expulsion?" he asked but his question was clearly rhetorical.

Miriam shut her eyes momentarily, sensing a scene to come.

"Dad?" Imogen's voice came on the line, sounding unusually tentative. Miriam strained to hear it.

"What's going on, Imogen?" boomed Max.

Miriam put a finger to her lips. It wouldn't do to broadcast this family row to Sharif, their cook and general help, who spoke passable English, and was already in the kitchen, preparing the evening meal.

"Don't make a fuss, Daddy," said Imogen. "I have to leave this school. Everyone here hates me. If you force them to make me stay, they'll find another reason to get rid of me. I'll save them the bother. I'll run away ..."

"For God's sake, Imogen," said Max, his face contorted with rage. "You're seventeen years old, not twelve. Pull yourself together."

The headteacher's explanation had erred towards the delicate and Imogen was content to leave her parents with a blurred outline of events leading to her expulsion. The school grapevine had carried the lurid details to her fifteen-year-old sister but Imogen had sworn Rachel to silence. Rachel resented the unfairness of having to stay on at Saint Jude's, while Imogen was about to escape. The sisters' dislike of boarding school life was one of the few things they'd agreed on in recent years.

Most of their teachers were nuns and none was qualified to teach drama – the only subject that interested Imogen. For that, they'd engaged a youngish resting actor called Mr Kane. With her mind set on a career in theatre, Imogen had persuaded him to give her extra coaching. She and Mr Kane met after school in a classroom, where the air was heavy with the floral scented deodorants adolescent girls used to conceal bodily odours. The school insisted the classroom door was kept open and passing schoolgirls stared in and giggled.

Imogen had a photographic memory and exceptional auditory ability. She rapidly learnt the dramatic speeches Mr Kane set for homework and they spent the coaching sessions working on her performance. After their hour was up, Imogen lingered. Mr Kane was a walking archive of information on theatre. He'd spent more of his acting career behind the scenes than strutting the boards and had special enthusiasm for stage sets – or the lack of them.

"For me, a blank canvas is the ultimate setting," said Mr Kane. "The magic happens when actors write their

154

performance in a minimal space."

"But surely you need a few props?" Imogen asked.

"Not as many as you'd think. Perhaps a few strategically placed objects. No more."

Reflecting on his words, Imogen decided this classroom setting was hampering her performance. "I can't concentrate in this stuffy room," she said to Mr Kane. "I've got a headache. Can't we go somewhere else?"

The 'somewhere else' that the headteacher had been too delicate to mention to Max Stapleton, was Mr Kane's flat in town. Once the coaching sessions had relocated, they extended late into the evening and Imogen had fond memories of the single occasion when her tuition lasted all night. Next morning her absence had been reported by a beady-eyed roommate and she returned to school, minutes before the police were called.

Mr Kane was quietly let go from his job but, as teaching was only a sideline for him, he was able to glide back into the life of the theatre. Between Mr Kane and Imogen, there were no hard feelings and they kept in touch for several months after she was summoned to Tunisia to join her parents.

***

Miriam was at Tunis-Carthage airport to meet the incoming Tunis Air flight. As she exited Customs, Imogen spotted her mother, with a driver, who was carrying a sign with her name on it. How ironic if her mother had forgotten what she looked like. She scanned the rows of meeters and greeters and guessed that holding a sign was something to do with the driver's personal prestige among his colleagues. She raised her hand in a wave and Miriam finally noticed her. A smile crept onto her mother's stern face, but she reined it back and the greeting they exchanged was tight-lipped and moody.

"Good trip?" asked her mother, brusquely, without offering a kiss.

"All right." Imogen shrugged.

The driver took her cases and they followed him out to the car park. Imogen settled into the back seat and Miriam sat in front beside the driver. He set off at a rapid pace and swerved to avoid a pothole, Imogen scrabbled for her seatbelt and fastened it. She gazed out at the featureless landscape dotted with billboards, several showing the face of a stern-looking dark-haired man.

"Who's that?" she asked.

Miriam turned in her seat. "That's President Ben Ali."

"Oh." Imogen shrugged. "What am I supposed to do here? Where do we even live? Not at some gas field at the end of the universe?"

"Your father's project is in the Gulf of Gabes," said Miriam. "But we don't live there. He travels there often but he also has an office in Tunis. We live in Sidi Bou Said."

"Sidi Bou what? I bet there's nothing to do there."

"Don't make this more difficult for everyone than it already is, Imogen. Sidi Bou Said is a beautiful town famous for its traditional white buildings with blue shutters and only about twenty kilometres from the capital. You can get into Tunis by a short train ride. And there are beaches all around us."

Imogen brightened. "That sounds good. Why did you choose to live there?"

"Your father's colleagues recommended it and it's popular with ex-pats. He was thinking of where would be best for me, because he's down at the Gulf so much. We make our own entertainment. There's the swimming club, volunteer work in the community, and parties."

Imogen yawned. As she'd suspected, this enforced kidnap to North Africa was a ploy. Her mother was clearly bored and needing a daughter to keep her company.

"How long are you keeping me here under house arrest?" she asked. "Why can't I stay in Oxford with Aunt Susan?"

"You know why, Imogen. After the trouble you've caused. You'll stay until we've worked out your future."

Angry tears stung Imogen's eyes. "My future! You're stealing it from me. If I'd wanted to be a beautician or a hairdresser, I'd be in an apprenticeship by now. That's it – I'll go home and train in hairdressing."

"And how will you support yourself?" asked Miriam.

"I'll live at home. At The Old Rectory."

"You don't drive, Imogen."

"Simon does."

"If you think I'm letting you create an open house at The Old Rectory for Simon and his mates, you can forget it."

Imogen leaned back in her seat and pulled a scarf over her face. Sister Marie-Clare, one of the teachers at Saint Jude's had told her that, in Tunisia, she'd need to cover her head with a shawl and wear a long skirt or trousers. But the women she'd seen in the airport had mostly been dressed like Europeans so Sister Marie-Clare was probably trying to scare her, in some hope she'd atone for her sins and the disgrace she'd almost brought on the school. She fell into a light doze, waking when her mother said, "We're quite close now. You might want to take a look."

Imogen pulled the scarf away from her eyes. The road dipped away to her right and beyond a line of palm trees she caught her first glimpse of shimmering, blue sea. Small fishing boats bobbed on the water and, as they rounded a bend, a marina came into view beside a triangle of beach.

Perhaps this place had possibilities. It could hardly be more different from Saint Jude's.

Chapter Thirty-Three

Imogen
Tunisia 1997

The car nosed its way into a small town of white-washed houses. The paved side alleys, snaking up the hillside, were narrow and bustling. Imogen craned her neck to peer out at late afternoon crowds.

"This is the centre of Sidi Bou Said," said Miriam, enthusiasm in her voice. "We live on the outskirts." She asked the driver to drop them off and wait for them for forty minutes. "Come on, let's stroll around."

Imogen followed her mother towards a market stall with a blue and white striped canopy. An elderly man, wearing a maroon skull cap and a light blue business suit, was purchasing some food she couldn't recognise. They turned into a warren of side alleys where the flat fronted houses were all painted white and windows had ornamental metal grilles in an identical shade of blue. Under the spreading branches of a tree, a group of men smoked and chatted – two were wearing traditional dress; the others wore suits with shirts and jumpers underneath, trussed up for winter. Imogen herself was wearing a sleeveless top.

From further away, the clanging of metal, suggested an industrial quarter but Imogen couldn't see it. They passed a group of young street musicians and paused to listen. Close by was a café where people of different nationalities sat or knelt on floor cushions, some puffing on hookahs. Imogen lingered, spellbound. "Are they smoking hash in public?"

"No, Imogen," her mother replied, smiling. "That's a water

pipe. They're smoking tobacco."

"Can we go inside?"

Miriam glanced at her watch. "Not today. It's a bit of a tourist trap, to be honest. We'll go to the lookout point and then we must head home."

At the end of the main street, an expanse of the Mediterranean unrolled before them, stretching towards an infinite horizon. Imogen gasped. The vastness was too majestic to fathom. All her senses strained to smell, hear and drink in the view.

"Stunning, isn't it?" said Miriam. "You can understand why this place has always attracted artists and writers. Paul Klee spent time here. And Simone de Beauvoir."

"Simone who?"

"Honestly, Imogen. When I think how feminists of my generation – and earlier – struggled to win the rights you girls take for granted..."

The driver picked them up and drove them to a large, modern house, set in a garden of jasmine and bougainvillea. Miriam showed Imogen to her room. The walls were white, as was the linen on the narrow single bed, and the only splash of colour came from the terracotta tiled floor, part-covered by a red and blue woven rug.

"I'll leave you to unpack," said Miriam. "Come down when you're ready."

"Mum," said Imogen in a small voice. "Is Dad still mad at me?"

She nodded. "But he's even angrier with Saint Jude's so let's stay away from that topic."

When Max arrived home, long faced, from his office in Tunis, he gave Imogen a hug, but his first words concerned workplace politics. "You wouldn't believe what that blasted Dixon did today!" he said to Miriam.

"Go and shower, Max," she urged. "You've had a hectic day. I'll have a drink ready for you when you come back down."

He nodded and headed for the bathroom while Miriam poured a strong gin and tonic for herself and a weaker one for

Imogen. They took their drinks out onto the terrace and sat on metal chairs, piled with cushions, at a mosaic-topped table, watching the trees shaking as collared doves flew in to perch in the branches and kick off their evening chorus. Cicadas joined in.

Miriam took a sip of her gin and set it down on the table, with a grimace. "I need to watch my drinking. In this heat, it's easy to slip into drinking every night. And sometimes at lunchtime."

"Hmm." Imogen swirled her drink and tasted it – ridiculously watery. She'd top up her glass with gin as soon as her mother left the room. "Who's that Dixon person Dad was complaining about?"

"He's your father's boss," said Miriam, taking an olive from a bowl that had appeared from nowhere. "He's finding it tricky because Howard's so much younger than him. Your father's spent so much of his working life running his own business. He's not used to taking orders."

The voile curtains parted, and Max stepped out onto the terrace to join them. "Where's that drink?" he asked.

Miriam got to her feet.

"Don't go yourself, Miriam," he said. "Ring the bell for Sharif. He'll fetch it."

"Honestly, Daddy," said Imogen. "What's got into you? Get it yourself like you did back home."

Max's brow crinkled, but Miriam was already strolling off in the direction of the kitchen.

"Mum's been telling me about your boss," said Imogen. "Why don't you like him?"

"Humph. It doesn't matter if I like him or not. He's bloody idle. Never in the sodding office..." realising his slip, he covered his mouth with his hand and added, "Oops, sorry. Pretend you didn't hear that."

As long as her father didn't want to rant about Saint Jude's, Imogen didn't care. "In what way is Howard idle?" she asked.

Miriam returned and placed a whisky and soda in his hand. "Howard's rarely in the office because his job is managing relationships with government and local contacts."

160

Max crossed his legs and took a gulp of Scotch. "Ah, that's better."

"I told Sharif we'd eat out here," said Miriam, as a lad of about Imogen's age appeared with place mats and cutlery.

Imogen stood up and held out her hand. "Hi, Sharif. I'm Imogen."

Sharif glanced at her hand and clutched the place mats to his chest. Miriam gave Imogen a stern stare. Sharif hesitated, then continued setting the table.

"Honestly, Mum. Why can't I chat to him?" asked Imogen when Sharif had scurried back to the kitchen.

"You can't. Just accept it."

Imogen sighed. "What will we do tomorrow?"

"I'll take you to the swimming club and set up your membership."

"I don't swim," Imogen pointed out.

"Trust me – in this heat you'll want to. The club has a spa, too, but the treatments aren't cheap so you'll have to ration yourself. You'll probably spend most of your days there until you get involved in volunteer work and study."

"What will I study?" asked Imogen, with genuine surprise.

"French for a start. There are a couple of good tutors in town."

"Not Arabic?"

"I can't see Arabic being much use to you," said Max. "But don't worry about making friends, you'll meet other English-speaking people here. There are several working on the gas field and a few of them have brought their spouses."

Her father didn't get it. What was she going to do with the other halves of gas field workers? They'd all be ancient. Why couldn't she hang out with young Tunisians like Sharif and his friends? Frustrated, she shuffled her feet under the table as Sharif set down a casserole dish, along with couscous and vegetables. Her mother said it was a local speciality, some lamb dish. She eyed it suspiciously and speared a chunk with her fork. The meat was tender but laced with fat so she pushed it to the side of her plate and served herself couscous and vegetables.

"Are there any people under twenty?" she asked.

"Yes. The Gorman twins and Melanie McFadden. But they only come in the school holidays."

"So you expect me to mooch around with schoolkids or a load of wrinklies!"

"They're not all old, Imogen," said her mother, in an irritable tone. "You'll meet them on Saturday. We're having a small party."

Imogen left her food to go cold and watched the garden view fade in the gathering dusk. A white flower was the last to stay visible and its heavy scent drifted towards the patio.

"What's that flower?" she asked.

"Jasmine," replied Miriam. "Gorgeous isn't it? It's Tunisia's national flower. I've heard that single men wear it in courting rituals to show they're available."

"I'll be sure to look out for them."

***

Her parents' party wasn't like the ones at The Old Rectory where she and Rachel had been press-ganged into taking round canapes, waiting endlessly for someone to stop talking and take a sausage. In Tunisia others were drafted in to do the work. Sharif took care of the catering and Miriam engaged two local men as cocktail waiters. The waiters circulated continuously with trays of pre-poured whisky and soda, gin and tonic, sparkling wine, and sometimes with beer. Only soft drinks needed to be requested.

Imogen hovered near their makeshift bar and offered to help pour drinks, but they declined. They were happy to chat between their rounds in a mix of French and English and she noticed them casting admiring glances at her pale legs.

The trees in the garden were decked with fairy lights and the path dotted with lanterns. Guests arrived in small groups, delivered in taxis or by drivers. A few men were in their twenties and thirties, sun-tanned and casually dressed in shorts but the older contingent was sleekly attired. Feeling overdressed to fit with the younger crowd, Imogen fumed. Lingering indoors, chatting to the waiters, she'd missed out on

162

the introductions. She took a second gin and tonic and gulped it rapidly watching younger gas field workers cluster under a tree, the tips of their cigarettes glowing.

"Excuse me," said a voice.

She looked up, embarrassed, as a tall man, with sun-bleached highlights in his brown hair, reached past her to take a drink from the tray.

He smiled at her. "And you are?"

At least he hadn't mistaken her for a waitress. "Imogen." He was the first person who had bothered to ask. "Max Stapleton's daughter."

"Delighted to meet you. Cheers." He clinked glasses with her. "I'm Howard."

"Dixon?"

"That's me." He grinned, and, behind his sophistication, she saw a boyish charm. "What have your parents been saying about me?"

"Nothing." Imogen felt her cheeks reddening.

"That's even worse." He laughed. "So, tell me, what brings you to Tunisia?"

She doubted her parents would share the humiliation that she'd been expelled. "I'm taking a break from my studies. When I get back, I'll be applying to drama school."

"You've made a good choice. This is a fabulous country with so much to learn and see. Carthage isn't far and you must get your parents to take you to Kairouan."

"What's that?"

"It's one of the most sacred cities of Islam – just behind Mecca and Medina as a pilgrimage site. I've heard it said that one pilgrimage to Kairouan equals one-seventh of a pilgrimage to Mecca." He paused. "Have you met everyone?"

"Not yet."

"Follow me. I'll introduce you. Not everyone here is middle aged like me." Howard led her out into the garden, and they joined a group of young engineers. The men greeted him with a back slap and, the women, with a kiss on the cheek. He wasn't old. He was the same age as them – early to mid-thirties – it must be only her father who disliked him.

Chapter Thirty-Four

Imogen
Tunisia 1998

Most days Imogen spent at the swimming club, stretched out on a sun lounger, holding up a magazine to shield her eyes from the sun. When her mother found a French tutor, her routine changed. The tutor wasn't local in Sidi Bou Said but in a suburb of Tunis so on Mondays and Thursdays, Mahmoud, their driver was tasked with taking her there and then he disappeared for two hours to visit his sister.

The teacher was a young Tunisian woman called Yasmine whose thick accent made Imogen giggle. Although the lesson wasn't too boring, Imogen rejigged the schedule from a two-hour lesson to one hour, so she could finish early and look around before Mahmoud picked her up. She soon discovered there was nothing to see or do. She strolled along shuttered suburban streets, trying to remember the way back to Yasmine's. In the distance was a marketplace and she headed towards it. Perhaps she could get a drink. Surely no one here would ask her for ID to prove her age. As she walked, she gathered an entourage of men, their white robes flapping around their ankles. They stayed at a respectful distance, calling out, "Laydee, Laydee – you come my brother's shop. Very good prices." How did they know she spoke English, not French? And even more surprising that they spoke it too. It turned out that they didn't. "Brother's shop" was the limit.

As she rounded a corner, there were six men in her retinue. The day was hot and sticky, and she felt slightly stressed. Up ahead of her a man was driving a donkey cart very slowly. As she drew level, she noticed the donkey was emaciated, its ribs visible. Without warning, the donkey collapsed, and the driver was jolted forward in his seat. He jumped down onto the road, face scarlet with rage, raised his stick and began beating the donkey. The animal didn't move.

"Stop that!" Imogen rushed forward, her goggle-eyed crew matching her step for step.

The driver turned and his face contorted into an ugly scowl. He raised his arm again.

"Stop it now." Imogen came up beside the driver and grabbed his arm. He twisted away and jabbed his elbow backwards, striking Imogen in the chest. Her followers took a step back, leaving Imogen facing the angry driver.

"This animal is sick. He needs a vet," she said in English. She tried to translate the sentence into French, remembering the word 'malade', but what was vet?

The man's eyes bulged. More people gathered. He flapped his hands and took a pace towards her, urging her to go.

She scanned the crowd. Surely someone would speak up for her and the poor donkey? Someone did. A voice: calm, sensible – and English. "What's going on?"

She spun round and found herself face to face with her father's boss, Howard Dixon.

Chapter Thirty-Five

Rachel
June 2019

The office wall clock glowered at Rachel but couldn't convince her to stay. It was only four-thirty as she packed up her papers and said good night to Michael and Carrie.

"Are you feeling okay, Rach?" asked Carrie, doing that goldfish open-mouthed stare which was so maddening.

"Sure." She swung her bag over her shoulder and headed off. *Rachel never leaves early*, they would say.

She joined the motorway, noticing in her rear-view mirror that the westbound traffic was building up behind her, and drove very fast to Junction 12, where she turned off. As she drew closer to Blakeswood, her spirits fell. To distract herself, she focused on earlier memories. Her childhood at The Old Rectory had been happy enough with a Blytonesque 1950s flavour rolled forward into the 1980s, as if the '60s and '70s had never happened. In those days, Miriam was a relaxed hands-off mother. In school holidays, she would give Rachel and Imogen a pack of sandwiches and encourage them to go wandering off all day. Miriam never worried about them climbing trees or being abducted by strangers. What she didn't like was the house being messed up so, when she set off for work, she would lock the doors, leaving her daughters stranded outside for the whole day. If it rained, they sheltered in the playhouse in the garden.

Rachel eased the car around the final bend and there on rising ground next to Blakeswood church, was the honey-coloured Georgian frontage of her family home. The house exuded an air of superiority as if, having survived wars, pestilence and floods, it was no longer content merely to be inhabited but must inhabit its occupants. At least that was how it often felt to Rachel – that the house was intent on devouring her. She swallowed hard as if a chunk of dry bread was caught in her throat and swung the car in through the iron gates. The sensors screamed that she was too close, but she often played chicken with them. She yanked the steering wheel, over-compensated and scraped her car's rear wing.

"Drat!" She got out of the car to examine the damage, licking her finger and running it along the scratch to see if she could make it disappear. Perhaps Jack would be able to polish it out. He was handy like that.

No one heard her arrive and she hadn't phoned ahead so she walked around the side of the house, reaching her hand over the top of the gate to unbolt it. They really should get a proper lock for that gate, she mused, but so far, no burglars had figured out that particular vulnerability.

The French doors were also unlocked, and she stepped inside, expecting to find Miriam preparing supper but the kitchen was empty. Pans and work surfaces gleamed like polished steel. It was like a stage set where food was a mere afterthought. She tiptoed across the hall and heard her parents' voices floating out from the drawing room. The folded back double doors formed a frame around the couple and Rachel lingered in the doorway and waited for one of them to notice her.

Max was lounging back against over-stuffed cushions, puffing on a cigar and following the curls of smoke up to the ceiling with his eyes. That was strange. Her mother had banned smoking indoors years ago.

Right on cue, Miriam said, "I wish you wouldn't! The smell lingers for weeks and you heard what Dr Hastings said about smoking."

"Honestly, woman! What's the point in extending my life if there's no pleasure left in it!" said Max, shifting position to massage his left hip with the flat of his hand.

"Sshh, it's time," said Miriam, hurrying across to the ancient stereo system and flicking the radio switch on,

Rachel announced her arrival. "Hi Mum, Dad…"

They turned rabbit-in-the-headlight eyes towards her and Miriam beckoned her to sit down.

"She'll be on air anytime now."

Rachel took the chair next to her father. Miriam turned up the volume on the stereo and techno music pumped out. Max seemed unfazed. His hearing must be failing along with his memory. The music faded out and the DJ's voice broke in to announce: "Now we're going over to Imogen Stapleton for our latest traffic and travel report. What's happening out there on the roads tonight, Immy?"

Rachel froze as Imogen's voice drifted across the room. A few days ago she'd returned from meetings in London to learn that Imogen had turned up at Stapleton Kumar's office, waited for forty-five minutes and then drifted away without explanation. "I don't get it!" Rachel had said to Carrie. "What did she do for all that time?"

"Nothing. She sat and flicked through some brochures and then said she had to leave."

Rachel had messaged Imogen but had heard nothing back.

Her parents fixed their eyes on the radio, as if willing it to turn into a television. They were decades behind with technology. Last Christmas Jack had suggested getting them an Alexa. "You can't be serious?" Rachel had replied. "No way."

Imogen spoke in a breathy drawl. "Well, Robbie, we've been experiencing long queues through the roadworks on the M25 in Hertfordshire, close to Junction 18. Those delays are starting to clear, and things are getting back to normal. A broken-down lorry is blocking the exit slip road at the junction of the M4 and the North Circular. Avoid it if you can. Overnight works will close Hammersmith flyover from midnight tonight until six tomorrow morning. Find another route. All underground services are running normally." Imogen's voice trailed off, DJ Robbie thanked her and faded in the next track.

"Doesn't she sound incredible!" said Max. "Just like an actress!"

This must be a daily ritual. Never once had it occurred to

168

her to listen to her sister on air but perhaps it reassured their parents that their prodigal daughter was still alive.

"Rachel, darling. This is a nice surprise!" said Miriam once she was ready to speak again.

Max balanced his smouldering cigar in an ashtray and pressed down on the arms of his chair to lever himself to a standing position. "Drink, Rachel?" he asked, meaning he wanted one but feared Miriam's disapproval.

"No thanks, Dad. It's a bit early for me but I'll get one for you."

There was no need to ask what he wanted; his routine was governed by the clock. A swift half of bitter on a weekday lunchtime, G&T at weekends and, if there were guests, wine with the meal and port afterwards. But always, once the sun was over the yard arm, a scotch and soda. As she poured it out, she noticed the bottle was a supermarket own brand. That must be why he used decanters when they had guests.

"We're about to have supper. Will you join us?"

"Why not? Let me help." It was salad. Again. Ham was sweating pinkly inside its cellophane wrapper with a sticker to show it had been marked down as an end of day bargain, but the lettuce and tomatoes were fresh from Miriam's own greenhouse. As she tore off some leaves and dunked them in a sink full of water, a microscopic caterpillar swam away. Rachel rescued it and popped it on the outside windowsill.

"Mum," she said without turning around.

"Uh huh?"

"Did Dad tell you he came to see me in the office and brought that revolting Dixon man with him?

Miriam paused. Rachel thought of the day she'd first met Howard Dixon. Her mother had been having a long talk with him on the terrace, but her father had hardly seemed to remember him. Now they were hanging out together, playing at being businessmen.

"No, he didn't mention it," said Miriam, with a firm shake of her head. "Why ever did he do that?"

"Honestly, Mum, it was outrageous. Neither of them thought to do me the courtesy of making an appointment. They strolled in to my office, pretended they wanted to take me out to lunch and hit me with the proposition that Howard wanted to invest in my business."

Miriam twisted the tea towel she was holding into a ball. "What was your father thinking of?"

"I was furious, of course. Not only did Howard offer to inject cash into my business, he asked for a non-exec directorship."

"What did you say?" Miriam scooped the lettuce leaves from the sink and dabbed them dry with the tea towel.

"What do you think I said? I told him to fuck off."

"I see," said Miriam. "I don't blame you." Her thin face tightened and lines became visible, running vertically and horizontally between her jaw line and her cheeks.

"There's something I've been meaning to tell you," Rachel began, mixing oil and vinegar to make a dressing. "When I met Howard here, that first time, he thought I was Imogen."

"Oh," said Miriam. "Well I suppose you did look a bit alike when you were younger."

"And then he asked me where Imogen was living now. Don't you think that's odd?"

"He was just being polite," said Miriam, leaving the kitchen to call Max to the table.

Over supper, her mother chatted about village events: the flower and produce show, making costumes for the AM Dram's production of *Private Lives*. She waited for the ball of conversation being tossed to and fro above her head – like a game of piggy in the middle – to drop so she could tell them what she'd come to say.

The shadows lengthened outside. "Summer will soon be over," Miriam remarked, inaccurately. Was she scared of an interruption in the small talk?

"That's ridiculous," said Rachel. "The school holidays haven't started yet."

"You need to do something about that leaky roof before winter, Rachel," said her father, giving her a solid stare.

That was her signal. She dropped her knife and fork with a clatter and rested her elbows on the table. "I need to talk to you."

Max lowered his eyes, while Miriam exclaimed, "Not a health scare?"

Rachel shook her head. "Not me, no. It's about this place." She circled her arms she couldn't seem to say the words 'Old Rectory', or 'your house', out loud. This heap of brick and stone was a millstone – and it was dragging her under.

"I've been thinking about the future and it's time we all moved on with our lives," she said. "But I can't do that with the mortgage and upkeep of this place. My advice is to sell it."

Miriam bowed her head and said nothing, but Max seemed to baulk at her words. Was it her tone? Had he understood what she'd said?

"Now listen here, young lady," he blustered. "You can't dodge your responsibilities."

There was a zinging in Rachel's ears at her father's belligerent tone. She linked her fingers and rested her chin on them giving him a cool stare.

"I'm telling you, Dad, I can't afford it." For almost fifteen years she'd been funding everything. On top of the monthly outgoings was the battle against dilapidation, endless damp and decay. The Old Rectory was diseased and rotting like its occupants.

"Nonsense," boomed Max. "A successful businesswoman like you – of course you can afford it." His face turned the shade of his favourite claret.

Miriam's eyes pleaded *Back off. Let me deal with this.*

"I'm sorry, Mum. I can't leave it any longer." She took a long, slow breath and continued. "I have to think of my own family. I see so little of Hannah and she's almost grown up. These last years before she goes to university are precious. I don't want to spend every evening and all weekend working."

She glanced at their faces but saw no glimmer of understanding. "I'm thinking of selling my share in Stapleton Kumar so I can go back to law school."

"Wha-at?!" They stared at her, as if she'd lost her mind. Miriam's lower lip quivered, Max's mouth fell open, so wide, she could see dark stains on the inside of his teeth.

"I'd be going back to the career I originally chose, Dad. I thought you'd be pleased. You always wanted me to be a lawyer."

"Well that was before," he blustered. "You're a businesswoman now. You can't throw all that away."

Miriam walked across to the windowsill, took a tissue from a box and blew her nose. The supper dishes sat greasy on the table amid crumpled paper napkins; the rustic wall clock showed it was only eight-thirty, but Rachel felt as if she'd been here for days. Why did it have to be like this?

"Look," she said, with a note of desperation. "At least tell Imogen the truth. She has a right to know. Businesses fail every day, Dad. Good solid businesses. It wasn't your fault."

Max leaned across the table and bellowed into her ear: "Not Stapleton businesses, my girl. We're not quitters. We stick with it through rough and smooth. Remember that."

He sank back onto his chair, wheezing and pressing his palm over his chest. His breathing turned rapid and shallow and Miriam hurried to the dresser and fetched a packet of tablets. "Take two of these," she commanded. She pressed two capsules out of their blister pack and filled a glass with water.

"I'd better leave," said Rachel, pushing back her chair and gathering up her things.

Max swallowed the tablets and they seemed to make him shrink. All the fight had gone out of him but, when she said goodbye, he didn't answer.

Miriam walked with her to the front door, her face a mask. She looked suddenly old. "I'm sorry, Rachel. I'll talk to him when he's calmed down and I agree with you about telling Imogen. The rift between my girls cuts me through."

Rachel strode towards her car. Scraping it on the gate hadn't been the best start to an evening that had spiralled downwards. She should have taken it as an omen and driven away.

She started the engine, her mother's words still circling inside her head. Her headache, as familiar now as an old friend, crept back inside her skull. She took a bottle of water from the side pocket and sipped it mechanically. She felt empty, defeated, all her ammunition spent.

Chapter Thirty-Six

Imogen
Tunisia 1998

On Howard's arrival, the men who'd been following Imogen
crept away into bustling side alleys but a crowd of locals
appeared in their place. She waited for Howard to speak but he
seemed to be taking his time to sum up the situation. Imogen
glanced behind her. A middle-aged man in a pinstriped suit
was holding a sheep on a lead. The sheep had a collar around
its neck and was watching its master with a soulful expression,
as trusting as any Labrador. The world was upside down. She
turned back to see the donkey was encircled by flies, eyeing
up the oozing wounds on its matted pelt.

Howard completed his recce and asked. "What's going on?"

Tearfully, Imogen explained about the cart driver beating
his donkey because it tripped over. The animal made a feeble
attempt to get up and the owner walked around it, prodding its
flank with his sandaled foot. "See that! He's so cruel. This
wouldn't happen back at home."

"We're not in England though, Imogen. I doubt this man
intends to harm the donkey. He probably depends on it for his
livelihood."

Howard scratched his chin and looked past the struggling
donkey to the cart driver, who dropped his gaze and backed
away. His load comprised wooden planks of assorted sizes and
some had slid forward and were jutting through slots in the
cart. The driver grasped a plank in his bare hands and tried to
push it back onto the pallet.

"Poor creature," said Howard. "He looks near the end to

me."

Did he mean the animal or the man?

Howard dug a hand into his pocket, produced some notes and offered them to the driver, speaking a few words in Arabic, then some in French. None of which she could understand. The man accepted the money, made a hand gesture and murmured thanks, not to Howard, but to Allah.

"Come on." Howard slid his arm through hers and turned her to face away from the ailing donkey. "We need to get out of here. It could still turn ugly."

"What did you say to him?"

"I told him to get some food and treatment for the donkey. But, you know, things are different here. Animals are never pets. They're here to work. You have to harden your heart."

Imogen nodded. Despite the warm day, she felt chilly and the adrenalin rush that had spurred her to action had subsided, leaving her flat and drained.

"Where are you going?" Howard asked her.

"I've just finished a French lesson. I was planning to wander round the market until our driver fetches me from outside the tutor's house."

"How long have you got? I'll take you for an ice cream."

"Ice cream!" she protested. "I need a drink!"

"How old did you say you were?"

"Seventeen."

"Definitely an ice cream."

"Why can't we go for a drink?" she asked, putting on her sunglasses so he couldn't read the sulk in her eyes. She fell into step beside him.

"First of all, you're too young. Second, we're not in the hedonistic holiday resorts you see in your brochures at home. In central Tunis, or Sidi Bou Said, you'd be fine to go into a bar or café – even alone – but this is a working suburb. I think you'll find only men go into bars."

"And if you do want a drink?"

"We drink at home, at parties or sometimes at an international hotel."

They walked some distance, Howard steering a path until

the crowds thinned out, pavements widened, and the houses seemed grander. They turned into a leafy side road with larger villas set back in gardens. "I live near here," he explained. "It's a popular area with wealthy Tunisians but there aren't many ex-pats. That suits me. Plus, it's nearer the office so I can get there fast in an emergency."

Over a salted caramel ice cream, Imogen cheered up and listened to Howard talking about his career in the international oil and gas industry. "This is the best project I've worked on," he said. "My first overseas posting was in Saudi and that had its challenges, but Tunisia is such a friendly country."

"Why did you choose the nomadic lifestyle? You're not married, are you?"

"I'm not. I expect I'll drift from one overseas assignment to the next, get very rich and retire at fifty."

"Fifty's ancient!"

He laughed and the corners of his eyes crinkled where his fair skin had been over-exposed to sunshine, but he didn't look old. "I know. But I'm nowhere near it yet. I'm only thirty-three."

"Did you see that man walking a sheep on a lead?" she asked. "A few days ago, I saw a family bundling a sheep into a taxi. Almost like it was being kidnapped. What's that about?"

His expression turned serious. "We're approaching the festival of Eid al-Adha," he explained. "It translates roughly as *feast of the sacrifice*. I'm sorry to tell you that those sheep will be pampered and petted for a few more days. And on the feast day, they'll be slaughtered."

"No!" Imogen's hand flew to cover her mouth, but she knew she was being ridiculous. It wasn't as if she was vegetarian. She ate lamb occasionally but the idea of a sheep being treated like a family pet and then slain ... She grimaced. "Explain it to me."

"Do you remember the story of Abraham in the Bible, being willing to sacrifice his son?"

"Vaguely. Didn't God provide a lamb in place of the boy? Stuck in a thorn bush?"

"Exactly. Here it's Ibrahim, not Abraham but it's basically

the same story. Afterwards, the lamb or goat is divided into three parts. One is for the family; a second share is for relatives and the third is given to the poor."

***

One week later, when Imogen left her French tutor's house, Howard was waiting outside in his red convertible with the roof down. He couldn't possibly have known what time she planned to leave. He must have seen her go in and waited. A shiver ran along her spine.

"Hop in, I'll drive you home," he said.

"I don't have to go straight home. No one's there." She'd leave a message for Mahmoud the driver with Yasmine. She wasn't going to pass up on a ride in Howard's sports car.

"Where are they?"

"Dad's at work down in the Gulf and Mum's gone home to England to visit Rachel, my sister."

"I see. I hadn't heard," he replied with a wink. "Tell you what, perhaps I can organise that drink you wanted. It was gin and tonic you were drinking at the party, wasn't it?"

"Gin or vodka." She stepped into the passenger seat and pulled the door shut.

During the weeks Miriam was away in England, Imogen abandoned her French lessons. Yasmine didn't care as long as she got paid and Imogen did a deal with Mahmoud, who was happy with extra afternoons off to spend with his family. Every Monday and Thursday he dropped her close to Yasmine's home, where Howard was waiting to whisk her off. He never took her to his house, though, in the weeks and months to come, she often asked him to. But, at the hotel, there were no restrictions on getting a drink. It was room service.

At seventeen, Imogen wasn't a virgin. There'd been Simon and Mr Kane, the drama teacher, along with a couple of conquests at parties. But now there was Howard and, when he removed his clothes for the first time in the hotel room, Imogen could see that thirty-three wasn't old at all. He was fit, rich and attentive. She was in love.

176

Chapter Thirty-Seven

Imogen
July 2019

The shine of Imogen's radio presenting job was beginning to tarnish. The late nights were no problem. Staying up into the early hours and often all night, had been a hallmark of her life with Simon. It was the early morning shifts that killed her. This job came as close as she might ever get to the theatre career she'd once craved but shift work didn't suit her. Working for a living was seriously overrated. It was all right for Rachel. Thanks to their parents' generosity she was her own boss and didn't have to jump at the orders of an idiot like Damien. Besides, Rachel had swallowed that Protestant work ethic crap fed to her by their parents, and Saint Jude's, and probably lacked the imagination to do anything else.

Since her visit to Stapleton Kumar and her talk with Carrie, Imogen couldn't get Howard Dixon out of her mind. What had brought him back to the UK? Where was he living, and did he remember her? The obvious way to find out would be to ask Rachel, or her parents, but she needed more time to think through her next step. For now, she needed a distraction and who better to arrange it than Gavin. She tapped a finger on his profile in her phone.

"Hey, Immy. Great to hear from you." His enthusiasm boosted her spirits. Why didn't he contact her more often? She was always making the running.

"What are you up to today?" she asked. "I have two days off. Can we get together?"

"Chichester," he mumbled.

"What did you say?"

It turned out he was taking his son, Luke, to an open day at the university in Chichester. "And afterwards, I promised him we'd head on down to the beach for a bit of a chill out and a barbie."

"What beach?"

"A place called West Wittering. Why not meet us there?"

"Don't be ridiculous, Gavin. How will I get there?" Imogen snapped. "I don't have a car and I assume it's some God-forsaken end of the earth type of place."

Gavin laughed. "It's secluded in parts," he concurred. "And it won't be busy on a weekday. But you and I like privacy, don't we? I tell you what, swing by my place and pick up the beamer. I'll leave the car keys on the kitchen table. You know where to find the house key."

Imogen thought for a moment. It would mean catching a train to Ferngate, a taxi out to Gamekeeper's Cottage and then a long drive to the coast but it might be worth it. She was intrigued to meet Gavin's son. "How are you getting there?"

"Luke's passed his driving test," said Gavin. "He needs some motorway practice, so I said he could drive us down in the Golf."

It was one of the hottest days of the year so far. Ideal for a trip to the beach but less so for crossing London by underground, pressed up against strangers with sweaty armpits, listening to station announcements urging passengers to carry water. But the train from Waterloo was airconditioned, a taxi was waiting on the rank at Ferngate station and, once she'd collected the car and was behind the wheel of GAV 1N, the BMW drove like a dream. She reached West Wittering and checked the instructions Gavin had texted her. When she wound down the window to pay her parking fee at the booth, she caught the sharp scent of ozone on the breeze. She left the car in the first vacant space, walked through a gap in a hedge and gazed out at sunlight shimmering on the water. It was her first glimpse of the sea since Ibiza and brought back some of the pain of losing Simon. She still thought of him most days and the memories were bitter-sweet with regret. She watched a family with two young children: a baby in a car seat and a toddler brandishing a bucket and spade and thought about the child she and Simon never had. Rachel had a lovely daughter. It seemed as if everyone had a child, except her. Even Gavin, who'd done nothing to deserve it, had a son.

Her phone beeped with a text from Gavin, telling her they had pitched up at the far end of the car park, away from the crowds. She drove along the bumpy track with the backs of small beach huts and the paths to the beach on her left. The parked cars thinned out, giving way to windsurfers and camper vans. Close to a clump of trees near the boundary, she spotted the Golf and drove towards it. Through her open car window, she sniffed the distinctive smell of weed and understood why Gavin had set up camp in this quiet spot. Even before she'd switched off the engine, he was on his feet, holding the door open and welcoming her with a kiss. Next to the Golf were two beach chairs and a picnic rug. A young lad and a girl were lying on their backs, blowing smoke rings into the sky. The girl shielded her eyes from the sun while the boy scrambled to his feet.

"Meet my lad," said Gavin. "Luke, this is Imogen."

She glanced at the lanky boy, but her eyes were drawn to the girl, who was levering herself up on one elbow and shaking back her blonde hair.

"Aunt Imogen!" The colour drained from the girl's face.

Imogen's heartbeat quickened. "Hannah, what are you doing here?"

"Her name's Harriet," said Gavin. "Do you two know each other?"

"She's Hannah, Dad. I keep telling you," muttered Luke. He stretched out his hand to help Hannah to her feet.

"Come here." Imogen drew her niece into a hug.

"I thought she was your girlfriend, Dad," Luke hissed. "What's she got to do with Hannah?"

"Sorry, Luke," said Imogen, turning to him and deferring to his choice of a brief handshake, not a hug. "It's a coincidence, that's all. Hannah's my niece."

"You never told me you had a brother," grumbled Gavin.

179

"I don't have a brother. Her mother, Rachel, is my sister."

Gavin shrugged. "Well now that's settled, let's have a drink. Then I'll get the barbie going." He opened the boot of the Golf and unloaded three disposable barbeques and a cool box. He handed a bottle of Prosecco and three beers to Luke, who flipped off the cap of a beer and sent it spinning through the air to clink against a small pile of empties.

Luke offered Hannah a beer and looked mildly surprised when she said, "I'll have Prosecco."

With a practised twist and tug of the cork, Gavin opened the Prosecco and poured Imogen a glass.

She noticed little rectangles scorched in the grass. "It looks like barbeques have scarred the landscape."

"Yes. They're not allowed but when did that ever stop anyone?" Gavin said, lining up his tinfoil trays and lighting them.

"Who's driving home?" Imogen asked.

"You are. And Luke. I've had too much already."

"Just a small one then."

While Gavin tended the barbeques, they stood around and Imogen tried to think of something neutral to say. Wasn't it still term time? Did Rachel know her daughter was here with Luke and Gavin?

"Shall I help?" Luke asked his father.

"No. You and Hannah go for a walk. Grub's up in thirty minutes."

Smoke drifted into Imogen's face. She moved her chair and watched Luke and Hannah stroll towards the beach, hand in hand. Gavin tended the barbeque and she sipped her Prosecco in silence. Plates heaped with meat weren't to her liking, but the aroma made her hungry. Perhaps she'd have a small burger. She looked in the cool box and found baby leaf salad, tomatoes, coleslaw and a bowl of Waldorf salad that looked suspiciously homemade.

Gavin grinned. "You thought I'd forgotten the salad, didn't you?" He gave her a quick kiss on the cheek.

"You're full of surprises, Gavin."

He watched her fold paper napkins and set out plates and

cutlery and smiled. A warm wind gusted over the tartan rug and Gavin weighted down the napkins with tumblers. He left the meat sizzling and reached for Imogen's hand, kissing her fingertips.

"Thanks for coming. It was a long journey."

"It was."

"I didn't think you'd bother, but I'm glad you did. It's hard to read you, Immy. What is it you're looking for?" His eyes wandered from her face to fix on a point beyond her shoulder. "Here come the love birds."

She twisted round to see Luke and Hannah shoving each other in a play fight. Hannah broke into a run, streaking ahead of Luke, who jogged behind and let her win the race.

"Slowcoach," Hannah teased. "You're the one applying for a sports science degree." They collapsed, giggling, onto the picnic blanket.

"How was your uni visit?" Imogen asked Luke.

His face brightened. "We weren't there long. Hannah and I walked round the campus and checked out the sports facilities and stuff, but Dad was kind of ironic about it all. He didn't want to go to the talks, so I picked up the brochures and we left."

"Can I see?"

"Sure." Luke strolled over to the Golf and fished out a prospectus from a bag of leaflets.

Imogen glanced at the shiny cover: glossy-haired students with confident smiles. Was this what university was really like? She'd never know. "I wanted to go to drama school, but I never made it. I hope it works out for you."

"Next year you must work on your grades," added Hannah. It was the longest sentence she'd spoken. It was clear she felt uneasy around Gavin, blushing or edging further away when he spoke to her.

Luke took another beer.

"Is it the summer holidays yet?" Imogen asked.

"Two more weeks," replied Hannah.

"Then you must come to London and stay with me. You promised, remember?"

Hannah nibbled on a charred sausage then left it on the side of her plate. "Yes, maybe."

"Here's my card – phone number, email and address on the back. Call me when the bright lights of Ferngate get too exciting."

"Thanks." Hannah eyed it suspiciously. "The Lazy Lucy? Is it – err – a club?"

"It's a houseboat. On the Regent canal at Little Venice. You'll love it."

Hannah's eyes lit up. "Sounds amazing. I'd love to." She slipped the card into the pocket of her shorts. Despite the sweltering weather, she was wearing black tights underneath.

The food ran out, Gavin reached for another beer and topped up Imogen's glass with Prosecco.

"Just half a glass, if you expect me to drive you home." Imogen moved her chair beside Gavin's but felt awkward under her niece's scrutiny.

"Hey, Luke. Why don't you take Hannah for a drive?" suggested Gavin. "Show her the coast."

"Cool, yeah." Luke threw a nibbled chicken drumstick onto his plate and wiped his hands on the grass. "Let's go." He twiddled his car keys as he waited for Hannah to follow him.

"Take it easy then." Gavin waved them off. He turned to Imogen. "This will be his first unaccompanied drive since passing his test. It reminds me of being his age – the open road, wind blowing through hair…"

Imogen glanced at the small pile of empties and felt faintly uneasy. "Do you think they should go?" she asked. Should she have stopped them? Was she responsible for her niece even though their meeting was entirely accidental? But the Golf was already weaving its way across the coarse grass of the car park towards the track.

"Are you sure he won't show off to her?" Imogen asked.

"Nah. He's a good driver and he'll take it easy. He's in love."

"With Hannah?"

"No – with that Golf."

When the car was out of sight, Imogen sat down and

182

reached for Gavin's hand. He pressed it gently and lifted his free hand to stroke her face. His touch was light and the smile he gave her was almost tender. A warm breeze lapped around them.

"It reminds me of Ibiza," she said.

"It's nothing like Ibiza."

"I suppose not. It's the soporific effect of the sea. The peace."

"Stop talking." He leaned towards her and kissed her. She felt oddly relaxed. Their silence was companionable, as if they were both years older and had settled into some kind of life together. And then, inexplicably, Imogen found herself confiding in him about Tunisia, about her first serious affair and about Howard. He listened intently, nodding at times, and sympathising when she described her mother's sudden determination to return home and the pain she'd felt when she realised she'd never see Howard again.

"He'll be an old man now," said Gavin, opening a discreet tin and taking out papers and tobacco to roll a spliff.

"Not that old," she countered. "Maybe fifteen years older than me. The age gap between my parents is over twenty years."

Gavin gave her a sharp look. He took a drag on the joint and offered it to her but she waved it away.

"You want me to drive you home, remember?"

"Sure." He looked at her through half-closed lids.

The wind turned cooler. Imogen shivered and gathered up the picnic rug to cover her bare legs. Her restless fingers plaited the fringe as she picked up the thread of her story. "I hadn't thought about Howard for years," she said. "Then last week, I heard, quite by accident, that he was back in England. He'd been in touch with my parents and was thinking about investing in Rachel's business, but no one thought to mention this to me. Can you believe it?"

Silence. She glanced at Gavin to see if he'd dozed off, but his eyes were fixed on her face. He was listening intently.

"So I realised, it was a sign," she said.

"What sort of sign?"

"That I must track him down and see him again ..."

Gavin sat bolt upright in the flimsy chair, holding the spliff out in front of him. White ash dropped onto his shoe. With a twitch of dismay, she realised he didn't want to know about Howard. When she reached for his hand, he pulled his away.

"Gavin, it's curiosity, that's all. It was unfinished business with Howard all those years ago. It doesn't mean ..."

"That you've been using me?" He turned his head away from her and took a long draw on the spliff.

She was taken aback by the bitterness of his tone but before she could reply, their mobile phones rang out in harmony. Imogen's first, then Gavin's. She didn't recognise the number, so she ignored it, while Gavin answered his.

"It's Luke," he said. "Something's wrong."

"What?"

Gavin raised a hand to silence her as he listened. Her own phone started up again and this time she answered. It was Hannah, her voice thick with sobs,

"Aunt Imogen. We've had an accident. Can you come?"

Chapter Thirty-Eight

Rachel
July 2019

Rachel paced the front path of Southerndown Cottage. Twelve strides, turn, retrace, repeat. The tenth time, she opened the gate, walked to the end of the close and peered along the main road, blinded by approaching headlights. Imogen had phoned with a curt explanation. Hannah had had a car accident. She wasn't badly hurt. They were on their way home and about half an hour away.

Sick and dazed, Rachel tried to piece together this scant information. What was Hannah doing on the Sussex coast? Why was she with Imogen? Why wasn't she at school and the sleepover she'd packed a bag for that morning? She returned to Southerndown Cottage where Jack was waiting on the doorstep. He held out a mug to her. "Coffee?"

Her throat was too constricted to drink but she accepted it anyway. Jack put his arm around her and she leaned against him.

"What the hell's going on, Jack? Why did Hannah lie about going for a sleepover at Ellie's? And Imogen – it feels like she's stalking us. Did I tell you she turned up at Stapleton Kumar's office the other day?" Although the night wasn't cold, she sensed Jack flinch.

"We'll have to wait and ask Hannah," he said.

There were no streetlights in their unadopted road and a tarry sky, punctuated by bursts of car headlights from the main road, stretched in all directions. As they craned their necks to look, a car indicated, pulled into the close and drew up outside Southerndown Cottage. Rachel froze. The BMW's distinctive number plate was familiar, but its tinted windows prevented her seeing inside. And then someone stepped out of the driver's seat.

"Imogen." Rachel ran to the gate as her sister opened the car's rear door and helped someone out. The someone was Hannah, dishevelled, trembling and wrapped in a tartan picnic blanket.

Rachel ran. She hugged Hannah tight and the car's headlights picked out a gash and bruise above her daughter's left eyebrow.

"Mum," sobbed Hannah. "I'm so s-sorry."

White paper napkins, wrapped around Hannah's left hand, were stiff with blood. Rachel stared at Imogen, who was standing, white-faced, beside the car.

"Why didn't you take her to hospital?" Rachel asked, but bit back the words and added, "Thank goodness you were there!" She studied Hannah's injured face. "What happened?"

"It's only bumps and bruises," said Imogen, tersely. "It looks worse than it is."

"But has she seen a doctor? What if she has a head injury?"

"Honestly, Rachel, don't fret. Hannah's been alert and lucid on the drive home. It's only because she dozed off in the car, and woke up suddenly, that she seems a bit shaky."

Jack came up beside Rachel and hugged Hannah.

"Daddy," Hannah whispered, pressing close to his side.

With an edge to his voice, he asked Imogen, "What's been going on?"

"Why are you attacking me?" fumed Imogen, her face taut. "I've just made sure my favourite niece gets home safely."

"Safely?" echoed Jack.

"Jack," warned Rachel. Whatever had got into him?

"Is that the car that was in the accident?" Jack pointed to the BMW.

"No," said Imogen. "That was Luke's Golf. It's still sitting in a ditch in Sussex waiting for a recovery truck to winch it out and bring it home."

Torn between learning what had happened and getting Hannah indoors to look after her, Rachel said. "Come in and have a coffee, Imogen. You must be exhausted."

Imogen glanced towards the car. The kerbside rear window was now open, and Rachel noticed Luke leaning out and making frantic sign language gestures to Hannah.

Imogen shook her head. "Can't stop, sorry. I need to drive these guys home." She hugged Hannah and gave her a peck on the cheek. "Take care, sweetie."

"Thanks, Auntie."

Someone rolled down the tinted passenger window of the waiting car and stared out. In the dim light, it was impossible to make out their features, but Rachel didn't need to see his face to know it was Gavin.

Chapter Thirty-Nine

Rachel
July 2019

As Imogen climbed back into the BMW and started the engine, Hannah broke away from her father's hold and scrambled along the path, waving frantically and calling out, "Luke." But the rear window of the BMW remained shut.

Jack caught up with her at the gate. "Come inside," he said, putting his arm around her and steering her back towards the house. Rachel waited until the car drove away and watched it turn out of the close onto the main road. As she tramped up the path, her panic seeped away leaving her bone-weary. Jack was in the kitchen making a hot drink.

"Where is she?" Rachel asked, tripping over the tartan rug Hannah had left lying on the hall floor in a heap.

"She must have gone up to bed."

"She's trying to escape the post-mortem," said Rachel, through pursed lips. "But I'm not going to let her." She thundered up the stairs. Hannah's room was already in darkness, but she flipped on the light.

"Ow. Switch that off," said Hannah, who had crawled into bed, fully clothed.

Rachel tweaked back the duvet. "Come on, Hannah. We must go to A&E and get you checked out."

Hannah put up a hand to shield her eyes from the light. "No. Please, Mum. I'm okay. Let me sleep."

Jack appeared with a mug of tea and set it down on Hannah's bedside cabinet. "Perhaps a good night's sleep would do her more good than a four hour wait in A&E," he suggested.

"Yes, please." Hannah sat bolt upright.

"I don't like it," said Rachel. "What if she's got a head injury?"

"My head's fine, Mum."

"Let me look," said Jack, changing places with Rachel and sitting on the edge of Hannah's bed. He scanned her face. "Her eyes are bloodshot, but the pupils look normal, there's no sign of confusion. That cut above her eyebrow isn't bleeding. Did Imogen bathe it, Hannah?"

Hannah nodded. "Yes. I've already told you."

Jack turned to Rachel. "Let her sleep. I'll call the GP's surgery in the morning."

"Well, if you're sure," said Rachel. As she bent to kiss Hannah's cheek, Jack switched out the light and beckoned her out of the room.

Overnight, the heatwave dissolved into a thunderstorm. Streaks of lightning played across the sky, but the air held on to its fetid warmth. Rachel lay rigidly sleepless, plagued by images of Hannah, bleeding, and trapped inside a smashed-up car.

"Are you awake?" asked Jack, as first light filtered through the curtains.

"Uh huh." She sat up and rubbed her aching head. It felt as if a band was being tightened around her skull.

"Did you find out why she was with Imogen?" asked Jack.

"I told you last night," replied Rachel. "She and Gavin are old friends from Ibiza days."

Jack's forehead creased into a scowl. "Not the most impressive choice of friend."

"At least she was there to look after Hannah," said Rachel. "This is our fault, not hers. We should have been tougher about Gavin. And I wish I'd told Karen."

Jack nodded. "This sneaking around has to stop. I can't believe she lied to us. Bunking off school. And a sleepover for heck's sake! Where was she planning to spend the night? I thought we'd raised her better than that."

"Leave it for now," said Rachel. "I need a shower." She

189

padded across to the bathroom.

"Should I wake her?" asked Jack.

"She won't be going to school if that's what you're thinking. I'm ringing the doctor as soon as the surgery opens."

When Hannah appeared, they were sitting at the kitchen table drinking coffee. She held up her left arm. It was wrapped in a towel. "It's still bleeding, Mum." She peeled back the towel to show cuts zig-zagging along her arm. One was oozing blood.

"Come on." Rachel led her back upstairs to the bathroom. "Why didn't you show me this last night?" she asked, unwinding the makeshift bandage and gently bathing the arm.

"I couldn't take any more. I had to sleep."

Rachel dabbed the wound dry and rubbed on antiseptic cream. "Does that hurt?"

Hannah winced. She shook her head. "Not too much."

"Will I have scars?" Hannah asked.

Rachel bit down hard on her lower lip. The cross-hatched pattern of cuts might heal into scars that looked like self-harm. Now wasn't the time to say. "How exactly did you do this?" she asked, wrapping a bandage loosely round Hannah's arm.

"Luke's car landed upside down in a ditch and the doors jammed. The windscreen smashed but the glass wasn't jagged. It was like small pebbles, so we pushed it out, but I didn't notice pieces of sharp metal sticking up from the bonnet." She sniffed. "When we crawled out, I cut my arm and my legs." She undid the belt of her bathrobe and showed Rachel two deep crimson gashes on her right shin.

"When they heal, they'll be invisible," promised Rachel with a firmness she didn't feel. "The surgery will put on proper dressings."

Hannah gripped the bannister, as if her legs might not support her. Downstairs, Jack was pacing the hall.

"Hannah!" His voice rang with emotion but, whatever he might have planned to say, he lashed out. "If you'd kept your promise not to go near that man, this wouldn't have happened."

Hannah clapped her hands over her ears and burst into tears.

"Don't shout at me, Dad."

"My God, Hannah. You don't get it, do you? Just think – your mother and I might have been driving down to Sussex to leave flowers at the spot where our beloved daughter died!"

Hannah ran into his arms. "I'm s-sorry. I was wrong. But don't stop me seeing Luke. Please."

"There, there." Jack hugged her tight, and kissed the top of her head.

The sound of a key turning in the lock snapped them all to attention. Karen let herself in, shaking rain from her umbrella, paused inside the door and stared at the scene in front of her. With methodical precision, she put her bag down on the floor, took off her outdoor shoes and changed into flip flops.

"Good morning," she said, heading along the hall. "Is it a special occasion? Someone's birthday?"

Hannah and Jack stayed rooted, but Rachel went with her into the kitchen. "Sit down, Karen," she said, piling mugs and glasses, abandoned in the panic of the night before, into the sink.

"What is it?" Karen's eyes grew round and startled. Perhaps she thought she was being let go from the job.

Rachel finished running hot water into the sink and asked. "How was Luke this morning? Is he okay?"

"Luke? How do you mean, okay?" Karen stared at Rachel. "I haven't seen him this morning," she confessed. "I'm not sure he came home last night. Sometimes he stays out with one of his new mates from sixth form college. Should I be worried?"

Hannah joined them in the kitchen. "Luke's okay," she said, taking her mobile phone out of her dressing gown pocket and holding it up. "He texted me an hour ago."

"I'll make us a coffee," said Rachel, realising Karen knew nothing about Luke's movements the day before. It would fall to her to be the messenger.

"I don't want coffee," said Karen. "Will someone please tell me what's going on?" She looked at Hannah. "Do you know where Luke is?"

"I – um…" Hannah was tongue-tied. Rachel abandoned the

191

cafetière, spooned instant coffee into two mugs and poured boiling water on top. "Here you go." She put a mug down in front of Karen. "Hannah was out with Luke yesterday," she began.

Karen lifted her eyebrows and frowned. "He told me he was going to a university open day. Chichester, I think."

"That's right. I went with him," said Hannah.

Karen seemed mildly puzzled but didn't probe but Hannah blurted out, "The thing is, Karen, while we were there, we had an accident. A car accident."

Karen's right hand flew to her throat and clasped the silver cross she wore on a chain. "Is Luke hurt? Where is he?"

"He's cut and bruised, like me," said Hannah, rolling up the sleeve of her robe to show Karen her bandaged arm. "But he wasn't seriously hurt. We were lucky."

Karen ignored the arm and her eyes flicked over Hannah's face. She pointed to the cut above her eyebrow. "Did you do that?"

Hannah nodded.

"So who was driving?" Karen asked, in a trembling voice. "Was it one of his entitled new friends from sixth form college?"

"Luke was driving," said Hannah.

Karen's mouth fell open and she moistened her lower lip with her tongue. She sat down hard on the kitchen chair. "Luke doesn't have a car! And he can't drive."

Rachel braced herself to step in. Incoherent questions flying between Hannah and Karen were making things worse. But did she know enough to satisfy Karen?

"Let me explain." She tried a soft question. "Did you know Hannah and Luke were – um – seeing one another?"

Karen nodded. "Luke didn't tell me out right, but I guessed. You only had to see them together to know they were besotted."

Hannah butted in. "It's been eight weeks." A smile lit up her face, pale from the recent trauma.

Rachel glanced at Hannah. Eight weeks! When and where had they been meeting? In town after college? Or at someone's

192

house? And, if so, how was Hannah getting home, because her school bus left promptly at three-thirty. Was Luke or one of his friends giving her a lift? Mentally she assembled a whole dossier of questions to ask Hannah when they were alone.

"Luke can drive, Karen," said Hannah. "He passed his test two weeks ago."

Karen's face grew pale and her hands trembled. "But how, when? Where did he get the money?" She let her hands drop and clasped them in her lap, then turned to Rachel with contempt in her eyes. "It was you, wasn't it? Have you been spoiling him?"

Rachel shook her head. "It was news to me, Karen. I didn't know about the driving until yesterday. But there's something else I should have told you." She paused, took a rapid in-breath and continued. "I'm deeply sorry I didn't tell you sooner. The fact is, Luke's father – Gavin – is back living in the area."

Karen's face tightened.

"I gather Luke's been seeing his dad, and it was Gavin who paid for his driving lessons and bought him a car – the car he was driving yesterday when the accident happened."

Karen gasped and a whistling breath pushed her mouth into an O-shape. She gripped the edge of the table as if she was drowning and it was a raft. "Gavin? Where?"

Rachel and Hannah exchanged a glance. Hannah leaned towards her mother and whispered into her ear, "Mum don't say any more. Please." Rachel batted her arm away. She took a sip of her coffee. "I'm sorry, Karen, but I don't know."

With the heel of her hand, Karen brushed her fringe back from her forehead. "Why did no one tell me?" She glared at Rachel.

"It was my fault," said Hannah, staring at the floor. "Luke made me promise not to tell anyone."

"That wasn't Luke's choice," said Rachel in a quieter voice. "Gavin insisted he didn't tell you. I'm guessing the driving lessons and car were an incentive to keep quiet. But I don't know where he lives."

"Nor do I," said Hannah, slightly too fast.

193

Rachel glanced at her sharply. Was she lying?

"I knew Gavin was back in the UK," said Karen slowly. "I've been looking for him for years. I wanted him to explain." A tear glistened in a corner of her eye. "Tracking him down on social media was easy, but he never answered my messages, so I gave up."

The tear fattened and spilled down Karen's cheek.

So Karen had never got over Gavin's betrayal. The missing years must have stoked her grief. "Talk to Luke," Rachel urged. But who was she, after all, to give advice. Failing to get over the past and move on was something she and Karen had in common.

Karen rocked in her seat, propelled by anger. "What the hell does he think he's doing – showering Luke with presents, poisoning my son against me?"

"I don't think it's that," said Rachel, gesturing to Hannah to leave the kitchen. Hannah nodded in gratitude and darted out of the door. "Can I help?" she asked, and she knew that it was futile. Karen must feel betrayed on so many levels: by her ex-husband, her son and even by the woman who had once been her friend.

"No." Karen shook her head and got to her feet. "I'm off. I need to find Luke and talk to him."

"Of course. Take it easy on him."

Karen didn't reply. She held her head high, jutted out her chin and made her way down the hall. At the door, she hoisted her bag onto her shoulder and bent to pick up her outdoor shoes, but she didn't bother changing out of her flip flops. She opened the door, turned and shot Rachel a look of deep animosity before walking out and letting it slam behind her.

Chapter Forty

Imogen
July 2019

Since that fateful day at West Wittering beach, Gavin had gone silent on her. Imogen knew his absence wasn't down to the car accident and its aftermath, terrifying though that had been. It was the conversation they'd been having before he answered Luke's call. Why had she confided in Gavin about Tunisia and Howard? At first, he'd seemed interested in hearing about her affair with an older man, admittedly in a slightly voyeuristic way, and when she told him how the relationship ended abruptly, his sympathy had seemed genuine. No, her mistake had been telling him that Howard wasn't quite as ancient as she'd let him believe – and that he was back in England.

Meanwhile, her compulsion to go to Blakeswood, confront her parents and discover Howard's whereabouts had slipped down her list of priorities.

Gavin might have been ignoring her, but Rachel was not. Imogen never answered her sister's calls, but she listened to her voicemails, thanking her for bringing Hannah home safely and updating her on their precautionary trip to A&E. She left a message to say Hannah was fine and had returned to school for the last week of term. Why had Rachel started confiding in her as if they were close like normal sisters? It made her uncomfortable.

"I'm worried about her," said Rachel in one of her voicemails. "Luke's not answering her messages. She's furious with me for telling his mum that Gavin's back. It's all a bit of a mess. You spent that day with them. Do you know if Luke's serious about her? If it's over, I can't say I'm sorry, but Hannah's heartbroken."

Rachel's message gave Imogen pause for thought. Hannah reminded Imogen of a younger version of herself. She was nothing like her mother. Perhaps she should have been my daughter, she mused.

She made another attempt to contact Gavin – perhaps he could shed light on Luke and Hannah's break up? But he didn't return her calls.

Slowly, the Gavin-shaped void in Imogen's life filled as she got to know her neighbours. In the early weeks on the Lazy Lucy she'd stayed aloof, nodding to fellow boat dwellers as she passed them on the towpath but one day she got talking to Jenna and Sam, a couple in their twenties, who worked in digital media, and they invited her for drinks. Later that evening two older men, Mark and Bill, who each lived alone on adjacent barges turned up. The five of them bonded and became a missorted social group. Their floating homes provided plenty of common ground and, on sultry July evenings, they gathered to drink red wine and smoke cannabis, as the sun went down. On the days Imogen wasn't on a night shift, she no longer headed to Selfridges to browse the fashion rails but hurried back to join her crew.

One Friday evening when the air had turned cooler, Imogen stopped at a local delicatessen to pick up olive bread, Serrano ham, and artichokes. She missed Spanish food, particularly tapas, but everything was available in London if you bothered to look. She would plate it up and take it to share with the others on whoever's deck they were congregating tonight. Sometimes Jenna and Sam worked late, or went out with shore-based friends, but Bill and Mark were sure to be looking for company. What would Gavin make of her new friends? Perhaps this would be the night when he decided to turn up and visit. That would teach him to be jealous and petty.

As she approached the Lazy Lucy, keys in hand, the wind picked up and tugged at her skirt and she spotted Mark leaning out of his boat and craning his neck as if watching for someone. When he waved and called out her name, she realised that someone must be her.

"Imogen!"

She quickened her pace.

"Hey, Mark. Everything okay?" She was out of breath and not in the mood for bad news.

Mark took the pipe he always carried with him, but never lit, out from the corner of his mouth and she noticed teeth marks, where he'd been chewing it. With his curly grey beard, he seemed to be channelling the look of the ancient mariner.

"You have a visitor," he said.

"Who is it?" she asked. "Gavin?" But why would he stop on the towpath to talk to Mark? He'd be lounging on the Lazy Lucy with his feet up on her bed.

"No. It's a young girl. Says she's your niece. Someone must have let her in through the gate and I spotted her, sitting on the ground beside the Lucy. She seemed quite upset, so I've taken her on board mine. Hope that's okay?"

"Hannah? How long has she been here?"

"About three hours."

In stunned silence, Imogen hitched her shopping bag over her shoulder and followed Mark to his boat, the Rosie Robin, where Hannah was sitting in the main cabin, fiddling with her phone.

"Aunt Imogen!" Hannah looked up but didn't move from her seat. Her eyes had a blank, miserable look, like a dead person resurrected.

"Drink?" Mark asked Imogen, in a hopeful tone, but one glance at Hannah's face told her that, whatever had prompted this visit, Hannah wouldn't want to discuss it in front of an audience.

She shook her head. "Come on, Hannah, let's go back to mine." She nodded to Mark, "thanks for taking care of her."

"Will we see you tonight?" he asked, wistfully.

"I don't think so. Maybe tomorrow."

She waited for Hannah to step ashore and laced her free arm through her niece's as they strolled along to the Lazy Lucy. She unlocked the door and wedged it wide open, feeling faintly annoyed that Hannah didn't show more enthusiasm for the boat. "It'll take a while to cool down inside. Sit here on deck and I'll get you a drink. I don't have any Coke, maybe elderflower?"

"Yes, that or water. Anything."

Imogen made two elderflower spritzers. Why not give alcohol a miss while she hung out with her teenage niece? She carried the drinks up on deck.

"So, how did you find me and what brings you here?"

"Your card, remember. You gave it to me at the beach and said I must come and visit. Anytime."

"Sure, I remember and you're welcome. But it's usual to ring first, you know. I often work night shifts; I might not have been around."

"I'm s-sorry." Hannah made a clumsy attempt to stand up, as if to leave. Her eyes looked unnaturally bright and moist. She sniffed. "I shouldn't have come."

"Don't be daft. You're here now, so you can answer my other question. Why?"

Hannah's face crumpled. She looked far younger than fifteen. "Everything's wrong. At home."

"How do you mean?"

"Dad's furious with me. While I was recovering from my injuries, he was fine but now he's angry because I lied to them. I'm grounded."

"That sounds harsh." Imogen tugged a tissue from a box and handed it to her. She could empathise with Jack's anger. Hannah had so narrowly escaped ending her young life in a ditch in Sussex before it properly began.

Memories of that day still haunted her. When they got Luke's call, she had driven Gavin straight to the accident scene. "You look on that side and I'll look on the left," he'd said, as the car crawled along the secluded country lane. A mangled road sign marked the spot where the Golf had gone into a ditch. Luke must have taken a bend too fast, braked, lost control and ploughed into the sign that warned of more bends ahead.

As they surveyed the wreck of the Golf, the road was deserted. "Where are the kids?" she'd asked Gavin.

"They scarpered," he said. "They're waiting a mile further down the road for us to pick them up."

"I don't get it," Imogen had said, shaking her head. "Why didn't they stay by the car, call the emergency services and wait for us?"

"Really, Imogen?" said Gavin, with a sneer. "Do I need to spell it out?"

And then it dawned on her. Luke, a young driver, who'd newly passed his test had been drinking – not to excess, he would have said, just a few beers – plus, when she'd arrived at the beach there'd been a familiar smell in the air that convinced her Luke and Hannah weren't smoking roll-ups.

"So Luke would have failed a drug and alcohol test and lost his licence?" she'd yelled at Gavin. "And I could have lost the niece I've only recently got to know." She felt a simmering resentment towards Luke and, by extension, to Gavin, the irresponsible father who had let him drive in that state.

Gavin had shrugged but his expression was sullen. They were both upset but couldn't find words of comfort for one another. When they picked up Luke and Hannah a mile further down the road, Gavin had told Imogen to drive into central Chichester and park by the Festival Theatre. She took Hannah to the theatre toilets and crafted makeshift bandages out of picnic napkins. When they returned, Gavin was phoning the police and calmly reporting Luke's Golf stolen from the car park at West Wittering.

"Yes," she'd heard him say, cool as you like. "My son and I were on a family day out with friends. We spent a few hours on the beach and, when we returned to the car park, the Golf was gone."

On the other end of the phone, the call handler must have been running through a script and Gavin, equally robotically, responded, "Yes, my lad must have left the keys in the car. Yes, it was a foolish oversight. Yes, I understand this may affect his insurance claim." And that was that. The crashed Golf, reported missing but hidden in plain sight, was recorded as a car theft and the finger of guilt pointed, not at Luke, but at anonymous joy riders.

How much of this would Hannah have told her parents?

"What does Luke say?" Imogen asked. "Has he recovered?"

Hannah's nervous calm shattered. "I haven't seen him, Aunt Imogen."

"Have your parents banned you from seeing him?"

"N-no. Mum said he could come to the house – but he won't come." She hiccupped and blew her nose. "I've been messaging and phoning, but he doesn't reply. Last time he texted was the morning after the accident. Ten days ago."

"It's very rude of him not to return your calls," said Imogen, reflectively, though it was something she often did herself.

"Do you think he's ghosted me?"

"Ghosted? What's that?" Then she remembered her younger colleagues using the word. It was the new way of breaking up – you no longer had to bother to tell a partner the relationship was over, you simply ignored their messages and deleted their social media profiles. The world was becoming a savage place.

"Have you checked social media? Has he blocked you?"

"If you mean Facebook – Luke and I don't do that, it's for old people like Mum. We do Facetime or Snapchat, sometimes WhatsApp. I use Instagram, but Luke doesn't bother much."

"Let me take a peek at Gavin's accounts," said Imogen, whipping out her phone and scrolling. "Perhaps it will give us a clue what the two of them are up to." The school holidays had begun, perhaps he'd taken Luke away for a few days. She clicked on Gavin's Twitter and Facebook but he hadn't posted in over a year. Except he'd changed his Facebook location. It used to read 'London and Malaga', now it said, 'rest of the world'. Odd. A small pulse beat in her forehead. Would Gavin take off without saying goodbye? Perhaps he was ghosting her, too.

"I'll give Gavin a call," she said, not wanting to admit to Hannah that their friendship had dwindled. She tapped his number; it went to voicemail. The message was new, and it was cryptic. "Leave me a message but expect to wait some time before I get back to you."

Imogen reflected. This was awkward. She was boat-sitting for an unknown friend of his. Surely he'd tell her he was going abroad? Perhaps there was no such friend – maybe the Lazy Lucy belonged to Gavin.

For a few seconds after the message ended, she kept the phone clamped to her ear knowing Hannah was looking on, trusting her to find a solution.

"I think Luke's punishing me," Hannah said, as Imogen put her phone away. "Because Mum told his mother, Karen, that Gavin is back and that Luke's been seeing him. Luke made me swear I wouldn't tell. He's only just found his dad and he's afraid of losing him again."

"What did Rachel tell Karen?"

"About the driving lessons – and Gavin buying Luke the car."

"Did she tell her where Gavin lives?" asked Imogen. She could understand Gavin wouldn't want anyone prying into his business.

"Mum doesn't know his address. Nor do I."

Well, that's a lie for a start, thought Imogen, but she didn't call Hannah out on it. "Do you really care about Luke, Hannah?"

"I do," sniffed Hannah. "I love him, and I thought he felt the same about me."

"I think I understand," said Imogen slowly, remembering the gut-wrenching feeling when her parents had separated her from Simon and sent her to Saint Jude's all those years ago. Simon had turned out to be 'the one' for her, hadn't he, even though it ended badly? Perhaps Luke was 'the one' for Hannah though, from what she'd seen, he'd need to sharpen his act.

"If you love him, Hannah, find him and force him to talk to you," she said. "He's caught in a conflict. I expect he's had a bollocking from Gavin, and probably from his mum, too. Whatever he's feeling, he owes it to you to tell you the truth." She paused. How to prepare Hannah for the negativity of life? "But if it's over, don't keep stalking him. Hold your head high and walk away."

"Thank you, Auntie." Hannah lifted her wan face and kissed Imogen. "It's what I needed to hear. No one at home understands." She tried moving her chair closer to the low mosaic table but something was tangled around the chair leg. It was a man's backpack. Hannah stood up and freed the strap. "How strange," she said. "My dad has one just like this." She fiddled with the zip. "In fact I think this might be …"

"Give me that, Hannah." Imogen snatched it from her. "Does your mother know you're here?"

Startled, Hannah shook her head. "She and Dad were both at work when I left."

Imogen spoke sharply. "You're going to have to stop all this sneaking around." But who was she to give advice? "Phone Rachel right now and tell her where you are. You can stay here tonight, and I'll get you home safely tomorrow."

She handed Hannah her mobile to make the call and went down the steps to the galley. When Rachel saw the number pop up, she'd probably think Imogen was finally replying to her messages but sorting out Hannah's problems was only an interlude. Nothing had changed between her and Rachel. Retribution had hardly begun.

She could hear Rachel's voice on the phone, probably bleating her thanks to be passed on.

"Mum wants to speak to you," said Hannah, coming to the top of the steps and holding out the phone. Imogen shook her head and mimed a charade of being busy in the kitchen as she laid out tapas on a plate.

"She can't come right now. She's making supper," said Hannah, returning her aunt's gesture with a conspiratorial wink.

Imogen felt a jolt pass through her, something between grief and longing. She stared at her niece and sensed a recognition that was almost visceral. Hannah should be my daughter, she thought, she's a risk-taker and much more like me than Rachel, with that rebellious streak. Her sister had been dealt a winning hand in life, but she didn't deserve it. Perhaps if something were to happen to Rachel …

An accident? But that would be impossible, and it would mean something happening to Jack too. She pushed the thought away.

Chapter Forty-One

Rachel
July 2019

Rachel turned the volume on her car radio up to full as she waited outside Ferngate station, Hannah's train was late. There was no information about delays on her phone app, so she strolled up onto the platform to check the signboard. As she reached the entrance, the train from London pulled in, and passengers trooped off. Hannah was the last to appear. She was out of breath so probably hadn't heeded the announcement that said Ferngate had a short platform and the doors of the rear carriages wouldn't open. She must have galloped through to reach the first eight coaches.

"Isn't Aunt Imogen with you?" Rachel asked. Why was she disappointed? She'd expected Imogen to come with Hannah on the train. She'd even prepared lunch. "Is she working?"

"Actually, she's not at the radio station today," said Hannah. "But she has to take her boat to have the loos emptied and she can only do it today because she needs Bill to steer it for her."

"Who's Bill? I thought she was seeing Gavin?"

"Bill's no one. No one important."

That sounds like Imogen, thought Rachel.

Hannah was subdued, but she was back, so Rachel didn't interrogate her about her trip to London. She'd wait for Hannah to confide in her. She was holding to her promise to put family first at weekends.

"What do you want to do today?" she asked Hannah. The garden of Southerndown Cottage was bathed in sunshine. Before driving to the station, she'd dusted down two loungers and manoeuvred a sun umbrella into position.

"Watch a boxset," replied Hannah, and so they curled up on the sofa with the curtains drawn so they could see the TV screen and munched chocolate brownies.

"Where's Dad?" asked Hannah.

"Out running. With Michael, I think." Jack's new routine revolved around his fitness regime. Already his body was leaner, and he had more energy.

It was supper time when Jack returned. He and Rachel exchanged a glance and she shot him a look that warned 'don't have a go at Hannah'. He nodded.

"Keep mine warm while I have a quick shower," he said and disappeared upstairs.

"Has Dad ever visited Aunt Imogen's houseboat?" asked Hannah, while they waited for him to join them at the kitchen table.

"Of course not. Neither have I. Why do you ask?"

"Oh, no reason."

"Why did you turn to Imogen?" Rachel asked. The barrier between her and her daughter felt like a physical pain.

"I had to talk with someone who wasn't family. Not close family."

"And did she help you?"

"Yes. She showed me a different way of looking at things."

"You know you can always talk to me."

"Yes, I know. When you're not at work."

Jack appeared, his face red and shiny from the shower, fetched a plate from the oven and joined them at the table. The chicken korma was already congealing in its tinfoil container, but the lamb pasanda looked edible. He helped himself to a large portion.

"Are we going anywhere on holiday?" asked Hannah.

Jack and Rachel exchanged a glance. Neither of them had given it a thought.

"West Wales," said Rachel, thinking quickly. "I'll sort something out next week."

Hannah groaned. "We went there last year. It's so boring."

"But you loved it, remember?" said Jack. "We saw grey

seals and puffins and thousands of kittiwakes."

"And you can go surfing," added Rachel. "That wet suit we bought you last year should still fit. Until we go, you can come into the office and do some work experience."

"Slave labour!"

"I'll pay you some extra pocket money."

"Am I still grounded?" Hannah asked, looking directly at Jack.

He cleared his throat. "Perhaps I was a bit harsh. But we worry."

"Aunt Imogen thinks you're over-protective," said Hannah, tucking into the last piece of naan bread. "Why don't you see each other more? I wish I had a sister."

Rachel paused with her fork in mid-air. The Stapleton family had buried more skeletons than a graveyard, even Jack knew only an edited account of their history. "I guess we've lost touch while she's been living abroad. But I'm glad you're getting to know her."

In a flash of inspiration, it came to her that there was something she could do to heal the rift with Imogen, if her parents refused to be honest about their situation. She would sell the London house and give Imogen half and then, perhaps, the bitterness between them could finally end.

Chapter Forty-Two

Rachel
August 2019

Every family in the country must have chosen West Wales for their summer holiday. All Sunday afternoon, Rachel scanned websites for country cottages, rang round farm stays in Pembrokeshire and Carmarthen and stayed permanently online with Airbnb. Everywhere was fully booked until September. So much for her promise to Hannah to prioritise family and book a holiday. She stood up from her laptop and stretched.

The house was eerily quiet. The aroma of roasting chicken reminded her she'd skipped lunch and was making a roast. It was already seven-thirty. Jack had gone to Ferngate to fetch Hannah ages ago. When they returned, she'd cook the broccoli and green beans. She laid the table and poured herself a glass of Sauvignon Blanc.

She heard a car stopping outside and went to open the front door. Jack's face was tense, and he looked straight past her, his eyes roving along the hall.

"Is she here?"

"Is who here?" asked Rachel. "Hannah? Of course not – you went to pick her up from the tennis club."

"This is getting beyond a joke." Jack stamped along the hall, flung open the sitting room door and peered inside, calling out, "Hannah – where are you?"

"She's not here, Jack," said Rachel with a flicker of unease.

Jack stared at her as if she was a stranger. "She wasn't at the tennis club."

"But I dropped her off there at two!" For the third time in as many weeks, Rachel felt a nameless panic gnawing at her. "She had all her kit and her tennis racquet ..." As if that meant anything. Ever since Hannah had started seeing Luke she'd been sneaking around, telling half truths about where she was going. But surely this time it couldn't be Luke. He and Hannah had split up in the messy aftermath of the car accident.

Jack banged his fist down on the kitchen table with such force, Rachel's wine glass rattled against a plate. "I've had more than enough of this. What the hell does she think she's playing at? I had to ask her friend, Abi if she knew where Hannah might be, and she hadn't the faintest idea. I felt a right idiot!"

Heat blasted from the oven but, under her thin t-shirt, Rachel shivered. "What did you do?"

"I rang her mobile, but she didn't pick up. So I texted, sent a WhatsApp, and waited. And then I called round at Karen's to ask if she was there or out with Luke."

"I thought you were gone a long time." Rachel pursed her lips. How had Karen reacted? She doubted he'd had a warm reception. Karen seemed to think she and Jack were to blame for Luke's accident. "Had she seen Hannah?" she asked.

"No. When she saw it was me, I thought she was going to slam the door in my face but she relented. She must see us as bringers of bad news."

"Was Luke there?"

"He wasn't. Karen told me he was at work. He's found a summer job as a kitchen assistant at the White Lion. So I went there."

"Did you see Luke?" Perhaps Hannah and Luke hadn't really split up. Maybe she couldn't say she was still seeing him in case Jack grounded her.

"The barman told me Luke was there," said Jack. "So I asked – politely – if he could come out and speak to me but the manager refused. So I threatened to walk into the kitchen and find him."

"Oh." Rachel covered her mouth with her hand. This wasn't going to end well.

"The stand-off lasted for a while. I learnt some new and

colourful language as the manager told me to leave, but I held my ground. The kitchen crew came out to view the drama. And Luke. I collared him and we had a brief word outside. Honestly, Rachel. I don't know what's up with him, but he was shirty with me. Wouldn't meet my eyes. But he was emphatic he hadn't seen Hannah. Not since the day of the accident."

Rachel's heart plummeted. She slumped down heavily on a chair, grabbed her phone and dialled Hannah's number over and over until she knew the recorded message off by heart. "So if she's not with Luke or Abi, where is she?"

Jack bowed his head then got up and went upstairs, his footsteps crossing the floor of Hannah's bedroom. She followed him. He was standing by Hannah's desk, holding her tablet computer and staring at its blank screen. He looked broken.

She put her arms around him. If she couldn't draw strength from Jack's usual stoicism, perhaps she could pass him some of hers. "Come on Jack. She's not actually missing. She just didn't go to the place she told us she was going. It's not late, it won't even be dark for another three hours."

"Then why can't we contact her?" he shouted, hurling Hannah's tablet down on her bed.

His words hit home so Rachel could no longer pretend to be calm. An idea was forming in her mind. It was hard to speak because her tongue was sticking to the roof of her mouth. Was this thought benign or threatening? "This is the third time Hannah's gone missing," she said. "And both times, Imogen's been involved. Do you think this could be something to do with my sister?"

Chapter Forty-Three

Imogen
August 2019

Imogen applied a fresh layer of sun cream and stretched out on the Lazy Lucy's top deck in the space she'd cleared, next to the solar panels. The panels were soaking up sunshine and recharging the boat's central battery. All around her, neighbours were at work: painting, varnishing, scrubbing and carrying out inspections, their comings and goings more hectic than a hive of bees. Bill had explained how summer was a vital time in the maintenance cycle. "You can't survive on a boat if you're not prepared to get your hands dirty," he'd said as Imogen glanced down at her immaculate polished nails and crossed her fingers. She was conscious of the fragility of her tenancy of the Lazy Lucy. It was weeks since she'd heard from Gavin and the fact that she missed him was beyond ridiculous. He'd even driven her brief obsession with tracking down Howard from her mind. Ghosting wasn't only a thing for youngsters. Gavin was blocking her. And then, as if her thoughts had summoned him up, her mobile vibrated and Gavin's name popped up on the screen.

It was a WhatsApp message, not a voicemail, but it was something. With trembling fingers, she tapped on the message and read.

Imogen Sweetheart. My spies tell me you're not working today. I have something for you at Gamekeeper's Cottage. Why not mosey on down and collect it? You'll be glad you did and sorry if it goes past its sell-by date.
Ta rah for now. G.

Furious, she slammed her phone down. How dare he send her stupid riddles that made no sense. She tapped his number but, instead of a ringtone, there was a continuous beep as if the number had been disconnected. Mildly alarmed, she checked her watch – five-thirty. Typical Gavin – expecting her to go haring down to Ferngate on a Sunday evening when there were probably engineering works and no trains. She was damned if she'd leap at his command. She read the message again. "You'll be glad you did and sorry if it goes past its sell by date."

Once more, her fingers scrabbled with her phone, but this time they were checking train times.

Less than two hours later, she alighted at the deserted Ferngate station and walked to the taxi rank. For the first time ever, no cabs were waiting. Should she take that as a sign? A notice on the wall gave a number for a minicab firm and she called it. A bonfire was burning in a garden nearby and acrid smoke wafted over and stung her eyes. She'd changed out of the shorts she'd been wearing to sunbathe but her cream linen trousers were already creased and her blouse felt stiff under the armpits. Finally a cab drew up.

"Where to?" asked the driver.

"Take me to Gamekeeper's Cottage. It's off the Old London Road, in the grounds of Stonehill Court."

The taxi driver glanced in his rear-view mirror, then swivelled round and looked at her appraisingly. "I thought I'd seen you before."

As the cab sped away from the centre of town, Imogen's phone beeped. It must be Gavin. On the point of accepting the call she noticed it wasn't him, but Rachel. She hesitated. She was never in the right frame of mind to talk to Rachel. Why was her sister forever badgering her? Hadn't she done her bit – more than – looking after Hannah, giving her advice and sending her safely home? She stowed her phone away, feeling her bag vibrate against her hip and guessed that Rachel was following up her call with a stream of messages.

The taxi made a sharp turn into Stonehill Court and braked hard, flinging Imogen forward until her seatbelt pinned her back.

"Careful," she warned. The driver nodded, then pootled along the winding driveway at five miles an hour. It was a couple of hours before dark, but trees formed an arch over the drive and blocked the light giving the place a twilight feel.

The driver drew up outside the cottage. Imogen paid and watched it drive away. The smell of an invisible fox reached her on the breeze. She couldn't see Gavin's BMW but in the space at the side of the house was the mournful carcass of Luke's Golf. It looked like it hadn't been touched since it was dropped off by a recovery vehicle. Why hadn't Gavin taken it to a body shop – or scrapyard?

She walked up the path to the front door and knocked hard. She waited. There were no lights inside, but it was still early. All her senses sparked on high alert as she rapped once more with her knuckles. She took out her phone and tapped on Gavin's number. Again, she heard the wailing tone of a number discontinued and no recorded message. She shuddered.

Gavin's message had said something about sell by dates and a horrific thought crossed her mind. But no. Gavin was the least likely person to commit suicide. Had she hurt him so much? She pushed the thought away. Gavin kept a spare key to the cottage in the window box, not underneath the terracotta trough as most normal people would do, but inconveniently, buried in soil beneath a loosely-rooted geranium. She lifted out the scarlet plant and scrabbled in the soil with her fingers. Nothing.

That's it then, she thought, rubbing her hands to brush off the potting compost. As she turned to go, she noticed an upturned flowerpot squashed into a place on the sill beside the window box. She hadn't seen it before. Perhaps he'd moved the key?

She lifted it up. Underneath was, not a key, but a mobile phone in a pink glittery case. Her heart pounded as she turned it over in her hands. This was definitely not his. Nor hers. Did he have a local girlfriend? Instinct told her that this phone was linked to Gavin's message and formed part of the puzzle. The screen was blank. She switched it on, but it needed a passcode. She tried 1234 and 1111 and 9999. Nothing.

From somewhere behind the house she heard a sound, between knocking and rustling. She froze.

Don't be ridiculous, she thought. It's probably an animal. Perhaps a deer. She'd had fleeting glimpses of them on previous visits and knew they roamed these woods, not in herds but in twos and threes. Gavin had told her they partied on the lawns of Stonehill Court at night, feasting on the bushes. Were deer dangerous? She didn't know.

There was only one way to get to the garden and it meant going around the side of the house and squeezing past the wrecked car. Holding her arms out in front of her, she made it through the narrow gap. Ahead of her, to the left, was the old game larder. The rustling and banging grew louder and mingled with the sound of an animal in distress. Or perhaps not an animal...

Imogen stared around wildly to pinpoint the source of the sound. The stout outer door of the game larder was shut. Could the noise be coming from there? She grasped the handle and turned it. The door juddered, indicating that the mortice wasn't locked. Gavin would never leave it like this. She put her ear to the thick door and felt a vibration of something or someone hammering against it from the inside. Heart in mouth, she scanned the door. At the top and bottom were simple latch-type fixings. She flipped up the bottom one, stood on tiptoe and reached up to open the top latch, yanking the door towards her. As she stood facing the inner black screen door, a strong smell of disinfectant wafted through the opaque metal mesh towards her. The screen door rattled as someone kicked and hammered on it from inside and a female voice shouted, "Help me!"

Chapter Forty-Four

Rachel
August 2019

Rachel laid her mobile phone face up on the kitchen table and turned to Jack. He'd been listening in to her phone conversation but could only have caught one side of it. For a moment they locked eyes then he drew her into a hug. She could feel his rapid heartbeat slowing as it fell into tandem with her own.

"What did they say?" he asked, letting go of her and sitting down heavily on a kitchen chair.

"I was worried they wouldn't take me seriously," said Rachel. "That the call handler would say that seven o' clock on a summer evening isn't late for a fifteen-year-old to be out with her friends. But they were great. Really supportive. They needed to know if she was vulnerable…"

"Yes – I heard you say there had been a couple of occasions lately when we'd been concerned. I thought you handled that well." The corners of Jack's mouth lifted as if to offer an encouraging smile, but there was no substance to it. Both of them were trying too hard to pretend it was a normal Sunday evening. "What happens next?"

"They're sending an officer round to talk to us. The operator told me to keep this line open." She gestured towards her mobile. "And to use another phone to keep calling round her friends and classmates. And they'll want a recent photo." A sob escaped Rachel's lips as her mind raced ahead to what this might mean. She had a vision of every photo of a missing teenager she'd ever seen on television news; one by one these pictures blended together into a single image of Hannah's smiling face.

"I'll get one," said Jack, unfolding his body and stretching as he stood up.

"You'll have to print it from the laptop. Use mine in the study. Or will they want a jpeg file, so they can share it?" A tear slid down Rachel's cheek.

Jack walked to the door, hesitated and turned. "Have you heard back from Imogen yet? If we could rule her out, it would be something."

Rachel scrolled through a list of the calls and messages she'd left for Hannah's friends. "Not a thing. Damn her. Why can't she just pick up?"

A thought occurred to her and she laid a hand on Jack's arm to detain him. "Perhaps it's me she doesn't want to talk to. Why don't you try calling her number?"

Chapter Forty-Five

Imogen
August 2019

"Who are you?" asked Imogen nervously, putting her face up close to the screen door and trying to peer through the microscopic holes in the black mesh to the darkness beyond.

"My name is Hannah Stapleton-Smith," recited a small voice. "Please help me."

Imogen's head spun. "Hannah, darling! It's me, your Aunt Imogen. What's going on? How did you get yourself in there? And speak up – it's not easy to hear you."

"Auntie! Thank goodness." Hannah's voice grew louder and stronger. "I thought I'd be here for ever. Gavin locked me in. I came to find Luke – just like you said – to try to talk to him one last time."

"But why would Gavin lock you in?" Imogen tried to make the connection with his recent message. It was obvious he'd sent her here to find Hannah. Was it a ploy to get back at her? Was it to incriminate her in some way? Her heart jumped in her chest.

"He accused me of spying on him," said Hannah through the black mesh. "But I wasn't. When I got here Gavin was carrying crates into a big transit van." Imogen could see her outline now but not her face or expression. "It seemed like he was moving out. He didn't notice me and then he started talking to someone on his phone, so I was scared to interrupt him. I hung around and watched him for a bit so it might have looked like I was hiding when he spotted me."

"What did he say?"

"He went ballistic. He accused me of creeping around. And he said some terrible things about you."

"Such as?"

"Something like you grassed him up? What does that even mean?"

Imogen swallowed but her throat still felt dry. If someone had blown the cover on Gavin's pathetic drugs empire it served him right. How dare he suggest that was her? As if she'd want to be associated with him and his dodgy dealings.

"That's not important now, Hannah. We need to get you out. Did you see what he did with the key?"

"No-o." Hannah's voice quivered with emotion making her next words hard to hear.

"He bundled me into this shed and pushed me, so I fell on the floor. When I turned round, he'd locked the screen and was shutting the outer door." Her voice was drowned in a fit of sobbing. "I shouted at him, begged him ..."

"Try and stay calm. I'll soon get you out." Imogen took a step back and examined the screen door. It was secured with three heavy locks. She ran her hands across it, feeling for a point of weakness but the metal was unyielding. This was going to need a specialist emergency service, like the fire brigade, to cut it open. But if she called them the police might get involved and there'd be all sorts of awkward questions connecting her to Gavin and his business dealings. The Lazy Lucy, for Christ's sake. Even the place she was living was polluted by Gavin's handprint. She remembered when Simon had carried that dodgy parcel from Ibiza to London for Gavin, years ago. She should have learnt that being linked to Gavin was a very unsafe place to be.

She swallowed and turned her mind to the immediate problem. "I found a phone, Hannah. Pink and glittery. Is it yours?"

"Yes, yes. He took it off me."

Imogen heard that animal sound again, coming from the cottage garden. On top of all this, there really was a deer and it sounded as if it, too, was trapped.

"Don't worry, Hannah. The screen door is locked, and I

can't see a key, but I'll take a look round and find something to smash the lock or cut through this wire."

"Auntie Imogen?"

"Yes, Hannah."

"Please ring my dad."

Chapter Forty-Six

Rachel
August 2019

Rachel read Imogen's phone number out loud and Jack keyed it into his phone contacts but, before he called it back, Imogen's name appeared on his screen. He must have tapped it before he was ready.

Both of them spoke at once.

"Imogen. It's about Hannah," said Jack. "Do you know where she is?"

"I'm calling you about Hannah," said Imogen. "I've found her."

Jack placed his hand over the mouthpiece and spoke to Rachel. "She's found Hannah."

"Where?" Rachel bounced up from her seat and came to stand beside him. "In London?"

"Where is she, Imogen?" asked Jack, parroting Rachel's words. "Is she in London with you?"

"It will take a bit of explaining," said Imogen, rapidly. "She's not in London. She's at a house on the outskirts of Ferngate. I'll explain when you get here. Listen – have you got any wire cutters? Or a sledgehammer. Or tools for picking locks?"

Jack's forehead creased into a frown. "Why?"

"What's she saying?" hissed Rachel, trying to pick up the conversation on the phone. "Can you put it on speaker phone?"

He flapped his hand to silence her. "Wire cutters? Why would I have those?" he asked. "I might have a sledgehammer.

But why?"

"Hannah's got herself locked into a shed," Imogen said briskly. "I can't find any keys, so bring tools. Whatever you've got."

Jack shook his head, perplexed. "Is she okay? Can I speak to her?" he asked.

"You can try but I don't think she'll hear you through the door. It's best if you get here as fast as you can."

"Where?"

Rachel glared at him. "Come on, Jack." She dug around in her bag for car keys and rattled them in his face.

"Gamekeeper's Cottage in the grounds of Stonehill Court on the Old London Road. Bring the tools."

"We're on our way."

Chapter Forty-Seven

Imogen
August 2019

Gamekeeper's Cottage was on lower ground than the main house and nestled into a hollow, so Imogen had to walk around to the front garden to get a phone signal. After ending the call with Jack, she went up the path again and pressed her face against the front window. The blinds were drawn but there was a small gap along the bottom edge. She focused on that. Wasn't there a high-backed sofa set against that window? She couldn't see it, but Gavin could have moved it. Or did he remove the furniture at the same time as he was emptying his stocks from the game larder? Gavin's absence, and her memory of his one-time presence, spread like a fog over the cottage and garden and sent a shudder along her spine.

She shook herself and hurried back to Hannah. As she squeezed through the gap between the Golf and the cottage wall, she heard a ripping sound as her nearly new cream trousers caught on protruding metal, but Hannah was calling out to her, her voice distraught.

"Where did you go?"

"Sorry, I had to move for a phone signal. Your dad's on his way."

"When will he be here?"

"I'm sure he won't be long. I've told him to bring tools. We'll smash these locks and get you out."

"Aunt Imogen," said Hannah.

"Yes?"

"Shouldn't we ring the police?"

Imogen blanched. When Jack and Rachel arrived, the police would be the second thing on their mind – after getting Hannah out. They'd be in full cry, wanting revenge and justice. Insisting Gavin be tracked down. No way would she be able to deflect them. But where did that leave her? Would they believe her presence at the scene was just accidental? That her visit to Gamekeeper's Cottage at this critical moment was a coincidence?

The police would be putting two and two together and making five. Every question and answer would become a road leading back to Gavin and linking him to her. She was as clueless as anyone else about Gavin's whereabouts but who would believe her? Her blouse was sticking to her, but she no longer felt hot and clammy. She felt a chill go through her.

"Listen, Hannah," she said. "I'm furious about what Gavin's done to you but I'm worried if the police investigate, it might get me into trouble." She bit down hard on her lower lip. "Because I knew Gavin, they might think I was involved."

"That's ridiculous," said Hannah, bristling in response to a perceived injustice. "I'll tell them it was nothing to do with you."

"Thanks, sweetie. But maybe we could just play down my friendship with him? I mean, I hardly know him. He's just someone I met a long time ago in Ibiza and I've bumped into him a couple of times since I got back." She cast a glance along the drive. Still no sign of Rachel and Jack. It couldn't be further than five miles. What was keeping them?

In an upbeat tone, mismatched to her mood, she said, "We're focusing all our efforts on getting you out, babe. We'll worry about the police after that."

"Don't go away and leave me, will you, auntie?"

"I promise. Let's talk about something more cheerful. If you could choose anywhere in the world to visit, where would you go?"

Hannah fell silent, thinking. Finally she replied. "Ibiza. I'd like to see where you and Simon used to live. And the clubs, of course."

Imogen gave a wry smile. Hannah was at an impressionable

age. Circumstances always seemed to make their meetings terrifyingly eventful, but it was clear she was becoming influential in her niece's life. Who needed a baby after all? She and Hannah could have some fun times together. From a corner of her eye, she noticed light moving along the drive.

"I see headlights! It must be your dad."

"Yes!" Hannah hammered her fist against the metal mesh and set it rattling.

"I'll go and guide them." She took a step away.

"No. Stay here. Please."

"Okay."

Car doors slammed and footsteps crunched on the gravel as Jack and Rachel headed for the front door of the cottage. She heard them ringing on the bell.

"Around here!" Imogen shouted but they didn't hear. "Hannah. They won't see us past the Golf. I'll have to show them. I won't be a minute." She broke into a run.

Jack was bending to peer in through the letterbox, with Rachel hovering anxiously behind him.

"This way!" Imogen shouted, lifting her hands in the air and waving.

They turned and saw her.

"Hannah's in an outbuilding. Come round here. You'll have to turn sideways to get past this car. Have you brought tools?"

"Yep." Jack lifted a toolbox from the ground and held it up above his head as he squeezed through the narrow gap. "Where is she?"

Imogen pointed. "Stuck in there."

"What the..?" Calling Hannah's name, Jack ran forward.

"Dad," she shouted, choking back tears. He gripped the handle and the door rattled like rail tracks when an underground train bursts from a tunnel into a station. "We'll have you out in no time," he promised, though his expression was more guarded.

Gaunt and strained, Rachel pushed past Imogen with a curt nod and took up a sentinel position in the place where Hannah's silhouette was just visible behind the screen door.

"We're here now, darling. Stay strong. Dad will soon have

you out."

Imogen watched Jack flip open his toolbox. "You won't make much progress with those," she said, as she viewed the fragile looking implements.

Jack eyed up the lock. Without turning round, he replied. "You'd be surprised. I've been defending youth criminals for almost twenty years. What they haven't told me about breaking into locked buildings isn't worth knowing."

He selected a slim, flexible blade, slotted it between the lock and the screen edge and jiggled it up and down. The door rattled and fought him back but gradually began to buckle. When the catch finally popped, Rachel cheered.

"Nearly there, darling."

Jack turned his attention to two sturdy padlocks and picked up a claw hammer. "Stand back," he commanded. "And you, Hannah. Move back against the far wall and cover your eyes. Bits of metal could go flying."

The murky twilight sky had darkened. Imogen tapped the torch icon on her phone and shone it on the lock. In the faint beam, Jack's face contorted as he alternately wiggled and bashed the lock. Minutes passed. Rachel crept closer and reached for Imogen's hand. She held it briefly, then busied herself adjusting the angle of the torch. They held their breath and waited.

The stench of disinfectant suggested Gavin must have cleared and scrubbed away all traces of his business empire before leaving. But what if something was left behind? Imogen shuddered. Did Hannah know what he kept in there? What had she seen?

With a cracking sound, the final padlock yielded. The screen door sprang inwards and Hannah stood blinking in the torch light, as three family members lined up to greet her. She put her head down and bolted, straight into the waiting arms of Imogen.

"Thank you, Auntie," she whispered, hugging her and kissing her cheek. "You've saved my life."

With a satisfied smile, Imogen watched Rachel's discomfort out of the corner of her eye. Finally, Hannah sidestepped away from her aunt into her mother's embrace and Jack joined them in a group hug. Loneliness swept over Imogen. She took a step back, distancing herself from the family trinity.

"Right," said Jack, dragging his gaze from Hannah to linger on Imogen. "Which of you is going to explain what the hell's been going on?"

Chapter Forty-Eight

Rachel
August 2019

Rachel stepped inside the game larder and gazed in horror at the stone floor and thick walls. Concrete had been layered over the original brick, making it soundproof and repelling the outside temperature to foster a permanent chilliness. Hannah was shivering. She was wearing the white t-shirt and denim shorts she'd left home in on her way – supposedly – to play tennis. But there was no sign of her sports bag or racquet.

"We can't talk here," she said. "Hannah's freezing. Let's sit in the car and put the heater on."

Jack helped Rachel and Hannah into the back of the car and went round to switch on the ignition and heater. Imogen opened the door and handed something to Hannah. "Here you go." It was her phone in its pink sparkly case.

"Thanks, Auntie." Hannah clasped it in both hands.

"Where did you get that?" asked Jack, sharply.

Imogen flinched. "I found it on the cottage windowsill, under a plant pot."

Through the open car door, Rachel noticed Jack was glaring at Imogen as if he didn't believe a word she was saying. Seeing Hannah's phone prompted her to dig a hand into her jeans pocket and take out her own mobile. She tapped on the last number dialled, put it to her ear and waited.

"Why are you here?" Jack asked Imogen. "Explain now, please."

"Don't shout at her, Dad," said Hannah. She leapt out of the car, clutching Rachel's jacket around her shoulders like tribal dress. "If Aunt Imogen hadn't found me, I'd still be locked in that shed. I'd have starved to death." Her eyes welled up and she broke into choking sobs. Jack took her hand, but she snatched it away to wipe her nose. "This was my fault. Not hers. I didn't go to tennis. I came here looking for Luke. Gavin was loading boxes into a transit van. He didn't notice me. As I was about to call out 'Hi' and speak to him, he made a call on his mobile, so I hid around the corner of the house."

"Why did you do that?"

"I know it was stupid because he saw me and said I was snooping on him. I tried to explain but he was in such a rage."

"Did that man hurt you?" asked Jack, his voice shaking with emotion.

Hannah shook her head. "He snatched my phone, pushed me inside that shed and locked it." She sniffed. "I begged him to let me out. Banged on the door and shouted and shouted, but he told me to shut the fuck up. Soon after, I heard his van driving away." Hannah's face was streaked with dirt and tears, her usually sleek hair hung around her face in matted clumps. "I was so scared."

"How long do you think you were in there?" Jack asked.

"I suppose six or seven hours. When he was talking on the phone, he said to whoever he was calling that he'd be dropping off the van at their place, picking up his car and heading on to Dover."

"Try to remember everything," said Jack. "What Gavin did is incredibly serious. When he's caught he'll be going down for a long time."

Jack turned to Imogen. "So how do you fit into this? Were you here?"

"Of course I wasn't here," Imogen snapped.

He fixed her with an angry stare. "Then explain," he demanded, and his hands curled into fists.

Imogen glanced at Rachel who had finished her phone call and was clambering out of the car, brandishing her phone as if it was a weapon. It gave her an uneasy feeling.

"I've spoken to the call centre," she said to Jack. "An officer came to our house and reported back that we weren't in. I've updated them and they're on their way here now."

"You've done what?" Imogen made a grab for Rachel's phone, but her grip was feeble and she clutched at thin air. "Why did you call the police? Hannah's okay, isn't she? We can all go home."

"I can't believe what I'm hearing," Rachel yelled. "Are you asleep? Don't you get it?" She rested her arms on Imogen's shoulders, giving her a shake and catching her off balance.

"Ouch." Imogen stumbled and twisted her ankle, muttering an expletive as she bent to rub it.

"Of course the police must be involved, Imogen. We've already made a report – three hours ago when we first realised Hannah was missing."

"But she's not missing any more. I've found her. Isn't that enough for you?" Imogen attempted to walk off, limping, but Jack held her arm.

"Tell the truth, Imogen. Were you with Gavin when he attacked her?" he asked, with a threatening edge to his voice. "Because I'm finding this hard to believe."

"Dad. Please," said Hannah. "Don't argue. Of course she wasn't here." She slunk up alongside Imogen and put an arm around her.

"Thank you, darling." Imogen stroked her niece's tangled hair.

"Hannah's right," said Rachel, with an effort. "Arguing among ourselves doesn't help." Imogen had found Hannah, so they owed her thanks, but the words stuck in Rachel's throat. What if it had taken days to find Hannah? Was there any water in that shed? She hadn't seen any. How long would Hannah have survived…

"All the same, this is serious," said Jack. "That man must be caught."

Hannah had remained at Imogen's side but now she shrugged off her niece's embrace and turned to Jack. "Look," she said, with a note of desperation. "I don't know what Gavin was up to. Probably some dodgy dealing but I'm sure he didn't mean Hannah to come to harm. And I'm not talking to the police. I'm off." She tossed her hair and hobbled a couple of

227

paces.

"Too late," said Jack, following her. The wail of a siren floated towards them on the night air.

Headlights flickered on and off through gaps in the trees as a patrol car wound its way up the drive and screeched to a halt just a metre away from where Jack and Imogen were standing. Two officers jumped out leaving the engine running. Ignoring Jack and Imogen, the female officer strode straight to Hannah, who was standing by the car with Rachel's arm around her.

"All right, love?" she asked, raising an eyebrow. "I'm PC Jenni Musgrove. Are you Hannah?"

Hannah nodded.

PC Musgrove turned aside and spoke into her radio, updating the control room. "Misper located," Rachel heard her say. "She's not injured. Just taking some details now. It might be worth giving the duty DS the heads up."

Jack took a step towards them, but PC Musgrove's male colleague blocked his path and addressed his first words to Imogen.

"Are you Miss Stapleton?"

"Err, yes. I mean no. I used to be. Now I'm Wilson." She jabbed a finger towards Rachel. "If you mean the Stapleton who phoned you, that's her. My sister."

Again, Jack attempted to join his family, but the officer stopped him. "Stay here, please sir. While we talk to these ladies." He walked up the drive to join his colleague.

"Is this the young lady who was – um – detained?" he asked Rachel.

"Yes. This is Hannah. She's safe now, thank god," said Rachel.

"And you are her mother?"

"Yes. I'm Rachel Stapleton."

The officer took out his notebook, flipped it open and scribbled a few words. He pointed his pen back along the drive at Jack. "Was he involved?"

Jack stood completely still, more rooted to the ground than a living statue. It struck Rachel that, in these kinds of cases, the father must often be the first suspect. As a solicitor, Jack would know this, but it wasn't in his nature to be passive for long. She must explain everything to the officers. Fast. When speaking to the police call centre, she'd only reported that Hannah was missing. In her second call, she said she'd been found, locked in an outbuilding but hadn't said anything about who might have been responsible.

"That's Hannah's father, Jack," Rachel explained rapidly to the male officer, who had yet to introduce himself. "No, he's not involved. Are you going to take a statement from Hannah? I'll need to be with her."

"How old is she?"

"Fifteen."

"She's underage and a vulnerable person. We won't be taking a statement now. Just an initial account to get the investigation under way. Specialised officers will take a full account later, but false imprisonment is a serious offence. We need to find out about the suspect quickly, so we can locate him or her."

"Of course."

"I'm PC Morrison, by the way," he said. "Before we talk to Hannah, can I have a quick private word with you? PC Musgrove will stay here with Hannah."

He led Rachel back along the drive to the patrol car. Her eyes met Jack's as she passed him on the drive, and she gave him a nod of encouragement. She noticed Imogen's eyes swivel to follow her but couldn't begin to imagine what might be going through her sister's mind.

The inside of the police car smelt of strong pine-scented air freshener and PC Morrison must have noticed Rachel wrinkling her nose. He wound one window down a couple of inches.

"Smells gross, doesn't it?" he said with a grin. "These vehicles are all round workhorses and sometimes, when we're transporting drunks to custody, they can't hold onto their booze, if you get my gist. Accidents happen."

He flattened out his notebook on his knee and asked, "Do you know who this property belongs to?"

Rachel took a deep breath. "I'm told that Gamekeeper's

Cottage was being rented by a Mr Gavin Winter. He's the father of Hannah's ex-boyfriend, Luke, but he's been estranged from his family and living abroad for years. We had no idea this was where he lived until we had a call from my sister." She pointed along the drive. "To say she'd found Hannah here."

"How was she involved?" asked PC Morrison, giving her a quizzical look.

Rachel shrugged and shook her head. "I really don't know. I wish I did. You'll have to ask her."

Chapter Forty-Nine

Imogen
August 2019

Stranded like film extras yet to be called, Imogen and Jack waited while the next phase of the drama unfolded out of their earshot. They watched mutely as Rachel was led past them to the patrol car.

"They probably think you did it," Imogen said to Jack. "It's always the father."

He scowled at her. "You'd better work on getting your own story straight. If anyone's in the frame it's you not me."

At that moment, Imogen realised how much she disliked him. She'd get him back for this, but he was right – she must work on her story.

When he'd finished his private talk with Rachel, PC Morrison left her in the car and walked up the drive to confer with his colleague, who pointed out the narrow passage between the wrecked Golf and the cottage wall leading to the game larder. Morrison wasn't overweight but it took him two attempts to cram his muscled torso through the narrow gap.

Imogen overheard PC Musgrove saying to Hannah, "Let's join your mum in the car and have a chat," and watched as Hannah slid into the back seat beside her mother. The officer sat in front and swivelled round to face them.

Imogen felt as if she'd been standing for hours. Through the thin soles of her shoes, she could feel the gravel; her twisted ankle throbbed and the little energy she had left was draining away. She remembered there was a wooden table and chairs in Gavin's back garden. Surely he wouldn't have taken those?

"I'm going round to the garden to sit down," she told Jack.

"I don't see why not," he said. "It's not as if we're leaving."

No one seemed to notice them moving away but, as they reached the game larder, PC Morrison looked up from fixing police incident tape across the open screen door and called out, "Hey there. Where are you going?"

"To wait in the back garden," said Jack, pointing at the gate. "I'm told there are seats."

"Okay," he nodded, shining his powerful torch into the outbuilding and illuminating racks of metal shelving, empty as far as Imogen could see. Why hadn't she seized the opportunity to wander round the game larder after they'd released Hannah? What if there were traces of her DNA inside from when she'd been there before with Gavin? The stink of disinfectant must be a clue that someone had done a serious clean-up and, if they brought in a sniffer dog, they would almost certainly discover what had been stored inside.

"Must have been quite a potting shed man, whoever owned this place," commented PC Morrison walking towards them. "I'm ready to talk to you now, sir." His earlier brusqueness forgotten, he held out his hand for Jack to shake. "If you sit in the garden and wait, madam. I'll be with you soon." He trained his torch beam on the garden gate to help Imogen find the latch then dipped it down to the drive and noticed tracks from a wheelbarrow or trolley. He sighed. "Hang on a tick while I widen the secured area." He set to work with his incident tape.

Temporarily blinded by the torchlight, Imogen fumbled her way into the garden, past overgrown shrubs, scratching her hands on a pyracantha bush. Her eyes and ears were on high alert for the deer she'd heard earlier. Weren't these thorny bushes meant to deter wildlife? The moon scudded out from behind a cloud and bathed the lawn in a pale, watery light. She found the garden table and chairs, still in position. It was eerily silent, apart from an occasional owl hooting in the woods. PC Morrison must have led Jack further away for his interview because she strained her ears to listen but heard nothing.

Time passed and, when the gate creaked and both officers

entered the garden, she looked up, startled.

"What's going on? Where's my niece and my sister?"

"They've gone back home," said PC Morrison. "The young girl – Hannah – needed her bed. We'll be talking to them some more in the morning, but we have enough to go on for the moment. It's a shame the girl didn't get the registration number of Mr Winter's transit van."

PC Musgrove broke in. "I don't suppose you know it?"

"I've never seen a transit van, but he had a BMW," Imogen replied. She might as well earn her Brownie points by cooperating while she could. "And it had a very distinctive number plate: GAV 1N."

"Thank you," said PC Morrison and, though it didn't take much remembering, both officers wrote the number down. "We should have spoken to you sooner. My fault – sorry."

"I'll run this registration through PNC," said PC Musgrove to her colleague, striding away from them and talking into her radio at the same time.

"Let's press on, Miss Stapleton," said PC Morrison.

"It's Mrs Wilson."

"Thank you. Now. Full name. Address."

Imogen shivered. Should she give the address of the Lazy Lucy? It was yet another thread linking her to Gavin and things she couldn't explain, such as, who was his mysterious friend who owned the boat. She took a deep breath. "I've recently returned from living in Ibiza, so I stay with friends in London, but my address is care of my parents: The Old Rectory, Blakeswood in Berkshire."

He noted it down. "I'm told this cottage was being rented by a Mr Winter. Tell me about your relationship with Mr Winter."

"We weren't close friends." Imogen shook her head vigorously. "We were acquaintances in Spain some time ago. When I moved back home, I didn't know many people, so I got in touch with Gavin. We saw each other from time to time, but we hadn't met up for ages."

"Tell me briefly what happened today. How did you know Hannah was locked in the game larder?"

Imogen paused. This was her theatrical moment and her acting needed to be convincing. "Like I said, I err hadn't seen Gavin for three or more weeks and he wasn't answering my calls or texts. I suppose I was worried. So, as I wasn't working today, I decided to catch a train out from London and visit him."

In the bleached moonlight, PC Morrison's expression stayed non-committal as he held her gaze. His pen was poised above his notebook. Why wasn't he making any notes?

"I'm sorry, Mrs Wilson. Could you repeat what you just said?"

Imogen repeated her lines.

"So." PC Morrison put his notebook and pen down on his knee and steepled his fingers. "You're telling me that, on the day Gavin Winter locked your niece in his game larder you just happened to drop by for a chat?"

Imogen felt blood rising to her face. Was he even allowed to ask her a question like this? Didn't she have rights? From somewhere out in the dense woodland, the other side of the garden fence, she heard the soft, long grunt of that deer again. PC Morrison didn't seem to have heard it. Was it a deer or was it a cry inside her own head?

"If you've been in contact with Mr Winter, I expect you have his phone number? Could you give me the number please?"

"I'm not sure if I have it," she replied, buying time.

"Let's have a look at your phone," said PC Morrison. His colleague's footsteps crunched back across the gravel. He caught her eye and they exchanged a look.

They didn't believe her. Imogen snatched a look at her watch. It was almost midnight. "Are there trains to London at this time?" she asked.

"I'm sorry, Mrs Wilson," said PC Morrison, fixing her with a hard stare. "But a serious crime has been committed. This is your niece we're talking about. I'd have thought you'd be doing anything you could to cooperate. This is an informal chat. We're talking to you as a witness, but the circumstances and your involvement don't seem to add up..."

234

Chapter Fifty

Imogen
August 2019

By the time she and the police officers had finished, the last train to London was long gone. PC Musgrove dropped her colleague at the police station and offered to drive Imogen to Blakeswood. The journey on empty roads took only fifty minutes but neither of them spoke.

"Will you be all right here?" the officer asked, eyeing the closed iron gates as she dropped Imogen outside The Old Rectory.

"Thanks. I have my key." She hooked it out of a pocket in her handbag and scrambled out of the passenger seat, waiting on the kerb until the rear lights of the patrol car disappeared from view.

Imogen pushed but the gates didn't budge. Miriam and Max had sealed themselves inside for the night. She remembered the outside handle had been broken for years and reached her hand in through the ornamental ironwork and felt around for the inside catch. She flipped it up, the gate yielded, and she went in.

She unlocked the front door, knowing her parents would have been fast asleep for hours. Since Max had started nocturnal wandering, they never activated the burglar alarm at night, so she padded up the stairs to her own room, lay down on the bed and fell asleep.

It was late when she woke next morning but the house was quiet. She looked out of her bedroom window at the lawn, mown with diagonal stripes, in keeping with her mother's fetish for a perfectly manicured garden. While she was staying there, she hadn't noticed a gardener. Did her mother do all the work herself? Were they too skinflint to pay a gardener?

She went downstairs and checked all the rooms. Empty. The French doors, leading from the kitchen onto the upper terrace were wide open so perhaps Miriam was outside gathering supplies for those endless salads. She walked outside, down the steps leading to the lower terrace and along the path, passing the walled kitchen garden. At the far end of the lawn, a flash of colour drew her eyes to the woodland. Someone was inside the playhouse. As she drew closer, she could see it was her mother.

Miriam was wearing sunglasses and seemed to be dozing on the bench. She didn't notice Imogen until she ducked in under the low doorway. Inside, the pitch of the roof was high enough for an adult woman to stand up. When it came to houses, even a playhouse, only the best had been good enough for the Stapleton children. Unless, Imogen reflected bitterly, you were the forgotten daughter living in a foreign country. When you were out of sight, no one cared if you had a house or not.

"Mum," she said. "Wake up."

Miriam stirred. She raised her hand and pushed her sunglasses up onto the top of her head and blinked. "Imogen?" she said in a voice, empty of warmth. "Were we expecting you?"

"I thought this was my home." said Imogen. "Do I have to make an appointment?"

"It is. Of course. You surprised me, that's all." She shuffled along the bench to make a space for Imogen to sit but Imogen remained standing.

"So where's the welcome? Tea and sympathy for Simon's grieving widow didn't last long, did it?" Why was she behaving like this? She'd come here to ask her mother for information but, within seconds, they were duelling again, returning to the touchy stand-off that began in childhood and erupted into a full feud in Tunisia.

"I don't know what you're talking about," Miriam snapped. "We offered you a place to live here with us, but you've moved on. We're glad you're making a good career. Your dad and I listen to your programme every day, you know. He refuses to miss it. If you're on late, I have to record it for him."

Imogen gave her a cold stare. "At least Dad cares about both his daughters."

Miriam refused to rise to the bait. She brushed away a spider's web dangling from a beam. Imogen's ankle was still sore from the day before and now the heel of her sandal caught on something. She looked down and noticed the floor of the playhouse was rotting.

"This place is falling apart and it's claustrophobic," she said, feeling a sudden urge to see the sky but, when she got outside, clouds had blocked the sun.

Miriam picked up her trowel and followed Imogen to the woodland copse where Imogen and Rachel had played as children, building dens and tree houses, hiding from their friends and from the grown-ups. The trees had reared up to reach their full height and the paths they used to run around were choked with ferns and brambles but the grass around the old bench had been trampled flat. Someone, presumably Miriam, still sat here.

"Sit down, Mum. I need to talk to you."

"If it's about money again, I'm afraid the answer's still no," said Miriam, a mix of emotions contorting her expression. "There's something I need to tell you. Rachel's been urging me to do it, but I couldn't face it. Until now."

"More family secrets? Should I be anxious?"

Miriam swept some leaves off the bench with the edge of her trowel before sitting and beckoned to Imogen to sit beside her. Her voice faltered as she recounted how, in the years after George's death, Max's consultancy business had failed.

"We were on the verge of bankruptcy," she said. "I thought we would lose everything." She twirled her sunglasses in her hand and took a breath before continuing. "Rachel was already a part-owner of that student house in London, so we transferred it all to her to shield it from our creditors. Had we been made bankrupt, that transaction would probably have been overturned and we'd have lost it, anyway, but Rachel came up with a solution." As she spoke Rachel's name, Miriam's expression softened.

Imogen winced. She hadn't even had coffee. Now she needed a drink,

"Rachel's property business was embryonic at that time," continued Miriam. "Hannah was a toddler and they were all still living in the London house and renting out rooms. But Rachel had invested in a couple of other properties."

Imogen shot her an angry look, but Miriam held up her hand for silence. "No Imogen, we didn't help her with those purchases. Rachel took out buy to let mortgages and it was due to her business success, she was able to raise a loan on The Old Rectory. It meant we could pay our creditors and stay in our home."

Imogen swallowed. "So you mean none of this…" She stood up and, with a sweep of her arm that took in the whole of the grounds and the house, said, "None of this actually belongs to you and Dad?"

"That's right. It belongs to the bank. And Rachel has been making the repayments."

"So The Old Rectory is nothing more than a stage set!" Imogen exclaimed. She and Simon had once made a trip to a desert region in southern Spain and seen the sets – all front and no substance – where spaghetti westerns were filmed. "There's nothing solid behind it."

"Yes. Rachel gives us money to supplement our state pensions. Your father and I are penniless."

Imogen paced, flattening grass in a semi-circle that took her halfway across the lawn and back, thinking rapidly. In the settling of her entitlements, her mother still owed her, but it looked as if Rachel would have to be the one to pay. But she mustn't let this distract her from her purpose.

She walked back to the bench. Her mother hadn't moved but she lifted her eyes as if beseeching understanding or forgiveness. Well, she could forget that.

Imogen glared down at her mother who was fiddling with her bracelet, twisting it round and round her wrist.

"I've heard Howard's back in England," she said.

Miriam's head jerked up. "Who told you that?" A slight inflection crept into her voice.

"Stop acting defensive. I know he went to Rachel's office, with Dad, and made an offer to buy into her business. What's that about?"

"No one told me anything about that, Imogen. Rachel was livid! I've seen Howard once since he came back. Your father invited him for lunchtime drinks around Easter time. Rachel was here. They must have discussed it then."

"So where is he? Why is everyone hiding this from me?"

"Not all this again!" said Miriam, clearly agitated. "Can't you leave the past buried as it should be?"

"No I can't. I want to see him. What's his address or number?"

Miriam groaned. "Honestly, Imogen, I don't know it."

"You're lying. You're trying to stop me seeing him. It was you who forced us apart."

"This has gone on too long. I'm not having this conversation." Miriam stood and headed up the garden with Imogen limping along behind her. When Miriam stopped to gather a lettuce and some tomatoes she'd picked earlier, she grabbed hold of her mother's wrist. Miriam dropped the lettuce. They both watched it roll under the broad leaves of a rhubarb plant.

"I'm serious," said Imogen, her fingers tightening on her mother's arm. "If you don't get Howard's contact details for me, I'll tell Dad what happened in Tunisia. I'll tell him everything."

Chapter Fifty-One

Rachel
August 2019

Rachel went with Hannah to the police station where her statement was recorded on video by specialist officers. As soon as the recording session finished and they were walking back to the car, Hannah breathed a huge sigh and said, "That's over. I never want to speak about it again."

"That's fine with me," said Rachel. She wondered if Hannah should have counselling or other psychological support? Perhaps distraction would be best, initially. "When do you want to start your work experience at Stapleton Kumar?"

"Tomorrow," Hannah replied. "But I'll need something to wear."

"Sure. We'll stop off in town," said Rachel with a smile, "we'll have lunch and do some clothes shopping."

Over the next week their half hour drive to the office became a safe space for talking, suspended between the pressures of home and work life. It was so long since Hannah had confided in her but now she shared her feelings about Luke and it was clear she accepted it was over. Rachel took the role of compassionate listener and held back from giving advice.

"Why doesn't Karen come any more?" Hannah asked.

Traffic was crawling towards the motorway and Rachel risked shifting her eyes from the road to glance at her daughter. Losing Karen had been inevitable. She must have felt Rachel betrayed her.

"She handed in her notice," Rachel replied. "After that day." There was no need to say what day that was. It was seared into both their memories.

"Was it my fault?"

"I don't think so. To be honest, she should have left years ago. To find a better job and move on with her life, I mean." But Karen had been stuck. Did she really expect Gavin to return? The thought of what that man had done to Hannah made her choke. She and Jack had given witness statements to the police and been assured Gavin would be caught, very soon, though if he'd been heading for Dover, he'd probably have driven down through France to Spain. She made a mental note to phone PC Musgrove for an update.

"You and Dad don't do much together, do you?" said Hannah.

"What do you mean?" What might have been intended as a harmless remark found its target. Rachel winced.

"He's been spending so much time away lately."

"It's his fitness regime, Hannah. He's obsessed with triathlons. Everyone's allowed a midlife crisis. At least he didn't get a Harley Davidson."

"And what about you, Mum?" continued Hannah. "You work, you hang out with me, you forget to book a holiday, even though you've been crazy-busy at work and need a break. Do you call that a life?"

"That's enough, Hannah," said Rachel in a sharp tone. Was that all Hannah thought her life amounted to? Why would her daughter choose this moment to attack her? The traffic started moving and Rachel focused on the road. The rest of the journey passed in silence.

In the car park, Rachel opened the boot to get her laptop and Hannah stalked off ahead into the building. She looked so grown up in her black jacket, bought on their shopping trip. It was the kind of jacket Hannah could throw on to transform her jeans, or a short skirt, into office wear. Why was it so uniquely easy for mothers and daughters to inflict guilt and pain on one another? she wondered and, with a jolt, remembered a phone call she hadn't returned.

It was impossible to make a private call in the office so she stopped in the lobby, sat down on one of the waiting area sofas, looking out through the plate glass windows at a strip of garden that had yet to be planted, and tapped her mother's number.

"Rachel. Thank goodness." The slight quaver in Miriam's voice made Rachel shiver. Her mother didn't do emotion. These days she operated within a limited range: brisk, stern, matter-of-fact or angry. She hadn't heard this much distress in her mother's voice since after George's death when her mother had suffered a breakdown.

Imogen had already left for Europe and Rachel was stranded on the peninsula between school and a future, now fogged, with no counselling or help. When she and her father visited Miriam in the clinic, they'd find her sitting in the garden, but she would only talk about the plants. As the summer stretched towards autumn, the nurses placed a rug over her mother's knees and left her outside, staring into space like an elderly lady. But the drugs she was on worked their miracle and, by early October, when Rachel was leaving to start her law degree in London, Miriam left the clinic and donned the mask she was to wear for the next twenty years. Even when Max's business failed a few years later, she shrugged, kept calm and carried on.

"Tell me what's wrong, Mum," Rachel asked.

"It's Imogen," said Miriam. "She's been threatening me." She sniffed. "I'm sorry, darling. I shouldn't burden you with this."

Rachel's heartbeat quickened. "What?"

"Imogen twists everything," said Miriam. "She always has. Did she talk to you about him..?" Her voice trailed off as if the weave of her sentence was unravelling.

"Do you mean George?" Rachel said her brother's name with an effort.

"No, not George. Howard. Did she tell you about Howard?"

"Howard Dixon? That dreadful man who thought it was okay to waltz into my office and offer to buy a share of my business?" The intrusion had been like an assault and she felt

242

the white heat of rage whenever she recalled it.

"I'm sorry that happened, Rachel. Your father forgets to tell me things. When he talks business he can be so convincing. I thought you must have discussed the investment when you met Howard at our drinks do."

"I told him to sling his hook."

"Yes," her mother's voice broke up again, "I can imagine you saying that. But he must have left you his contact details – you know – in case you changed your mind?"

"For heaven's sake, Mum! What are you saying?"

Miriam continued in a flat voice. "I need Howard's number, Rachel. Urgently."

Rachel remembered Howard sliding his business card to her across the table in the meeting room. She'd left it there for the cleaners to throw away. But didn't Howard give his business card to Michael Kumar when they bumped into him by the lift?

"I don't get why you're asking me. You invited him to your party. You must have it."

"It was your father he contacted and who invited him to drinks – though when he turned up, Max didn't have a clue who he was."

"Well, get his number from Dad," said Rachel. She had a ton of work waiting, her finger itched to tap the red button and end the call.

"I can't," said Miriam. "There are reasons…"

"What do you need it for?"

Miriam sighed. "Imogen wants it. In fact she's demanded I get it for her."

Far from getting answers, this was turning into a cryptic mental wrestling match.

"Howard was in Tunisia, Rachel, when your dad was working there. He and Imogen became close. Perhaps too close."

"Wha-at?" An earlier memory returned – Howard following her into the kitchen and asking for her sister's address. Now, it seemed, Imogen wanted to contact him. What was going on?

"Are you saying…" asked Rachel, slowly, "that Imogen and

243

Howard had an affair?"

"I suppose that's what you might call it."

"But Imogen was only a child!" exclaimed Rachel, feeling sick.

"Not really. She was seventeen and he'd have been around thirty-three."

"All the same ..."

"Listen, Rachel. A lot of things happened in Tunisia and there's more I need to tell you. Some of it your father knows, some he doesn't but if Imogen talks to him I don't know how it would affect his condition. He might not understand or perhaps it might destroy him."

An idea flashed into Rachel's mind – so shocking that she pushed it away.

"Did you cover something up, Mum? Something huge?"

From the other end of the line she heard a haunting sound like a sob. "I'll tell you when I see you, I promise, but not on the phone. Do you have Howard's contact details or not?"

Rachel relented. "I didn't keep them, but I think he gave his business card to Michael. I'll ask him when he gets back from holiday."

"Please, Rachel. Ring or email Michael now."

"All right, Mum. I'll do it." She ended the call and let her phone lie in her lap. Her parents had spent two years in Tunisia and Imogen must have been with them for almost eighteen months. In all that time, Rachel had never visited. The first summer her mother had come home, but by the second year, Miriam was expecting George and was too exhausted to travel. She hadn't seen either her mother – or Imogen – at all that year. That second summer, her father came home for a month and during other school holidays she was shipped off to stay with Aunt Susan and, once, to volunteer on an archaeological dig organised by the school. At the time, she'd accepted this was the status quo. If they'd wanted to see her, she could easily have travelled to Tunisia. But what if they didn't want *her* to see *them*?

Chapter Fifty-Two

Imogen
September 2019

Miriam didn't ring. Howard's address and phone number arrived by email and sat for two days in the Hotmail account Imogen rarely checked. She stared at the number and, for a heart tensing moment, her fingers itched to dial it straight away but, after two decades, what would she say? She tapped the address into Google maps, stuck her feet into flat-heeled boots and locked the Lazy Lucy.

"Drinks at mine tonight?" Bill called out to her as she walked along the towpath past his boat. "Seven o'clock."

Imogen didn't commit. She raised her fingers to her lips and blew him a kiss. Bill reached up to pluck it from the air. He was in touch with his inner child, for sure. She'd grown fond of him. She sensed Bill had spotted a vacancy in her life and, in his clumsy yet endearing way, imagined he was edging closer to filling it. He'd invited her to spend a weekend with him in Dartmouth where, it appeared, he owned a quayside cottage but no boat. So, being a boat obsessive, he rented out his cottage and lived most of his time in London on the canal. What was wrong with some people?

At the junction of Blomfield Road and Warwick Avenue, she turned left and crossed the hump-backed canal bridge. September's weather was outshining August and the silver tables, on the quayside at the Waterside café, glinted. Hanging baskets were overflowing with trailing blooms and the daily specials, chalked on the blackboard, tempted her. With an effort, she picked up her pace and marched on towards

Paddington station.

At Oxford Circus, Imogen followed the directional arrow on her phone's map beyond familiar department stores into the smart, moneyed streets behind. She walked on until the crowds dispersed and entered a street of white houses, Guildford Terrace. Getting Howard's address, as well as his phone number, was a coup. It saved the awkwardness of playing telephone tag or sifting through social media with the risk of being ignored or blocked.

Despite the pristine elegance of its buildings, Guildford Terrace felt faintly claustrophobic. She slowed down to read the brass plaques of doctors and dentists; architects or solicitors, unsure whether she was approaching Howard's office or the flat where he lived. Her mother had emailed a photo of Howard's business card, with no covering message. The card had a business name 'Dixon Enterprises' and an address, 44D Guildford Terrace. What if it was a false frontage – mailing address for business use? Her heart sank.

She dawdled the last few paces to number 44. The front door was painted black, with Grecian-style columns on either side and an array of name plates each with a doorbell entry system. The ground floor was a dental surgery. The first-floor names were more discreet about their professions but, from the second floor upwards, the buzzers were name-tagged with a hint of domesticity: *Mr A S and Mrs W V Johnson, Philippe de Courcy* and, finally, not 'Dixon Enterprises' but 'Mr H L V Dixon'. So the enterprises, whatever they were, must be run from his home.

With her finger poised to jab the buzzer, Imogen hesitated. What if there was a Mrs Dixon? Or a girlfriend? What did she intend to say to Howard after all this time? Yet this was a performance she'd been rehearsing for since she was a teenager. She'd fantasised about it during the darker days with Simon. But her rehearsal had been sketchy, she hadn't learnt her lines.

Tentatively, she pressed. A light flashed and she realised a video entry system was filming her and projecting her image. What's more, it was probably being monitored, not only from inside the flat, but remotely, perhaps by Howard from his mobile phone. She felt a rush of humiliation. What if he'd seen her? What if a Mrs Dixon was inside and deciding whether to answer the door?

She smoothed back her hair and jutted her chin towards the camera as she pressed the buzzer again. She waited, feeling a tightness in her chest. No response. She turned to leave. She had Howard's phone number. She could make something up - pretend she was involved in Rachel's property business and was making contact to further discussions. That was it, she'd do that.

She clumped back down the steps to face another Friday night with only Mark and Bill – the Tweedledum and Tweedle-dee of her middle years, as she thought of them – to fill the emptiness. Jenna and Sam had been ordered to move on. They'd been living on their boat for almost a year, but it turned out they only had a continuous cruiser licence and were supposed to move on every fourteen days and travel a set distance.

"Does that mean your licence won't be renewed?" Imogen had asked Jenna, wondering what she would do in similar circumstances.

Jenna had nodded, her face shiny with recent tears. "It could get even worse. The letter says enforcement proceedings have started. I've heard through the online forums that they can confiscate your boat."

"What will you do?" Imogen had asked.

"We're heading for the Midlands tomorrow. I'll have to leave my job but we're hoping Sam's boss will let him work remotely. Or at least bung some freelance projects his way."

Imogen had poured Jenna two strong gins and given her a bottle of champagne as a leaving gift. It was a relic of Gavin, she no longer had a taste for. She watched Jenna stumbling along the tow path, her shoulders hunched in defeat, and thought about the meaning of home: her parents rattling around in The Old Rectory, the grim tower block flat she'd shared with Simon, her sister's picture-perfect cottage. The Lazy Lucy had given her respite, but it hadn't healed her.

She paused on the pavement outside number 44 Guildford Terrace, pulled out her phone and messaged Bill to ask if he had food for the evening. He pinged straight back, accepting her offer to do some shopping on the way back. At least she would get to choose the menu. Mark had once served up a whole casserole of offal. The memory of it made her want to puke.

As she stashed her phone away and slung her bag over her shoulder, a tall man with silver grey hair rounded the corner and stared at Imogen. Since hitting forty she'd become a magnet for men of a certain age. She turned and walked swiftly in the opposite direction. If she took the long way round, she could swing by Selfridges and buy supper in their food hall. It would be pricey but Bill and Mark would chip in towards the cost.

"Hey!" A voice called out.

She glanced behind her. The man had caught up with her and was a few feet away. Imogen's jaw dropped open with surprise.

"Wait!" He strode towards her. "Imogen! It is you. I caught you on my door phone camera."

She stopped. "Well, here I am," she said, conscious of her rapid heartbeat.

Howard's brown eyes locked onto hers. He held out his arms. She hesitated. Was this ever after? And was it even happy? Her feet edged forward. She let his arms encircle her and pull her closer. His after shave had the spicy scent of hot countries, but the citrus notes were a little too feminine.

She thought of Bill and Mark. Soon they would carry their folding garden table along the towpath and set up chairs beside the Lazy Lucy, waiting for her to appear with their supper. Bill would go hungry from now on.

Chapter Fifty-Three

Rachel
September 2019

Rachel agonised over her mother's revelation about Howard and Imogen's relationship. Howard repelled her – an arrogant silver fox, worming his way into the Stapleton family, mounting an assault on her business when it was in difficulties. She had to concede he might have been good looking twenty years ago but all the same …

The more she thought of it, the wilder her suspicions became until she felt as if she was going mad. The only way forward was to test the evidence with an expert and who better than Jack. Except, as Hannah had pointed out, Jack was hardly ever at home. Even though there were numerous triathlons in Surrey, Hampshire and Berkshire, last weekend he'd travelled all the way to the Lake District and arrived home late on Sunday night, too tired to do anything but shower and fall into bed. The following evening he was out again, training.

By Tuesday morning Rachel could wait no longer. They rarely discussed anything important over breakfast, but Hannah had finished her work experience and was having a lie-in, so it seemed a good time.

"When I was at Mum's last week she told me something shocking," she began, handing Jack a mug of coffee.

"What was that?" asked Jack.

"Remember that man I told you about? The one who was at my parents' drinks do and then turned up at my office with Dad?" For some reason her jaw clenched, and she couldn't force out his name.

"Um, maybe. I think Michael mentioned him to me. Didn't he want to buy into your business? Howard something."

"Yes, him," said Rachel. "They worked with him in Tunisia." She paused to check she had his attention. "And while they were there, Howard and Imogen had an affair."

Jack's head jerked up and he gave her an odd, almost shifty, look. "With Imogen, nothing would surprise me."

"What do you mean?" Suddenly Rachel was feeling defensive of her sister. "She was only seventeen, Jack. Don't you think it's wrong she was seduced by this smooth-talking older man?"

"She wasn't underage."

"What are you saying?"

"Nothing." Jack got to his feet, dusting toast crumbs off his lap onto the floor. "Listen, I have to shoot. My first meeting's at eight-thirty."

Rachel sighed. There was no point in talking to him in this mood. "Okay. See you later."

She watched him leave. Why had he reacted so strangely? There was more she wanted to say to him, but the moment had passed.

All day she thought about when to tell Imogen about her planned peace offering of a half share of the proceeds of the London house. It might not fix the past, but perhaps it could mend the future.

Meanwhile, her own future plans were slowly taking shape. Leaving Stapleton Kumar would be scary but, now Michael had returned from holiday, it was only fair to share her thoughts with him. She booked a meeting room where they could talk privately away from Carrie's watchful eyes and Michael joined her, bringing his Tupperware box of sandwiches and put it on the middle of the table. "Help yourself, Rach. There's plenty."

"Thanks. Just the one." She helped herself to a chicken and avocado sandwich. The meeting room no longer smelled of polished wood but like a works canteen.

"How's Carrie been?" asked Michael, biting in to his second sandwich.

"I'm pretty sure she's job hunting," replied Rachel. "But with the economic uncertainty she must have decided to stay put. For now. While Hannah was here, she cheered up. I guess it's me she can't get along with."

A lock of her hair swung into Rachel's face and she raked it back behind her ear. Over the summer, she hadn't even made time for the hairdressers. "It was hectic while you were away, Michael," she said. "But there's plenty of good news. The bank loan's agreed and the terms are acceptable. I've left the paperwork in your in tray for your signature."

"You did a great negotiation, Rachel."

"Thanks." She blushed. "That's not all. We've sold two more of the Elmglades properties at only a small discount, including the one we've had fixed up after the Higgins family trashed it."

Michael whooped with delight. He must feel his vision for the future of the business being validated. Now she was going to dampen his celebration.

"How would you feel," she began, feeling her way, "if I decided to sell my share in Stapleton Kumar?"

His eyes widened into a horrified stare. "Come again?" He fumbled to straighten his tie but, for once, he wasn't wearing one. "I never expected that," he began. "I mean, it's your business."

"The thing is, Mike," she said. "It's been costing me. And I don't just mean in the financial sense. I won't pretend that our fragile cash flow position didn't stress me. But, mainly, it's because I'm seeing my life clearly for the first time and it's passing me by. I want to go back to practise law. And there are family reasons too. Hannah's practically grown up. In two years, she'll be leaving for university."

Michael listened intently. "Go on."

"I've spent so little time with my daughter. I want to change that. A couple of times this year I've almost lost her."

She thought about the times Hannah had lied to her, skipped school and ended up in life-threatening danger. Would that have happened if they'd been closer? What hurt her most was how, when Hannah had needed emotional support, she'd run

251

away to London to confide in Imogen, reaching out, not for her mother, but for a facsimile of her.

"How would you feel about putting out feelers," she asked Michael, "to see if anyone's interested in buying out my share?"

Certain properties in their portfolio were ring fenced and belonged to Rachel only, including the London student house and the debt-laden Old Rectory. When Michael joined her, he'd raised his own funds to buy into the business and now owned a forty percent share of the remainder.

"Who were you thinking of?" asked Michael. "Someone to take over your role? Or a more arm's length investor, like your father's friend, Mr Dixon?"

Rachel felt a rush of nausea. She swallowed. "Absolutely not. I wouldn't force a charlatan like Howard Dixon on you."

"I don't know," said Michael, leaning back in his chair. "He didn't strike me as that bad. He has a forensic brain and decades of business experience. Admittedly he's from a different industry but a fresh eye might be helpful. He could be an asset."

Rachel gaped at him. "You don't mean that?"

Michael must have read the shock on her face. He ploughed on, "The thing is, Rach, and I need time to think, if it's not me and you taking Stapleton Kumar forward, I wouldn't look for someone with a property background. I could hire in that expertise. A numbers person is what we need for the next stage of expansion."

Rachel averted her eyes. "It sounds like you've already had a private conversation with Howard."

Michael made a quick nervous movement. "I admit he rang me, and I agreed to meet him for an informal chat." He cleared his throat. "He asked about your reaction to his offer. Wanted to know if your blunt refusal was a final word."

"And you never mentioned it to me?" Michael was the person she trusted most, after Jack and Hannah.

He shook his head. "I knew you were dead against it so I didn't think you'd want to hear. But I got the impression Mr Dixon was more closely acquainted with your family than you'd said."

"Why was that?" asked Rachel.

"Do you remember ringing me, while I was on holiday, and asking me to email Dixon's contact details urgently? It was lucky I had his business card in my wallet."

"Yes."

"You said a member of your family wanted to contact him, but that made no sense because your father brought him to the office. When I had that meeting with Dixon, he asked if I'd ever met Imogen. He wanted to know where she was now."

There was something relentless about the way Howard and Imogen were circling round each other, edging closer after all these years. A terrible suspicion had been nagging at Rachel, ever since her mother's revelation. It would make sense of why she'd never been invited to spend any of her school holidays with them in Tunisia because, if her hunch was right, they wouldn't have wanted her to see Imogen.

What if Imogen had become pregnant and George wasn't Miriam's child after all? Was it possible the baby was Imogen's and her parents had persuaded her not to ruin her future? Might they have covered it up and registered George as their own son?

Chapter Fifty-Four

Imogen
September 2019

"Have you ever been married?" Imogen asked Howard on that first evening when he swept her up from the kerbside and ushered her into his flat, as if he was Professor Henry Higgins and she was Eliza Doolittle. There were other things she needed to ask him – unfinished business from their time in Tunisia – but, for now, those could wait. She held out her champagne flute for Howard to refill. The champagne was vintage, but she didn't comment. For now, she would hide her sophistication in case Howard preferred a naiver version, reminiscent of the girl he'd known in Tunisia.

"I was married, briefly, when I lived in the States," he said. "Does it matter?" He gazed at her over the rim of his glass as he savoured the champagne.

"And will the first Mrs Dixon come to reclaim you?" It sounded clumsy but she had to ask. At this stage of her life there was no room for false moves.

"I settled my account over there, if that's what you mean. My ex-wife, Sasha, and I owe one another nothing." He lowered his eyes. "I don't think I ever properly got over you."

What bullshit, she thought, not letting her smile slip. They were sitting facing one another on his identical grey suede sofas, Howard's brown eyes gleamed and his face had a satisfied, pinkish glow. Every time he topped up her glass, or offered a bowl of cashew nuts, he let his hand brush hers or stroked her cheek. If this gave him a charge of sexual electricity, the circuit didn't complete. Imogen felt nothing.

No matter. This was the role she'd cast for herself and she'd already passed the audition. Out of nowhere, it sparked a fresh resentment towards Rachel who could support herself and her family; had a delightful daughter and a good, uncomplicated man, Jack, who loved her. Recalling the evening Jack had spent on the Lazy Lucy, Imogen remembered she still had the backpack he'd left behind. It would make a useful stage prop. She'd bring it with her when she moved her stuff into Howard's flat.

Shadows filtered in through tall sash windows and lights came on in trees in the square beyond, so the late September evening hinted at Christmases yet to come. Howard stood up to draw the curtains.

"Leave them open please."

Imogen walked across to the window and put her arms around his waist. She needed to see outside.

***

Imogen made Howard wait a fortnight before agreeing to move in with him and shared her plans with no one. Throughout her adult life, she'd chosen when to step off grid and when to resurface. Soon her parents would switch on Radio Denim for their daily listening vigil and wonder why her voice no longer featured. Did her mother still listen? She wasn't proud of her tactics at their last meeting, but she'd achieved what she needed, and it was too late for regret.

She wrote a decorous letter of resignation to Radio Denim but, when she saw the relief in Damien's face at the news of her departure, she insisted on working her notice so she could plague him for a while longer.

"Do you know, Damien," she said, "I reckon your father named his radio station after you." She'd arrived late for her night shift and he was pacing the studio like a caged leopard, with spots to match, though his were pink.

"What do you mean?" he asked, taking her jacket away to hang up and pushing her into the broadcaster's chair.

"Well 'denim' is practically an anagram of Damien, isn't it? Maybe your dad can't spell. He should have called it 'A

Denim'." She put on her headphones to block out his voice, adjusting the headband to reduce the clamping force.

Damien scowled and his acne-scarred cheeks turned pinker. Perhaps she'd plant a few gremlins in the systems as a leaving gift. But technology wasn't her strongest skillset. She let the thought pass.

Rachel continued to ring, and Imogen let her messages roll over to voicemail. One message had hinted, in that old-fashioned prose newspaper personal columns used to use, that, if she got in touch, she might 'learn something to her advantage'. It must be a trap.

Behind the hushed walls of Guildford Terrace, Imogen found the leisured life she'd craved and it sparked inertia. She drifted from room to room, sensing life going on elsewhere and pined for the carefree days on the Lazy Lucy: the swish of water; the neighbours, so close she could hear them arguing or brushing their teeth; the sizzle of olive oil hitting the pan as someone cooked dinner.

Now she was securely in residence she decided to tackle Howard.

Most evenings, when she wasn't working, she and Howard ate out at local restaurants. He had a taste for fine dining and Imogen sensed she would have to fight against the creep of calories. On the evening after her final shift at Radio Denim, she bought fillet steak and green salad for supper, served herself a postage stamp sized piece of meat and gave the rest to Howard. It reminded her of her childhood when Miriam would buy two steaks and give one to Max, cutting the second steak into three pieces for herself and her daughters.

"That was excellent, darling," said Howard, picking a shred of beef from between his teeth with his fingernail.

Imogen averted her eyes. "Come and sit with me," she said, taking her glass of red wine across to the sofa and patting the place next to her. "Tell me about your business projects. Are you thinking of taking a directorship? Or simply investing?"

Howard settled down and stretched his legs out in front of him. A smile hovered on his lips. "I'm still turning over options," he said. "I have the money to invest when the right opportunity comes up."

"You were interested in Stapleton Kumar, weren't you?"

"How did you hear that?" He turned to look at her, his voice surprisingly sharp.

"Don't fret. It helped me to find you."

"I don't think Rachel was receptive to my advances." He gave a weak grin. "Sorry – bad joke."

Imogen winced but she'd nudged the conversation in the right direction, so she pushed on. "There must be a way. I'll talk to her. I'm sure I can persuade her." There was a poetic symmetry in the idea of Howard – and herself by extension – taking a stake, or preferably ownership, in Rachel's business. Not that she could tolerate a close connection between Rachel and Howard. One way or another, he would need to supplant her.

Howard changed the subject. "I don't want to get embroiled in a business that draws on too much of my expertise and time," he said, stroking her hand. "I've grafted all my life. I want to relax. I want us to travel. I thought I – we – might buy a place in the sun. Perhaps Spain – or Ibiza, if you like?"

Imogen shuddered. "Not Ibiza." She was never going there again.

"Tuscany then?"

Imogen nodded. "Tuscany would be perfect." But she wasn't ready for Tuscany. Not yet. With Howard as an ally, she could move forward with her plans.

Chapter Fifty-Five

Rachel
October 2019

As October arrived and students returned to university, the house Rachel owned in Streatham stood empty of tenants when it should have been bringing in rental income. The estate agent had recommended a presale facelift before putting it on the market.

It was time to tell her parents about her plan to sell it and give half the proceeds to Imogen. And at the same time, she could confront her mother with her suspicions about what happened in Tunisia.

Overnight an early frost had settled on her car's windscreen and she sat in the driving seat with the fan and heating on full blast waiting for it to clear. As she drove to Blakeswood, she thought of her seventeen-year-old sister, whisked away from school and her dreams of drama school, to live in a foreign country with nothing to do. Her parents should have looked out for Imogen and kept her safe. The idea that George was Imogen's son wouldn't leave her mind. Had Imogen covered up her pregnancy until it was too late? Perhaps, in Tunisia, abortion wasn't possible. Did they make a family decision for Imogen to lie low, perhaps give birth at home, and that their parents would register George's birth and bring him up as their own? Yet surely, if that was the case, Imogen would have seemed fonder of George? Or had she hardened her heart when she agreed to have her child taken from her?

She reached The Old Rectory, parked and let herself in with her own key. Her mother was pacing the hall, wearing a shabby pink cardigan. Behind her, on the console table, yellow chrysanthemums were drooping in their vase, shedding shrivelled leaves onto the floor. Her mother didn't seem to have noticed.

"What is it?" Rachel kissed her mother's cheek, but Miriam shied away and pulled the cardigan tighter.

"You haven't visited in weeks."

"Well, not quite weeks but I've had a lot to think about."

Miriam flinched. "I was wondering when you'd ask. What took you so long?" She ran water into the kettle and took a cafetière out of the cupboard. "I have something to tell you," she said. "I've finally told Imogen about our near bankruptcy and how you took on the mortgage on The Old Rectory. So you don't have to worry any more. She knows the truth."

Rachel laughed out loud and flung her arms around her mother. "Thank you, Mum. I so want to make everything right between us. That's a huge step."

"I don't believe that, Rachel. Nothing will fix it."

"I have a plan, too," said Rachel, her smile widening. "I'm selling the house in Sunnyhill Road and I'm going to split the proceeds with Imogen. She'll have exactly the same as you gave me to get started."

Confusion passed across Miriam's face. She touched her chest, moving her hand in an unnatural motion – almost as if she was making the sign of the cross but she'd never been religious. "Well it might help but I'm not sure. Knowing Imogen…"

"Yes, it will. It must," said Rachel.

"Have you told her?" Miriam prodded.

Rachel shook her head. "Not yet. I know the first thing she'll ask is 'How much?' But the house is in a poor state and wouldn't fetch its full market value. I'm getting some work done – a new kitchen and bathroom, plumbing, ceiling repairs. Imogen's always asking about it, so I thought I'd ask her round to see the house and tell her my plan then."

The kettle boiled and Miriam turned away to make coffee while Rachel pulled out a kitchen chair and sat down, gathering her thoughts. She noticed how her mother's hand shook as she poured water into the cafetière and pushed down the plunger without leaving it to stand.

Miriam took the seat opposite Rachel and folded her hands in front of her on the table.

"Those things you told me on the phone about Tunisia," Rachel began. "They really shocked me."

On sunless days, the tall French windows kept the kitchen colder than the air outside. Miriam's face had a blueish tinge. Rachel poured the coffee and slid a cup across to her mother. She curled her fingers around her own cup, letting the welcome warmth seep into her hands. When Miriam didn't reply she prompted. "You promised to tell me about Imogen's 'affair' with Howard."

Miriam stared down at her drink but didn't pick it up.

"Mum, is there something else you haven't told me? I mean, did Howard abuse her in some way?"

"No." Her mother shook her head emphatically. "Nothing like that."

Rachel paused. Miriam had promised to tell her when they met in person. Perhaps she needed silence. Time to think. Minutes ticked by. Whenever their eyes met, Miriam dropped her gaze.

"Okay," said Rachel, finally. "It looks like I'll have to ask the questions. Did Imogen get pregnant?"

Miriam gave a quick shake of her head. Rachel pressed on. "You're making it hard for me to say, but I've been wondering – was George Imogen's son? And did you and Dad cover it up and adopt him?"

Miriam blanched and found her voice. "No, Rachel." She pulled the sleeve of her shabby cardigan down over one hand and fidgeted with it. "I can see how you might come to that conclusion," she said. "But it's far from the truth. As I told you, Imogen did have an affair with Howard. She was very young and imagined she was in love with him."

"So George *wasn't* her son?" She wasn't ready to abandon the idea. It would explain so many things, including why her sister came home from Tunisia brimming with resentment.

"No Rachel. The truth is worse – if that's possible."

Rachel inched her chair away from the table and gazed coolly at her mother over the rim of her cup. "Then tell me. I need to hear it."

A shadow crossed Miriam's face and she buried her head in her hands. When she looked up, her eyes were red and inflamed with no trace of mascara.

"I love you, Rachel. You've been a wonderful daughter to us. Don't judge me harshly."

"Don't be silly," said Rachel, giving what she hoped was an encouraging smile.

"Part of your suspicion is correct," Miriam continued. "Howard was George's father."

"I see!"

"No, Rachel, you don't see. George wasn't Imogen's child. He was *my* son."

"What! No." Rachel tasted acid bile in her throat. She swallowed. She got to her feet, turned her back on her mother and paced. "I don't believe you." But she did. The map of her childhood had been shredded. Everything was tainted, a sham. Her mother! The woman she'd supported, emotionally and financially, for most of her adult life. Never mind the collateral damage to teenage Imogen. Before Tunisia, her sister had been wild and unruly, but she came back embittered. Something that happened there had moulded her.

"Rachel …" Her mother's voice faltered. "Don't look at me with such disdain. I know it must seem bad to your eyes, but I was young myself – just six years older than Howard – he and I were the same generation."

"So you're saying your marriage to Dad didn't matter?"

Miriam hung her head.

"Does Dad know?"

"Max knows about Imogen's affair with Howard, but not about George. Think about it, Rachel. Your father was in his sixties and thrilled to have a son. I've always believed it would destroy him to learn the truth." Her eyes took on a faraway look. "George was very much a wanted baby. A love child. Imogen wasn't the only woman who was in love with Howard Dixon."

Rachel felt sick. No wonder The Old Rectory thronged with wandering ghosts. Nothing had ever been as it seemed.

She narrowed her eyes and asked, "Are you sure Dad never suspected?"

Miriam shook her head and her expression shifted from wistful to sad. How many times had she seen this expression on her mother's face and imagined she was thinking of George? Perhaps she'd been dreaming of her former lover? She remembered the drinks party when Howard and Miriam had a lengthy private talk on the terrace and her mother's flushed face when she came indoors, with Howard following behind.

"I was in an impossible situation, Rachel. I know what I did was wrong and I'm not making excuses. I didn't want to break your father's heart. I've lived on the edge, expecting him to find out."

"How? If you covered it up?"

"Imogen blackmailed me. Can you believe a daughter would do that to her own mother? And when I challenged her account of George's accident, it got worse."

"Go on," said Rachel, finding it hard to breathe.

"Imogen always insisted you were the one looking after George that afternoon and she was at Simon's. When you finally came home in the early hours from wherever you'd been hiding, you emphatically denied it. I was torn between my daughters, but Imogen threatened, if I challenged her account, she'd tell your father George wasn't his."

A flicker of hope penetrated the place in Rachel's heart where guilt and sorrow had festered for decades. "So, you didn't believe I was responsible?"

"I didn't want to believe it was you, Rachel, but everything seemed to point to it. Your revision notes, books, and your flip flops, were on the sun lounger beside the pond where George drowned. And when we got back from the hospital, where George was pronounced dead, you'd disappeared. I was too distraught to notice but your father was out searching for you for hours."

Tears gathered in Rachel's eyes and slid down her cheeks,

unchecked.

"Simon corroborated everything Imogen said," continued Miriam. "She was at his house. But by then it didn't matter because I'd already given my initial statement to the police. I couldn't let suspicion fall on either of my daughters. So, as you know, I lied. I told the police officer I was at home all afternoon and George must have wandered away without me noticing. Your father agreed to say the same thing."

"But how did George drown in the pond, Mum? He could only toddle a few steps."

"He was a fast crawler. He used to pull himself up on chairs. Don't you remember how he could grab onto his cot rail and fling himself over the side onto the floor?" Miriam wiped away a tear. "George loved water. I've always thought he must have hauled himself over the fountain wall into the pond. Once he was in it, the slimy weed would have stopped him getting a foothold or hand hold to climb out."

"Stop!" said Rachel, her chest too tight to speak. She still dreamt of George – his elflike smile, his little arms outstretched for a cuddle or a carry – but always those memories shaded into a nightmare as she pictured his chubby little legs sliding from beneath him, scrambling to hold his head above the deep, scummy water. Gasping and choking...

She laid her head down briefly on the kitchen table, waiting for the horror to fade. With an effort, she shook herself and lifted her head. "Do you still worry Imogen will say something to Dad?"

Miriam shrugged. "I worry less. With his memory problems. Sometimes he mentions George, but we rarely speak of him now. Perhaps if Imogen did tell him, it wouldn't ruffle him at all."

Chapter Fifty-Six

Rachel
November 2019

The conversation with Miriam about George's death and why she'd kept silent, left Rachel no closer to the truth. She craved relief from years of guilt by proxy and fake memories.

The idea of her mother having an affair – and a child – with a man who was also in a relationship with her teenaged sister plagued her. Howard Dixon, who had bullied his way into her office, no longer seemed a comical figure, but a poisonous arch-villain.

"Have you heard from Howard Dixon?" she asked Michael. "Is he still interested?"

Michael's reply was evasive so she didn't press him. If she followed through with her plan to withdraw from Stapleton Kumar and Howard turned out to be the only interested buyer, did it really matter? Wasn't it for Michael to decide? If she returned to study, she'd have no income to keep up the mortgage repayments on The Old Rectory. But why should she? Soon, her father would neither know nor care where he lived, and her mother's confession had hardened Rachel's heart.

She spent less time in the office and more with Hannah. Jack was forever out, training for half marathons or triathlons, and driving all over the country to compete. But she had urged him to follow his interest, so why should she be surprised if they weren't as close as before?

And then she heard from Imogen.

"I thought you were in Tuscany?" she said, trying to

remember exactly what her mother had said. Something about Imogen house hunting? But it seemed an odd choice for a single woman.

"I was. But I'm back now. When can we go and see that house?"

Rachel hesitated. Had their mother already told Imogen her plan? "What made you ask that?"

"You left me a voice message three weeks ago, remember? You said if I wanted to see it, now was a good time because there were no tenants living there and you were having it refurbished ready to sell."

"Oh yes, I did." She'd left the message when she first thought of selling the house, but she hadn't told Imogen her plan to share the proceeds. She was still convinced Imogen was the victim of events in Tunisia but her mother's allegations of blackmail had disturbed her. Their conspiracy of silence had blighted her own life. What did Imogen know? Now could be the time to ask her.

"How about next week?" Rachel suggested. "Early Tuesday evening?"

"Good. After we've looked round, I'll take you and Jack out for dinner," said Imogen, sounding almost naively grateful they were going to spend an evening together. Rachel felt pleased. It wasn't as if they were suddenly going to transform into proper sisters, like Meg and Jo in Little Women. Or Elizabeth and Jane Bennett. But it might be a start.

"Let's you and I meet at six-thirty," said Imogen. "We can ask Jack to arrive later. Say, seven-thirty? We'll have a look around and a proper chat first. Just the two of us."

***

Jack agreed to drive up to London after work, so Rachel travelled by train. She'd forgotten the frustration of living in an area with no underground station. When she was a student, it hadn't bothered her. Even when Hannah was a baby, she'd managed to get around but today the decision between a train to Streatham Hill and a ten-minute walk or taking the Victoria Line to Brixton and catching a bus perplexed her. She opted

265

for the bus.

The bus ploughed up Brixton Hill, passengers gradually thinned out and Rachel got a seat. She stared out of the window across the landscape of her youth, remembering when she and Jack were first together. She got off the bus at the Odeon cinema, happy to see it hadn't been turned into a warehouse or a row of chicken shops. The area had once been marketed by estate agents as Streatham Village and still had the feel of an established community. The clocks had gone back, and darkness collected in the gaps between windows and streetlights. As she strolled the last few paces, the windows of her house stared back at her, blank and insolent under the pallid sickle moon. She entered through the side gate, unlocked the back door and tripped over a pile of floorboards and a plumber's bag. She groped for the light switch and blinked.

The old kitchen had been ripped out. The plumbers had torn up floorboards and replaced ancient pipes with shiny new copper. Rachel stepped cautiously over stacked up boards. The builders weren't the neatest of workers, but they didn't know she was coming to the house this evening. Her foot clipped a power tool. There was some valuable kit lying around. What if the house was broken into? Hopefully they were insured.

The front doorbell clanged into the silence and she strode down the hall to answer it. Imogen was standing on the doorstep, wearing a cashmere winter coat that looked brand new and holding a large Harvey Nicks carrier bag. Perhaps she'd been shopping for a coat and put it on straight away. It was certainly chilly enough.

"You found it," she said. What an inane greeting. "Welcome."

"It's exactly as I imagined," said Imogen, clasping her coat tighter as she stepped into the draughty hall. "Outside at least. Inside it's worse. Come on, show me round."

Rachel led the way along the hall, past two closed doors and down a flight of three steps into a large open plan kitchen. Harsh overhead lighting illuminated a dark stain on the ceiling.

"What's that?" asked Imogen, pointing at the stain.

Rachel grimaced. "A flooding disaster. One of the tenants let the shower overflow. The ceiling's lathe and plaster. If it had collapsed with anyone standing underneath, they could have been killed."

Imogen took a step back. "Is it safe now?"

"Sure." Rachel nodded. "Kevin, my contractor, has made it safe. He'll replace it after his guys have finished the upstairs plumbing."

Imogen looked startled. "You said Kevin, didn't you?

"Yes."

"It sounded like Gavin. Have you heard anything from the police?"

Rachel shook her head. "Not recently. They tracked him down quite quickly. In Spain. The last I heard was they were working on a European arrest warrant, or extradition, or something like that, but I don't think it's straightforward. Has he been in touch with you?"

Imogen shook her head. "Not a word."

"You still haven't told me how you knew Hannah was there," said Rachel. "I'm grateful, of course, but it would set my mind at rest to know."

"Leave it, Rachel." Imogen's head jerked up and her eyes flashed with anger. "I've told the police everything I know. I don't believe Gavin intended to hurt Hannah. She must have got in the way of his escape. Tell me about your plans for this kitchen."

A brochure from the kitchen company was lying on the windowsill and Rachel picked it up and flipped through the pages. She pointed to a double page of photographs. "It's this design – Nordic. I should have brought the drawings to show you. This is how it will look when it's finished."

"It must be good to have the money to make those choices."

Rachel flinched. Why did Imogen lash out all the time?

Imogen stumbled over a pile of tools and dislodged a blow torch from the heap. She picked it up and placed it on the kitchen counter.

"Careful with that," warned Rachel.

"Oh yeah. It's a blow torch, isn't it? Gavin told me he had an incident in his cottage with one of those … It started a fire without even being left on. This kitchen looks a real mess."

Rachel gritted her teeth. Imogen was right. Kevin had ripped out the white melamine units and broken them up but hadn't taken them outside to the skip. The polished beech kitchen counter, that she'd thought so sophisticated in her student days, was covered in marks from hot pans and sagged in the middle. Some of the floorboards, where the new pipework was being installed, had split and would probably need replacing.

"Show me upstairs," said Imogen.

There wasn't much to see in the family bathroom, which had been stripped of sanitaryware.

"We're putting an en-suite in the master bedroom," said Rachel and led the way along the landing. The framework for the en-suite was under construction.

Imogen smiled. "It's like a set for an Alan Ayckbourn play," she remarked, her face flushed with enthusiasm. "You know, they use open frames for the rooms and warring couples step between them to act out different scenes."

"Do you still wish you'd gone to drama school?"

Imogen arched her eyebrows. "Of course. But my life hasn't been exactly free of drama: high emotion, death, destruction, family fallout."

That was true, thought Rachel. By any standards, Imogen's life had been high drama. Perhaps there was time to ask her about George before Jack arrived.

The bedroom furniture was sparse. There was a mahogany wardrobe and a double bed with a stained black and white striped mattress. She felt ashamed at the squalor on display. "This will all go to the house clearance people before it goes on the market," she said.

"It's not exactly a selling point," agreed Imogen, running a hand across the mattress, perhaps to check it was clean enough to sit on in her new coat.

"Come and sit with me, Rachel. There's something I need to talk to you about."

"Sure, but tell me, what do you think of the house? It will be smart, I think, when it's finished. Kevin told me the buyers would probably be a family upsizing from a flat or a two-bed cottage, which is great, because this street has a proper community feel."

"Lucky them," said Imogen with an angry glare. "Do you never think of anything but property?"

"I don't know what you mean." Rachel reeled away from her sister's attack.

"What about people? Your family. Jack - your partner, or whatever. How much thought do you give him?"

"Of course I think about him!" said Rachel. "He's my rock."

"But you spend all your time working. That's what Hannah told me."

Had Hannah betrayed her in such a brutal way? Underneath her quilted jacket Rachel felt a chill seep through her. "Jack and I are both busy with our work, of course," she said stiffly.

"But think, Rachel," urged Imogen with a new intensity. "Has his behaviour changed? Does he spend a lot of time away from home?"

She thought about Jack's half marathons and triathlons and his overnight trips to compete in different areas. But that was with Michael, wasn't it? Though, recently, Jack had joined a club and was pulling ahead of Michael in the number of events he'd competed in. "What are you saying?" she asked, slowly.

"Let me show you something," said Imogen. She took her phone out of her handbag, tapped on the photo icon and held it out to show Rachel a picture. "That's Jack."

Rachel stared. He was standing next to a feminine-looking bed, with white linen and a jumble of cushions, in a room lit by a Moroccan lamp and fairy lights. "Where was this taken?" she asked. "What's going on?" With shaking hands, she took the phone from Imogen and turned it sideways, stretching the screen to enlarge the image. "That's a boat isn't it? Your houseboat?" She sensed a stab of foreboding.

Imogen nodded. "You can't trust him, Rachel. I felt I should warn you."

"What are you saying? When was this?" Rachel's throat felt parched and her voice cracked as she spoke.

"Do you remember a night back in the spring, when trains from Waterloo weren't running? Did Jack make it home?"

"No, he was stranded and stayed the night in London."

"Jack spent that night with me."

Rachel gasped. "I don't believe you!" Shock ricocheted through her and she gave a nervous laugh.

"Perhaps you'll believe the evidence." Imogen lifted the Harvey Nicks bag onto the bed, opened it and took out - not shiny, new clothes – but a scruffy backpack. She held it up. "Recognise this?" She unzipped it and emptied out the contents. There was the Fitbit that Jack claimed to have lost; his Kindle and a dog-eared paperback. The bag was Jack's, sure enough. It was the one he'd said he'd left on a train...

Rachel's face grew warm but, inside she was shivering. Unable to meet Imogen's eyes, she let her gaze wander to the window and peered out at a night sky, turned foggy.

"I'm sorry, Rachel," said Imogen. "We'd both had too much to drink. But he was so insistent. It was just one night. It meant nothing to me, but, ever since, I've been turning over in my mind, trying to decide whether to tell you." She gave a high-pitched laugh. "Why do you think I haven't been returning your calls?" Her fingers played with the zip of the backpack, "I couldn't decide if I should tell you but then I thought, if he can have a casual fling with me – your sister – there might be other women."

Rachel stared at the wall and said nothing.

"I thought you should know you can't trust him."

Chapter Fifty-Seven

Imogen
November 2019

"I'm sorry," Imogen repeated, standing up and shuffling her feet. "I'll leave this here, shall I?" She crammed the backpack into the department store carrier bag. "If I've done the wrong thing in telling you, I'm sorry. But now you know, you can decide."

Rachel twisted her head round and stared at Imogen, her face a mask of misery.

"It's best if I leave now. I'll cancel the restaurant." Imogen felt a giggle bubbling inside her and turned it into a cough. "You and Jack will have some talking to do."

She strolled across to the door, put one hand on the doorknob and raised the other in a limp wave.

"Wait," said Rachel, hauling herself to her feet and walking across the room. She grabbed Imogen's arm and spun her sister round to face her. "What's your problem? Why do you hate me so much?"

Imogen's eyelids twitched but her expression stayed deadpan. "I don't," Imogen replied, in a solemn tone. "Sure. I resent you and your charmed life. But I don't hate you. I hate Miriam, our mother."

Rachel stared with mute incomprehension and slowly shook her head.

Imogen tugged the door open and skipped down the stairs, feeling more alive than she'd done in ages. A light draught was blowing along the hall and she noticed the back door was open and tapping in the wind. She'd go out that way to avoid the risk of bumping into Jack on the front doorstep. She glanced into the kitchen. On the work surface, among the tools she'd kicked over earlier, was the blow torch. She picked it up and turned it over in her hands. It wasn't hot like the one that Gavin had described.

Gavin! She missed him, in spite of everything: what he'd done to Hannah, how he'd almost implicated her in his dodgy drug dealing. Gavin understood how it felt to be fully alive. Howard was too strait-laced – in contrast to his louche younger self, who'd seen nothing wrong in simultaneous love affairs with a mother and daughter. In all those years in foreign parts, he'd never taken a drag on a spliff or snorted a line of coke. Howard was strictly a whisky and champagne man.

Holding the blow torch made her feel strong and powerful. It was like cradling a Kalashnikov. She remembered Gavin's health and safety briefing about the danger of fire on boats and how old houses, with their seasoned timber, were tinder boxes, full of dust ready to go up in flames. She examined the switch and tried to work out how to turn it on.

Chapter Fifty-Eight

Rachel
November 2019

Rachel sank down on the bed and buried her face in her hands. Grief and guilt were familiar to her, but this anguish was new. Pain settled inside her like a stone, more agonising than giving birth. Jack had always been her rock, the beacon that lit up their family life. And now he had betrayed her – with her sister.

A headache pulsed above her left eye and she searched in her bag for a paracetamol. The blister pack was empty but there were some in a small tin. She broke a fingernail opening the lid, swallowed two and retched because she had no water to wash them down. A sour taste stayed in her mouth and pooled in her stomach. She lay back on the mattress, smelling the ingrained sweat of her student tenants' bodies, closed her eyes and waited for Jack to arrive.

When she heard him calling her name from downstairs, she didn't move. His footsteps pounded up the uncarpeted stairs and he barged into the bedroom, asking, "Did you know the back door was open? There are some pricey tools lying around," followed by, "Why are you lying down?"

Rachel lay totally still. He squinted down at her. "Are you feeling ill?"

She raised herself and struggled to a seated position, meeting his concern with a dull stare.

He hesitated and thrust his hands into the pockets of his anorak. "What's wrong? Where's Imogen? Didn't she turn up?"

"Oh yes. She was here." Rachel shaded her eyes from the light. "She told me something quite shocking." She scrutinised Jack's face. He looked puzzled, but not guilty.

"What sort of thing? Not Ibiza again? Or Gavin?"

"No, Jack. Not Gavin. You."

"Me!" Surprise flickered across his face, then he flinched. He curled his hands into fists and brought them up level with his chest. "What did she say?"

"That you spent the night with her. That day when all the trains were cancelled."

Her words echoed like pebbles dropping into the void between them.

"Why, Jack?" Rachel couldn't hold back her tears. "With *her* of all people. You know how she hates me."

Jack reached out and touched her arm. "She's lying."

Rachel shoved his hand away. "Then how do you account for this?" she thrust her hand into the carrier bag Imogen had left behind and pulled out the backpack.

"Where did you find that?" Jack asked, scanning the room, as if she had somehow unearthed it in some corner of a bedroom, in a house he hadn't visited in years.

"You left it behind on her houseboat. She also had some soft-focus photos of you, posing beside her bed. Gross – and seedy – it made me want to puke. How many more did she take? Selfies of you both with no clothes on, perhaps?" Anguish turned to fury. She moved her face within inches of his and yelled. "How. Could. You!"

"Rachel." Jack uncurled his fingers, so his hands flapped, without coordination. "It's not what you think. Whatever she said, it's all lies."

"Then tell me the truth!" A fleck of her spittle landed on Jack's chest. They both ignored it. "Why has she got a photo of you in her bedroom?"

Jack rubbed the shadow of stubble on his chin and reached for her hand. He pulled her down to sit beside him on the bed. She let her hand lie limp in his palm but didn't snatch it away.

"I bumped into Imogen at Waterloo. She was getting off the train while people were piling onto the concourse, trying to get home. We were told there'd be no trains running for hours, so Imogen suggested something to eat. Everywhere near the station was rammed with stranded commuters. She said she had food at her place. I should have known it was a bad idea." He ran his free hand through his hair so it stood up in odd tufts.

"So you went with her to the Lazy Lucy," said Rachel. "If it was all innocent, why didn't you tell me?"

He hung his head. "I was embarrassed. She didn't have any food, only some cheese, but she had alcohol – lots of it. I got horribly pissed."

"Are you seriously telling me, Jack Smith, that Imogen got you drunk and took advantage of you? Give me strength!" Rachel stood up and strode out of the room. She slammed the door and headed for the bathroom, but she'd forgotten all the sanitaryware had been ripped out: no basin, no bath, no toilet. She needed the loo urgently. In desperation, she crouched down on the floor. Jack caught up with her and hovered in the doorway.

"If you want to do something useful, stop staring and get me a bloody bucket or something," she yelled.

"Of course." He clattered down the stairs and returned with a bright orange builder's bucket. He held it out to her and, tentatively, she took it. Something about the ridiculousness of the situation made a giggle rise in her throat. Soon, both of them were howling, tears of laughter mingled with pain as they gripped the cement-smeared bucket between them.

"Honestly, Rachel," Jack put a hand on the wall to steady himself. "I didn't sleep with her, I swear. I was stranded and incapable, so I stayed overnight, curled up on my own on a microscopic sofa. First thing in the morning, before she was stirring, I picked up my laptop and left, but I must have left the backpack behind."

"Forget it, Jack. I know she's hard to resist." Rachel snatched the grimy bucket from him and pushed him out of the door so she could pee in private. There was no paper, no towel, and not even any cleaning cloths, so she spat on her hands and rubbed them dry on her jeans, while her mind picked apart what Imogen had said and weighed up Jack's excuses. She took a deep breath and prepared to open the door.

Jack was leaning against the wall, ashen faced. "Rachel?" He spoke her name as if it was a question.

She took a deep breath and answered.

"I believe you."

He stared at her. "Really?"

She nodded. "Why would I believe anything Imogen tells me? For the whole of her adult life she's massaged facts, hidden the truth and blamed others." She didn't mention blackmail.

"I don't like her," Jack confessed. "But I think Hannah's become fond of her."

"Then we must stop that. I won't have Imogen messing with our daughter's head."

Chapter Fifty-Nine

Imogen
November 2019

Imogen laid the blow torch back on its side on the wooden kitchen work top. This house was innocent. And there were other ways of starting fires – conflagrations large and small. She had a feeling the one she'd just lit might rage into an inferno.

She walked briskly down Sunnyhill Road, picking up her pace and feeling in her coat pocket for her phone to call a taxi. The sickle moon dodged behind cloud and it was too dark to make out the number. Ahead of her, the lights of a small pub, standing on a triangle of land, where two roads met, beckoned her in. The bar was empty, apart from an elderly man with a Jack Russell, morosely drinking a pint of something thick and brown. His eyes lit up when he saw Imogen. She guessed he was one of those locals who chatted to everyone. She ignored him, ordered a glass of red wine and took her drink to the table nearest the door. She wasn't in any hurry. Howard thought she was having dinner with Rachel and Jack. That morning he'd asked her if he could join them for the meal and seemed crestfallen when she'd said no.

Once her glass was half empty, she took out her phone again and saw there were several Ubers close by. She could wait here a little longer. The events of the evening had left her feeling twitchy. She needed to calm down. The lone drinker and his dog departed, and she had the saloon bar to herself. Perhaps she'd ring someone, but who? Not Howard. Her finger hovered over, and tapped, the number of The Old

Rectory.

"Imogen!" Miriam articulated all three syllables of her name. Since the brief tussle over Howard's address, they'd barely spoken. "I thought you were seeing Rachel this evening," Miriam continued stiffly. "To look around the house in Sunnyhill Road."

"I did. I saw her earlier."

"Rachel told me you were all going out for dinner afterwards. What did you think?"

"About the house? It was a bit of a wreck. Typical student house but I can see she's investing some money to improve it." Keeping the phone clamped against her ear, Imogen left her empty glass on the pub table and went outside to light a cigarette. She glanced back up the road, but Rachel's house was out of sight, beyond the brow of the hill.

"No, I meant, what did you think about Rachel's offer?" said Miriam. "Wasn't it generous of her? I must admit I was against it when she first mentioned it, but I've come to see that this could be the way to put things right between the two of you."

Imogen took a long drag on her cigarette. "What are you saying, Mum? What offer?" She couldn't recall any gesture of generosity by Rachel, but then she had rather hijacked their conversation to talk about Jack's overnight stay on the Lazy Lucy. Rachel hadn't said much after that.

"Didn't she tell you?" asked Miriam. "I wonder why. Perhaps I shouldn't say anything."

"Come on, Mum. You can't leave me in suspense."

"Well, she did seem totally set on it," said Miriam, slowly. "I can't think why she'd change her mind after organising all that renovation work. It's costing her a fortune."

It wasn't a particularly cold night but Imogen's hand, holding the lighted cigarette, trembled as she waited for her mother to continue.

"She's doing up the property to sell at the best possible price," said Miriam. "And – isn't it wonderful – she's planning to share the proceeds with you ..."

Chapter Sixty

Imogen
November 2019

Imogen lay in bed, chasing sleep. She must have dozed for a while because, when she woke, she'd chewed the inside of her cheek and it was raw and bleeding. She tried to guess what Jack might have said when Rachel confronted him with the backpack. Had she thrown him out? How would it affect Hannah? Perhaps her niece would run away from home again. Soon.

How ironic that the evening had ended with her mother revealing Rachel had been planning to give her half of the house. It had diluted her joy in being the bearer of bad news. Now Rachel would, presumably, change her mind and renege on the act of generosity. A financial windfall would have given Imogen control of her own future. For now, she was dependent on Howard, but what if she wanted to break free from him?

Imogen and Howard had few friends between them. When they ate dinner at home, or in fancy restaurants, she groped around for conversation while Howard focused on his meal. How fascinating he'd seemed in Tunisia when she was seventeen and eager to soak up his travellers' tales and learn the customs of the country and of Islam. The thrill of their secret meetings in places where they could hide from the ex-pat community, and her parents. Back then, Howard's love making had been adventurous, enticing her to push boundaries way beyond the mechanical sex she'd learned with boyfriends her own age. Now he was only too happy to settle for vanilla sex and an early night.

She rarely thought about Simon now but sometimes when she was half-awake, Gavin, who embodied the rock n roll lifestyle and was a damn good lover, would force his way into her dreams and she would wake furious with the memory of the trouble he'd caused her.

During her interview with the police, she'd had to show them Gavin's cryptic message summoning her to Gamekeeper's Cottage. It was the only way to throw off their suspicion. Surprisingly they'd accepted her explanation that he'd contacted her because Hannah was her niece. They reckoned his escape plan would have needed at least six hours from the time he locked Hannah in the shed. Piecing together the phone conversation Hannah had overheard and what she'd gleaned from the police, it seemed he must have dropped off his transit van, driven his BMW to Dover and messaged her from there before catching a ferry to France.

The remaining evidence from Imogen's mobile phone was unflattering to her ego but backed up what she'd said – that she'd been attempting to contact Gavin for several weeks, but he'd never replied. Her phone showed multiple, unanswered calls and messages. It looked as if she was pursuing him and not the other way around and there was nothing to suggest she'd been involved in any of his business dealings. She'd given a witness statement and the police had backed off.

Thinking of how Gavin had treated her filled her with rage. And Hannah. What if she'd ignored his message and hadn't travelled to Gamekeeper's Cottage? How long would Hannah have stayed locked in that shed? She might have died. Imogen felt hot and cold at the thought. If Gavin was here now she would kill him; tear him apart with her bare hands. But Gavin wasn't here and the only person around for her to pick a fight with was Howard.

"We need to talk about what happened in Tunisia," she said when he emerged from his morning shower and joined her at the kitchen table. The gel he'd used had a faintly feminine scent, perhaps jasmine, and this increased her irritation.

"How d'you mean?" he asked holding out his mug, expecting her to pour coffee. She made him wait.

"The way you treated me, for a start."

"But we've talked about that." Howard strolled across to the counter and poured the coffee for himself. "I was in love with you, but you had to leave with your family. What could I do?"

"You could have asked me to marry you."

He cradled his coffee mug and stared at the floor.

"So was it, by any chance, because you were having an affair with my mother?"

Her words landed like a small explosion. Howard's head jerked up, his hand shook, and coffee spilled down his immaculate white shirt. "How did you know?" he stuttered.

"Don't take me for an idiot," she hissed.

Howard's mask of self-satisfaction slipped. Underneath, his face was haggard. With a despairing look, he headed to the bedroom and shut the door.

She waited ten minutes, sipping her coffee, then another ten, before following him He was lying on his back in the centre of the emperor-sized bed, staring at the ceiling. She climbed onto the bed next to him, took his hand and waited for him to speak.

"I know it looks bad," he began. "I'd spent too much time as an ex-pat. Think about the life I'd been leading up to then, working in Saudi, living on a compound, no women around."

"I don't believe you," said Imogen.

He rolled onto his side and gave her a rueful smile. "Perhaps one or two nurses."

"You see. It's better when you tell the truth."

"In Tunisia your father was often down at the gas field while your mother stayed behind. I remember she was deeply unhappy, missing you and your sister. Max encouraged her to socialise and meet other people. She and I were a similar age. I think she was six or seven years older than me. It was a friendship really. A friendship that went too far."

"So after you'd taken advantage of my mother, you seduced her child?" said Imogen.

"Not seduced, Imogen. And you weren't a child. Eighteen I'm sure."

281

"Seventeen."

"When I met you I didn't continue the relationship with Miriam because I was falling in love with you."

"That's a lie."

He blustered. "I couldn't drop her immediately, could I? She'd have become suspicious. But the more I pulled away, the more clingy and tearful she became."

That would make sense, mused Imogen. Her mother would have been pregnant with George and torn about what to do.

"Don't fight with me, Immy." Howard embraced her so tightly she could hardly breathe. "Now we've found each other again, let's not spoil it."

They lay still for a while, then Howard rolled onto his side and checked his watch. "I'm late."

"Where are you going?"

He loosened his tie and undid the top button of his shirt. "That's better. It was strangling me. I have a meeting with my broker at nine, and after that I'm off to the bank."

"Is that for our house in Tuscany?" she asked. They'd spent ten days trudging round properties in sleepy villages with cobbled streets, a fountain in the main square and pigeons – lots of them. After a while, the villas blurred into one, as did the local trattorias, where they chose from a menu, identical to the one the day before, drank local wine and gazed at views down steep hillsides into the valley below. There was no evening entertainment, few shops and nothing much to do. She'd begun to wonder if Tuscany was for her.

"Not Tuscany," said Howard, clearing his throat. "A couple of potential business opportunities have come up. I'm valuing my portfolio to see how far the funds will stretch."

"You promised me you'd focus on buying into Stapleton Kumar," Imogen retorted.

Howard glanced at his watch. "Have you told your sister about us yet?" He shifted in his seat. "It's uncomfortable for me to pursue it otherwise. I thought you might tell her when you went out for dinner the other night?"

"That wasn't the right time," said Imogen, reining in her irritation and smiling sweetly. Howard liked it when she was girlish and compliant, but it was testing her acting powers. Was it because she was so young that he'd gone after her in Tunisia? His American wife, Sasha, had been nineteen years old when they married. The thought troubled her.

"Come here," he said and put his arms around her. "I love you, Immy, but I worry that you push away people who care about you."

"If you mean my family, I have my reasons."

"I know," he said and kissed her gently on the cheek. "But perhaps you could be a little bit kinder?"

After Howard left for his meetings, she wandered around the apartment straightening cushions and topping up flower vases with fresh water. A cleaner came in three days a week. She was bored. Why did she give up her job at Radio Denim? One day soon she'd go down to Little Venice and catch up with Bill and Mark. But today there was something she had to do. She flipped open her laptop and clicked into Word.

Dear Hannah

I'm writing to answer some of the questions you asked me about what your mother and I were like when we were younger, and why we're no longer close. I don't think your mother will ever tell you but you deserve to hear the truth.

As you know, Rachel and I had a baby brother, George, who was born while your grandparents were working in Tunisia. You will have seen his photos on the mantelpiece at The Old Rectory and in your grandma's albums.

She glanced around the sitting room, struck for the first time that neither Howard, nor she, had any family photos on display. She remembered there was one of her holding George aged four months, shortly before they left Tunisia. She'd steal that one from her mother's album and frame it. Perhaps she could find a photo of Hannah to put on display, too. And one of Simon when he was young and gorgeous. Why not?

She turned back to her letter.

George adored me. Sometimes it felt like I was his primary carer because, when we returned to England, your grandma had to go back to work to help your grandad get their business re-established.

On the day George died, I was looking after him in the morning but we'd arranged that Rachel would take over from me at two o' clock. I was due to go to Simon's house. He was my boyfriend back then but, later, we got married. Simon lived in Blakeswood with his parents, not far from us. He and I were already planning to go to Holland on tour with his band.

So you see, after I left for Simon's house, your mother was in charge of George. But she had other things on her mind because she was revising for her exams. Rachel didn't have my experience of caring for such a young child. If you take your eye off a small child, who can walk a few steps, they wander. Sometimes they get lost or, as in George's case, they drown.

Your mother didn't mean it to happen, of course. But I'm sure the guilt has stayed with her to this day. That must be why she's so strict with you…

She printed out the letter, signed it and added a P.S.

If things are difficult at home, you can come and stay with me any time. My new address is on the letter.

Using Howard's fountain pen, she added a row of kisses, addressed the envelope and walked to the post box.

Imogen dangled the letter through the posting slot. Once she sent it, that would be it. She opened her fingers and let it drop. But if she'd expected the letter to be a neat exorcism of the past, she was wrong because memories of that day in May 1999 came flooding back to taunt her.

Chapter Sixty-One

Rachel
December 2019

The Saturday post arrived early. Jack scooped three letters up from the doormat when he came in from his run and tossed them onto the kitchen table. Rachel was sitting in her dressing gown, with a towel around her shoulders and water dripping from her wet hair.

Hannah must have heard the door and joined them in the kitchen, yawning.

"Coffee?" asked Rachel. "Or tea?"

"Tea, please," replied Hannah. "Have we got any peppermint?"

"Have a look in the cupboard."

Hannah pulled out boxes of herbal tea bags and checked them. "This one expired in, like, 2016," she said.

"I doubt they've gone off."

"There's a letter for you, Hannah," said Jack, flicking it across the table to her.

Hannah abandoned her quest for mint tea. "Yay – how quaint. It must be from Grandma. I mean, who else would write to me?" She paused with the envelope in her hand. "Now I feel bad because I haven't visited them in ages."

Jack slid a knife towards her, and she slit open the envelope, pulled out two sheets of typewritten paper and began to read. She scanned the first page rapidly and looked up with a frown.

"What is it?" asked Rachel, refastening the belt of her dressing gown. "Is it from Grandma?"

"No. It's from Aunt Imogen." Hannah was holding the letter loosely in her hand as she looked at her mother, with a perplexed expression. "I'd asked her a few questions about when you and she were young and she's writing to answer them. She says I need to know about what really happened to your little brother, George."

"No!" Rachel let out a yell of fury and Jack added his voice to hers. She lunged for the letter, ripped it from Hannah's hand and began tearing it into diagonal strips.

"Hey. That's mine! Give it back. It's private," shouted Hannah, trying to gather up the shreds of torn paper.

Rachel crumpled the remains of the letter in her fist. "She's a witch, Hannah. Anything she tells you is untrue. She's out to cause trouble between us. Imogen wants to break me. She's tried everything she can think of and now she's using you."

"I don't believe you," said Hannah, her face flushed with anger. "You're not being fair! If there's something I should know about George, tell me."

"No!" With a cry of anguish, Rachel fled the kitchen and ran to the sitting room, slamming the door, before Hannah could see her tears. Imogen's mind games were a torment. The Stapleton family consensus was that Rachel was responsible for his death, even though her mother had expressed doubts. For twenty years she'd been under attack and had her voice muted.

During the police investigation into George's death, she'd been instructed to say she hadn't seen what happened. But at home, two different stories were bellowed at her: the official story Miriam had told the authorities, and the poisonous one Imogen had poured into her ear. Later, when her mother was in hospital and Imogen had left for Holland, Rachel had told her father she was going to contact the police and tell them she'd lied – that she, and not Miriam, was responsible for George's death. Her father wasn't an emotional man. He'd taken her in his arms and hugged her tight. "What good would that do, Rachel? It won't bring George back. The case is closed and reopening it would only add to your mother's grief."

She heard a scratching at the door and opened it to let

Jensen in. Normally she made him lie on the floor but today he clambered onto the sofa and settled with his head on her lap. She let him stay, drawing comfort from stroking his sleek coat and his unwavering trust in her.

She lay back, on the sofa, arms around the dog, and shut her eyes.

"Are you okay, Mum?" asked Hannah, coming into the room an hour later with Jensen's lead. "I'm sorry I shouted at you. Dad told me things were tricky for you just now."

Jensen opened one eye and spotted his lead. When he saw any of them putting their coats on, he bounded towards the door but, today, he snuggled back down and nuzzled Rachel's knee.

"There have been secrets in my family for too long, Hannah," said Rachel, risking a faint smile. "I promise I'll tell you. But not now. Not like this. And don't believe what Imogen says."

"Your mother's right, Hannah," said Jack, appearing in the doorway. "Imogen is on a mission to destroy our family."

Chapter Sixty-Two

Imogen
May 1999

Imogen picked George up in her arms and carried him out into the garden. She noticed Rachel's A level books and flip flops abandoned on the sun lounger, as she set George down on the grass. He grabbed the lounger with both hands and hauled himself up to standing. It wobbled but didn't collapse. George swayed as he balanced on his chubby legs, then struck out on an adventure. He tottered away from the lawn, across the gravel towards the fountain, plumping down on his padded bottom every so often, cackling with laughter and holding his hand out for Imogen to come and raise him up.

She made him wait. George sat contentedly, scooping up gravel with his hands and letting the stones pour out between his fingers.

Imogen walked into the centre of the lawn and called out, "Rachel. Where are you hiding? Come here, lazy cow. I'm off to Simon's. It's time for you to look after George."

Being used as George's childminder was the ultimate insult. If she hadn't been planning her escape to Europe, she would never have let herself be so abused, but she needed money, and her mother was paying her to look after him.

Within the family, Rachel's A level exams were given such status and priority, it felt to Imogen as if her sister was poised to leap forward several decades and be awarded a Nobel Prize, while her own career path into acting had been blocked.

On that day, Imogen had struck a bargain with her mother at the breakfast table. George was sitting in between them in his highchair, gripping wooden blocks in both hands, and banging them down on the tray in front of him. Imogen felt the beginnings of a headache.

"I'm only looking after him for the morning. I'm due at Simon's by two-thirty. Rachel will have to take over."

"Where is Rachel?" Miriam had asked, spooning milk-sogged cereal into George's mouth.

"Revising in her room," she muttered. "Or pretending to."

"Now, Imogen, that's unfair," said Miriam. "Are you sure you girls have agreed the plan for today?"

"Yes," said Imogen. "Rachel's taking over at two."

"That's fine then. I'll be back around four," Miriam said, rising from the table and kissing George's forehead. "Be a good boy for your sisters today, Georgie." She picked up her car keys and tip-tapped across the hall towards the front door and her waiting Alfa Romeo.

As soon as the door closed behind her mother, Imogen wiped George's sticky mouth and carried him upstairs. She laid him on his mat and he gurgled happily as she changed his nappy. Then she put him back in his cot, pulling the curtains to block out the sunlight. "Go back to sleep, Georgie. I'm busy. Night, night."

George was a good-natured baby. "Ny ny," he said and snuggled down.

The morning dragged but suddenly it was time. She mustn't keep Simon waiting. After Ibiza, he might not have expected her to come back to him, but he'd accepted it. Persuading him to let her join his band's first European tour had been a tougher challenge. She mustn't put a foot wrong. This afternoon they were meeting at Simon's parents' house to book the ferry and their first few nights' accommodation. No way was she going to miss it.

Shielding her eyes from the sun with one hand, Imogen scanned the lawn and looked beyond it, to the rough meadow grass and the fringes of the woodland. There was no sign of movement. Rachel had been wearing a white top earlier on, so she'd stand out against the trees if she was there. Where was she?

She called again. "Rachel. Come on. I've been childminding George all morning. Now I'm off to Simon's." In a lower voice, she added, "I've told Mum you're taking over from me at two."

Behind her, George made a few more tottering steps and reached the edge of the pond. He gazed up at the water pouring from the stone fish head. When the spray hit him, he laughed out loud. Imogen thought of his father, Howard, and a wave of bitterness hit her.

"Shush, baby. Horrible baby."

George laughed back, a dimple forming in his podgy chin. He reached up his arms to her. "Carry!"

She scooped him up. "You like the water, don't you, Georgie. See this lovely wall around the pond? If you hold my hand tight, I'll show you how to walk on it."

She hefted him up and onto the wall. "Round we go. Round and round the garden, like a teddy bear. Round and round the edge of the deep pond. One step, two steps and a slip."

She pretended to drop him in the water. George looked at her, bewildered but when she swooped and lifted him, laughing, into her arms, he joined in. She kissed his cheek.

"Eegen, Eegen," he cackled. "Again." He grabbed hold of her necklace and pulled it.

"It's Imogen," she said, disentangling his fingers from her beads. "There you go, Georgie." She set him down on the lounger. "You stay here and mind your sister's books. Rachel will be here in a moment to play with you. You'll like that, won't you?"

George jerked his body excitedly, so the sun lounger bounced like a trampoline. His head bobbed up and down in delight.

Imogen threw another glance down the garden as the sun slid behind a cloud. Still no sign of Rachel but her presence was everywhere – imprinted on the scene: the set books, the flipflops, the sunglasses…

Imogen took a deep breath and lifted her chin. "Bye bye, Georgie." She waved and strode rapidly up the stone steps onto the terrace, without looking back. She entered the house through the French doors leading into the kitchen. The grandfather clock in the hall showed two fifteen. She hurried through the house, out of the front door and pelted down the drive and ran the half mile to Simon's house.

***

If she'd gone to drama school she might not have become an actor. Perhaps she'd have ended up as a director or stage manager. No one knew better than Imogen how to arrange a scene. All those endless months in Tunisia when Howard was working or had some feeble excuse – such as shagging her mother – so he couldn't see her, Imogen had read her way through the swimming club library's collection of Agatha Christie novels. She knew all about timings, and alibis, and of tracking the movements of any characters, who might be implicated in a scene. And what books had Rachel been immersed in during that time? King Lear and Dostoyevsky. Dosing herself on family feuds, intrigue and – above all – guilt.

Chapter Sixty-Three

Rachel
December 2019

A week after Imogen's letter to Hannah, her grandmother made an unscheduled visit to Southerndown Cottage. When Rachel arrived home from work, Miriam was in the kitchen drinking tea with Hannah.

"This is a surprise, Mum," said Rachel, glancing around her kitchen at pans from the night before, piled high in the sink; dirty mugs on every surface. She frowned. Hannah could have made a small effort to empty and restack the dishwasher when she came in from school.

"I'm sorry we're in such disarray," she said. "Karen doesn't come to clean anymore." In many ways it was a relief. It spared her from painful reminders.

"How are you, Mum? Nothing's wrong with Dad, I hope." There must be a reason for this unexpected visit.

Miriam took a bourbon biscuit from the plate Hannah had put on the table. "Far from it. Last week we went to the memory clinic and he sailed through most of the tests. They made him count backwards from a hundred, subtracting seven from the previous number each time – I couldn't have done it!"

"A hundred, ninety-three, eighty-something. That's hard!" said Hannah. "What else?"

"They gave him word lists to remember – and twenty minutes later they asked him questions." She took a sip of her tea. "The only part of the test he didn't do well on was people. He knew the name of the prime minister but, when they asked him if he had any children, he said he had two: a daughter called Rachel. And a son called George."

Silence reigned in the kitchen as they absorbed this. Eventually Rachel asked, "Did he get a diagnosis?"

"The doctor said he has a form of mild cognitive impairment. It's a bit more serious than age-related forgetfulness – but it's not full-blown dementia. Not yet."

"Will he get better, Grandma?" Hannah asked quietly. "I mean is there some medication he could take?"

"I don't think so, darling. We should all spend time with him now, when he's mostly well, and create memories. He'd like that."

"Will you talk to me about George one day, Grandma?" asked Hannah.

Rachel gave her a sharp look, but it seemed the question was innocent. How much of Imogen's letter had Hannah read? She shouldn't have torn it into indecipherable strips. She could have read it herself. How could she guess what venom had poured from Imogen's pen? She seemed to want to rip apart every strand of Rachel's life, piece by piece, hoping the supporting scaffolding would collapse.

Miriam's face lit up as she answered Hannah's question. They'd always needed permission to feel safe talking about George and now Hannah had granted it. "Next time you come over; we'll look through my old photo albums together."

"Are you staying for supper, Mum?" asked Rachel.

"I'd better not. I mustn't leave your dad on his own for too long."

"See you soon, Grandma," said Hannah. "I'm off to do my homework," she added with a grimace.

Miriam's face relaxed into a smile. "She's so like you, Rachel."

"Do you think so?" Did Miriam mean Hannah was a girly swot?

"Absolutely. It's lovely that you don't have to nag her about homework, but I was thinking of her sunny, open temperament."

"Thanks, Mum." Rachel kissed her mother's cheek and, for

once, Miriam allowed the brief show of affection and didn't pull away.

"Now, you must have guessed I've come for a reason," said Miriam when they heard Hannah's bedroom door closing. "I have news. It was a shock to me but I've got used to it and I'm hoping it might finally end all the unpleasantness."

Rachel clasped her hands together as she leaned forward to listen.

"Do you remember how anxious Imogen was to get Howard Dixon's contact details?"

Rachel nodded. "How could I forget?"

"Well it seems she tracked him down and, not only was he delighted to see her after so long, they've already moved in together!"

Rachel gaped. Perhaps Miriam had suspected this outcome, but Rachel could never have guessed it. Imogen seemed so full of bitterness. If she'd been asked to put money on the reasons for her sister's determination to track Howard down, she would have said "revenge." It was the only motive that seemed to fit. She'd even taken some small-minded pleasure in imagining Imogen calling him out about his behaviour. Her sister might not have been underage when Howard seduced her, but she could probably have done his reputation some damage. Or perhaps she'd have blackmailed him. It was another of her specialisms.

"She's a quick operator," said Rachel. "When did this happen?"

Miriam gave a tight smile. "Quite some time ago, it seems. Before she left her job at Radio Denim. She's moved on fast from the tragedy of Simon's death and found herself a…" Miriam gulped. "A millionaire."

"Actually, Mum," said Rachel, "I'm not sure it does end here. I suspect Imogen's little drama has a few more steps to play out. We don't have to have anything to do with her – and Howard." It seemed that Miriam still yearned for a happy ending, but Rachel had ruled it out. Staying away from her was the only way to keep her family safe.

Miriam groped inside her handbag for a tissue. "You're

right. So much of this is my fault."

"Tunisia is in the past, Mum. You can't do anything about it. But tell me." She looked into her mother's red-rimmed eyes. "Do you honestly think I would have gone off and left George?"

"I don't, Rachel. I didn't think so at the time and I don't believe it now. But what else could I do? I'd already taken responsibility – perjured myself, if you like, by giving a false statement to the police. I did it to protect my girls. Perhaps, if I'd had another young child, I might have hesitated in case social services stepped in and checked up on my fitness as a mother. Maybe I'd have been prosecuted for neglect, or worse? But I don't know what happened on that day, and it seems like you don't either. All I can say is, you've proved your trustworthiness to me over and over again for years."

"Thanks, Mum. I feel lighter now," said Rachel. For the first time in years, they hugged one another and, when Miriam left to drive home to Blakeswood, Rachel stood on the doorstep, waving, until her rear lights disappeared from view.

Later that evening, when Jack arrived home, Rachel led him into the sitting room and put a bottle of beer in his hand. "You'll need this," she said, and told him the full story of Imogen, Howard - and Miriam. She explained everything she'd recently learned about what had happened in Tunisia, including George's parentage.

Jack listened in stunned silence and, when she had finished, he didn't do his usual trick of testing the evidence. He took a long drink from his bottle.

"I'm lost for words," he said, scratching a graze on his chin where he'd cut himself, shaving. "What can I say about George?"

"It was a huge shock to me," said Rachel.

Jack shook his head. "How did your mother take the news about Imogen shacking up with her old lover?"

"She seems to have taken it in her stride. If anything, she's softened. I was furious with her for betraying Dad but now I only feel pity. The best thing is I no longer feel responsible for helping them stay in The Old Rectory. They'll be better off living somewhere without the ghosts and, if they don't move, Imogen will force them out."

"Whatever are you talking about, Rachel?" asked Jack.

"Sorry. I'm getting ahead of myself. There's so much I haven't told you."

A shadow crossed his face. "I wish you'd trusted me."

"I did. I do. But it's complicated. First of all, my parents don't own The Old Rectory. Fifteen years ago they were on the verge of bankruptcy so I had to rescue it for them."

Jack steepled his fingers and stared at her as if she was a stranger. "Why didn't you tell me?"

Rachel dropped her gaze. "I tried to keep it as a business matter. Not a personal one. I took The Old Rectory into Stapleton Ltd – as my company was called then – and it still sits in my portfolio. It's mortgaged up to the hilt and I've been servicing that debt ever since. My parents have never been in a position to contribute a penny towards it. Originally it was a huge drag on the company's cash flow but, these days it's insignificant, compared to the new risks we've taken on and the money Michael and I have borrowed to fund our housing developments."

She risked a smile, relieved to have Jack's attention again.

"So Stapleton Kumar has financial problems? I never realised."

"Why should you? It's not your problem but you'll see it would have been impossible for us to create a role for you in the business. Things are improving but we've needed quite a large cash injection and that's increased our bank borrowings. Remember I told you my father turned up at the office out of the blue and brought Howard Dixon, who was offering to buy a share in the business?"

"Yes."

"He started talking to Michael behind my back. For a few months he backed off but, in the last couple of weeks, he's been back in contact, raising his offer and increasing the pressure. That can only mean one thing."

"What?" asked Jack.

It wasn't usual for Jack to struggle to keep up but perhaps

the volume of secrets she was sharing would overwhelm even the sharpest brain.

"Imogen," she said. "It all fits. She's putting him up to it. Michael's getting twitchy because he sees this new stream of money to invest and I'm saying no. I couldn't stay in the business and work alongside Howard but now I know he and Imogen are an item, it all makes sense. She's the one driving this forward."

"Why would she do that?"

Rachel took a deep breath and divulged her final secret. "When George died, my mother took responsibility for it, as I've told you. But that was only the official story for the police and coroner. At the time, and for years afterwards, my parents and Imogen persuaded me I was responsible for George's death."

"Rachel!" He hugged her close. "How dare they! Of course you weren't."

Rachel bowed her head. "The thing is, Jack, I have no memory of that terrible day. Only what I was told. I tried to tell the truth, as I recalled it, but no one would listen. I found I no longer knew the truth. It was as if my own memory had been recorded over.

"When Imogen sent that spiteful letter to Hannah, and when she pretended she'd slept with you and showed me fake evidence, I knew, beyond doubt, she would go to any lengths to destroy me. Nothing will placate her. Not giving her half of the house in Sunnyhill Road, not finding a new rich man. Imogen still believes everything that should have been hers was handed to me on a golden plate."

"But the truth is that you've been grafting for years and looking after your parents and their house," said Jack.

"And missing out on valuable time with you and Hannah," added Rachel. "Believe me, Jack, Imogen won't stop until she's taken everything from me."

Jack reached for her hand and kissed it. "And you're going to fight her – every step."

Rachel shook her head. "No. I'm not going to fight. I'm going to let her have it."

Chapter Sixty-Four

Imogen
December 2019

Imogen sometimes wondered if Rachel and her mother suspected her of having a part in George's death. Might they even imagine she'd killed him? She'd never do that. Murderers are stupid – they're bound to be found out. But accidents happen all the time. Some lead to death and some don't. It's all about theatre: acting, stage managing, gathering and directing the right cast of characters and props. As Mr Kane had told her, if you set the scene and put the actors in place, things happen of their own accord.

Although she'd had no hand in Hannah's car accident, she could have stopped Luke from setting off. She'd seen Luke drinking, and smoking weed. That day might have ended so differently and Rachel would have been devastated at losing her daughter. She would never have recovered and her relationship with that prissy Jack – the only man who'd ever said no to Imogen – would have imploded under the strain. Rachel's business would have gone belly up, for sure. She'd have turned inwards and become a sad hermit. Perhaps she'd even have killed herself and Imogen would have inherited everything. Except that there was nothing to inherit. And how ironic was that!

Imogen was glad Hannah had survived. She was fond of her niece. Once she and Howard were set up in their house in Tuscany, she would invite Hannah to stay and cultivate their relationship. Hannah had a wild streak in her; a streak that Imogen recognised. In years to come, when she threw parties in her homes in London and in Tuscany, she'd invite beautiful people and, maybe, celebrities. She could show Hannah a different sort of life. And who knew what would happen.

For the moment, Howard's negotiations to buy into Stapleton Kumar were proceeding smoothly. Michael Kumar seemed to like him and had outlined his future plans for taking the business to the next stage when it was reinvented as Kumar Dixon. Imogen was almost sorry that the Stapleton name was going to disappear but then, officially, she wasn't a Stapleton. Although she used the name when it suited her, she was Mrs Wilson and, maybe, one day soon she would be Dixon. Imogen Dixon had a nice ring to it.

Sometimes in the evenings, when she and Howard sat finishing the bottle of wine they'd started with their meal, she'd notice Howard watching her, with a troubled expression, and try to guess his thoughts.

"Did you ever think of having children with your ex-wife?" she asked him, trying out different tacks to find out what was on his mind.

"Never," he replied.

"Would you have liked them?"

"I'd have liked a son," he confessed. "But it wasn't to be."

So Howard had never known George was his child! Much as Imogen despised her mother, she admired her ability to keep secrets. Imogen had filled Howard in on brief details of George's tragic death but he began to show an unhealthy interest in the accident-proneness of the Stapleton family.

"Tell me again about Simon's death," he said.

His obsession was beginning to feel ghoulish, but she always answered his questions, clearly and promptly. She even showed him the investigator's report.

"So you see, on that evening," she said, "Simon had drunk too much, as he was in the habit of doing, and fell off the balcony. It was a terrible accident."

Imogen had always loved accidents and mysteries, not just Agatha Christies, she liked locked room puzzles, too. Watching Howard finish his glass of Chateau Lafitte in the soft lamp light, she cast her mind back to that night in February when Simon died. It was less than a year ago but, already, it seemed to belong to the distant past.

Not content with dragging them both towards the gutter, Simon had been gradually drinking himself to death. His liver scan was showing early signs of disease but the path to self-destruction Simon had chosen could take years, and meanwhile her life was wasting away.

After Simon failed to attend the clinic rehabilitation programme, Imogen stopped protesting about his drinking and actively encouraged it. The less she saw of him, the fewer arguments they had. Sometimes she stood watching him from the balcony of their flat in San Antonio, as he weaved his way along the main road and thought how easily he could step out in front of a car.

That fateful day had started positively. Their neighbour, who lived in Madrid, had asked Simon to redecorate his holiday flat. All winter, Imogen had nagged him to get on with it.

"If you do a decent job, he might recommend you for other work and more income," she urged.

Finally, that morning he'd made a start. Being Simon, he didn't bother rubbing down the woodwork or filling in cracks; he washed the old gloss paint down with sugar soap and covered the doors and window frames with a thick layer of brilliant white. When she went next door at twelve-thirty to take him a sandwich and a coffee, she gagged on the paint fumes.

"Open the window, why don't you?" she said.

Simon slid the balcony doors wide but, when he took the coffee from her, his hand was shaking so badly he spilled some on their neighbour's Aztec-patterned cream rug.

"Look what you've done!" she exclaimed.

"Bitch," he yelled, bringing his contorted, red face close to hers. "It's your fault. You always blame me."

In a way it was her fault because, most days, Simon would have started drinking at nine o' clock and, by midday, his hands would be steady. He abandoned the decorating, along with the coffee, and stormed out to one of his drinking haunts.

He'd gone out angry and returned, wrecked, long after midnight but Imogen had waited up for him. As he came in through the door, she poured him another whisky, a treble to add to those he'd sunk earlier in the day and handed it to him with a smile.

"Sorry, Immy," he said, slobbering a kiss onto her cheek.

"Let's take our drinks out on the balcony," she'd suggested, holding out the whisky bottle to him. "You can cool down before you try to sleep."

Simon took the bottle in his free hand. She noticed the yellowing of his eyes and an angry sore on his lip and felt nothing for him. He trudged out through the sliding doors and she followed. They leaned over the balcony railing and stared gloomily down at the dark windows of the apartments in their block. Simon's still-black hair had grown longer and curled onto his shoulders; sometimes he wore it in a ponytail. She'd always admired his hair. As he leaned over the parapet, swirling his drink morosely, Imogen stepped back inside the flat, swiftly pulled the double-glazed balcony doors shut and drew the upper and lower bolts. Simon turned around; his expression shifted from sullen to a mask of fury.

"Let me in," he shouted, hammering on the door with his fists. "Bitch." She paid no attention. There was no one else to hear him. Earlier in the day, she'd walked along each corridor, knocking on doors and knew every flat was empty. Better apartments could be rented cheaply over winter. Why would anyone choose this shithole?

Simon swung his fist, thumping it rhythmically against the window, like a bird flying headfirst, to attack its reflection in a window pane over and again. He can't have realised how hard he'd been hitting or how solid the double-glazing was. He rubbed his hand. She grew weary of watching him. He moved away from the window and paced like an animal in a zoo. She drew the curtains leaving only a crack to watch him through and perched on the arm of the sofa. The double glazing blocked out Simon's shouts, but she could see he was necking whisky straight from the bottle.

Twenty minutes ticked by. Simon's pacing stalled and he

looked around. Through the gap in the curtains, she followed the direction of his gaze, sensing what would come next. She turned her back to the window. Moments later, she heard an anguished scream followed by a thud. She fumbled to unbolt the balcony doors, raced outside and stared down at Simon's broken body spatchcocked on the concrete terrace six floors below.

That's the thing about accidents. They lurk everywhere, waiting to happen. As she'd anticipated, Simon had glanced across to their neighbour's flat and noticed the wide-open balcony doors he hadn't closed after abandoning his painting job. Like so many, much younger, men before him, their judgement impaired by booze, he must have assumed it would be an easy climb across from their own apartment's balcony to next door's. The open windows giving access to their neighbour's flat would have beckoned him to try.

Imogen's eyelids drooped as she gazed at Howard and stifled a yawn. All that was in the past. Thanks to Howard she had a new life. When she set out to track him down, she was unsure of her feelings towards him. Was he the love of her life, kept apart from her by her treacherous mother? Once they were reunited, she'd soon discovered that any feelings she might have had for Howard belonged to the distant past. It was a simple equation. Howard owed her and now she was making him pay. With his help, the balance on the Stapleton family's account, stolen by her sister, would return to her, too. Once they were all square, she needn't see any of them again. It was obvious that Howard adored her, but it would be better for everyone if he stopped asking questions about Simon. Accidents could still happen.

Chapter Sixty-Five

Rachel
December 2019

The December sky was heavy with clouds, but Rachel's heart felt light as she prepared to meet Michael at the offices of Stapleton Kumar's solicitor, where she would sign over her share of the business to Howard Dixon. She dressed carefully in black trousers, brown suede ankle boots and a shiny gold blouse but, when she looked at her reflection in the mirror, she felt drab. She changed into a red dress; the kind of vivid dress Imogen might wear. Red was the colour for celebration.

It seemed Howard had done surprisingly little due diligence on the portfolio of properties he was taking over from Rachel. His solicitor's pre-sale investigations had barely raised a query about the massive loan against The Old Rectory. Michael would never let him subsidise it through the business so, once he owned it, he could carry on paying the loan from his own pocket, as Rachel had done, or force the sale of the house to clear the debt, in which case her parents would have to move out. The thought that this decision was no longer her responsibility, lightened her step. A snatch of lyrics from an Elbow song *One Day Like This* floated out from her radio and she hummed along.

Everything was changing. No longer trapped in the past, she could finally move on. In conversation with her mother, she'd discovered Miriam's dogged attachment to The Old Rectory was fading. Was it because of the damp, the constant repairs and the remoteness of Blakeswood, a village without shops and no public transport? Or could it be because Miriam's secret, nursed for two decades, was finally out and she no longer needed to barricade herself into the house where George had died? She and Max would be better off moving to a small town near the shops before his condition took a turn for the worse.

The relief of no longer having secrets from Jack had rebalanced the occasional prickliness between them.

"I won't get as much money from the sale as you might think," she warned him. "Not a lot to show for all those years of work. My share of the portfolio is laden with debt, but I guess Howard's pockets are deep enough to sit it out until the market recovers."

"You'll have half the proceeds of the Sunnyhill Road house, though. Once the sale goes through?"

"Yes. Once I've paid the builders and given Imogen her share. I'll have plenty to pay for my law school and to live on for a couple of years."

"You're still determined to pay her?"

Rachel nodded. "I am."

It would be difficult to continue helping her parents in any significant way. They had only their state pensions to live on because their savings had gone on fending off their creditors. Unless Imogen persuaded Howard to be generous, they were in for a lean time. She would think about it and discuss it with Jack. If she did decide to help them, her decision would be driven by love and not by guilt.

"How do I look?" she asked Jack, as she emerged from the bedroom in the red dress.

"Magnificent!"

"Would you like to marry me?" she suggested, testing out the smile she'd been practising to Elbow's song lyrics.

"You're joking?" His smile broadened into the carefree, boyish grin she remembered from their student days. How lucky she'd been to go to university, escape her dysfunctional family and find someone so normal to fall in love with.

"I'm perfectly serious," she said. "I'm ready to become a Smith. I've been Stapleton for too long."

"Come here, Mrs soon-to-be-Smith." Jack drew her into his

arms and they shared a long kiss.

"Aw, you love birds. That's sick!" said Hannah, padding out onto the landing in bare feet so neither of them heard her approach.

"Hey - watch it or I'll send you to Saint Jude's boarding school like your mother before you," said Jack, still grinning.

"You wouldn't dare!"

"I think sick has a different meaning now, doesn't it?" said Rachel. "It means something's good or cool."

Hannah raised an eyebrow. "It did, back in, like, the noughties but now it's just – well – sick. I came to tell you something."

"Spit it out," said Jack.

"Aunt Imogen messaged me this morning. She and her new bloke, Howard have bought a place in Tuscany and she's invited me to spend next summer in Italy with them."

"No!" chorused Jack and Rachel in unison.

Hannah grinned. "I guessed you'd say that. She did sort of save my life though."

Rachel gave her a bemused look. How could Hannah still believe this? After the car accident, Imogen hadn't even taken Hannah to A&E and Rachel had blocked the terrifying kidnap incident at Gamekeeper's Cottage from her mind. Neither Jack, nor Hannah, seemed to have grasped how badly that could have ended. Rachel shuddered. She'd had enough of ghosts. From today she'd be free.

"Anyway, you're not available to go to Italy next summer," said Jack. "You're coming abroad with us. Your mother and I are getting married."

How would Hannah react? Would she be happy? Shocked? But Hannah had no questions. She was ready to celebrate. "Can I tell my friends?"

"If you like."

Hannah headed off to her room.

"Do you think she'll tell Luke?" Rachel asked.

Jack put a finger to his lips, pulled Rachel back into their bedroom and closed the door. "There's one final secret between us and, this time, it's on my conscience," he said. "I

305

shouldn't tell you because of client confidentiality but for family reasons you need to know."

What could it be? Jack never kept secrets. His weekend absences to run marathons and triathlons turned out to be exactly that, not trysts with other women as Imogen would have had her believe – he had a drawer full of medals to prove it.

Jack swallowed. "I could lose my job for telling you this. Two weeks ago, I was in court, representing someone we know."

"Who?"

He didn't smile. "Luke."

"Oh my God," Rachel's hand flew up to cover her mouth. "What happened? What had he done?"

"It's rather a tragic tale and it relates to Gavin – the loving father, who came back after ten years and bought his lad a car and driving lessons. It seems Gavin was carrying out a pernicious form of grooming. On his own son." Jack's eyes clouded and he turned his head away. "I've seen some shocking things in my job – but this…"

"What sort of grooming?" asked Rachel, horrified.

"Drug dealing. It seems the delightful Gavin, who, I gather, Imogen was so fond of, was quite high up the food chain. He ran his UK distribution network from Gamekeeper's Cottage. Being Gavin's son didn't spare Luke. His father had him selling into the sixth form college and to his friends in the football club. When Gavin did a runner, he left his son with a sizeable haul of merchandise hidden under his bed at Karen's house."

"That's horrendous," said Rachel, feeling as if her heart had stopped beating as she tried to take in the enormity of what Jack had told her. If Hannah had stayed with Luke she could so easily have been drawn in and implicated. Her life would have been ruined before it properly started. "I've heard of 'county lines', where vulnerable kids get duped into supplying drugs from the cities out into rural areas but his own son! I can't believe it."

"Grim, isn't it."

"How did you get involved in defending him?"

"Karen came to see me at the office. Distraught. Do you remember Luke had a part-time job at the White Lion?"

"Yes, he was a kitchen assistant. You went there to talk to him when we were searching for Hannah."

"It seems Luke was selling to the guys in the kitchen, but they weren't as discreet as his sixth form college mates. When one of them was caught in possession of a tiny amount of gear, he immediately disclosed Luke's name as his dealer. The police raided Karen's house and found quite a stash."

"Poor Karen." She could have done more to help her, but Karen had always been resistant.

"Remember, you don't know this, so you mustn't say anything. Luke's still only seventeen, his name hasn't been published. It's not officially in the public domain."

"Does Hannah know?"

"I think so. She asked me questions about what would happen in a scenario that could only fit Luke's case. I didn't press her, but I guess the news is all around the youngsters of Ferngate…"

How do you keep your children safe? Accidents happen and Hannah had been lucky on more than one occasion. Unlike George…

The years peeled away, and Rachel was back on that sunny, hazy afternoon in May 1999, smelling the undergrowth and listening to the raspy chatter of the magpies. And there was something else she heard too. A voice. She clamped her hands over her ears, just as she'd done back then, blanking out those words and the outside world with her headphones and Eminem's music.

The voice was her sister's, the words strident and crystal clear. "Rachel. Where are you hiding? Come here, lazy cow. It's time for you to look after George. I'm off to Simon's. Come now!"

Rachel had stayed put. She was a few weeks short of her eighteenth birthday, hardly a child, but fixated on her own concerns, her studies, her exams. Nothing like the responsible adult circumstances had forced her to become…

From now on, she would always be there for her daughter. It wasn't too late.

Rachel stood up and slid her feet into shoes with heels much higher than she normally wore. She practised walking in baby steps, gaining confidence as she strode down the path and out of the gate to her car. She drove into central Reading towards the solicitor's office, where she would sign away, not just her share in Stapleton Kumar, but all of her past. She'd paid the price. She was starting over.

Fantastic Books
Great Authors

darkstroke is
an imprint of
Crooked Cat Books

- Gripping Thrillers
- Cosy Mysteries
- Romantic Chick-Lit
- Fascinating Historicals
- Exciting Fantasy
- Young Adult
- Non-Fiction

Discover us online
www.darkstroke.com

Find us on instagram:
www.instagram.com/darkstrokebooks

Printed in Great Britain
by Amazon